JOURNEY
OF A
LOST SOUL

J. ROBERT BRANDTS

ISBN: 978-1-7347402-0-2 (paperback)
ISBN: 978-1-7347402-1-9 (eBook)

Book Cover Design by ebooklaunch.com

Book Cover Photograph by Jennifer Reed

Printed in the United States of America

Visit the author at www.bobbrandtsbooks.com

*This book is dedicated to my amazing wife, Patty,
and my two wonderful daughters, Jen and Amber.
Thank you for your unwavering faith, support, and love
throughout my writing journey.
I couldn't have done this without you.*

"*Fear not that your life shall
come to an end,
but fear rather that it shall
never have a beginning.*"
Hawthorne

"*Veni, vidi, vici.*"
"*I came, I saw, I conquered.*"
Julius Caesar

PART I

Veni

*"The tragedy of life is what dies
inside a man while he lives."*
Albert Schweitzer

CHAPTER 1

My story begins in May of last year.

I had just entered a period of "Men's Pause" – that time in life when a man stops his life for a moment and asks himself; "Is this all there is?" I was 42 years old, unmarried, and employed as a manager of a popular Boston restaurant. I had been telling myself for years that "Life was good" and "Everything will be all right" but I'd reached a point where the words rang too hollow to ignore any longer.

It was a visit to my doctor's office that finally pushed me over the edge. I went to him – it was my fifth such visit since the beginning of the year – with symptoms that included a nagging cough, a dull ache in my lower abdominal area, a tightness in my chest and unrelenting fatigue. I could barely keep my eyes open long enough to close the restaurant each night. I played the silently suffering tough guy in front of my employees and customers, but deep down I knew the terrible truth and all I needed was for my doctor to confirm my diagnosis: I had cancer. I didn't know *where* I had it – intestinal, testicular, pancreatic – but I knew it was in there somewhere and it was spreading at an alarming rate.

Looking back now, the truth is that I *wanted* to have cancer. Twisted but true. I had become desperate to find a life preserver to pull me out of the thick, sticky mud that had become my life. Instinctively, I knew that changes had to be made and yet I felt so powerless and so afraid that I was looking to a life-threatening

1

illness to save me from myself. As at birth, I was looking to my doctor to give me a hard slap and bring me to life.

Dr. Fugere had been my doctor for many years. He was a younger, new age kind of doctor who wore a beard and had a diamond earring in his left ear. I liked him because he had always been open to alternative therapies such as acupuncture, homeopathy, and the like; he probably even had a few leeches tucked away somewhere in a back office. I also liked him because he never laughed at me when I complained about my symptoms or when I told him about my deepest fears regarding my health. He would just listen intently, order the necessary tests to quell my fears, and then send me on my way with some gentle reminders regarding diet, exercise and stress. The perfect doctor for a closet hypochondriac.

This visit went pretty much to form – I talked, he listened, he poked and prodded a little bit, he mumbled a few "hmmm" noises and then he sat down in a nearby chair. I braced myself for the upcoming bad news.

"Well Dan," he began, "this is the sixth time I've seen you in the past five months, so I think it's time to prescribe something a little different for you."

I held my breath.

"Your symptoms continue to persist despite my previous recommendations regarding diet, exercise and stress so…" his voice trailed off. Then he paused and took a deep breath. Looking back, I could see he was setting me up. It was probably all he could do not to break into a fit of laughter right then and there. "…I'm going to have to go with a more aggressive therapy."

I knew it! I thought. *It was time for the chemotherapy.* I flashed on thoughts of my hair falling out and my body wasting away but I felt ready for the challenge.

He grabbed a prescription pad from the counter and scribbled a single word on it, then turned the pad so I could read what he'd just written.

"Change?!?" I asked, feeling both insulted and disappointed with his single-word prescription. "All of these symptoms and the best you can do is recommend *change* to me?"

He shrugged. "It's obvious to me that you're not happy right now," he told me. "I'm not a psychiatrist but I know an unhappy person when I see one. Physically, you're fine. It's something beyond the physical that's hurting inside of you and I just can't help you with that. I see it in men your age all the time. You're feeling unhappy with your life, maybe even a little depressed, and you're looking to me for some validation for your fatigue and lack of motivation. Usually I'll just keep listening and doing the diagnostic tests to address their fears, but with you I only see it getting worse with time. So, I'm going to do you a favor and tell you: you're 100% healthy. What you need can't be found in a doctor's office."

I was stunned. I had come looking for some validation and instead got my legs knocked out from underneath me. It was just what I needed, and I owe that doctor my life.

CHAPTER 2

I staggered home that day and thought about what he'd told me. I thought about the boring circle my life had become – work, eat, recover from work, sleep, then repeat the cycle – and the word "change" kept repeating itself in my head. I thought about how "change" had evolved into buying a different color toothbrush or trying my morning latte with whole milk occasionally instead of my usual 2%. I finally saw my life's track for what it was – predictable, safe, unchallenging and absolutely deadly to my spirit – and saw too that nobody was going to make changes for me; for better or worse, it was my ship to steer.

I then came to a second conclusion: it was time to make a move.

The move came in the form of a decision to sell the bulk of my earthly accumulations, pack a small backpack, and just start walking. Nowhere in particular, just slap on my shoes and my pack and put one foot in front of the other. I'd read about the tradition of aboriginal walkabouts and the concept had infinite appeal to me. Simplify my life to its bare essence – food, health, clothing and shelter – and begin the excavation process to uncover a soul that had quieted to a whisper in my chest.

My condo sold quickly, as did the bulk of my furnishings, and the rest – photos, important documents, favorite CD's, baseball card collection and the like – I put into a $50 per month storage unit. I tucked all my money into one account, accessible through the miracle of ATM, and packed my fears regarding an uncertain future into a cardboard box that I tucked into the back of my storage unit. The question of, "What will I do when I get back?" could wait until my return.

On the morning that I began my journey – a beautiful spring morning with endless blue sky to match the vast spectrum of possibilities that lay in front of me – I felt as excited and alive as any time I could remember as an adult. As I took my first steps that morning, toward my unplanned and unknown future, I thought back to when I was a young boy growing up in Western Massachusetts. I remembered waking up on a Saturday morning feeling like I had millions of dollars in time currency to spend that day. I didn't know what adventures I would have that day, but I knew with certainty that they would be new and exciting and infinitely better than anything school could offer me. Substitute the word *work* for *school* in that sentence and that's what I felt on that first morning. It was absolutely intoxicating.

I had intentionally packed light for my journey, eschewing the typical frame pack in favor of a much smaller day pack. I didn't want to attract the attention that would come with appearing as if my life were thrown on my back, so I decided against bringing a sleeping bag, tent, and all the other assorted outdoor camping paraphernalia. I instead packed a single wool blanket, a change of clothes and rain gear. My only concession to boy scout preparedness was my Swiss army knife and a small compass. I figured I would sleep under the stars when weather permitted and make use of cheap hotels when Mother Nature didn't cooperate. I had enough money in the bank to allow for a year of frugal, stress-free wandering with some left over for a semi-soft landing at the other end. I felt ready to explore the sights, sounds and experiences of the physical world and the tunnels, caves and chambers of my inner world.

CHAPTER 3

The first few days were everything I'd envisioned. I had a friend drop me just outside the Boston city limits at the start of day one and I strolled the back roads of rural eastern Massachusetts. The weather was nothing but perfect – lower 60's with light, fragrant breezes – and everyone seemed to have a smile and a wave for me along the way. I walked at a comfortable pace and my legs and feet held up well. It felt good to have my body serving a purpose beyond digesting food and taking an occasional trip to nowhere on the treadmill at the gym. Each night I would find a small patch of woods and curl up to sleep. It took me a couple of days to get used to my new "mattress" and the little nighttime noises, but all-in-all it was a smooth and enjoyable beginning to my journey.

All of that changed on the fourth day.

The day began innocently enough – a sliver of light and chirping birds acting as my alarm – but the sinking temperature and heavier winds spoke of the changes to come. I was just an hour into my walking that day when the raindrops began to fall. I slipped into my rain gear and it wasn't long after that that the raindrops turned into rainboulders. My rain shell was rendered useless under the onslaught and I was forced to find cover. It was another hour of uncomfortable walking before I came to a small town and was able to find a restaurant to act as my temporary shelter. This pit stop marked the true beginning of my journey.

I sloshed into Donny's Deli and Restaurant, found a table in the restaurant section, peeled off my soaked shell and hung it to dry on the back of one of the chairs. I used napkins to wipe my face and head and began the process of drying out and warming up. I did my best to ignore the disapproving looks that were being lobbed my way by my waitress and my neighbors at the surrounding tables.

It was while sipping the hot coffee I'd ordered that I first noticed "Eddie the Entrepreneur" at work. He was a young guy – probably in his early twenties – who had the look and air of a city kid. He was in the middle of a bustling crowd of people, all of whom were waiting in line at a large deli that occupied one whole side of the restaurant. It was lunch time and the deli was overrun with office workers who were obviously feeling the pressure of having to order and then eat their lunches within their allotted half hour. Eddie was capitalizing on this pressure.

I would learn later that he had collected a series of numbered tickets from the deli counter and he was now selling them to interested individuals in line. I watched as he worked his way through the crowd, tickets in hand, offering to sell his lower numbers to people who had just walked in the store. It appeared that business was good as I witnessed many people dig into their pockets, hand him some cash, and then proceed immediately to the front of the line. Ingenious.

After a while, our eyes met for a second time and he wandered over to my table. He postured in front of me and asked, "Yew godda problem?" His Brooklyn accent was unmistakable.

Not accustomed to anyone breaking the shell of silence that had enveloped me over the previous few days, I was initially taken aback by his frontal assault. I recovered quickly however and simply said, "No, I was just admiring how you work." He looked at my wet pack and my drowned weasel appearance and seemed to determine that I was not a threat to his business. He smiled broadly at my compliment and sat down at my table. It was then that I felt the front door to my life swing open wide – a door that had previously been closed and locked, a small peep hole my only way to see what was happening on the other side. I would have kept a person like Eddie out on my doorstep, talking only through the peep hole in my door, prior to this journey. For whatever reason, I felt ready to have visitors and so I opened the door and welcomed him into my world. It was a little later in my journey that I realized that once you opened that door, there was no telling *who* might walk into your living room for a visit.

Eddie was quick to share the logistics of his small business with me. He said it was an improvement over his previous job, which was stealing cars at video drop off sites around New York City. "Jest stand dere and wait fer 'em ta hop outta dere cars wit da motah runnin' 'n boom! Ya got yerself a bran' new cah!" He told me that he would make $500-$1000 per car but that he got tired of watching all his co-workers carted off to jail and decided to find a new line of work. "Now I jest duz dis kinda thing 'n some udder small stuff ta pay da bills," he smiled, "but nuttin' dat's gonna put me in da slammah."

I liked Eddie. He reminded me of a puppy – lots of frantic energy and wide-eyed optimism – and he was extremely honest about who and what he was; no apologies. We talked for a while longer and then I noticed that the rain had subsided. I decided to hit the road again and just let my body heat dry out my still-wet clothes. We said our goodbyes and Eddie went back to work. I grabbed some cash out of my pack, paid the bill at the front register and made a quick visit to the bathroom. When I returned to my table Eddie was standing there again and he was patting my pack.

"Dis izza a nice pack ya got heeyah, mistah," he said to me with a too-friendly smile.

At the time, I simply thanked him for his observation and went on my way. It wasn't until later that night, when I was bedding down next to a remote stretch of road, that I realized what Eddie had been doing next to my pack. He was displaying another one of his many talents and had quickly and smoothly removed my wallet from the front pouch in my pack. Strange as it sounds, I actually smiled at the realization that Eddie had successfully stolen my wallet. I admired his skill and his ability to do his nefarious work without raising so much as an inkling of suspicion within me. That feeling of admiration would last less than 12 hours.

CHAPTER 4

The following morning, I wandered into the next town and placed a call to my bank to report the stolen ATM card. The woman on the other end was polite enough but her voice didn't carry the right level of sympathy and emotion to be delivering the next bit of news.

"I'm sorry Mr. Barnes but I show that account as having a balance of $14.52 at the moment."

I froze. I held the phone in my hand and just shivered, unable to fully assimilate the information that she had just given me.

"Sir? Sir?"

"How can that be?" I finally muttered.

"I realize this isn't the best time to be asking this," she said without sounding apologetic at all, "but if you used your birth date as your access code and someone stole your entire wallet, then it's a pretty easy thing to get your birthday off your driver's license." I flashed on my code – 0707 – July 7th, my birthday. "We see it all the time," she said.

"Now she tells me!"

"Why didn't you call us right away, sir? That way all of your money would have been insured from the time you reported it to us."

"Now she tells me!"

Knowing that she didn't want to hear my tale of Men's Pause and sleeping in the woods, hours from any phone, I just hung up.

After hanging up the phone, I quickly considered my options. I could call my mother and have her wire me some money. Knowing just how tight money had been for her since my father passed away ten years ago, I quickly eliminated that option.

I then thought, for just an ever-so-brief moment, about calling my ex-wife, Mary, and asking her for a short-term loan. She had, after all, become an extremely successful realtor in San Francisco following our divorce. But the water bucket of reality gave me a good, cold dousing with the realization that Mary probably wouldn't even give me a needle and thread if she saw me laying on the ground with my intestines spilling out onto the pavement. Our divorce had not been amicable.

When I realized that I was on my own – and after kicking myself soundly for cutting up my charge cards before leaving - I spent several minutes obsessing on the thought of Eddie's $20,000 24-hour spending spree. I imagined him being slightly annoyed at the daily cash withdrawal limits but then recovering quickly and heading to an electronics store to buy all manner of appliances and gadgets that he could then sell on the street. I took a small measure of satisfaction in thinking that I was probably his all-time biggest payday. It was a *very* small measure of satisfaction.

Numb with shock, I began walking aimlessly. I didn't care where I went or what I did; I just wanted to try to walk away from the sense of dread that had crept into my stomach. It proved to be a stubborn travel companion. I had no training for truly living by my wits, and the prospect of life without money, food, shelter or employment scared the crap out of me. I was forced into living life without a parachute and had just been shoved out of the airplane. Plunging downward, I kept on asking the panicked question of " *What now?!?!*"

During my free fall I began a running dialogue with myself in an effort at keeping insanity at bay. Though I understand that talking to oneself is not often equated with maintaining sanity, it was truly my saving grace. During these on-going dialogues I often had some heated battles between my base instincts, the ones that worried about food and shelter, and my higher self, who was constantly worrying about doing the right thing. Soon after losing all my money, these two got into a particularly heated battle.

CHAPTER 5

Much like Alexander Haig back in the 80's, my base instincts had quickly moved in to assert their leadership. My basic physical needs were being threatened and so these instincts were on high alert. They would chatter at me non-stop as I obsessed on where to find food and what to do next. Eventually, my growling belly pushed me over to a more instinctual view of the world and I decided to take desperate measures.

I strolled into a roadside diner and sat at a table near the door. I had purposely left my pack outside, hidden in some bushes, so as not to draw unwanted attention my way. My waitress brought me a menu and I thought for sure that she saw right through me. She placed the silverware and water on the table without making any eye contact and I glanced at her nameplate. Her name was SynDee.

I ordered a deluxe cheeseburger with fries and a chocolate shake – the All-American meal. I savored every bite, even going so far as to lick the grease and ketchup from my fingers when I was done. It was delicious. Not feeling fully satisfied, however, I ordered a big slice of apple pie a la mode for dessert. I felt like somebody had blown up a weather balloon in my gut.

It then came time to make my move. The waitress had wandered back to the kitchen and I was getting ready to stand up and bolt out the door when my higher self decided to have a few words with me. Guilt took over my insides as I asked myself if I had really stooped this low. I had run a restaurant for many years, so I knew what it felt like to have someone run out on a check. And yet here I was preparing to do that very thing to some poor, unsuspecting waitress.

Then my instincts gave me a cold, hard slap, reminding me that I had no way to pay for the meal that I'd just eaten, and if I was going to make a move, I'd better make it soon. One last squirt of adrenaline got me up out of my seat and I dashed out the door. I grabbed my pack out of the bushes and ran for as long as my legs and sloshing, grease-filled stomach would allow.

Later that night, when I knew I was in the clear, I felt a kind of exhilaration that I hadn't felt for many years. I thought back on the times that I had stolen comic books and baseball cards from a local store with some friends when I was ten years old. The feelings were identical. Risk could be an exciting playmate sometimes and the surge of energy that came with dodging a bullet occasionally was positively addicting.

But then my higher-self came in and, as he had when I was a kid, spoiled the party. He dumped an ice-cold bucket of guilt on my head and all thoughts of risk and adventure momentarily left my brain. That seemed to be his way of making sure that these types of things didn't become habit-forming.

CHAPTER 6

I wandered without any real plan for the next few days, completely immersed in a cesspool of self-pity. I managed to avoid any further dine-and-dash episodes by learning the centuries old art of gleaning. I became quite adept at picking through restaurant garbage cans and finding edible scraps that had been discarded. In some towns the competition became quite stiff as the local gleaners had staked out their territory around the more productive restaurants.

"What da hell ya doin' wit'cher nose in m'can?!?" came an angry voice from behind me one day. I had just laid my hands on a practically untouched roast beef sandwich when I was forced to turn around and face the angry voice. I knew that, to the average person walking down the street, I certainly looked the part of a homeless bum, but it hadn't taken me long to realize that I would never be allowed to enter the fraternity of true bums. They saw right through me. Some of them took pity on me and offered small pointers and a helping hand when they could. Others, like the man in front of me, had no patience for any outsiders who didn't know the rules of the road. All he saw was competition.

He was a small man, probably pushing sixty and missing most of his teeth, and I probably could have taken him; but I also knew that I was not much of a fighter. Besides, teeth-wise, I had a lot more to lose than he did. So, I did what I had always done in those situations: I tucked my tail between my legs and simply said, "Sorry, I didn't know it was yours." Total acquiescence. I offered him the sandwich in my hand, but he just brushed by me with a loud "harrumph" of contempt and went about searching for his lunch. I gobbled down the sandwich as I walked away.

It was then that I realized that I couldn't go on living that way forever. My self-respect started to feel a little bruised.

That was when I came up with my Work Across America plan. The general idea was to get a series of odd jobs when I had to and then walk until I ran out of money. The process would then repeat itself until I made it to the West Coast. Once there, god only knew what the plan would be.

My higher self seemed to like this plan much better.

Encouraged by a kind-hearted cook who had fed me a couple of times, I took my first part-time job as a dishwasher in a diner just west of Worcester. The owner was more than happy to pay me cash – a sentiment shared by a good many business owners I would soon learn – and he didn't much care that I didn't come equipped with a resume and references. *Could I stand* and *could I scrub dishes* were the only questions he wanted answered. I answered in the affirmative to both questions. I stayed there for a couple of weeks and managed to collect close to $400 in wages and shared tips – more than enough to fund another couple of weeks of walking.

This became my pattern. Work two weeks, walk two weeks. I came to enjoy them both at a deeper level through this routine. I could enjoy the social contacts and creature comforts of the work world and then, just when it was beginning to feel suffocating, I could head for the solitude of the open road. When I found myself tiring of sleeping on the ground and missing hot showers, I could settle into a more civilized existence for a while. It was a perfectly balanced life.

CHAPTER 7

My balance was disrupted a little bit during a short stopover in a town in upstate New York. I had just finished eating my lunch and was walking through a warehouse section on the outskirts of town when I heard a muffled cry for help. It was a Sunday afternoon so the surrounding businesses – most of which seemed to involve asphalt, sand, construction and the like – were empty and quiet. The first moans that I heard shot straight to the more instinctual sections of my brain, and they were telling me that I should keep on walking.

"Don't get involved," I thought. *"It's probably some scam to get you over by the buildings so some guy can nail you on the head and steal everything you've got."*

Then came the second series of cries and moans. This is where my higher self jumped into the fray.

"How could you just walk away from a cry for help?" asked the voice in my head. *"Someone is suffering over there – maybe even dying – and you're thinking about ignoring it?"*

The third cry was louder still and stirred me to action, the conflicting voices in my head be damned. I hurried over in the direction of the sounds, my Boston-bred antennae extended fully looking for any signs of danger.

Once next to the buildings, I stopped and listened again. I thought I was close to the spot from which the sounds had come but I saw nothing. A few moments later I saw some boxes moving a few yards away and I went over to investigate.

Buried under the boxes and stacks of old newspapers I saw the face of an old woman. Her face was so dirty and smeared with oil and grease that she all but blended in with the ground. I went down on one knee and raised her head, propping it up on a nearby stack of old rags. She was hacking non-stop and I noticed when I put my hand under her neck that she was burning with fever. Even through the dirt I could see that her skin was pale, and her eyes were sunken almost out of sight. She was dying, that I knew, and my mind went into scramble mode, searching for an answer regarding what to do.

I looked at the old woman more closely. I guessed her to be in her late 60's, though all of the grime and the effects of an obviously hard life could have skewed that 10 years in either direction. Her face was etched deeply with wrinkles and the few teeth she had were yellow and black with disease. She had dried spittle up and down her cheeks and chin and all I could think for the longest time was: *"I'm not performing CPR on that mouth!"*

Her face began turning strange hues of grey-blue as her hacking deepened. She made no effort to cover her mouth and sputum flew everywhere. I recoiled, repulsed to my core. Through her coughs she kept on trying to speak, but she couldn't get enough breath to form any words. Frustrated, she reached under her rag blanket and pulled out a dirty cloth that she held up for me to take. Not wanting to touch anything that may be infected with TB or some other exotic disease, I put my hands up and smiled weakly, trying my best to say, "thanks, but no thanks." This rejection seemed to make her angry as she thrust the cloth closer to me. This sudden movement caused two things to happen simultaneously.

First, she went into a coughing fit that was so deep and so violent that she started spewing blood from her mouth.

Second, I panicked. The sight of the blood and her wild, death-is-so-close-I-can-taste-it eyes, spurned me to action. I got up and made a dash for the nearest road, leaving her lying there hacking and gasping for air.

It took me just a few minutes to get to the road and the first car I saw stopped immediately. I must have looked like an honest man despite my flailing arms and my wide-eyed, panic-filled face. The man had a cell phone and he called an ambulance. The ambulance arrived quickly enough and, upon their arrival, I led them to the spot where I had left the old woman. I noticed as we approached that there were no longer any hacking noises. Nothing but silence. The kind of silence that sneaks into your belly and sits there like a rock. Unlike the paramedics, I knew exactly what was waiting for us as we approached the building. The old woman was dead.

As we stood over her now lifeless body, I saw that her face was deep blue, and her eyes were wide open with a permanent "What happened?!?" look etched on her face. She was lying right where I had left her, and her hand was still extended outward with the dirty cloth spilling out of it. The paramedics knelt and did a perfunctory check of her vital signs but there was no doubt as to her fate. They hoisted her up and placed her on the gurney. As they did, the cloth spilled out of her hand and fell to the ground. I looked around and saw that nobody had noticed it except me. After they'd loaded her into the ambulance and took down the little bits of information that I had to offer, they packed up their equipment and left. As they drove away, I looked down at the cloth on the ground.

I walked over and gave it a small nudge with my foot. I noticed something silver-colored peek out at me from behind the soiled cloth. I nudged it harder, still not wanting to touch it with my hands. A silver chain and locket scooted across the ground. I went over and picked it up and examined it more closely. I could tell by the color and weight that it was made of real silver. It was worn smooth, but I could still see evidence of the expert craftsmanship that had fashioned the locket. I wiped the necklace on my pants and then opened the locket. Inside were two small pictures, one on either side, that had obviously been tucked inside this locket for many years as they were very worn and faded. I could still make out the pictures, however, and saw a man's face on one side and a woman and a small girl on the other.

I looked down at the spot where the woman had been lying and wondered to myself what the story was behind these pictures and why she wanted me to take the locket from her. Now I would never know. I looked again at the greasy cloth on the ground and noticed a piece of paper tucked inside of it. Emboldened now, I reached down and picked up the cloth. I pulled the piece of paper out, shook the cloth to see if anything else was inside, and then threw the cloth away.

The paper was folded several times and I saw that it was a flyer for some miraculous new weight loss program. On the back, in neat handwriting, was the following message:

Please deliver this locket to my daughter

Nancy Taylor
321 Pleasant Street
Enfield, New York

Thank you for fulfilling a dying woman's last wish

I looked again at the locket in my hand and realized that it suddenly felt much heavier. It carried the weight of a woman's life and I wasn't sure I was worthy of the task of delivering it to its destination. Sheepishly, I tucked it into my pocket.

I walked toward the next town and toyed with the idea of delivering the locket in person to the woman's daughter. It was the least I could do, I figured, after abandoning her in her last moments like I had. I even went so far as to consult a map at a gas station along the way and saw that Enfield, New York wasn't more than a couple days walk from where I was. Eventually, however, I settled on the more conservative - translation: *cowardly* - approach of just mailing it to her at the next town.

CHAPTER 8

My actions with the dying woman weighed heavily on me for the next many miles. I viewed it as a weakness of character, always a hard admission to make, and I had a hard time reconciling the whole thing. I tried to convince myself that I had acted rationally, seeing as I hadn't known the entire situation at the time it was happening, but my words rang hollow. I had always viewed myself as being a nice guy, and helpful, and all that crap and yet when I had the opportunity to pull that quality of nice-guyness out of the sanctuary of theory and really test it in the harsh environment of reality I had failed miserably.

Why did I run for cover at the first sign of real danger? Was I that scared and weak? I reminded myself of the risk of disease, but my higher self countered with names like Mother Teresa, Gandhi and other people who had managed to put aside thoughts of personal safety in order to do what was right.

This was a familiar debate for me. My desire for greatness versus the realities of my entrenched fears and insecurities. I engaged in this internal debate quite often. Somewhere inside of me was a kernel of desire to leave a lasting mark on the world. That desire raised its head from time to time and came close to convincing me at times that I had a cancer cure or change-the-world book hidden within me. The feeling rarely lasted longer than a few minutes, however, as it would soon get dragged back into the quagmire of self by an army of self-doubting, fearful voices.

"You're a failure, face it!"
"Don't get involved!"
"What if something happens to you?!?"
"Don't let people get too close!"

I knew my enemies well, if only from a distance. Like the general on the mountaintop above the battle, I preferred to view the fighting through binoculars from a safe distance. And yet there was one enemy that I hesitated to look at even through binoculars.

My fear of death.

After some thought, I realized that this one, big fear hovered above all the others. It cast a large, gut-wrenching shadow over my entire life and many of my other fears were nothing more than offspring of this one Father Fear. My fear of failure was merely a small spokesperson for my fear of dying without having lived up to my potential. My fear of pain was just a whisper that hinted at my fear of life-threatening illness and dying an ugly death. My fears of intimacy and discovery by others were a direct result of the inner shame I felt as a result of all the above. Death ruled over my inner kingdom. I knew this, and yet I felt powerless to change it.

I soon realized that the dying woman represented all these fears rolled into one resolve-testing package. She had died the death that I envisioned for myself in my worst nightmares - alone, homeless, wracked with pain, no hope for any miraculous cure. I turned away from her in the very same way that I averted my inner eye from the faces of the fears inside of me whenever they raised their demonic heads. I ran for cover in the same way that I hid behind work, TV and other distractions in order to avoid the unpleasantness of facing down my fears. She was nothing more than a physical version of the very same inner tests that I'd been facing all my adult life. And, just as I had always failed those inner tests, so too did I fail this external test. Showing no desire to dirty my hands with the messiness of the reality lying in front of me, I took the easy way out and avoided the problem all together, preferring instead to just hand it off to someone else.

I felt small.

As a morose exercise in masochism, I continued to roll the events surrounding the woman's last minutes on Earth around in my head. I would flash on her emaciated body struggling for each precious breath. I would see her bulging eyes and protruding veins as she coughed and hacked her way through her final moments, trying desperately to communicate her last wishes to me. I stared at the ghastly pictures on my mind's screen, ignoring my impulse to look away. I was determined to face down these voices of weakness and perhaps salvage a few positives amidst the rubble of my pulverized ego. It got me thinking about the power of legacies.

The worst fate for any of us would be to be lying in that old woman's position and realizing that nothing in our life had truly mattered. We came and we went and there was nothing of consequence in between, nothing to say, "I was here world!" We'll just be another forgotten soul in the long history of forgotten souls. There will have been birth, then the scramble for small moments of pain-free existence, and, finally, an unceremonious death. No footprints or fingerprints left behind as a testament to our existence. Period, end of sad story.

That poor woman, lying there in the middle of nowhere, wracked with fever and knowing she had just minutes to live, had been hoping for someone to serve as a messenger for her final legacy. As humble as it was – an old locket and a few scribbled words – it was her entire life distilled into one small package. It must have felt to her, in her quiet desperation, like I had fallen from the sky in answer to her prayers. I suddenly felt very honored to have been entrusted with the locket and felt another twinge of regret for not having the guts to deliver it in person.

It was then that I decided to finally take a stand on the side of what was right, no matter the consequences. I decided to go to Enfield.

Following this shift in thinking – from viewing the locket as a burden to more of a blessing – I became quite anxious to meet her daughter and deliver this small legacy. I imagined Nancy's look of surprise upon seeing the long-lost locket. I could hear her sobs and see her tears as I told her about her mother's dying wish. I rehearsed in my mind my answers to her inevitable questions surrounding her mother's last moments, electing to avoid any details that pointed to my cowardice. I figured it wouldn't serve any useful purpose to drag such unpleasant details into the daughter's last memories of her mother. Besides, despite my many shortcomings, I still had some pride.

I strolled into Enfield after just a couple of days and had no trouble locating Nancy Taylor's house on Pleasant Street. Not wanting to miss the look on her face, I decided to walk to her house rather than call beforehand. I walked up onto her front porch and knocked on the door. Not once during all my daydreaming did I play out the scene that soon followed on Nancy's front porch.

The woman who answered was a large woman in her 40's who had a scowl that I imagined never left her face. She had two small children clutching at her legs and what sounded like a third one wailing behind her somewhere in the house. "Yeah, what is it?" she asked me with extreme indifference.

This was my big moment. The time to deliver the lines that I'd been practicing for the past couple of days. I took a deep breath, determined not to let her initial reaction throw me off my course. "I have a present and a message from your recently deceased mother," I began. I noticed her body stiffen. "She gave me this locket," I pulled it from my pocket and extended it to her, "and she wanted me to tell you to take it along with her undying love." I'd spiced it up a little bit, but the message was the same. I stood there waiting for the onslaught of questions regarding how her mother died, where she died, what else did she have to say and the like. No questions came.

Instead, she spit the next words at me like verbal darts. "Well you can just take that locket back where you found it mister because I buried my mother in my mind over 30 years ago." Her anger gathered steam as she said to me, "I don't want any of her so-called love and I certainly don't want a piece of jewelry that's gonna remind me of a mother that tossed me aside like an old rag doll that she didn't want anymore!" With that she slammed the door.

I stood on her porch for several minutes debating whether I should knock and try again. Feeling convinced that she'd probably come back with a gun, I decided it was best to just leave. Before leaving her porch, I jotted down the name of the town where she could find her mother's body on the same piece of paper on which the mother had scribbled her final words, then stuffed it, along with the locket, into her mailbox and walked away.

After getting over my initial disappointment at not being able to deliver the old woman's dying message as intended, I spent several walking hours thinking about the anger and hate that Nancy had thrown my way. I thought about how we seemed to be living in a world where hate and anger were just as acceptable as love and kindness used to be. Just another couple of emotions that are all part of being human. Things like yelling at a waitress, venting your anger on a TV show, or honking your horn and flipping off a stranger are not only considered to be well within your rights as a human being, they're actually considered to be healthy and cathartic. When did all this become okay? Love thy neighbor seemed to be slipping out of the top ten list as far as commandments go.

CHAPTER 9

It was soon after "the locket incident" that I stumbled on The Shady Glen Funeral Parlor. It was in a small town in eastern Ohio and I noticed that there was no shade, there was no glen and, truthfully, there wasn't even a parlor to speak of. I was walking by one afternoon and I happened to notice a long line of cars on the side of the building. Figuring that they were just waiting for a funeral procession to begin I didn't give it much of a thought. Then I saw people pulling away one car at a time and it piqued my interest. After closer inspection I noticed that some of the people were reaching out of their windows and putting things into a machine much like the ones you find at bank drive through windows. I wasn't truly prepared for what I saw next.

I walked up to where the cars were waiting and saw what it was that they were doing: it was a drive-thru wake. It was indeed set up like a bank drive-thru but where you would normally see a teller looking at you through a plate glass window you were instead greeted by a dead body lying in state in a propped-up coffin. And where you would normally send your checks and deposit slips through the vacuum tube, people were instead sending through flowers, cards and other gifts and remembrances. How touching.

There was a man on the other end of the tube emptying out the contents of the canister, arranging the items around the casket and then sending the canister back for the next person in line. I went in for a closer look. The man behind the window gave me a solemn nod that he'd probably practiced hundreds of times in a mirror in order to get just the right effect. I surveyed the casket and the surrounding area. There was a short obituary at the foot of the coffin, several canned, but appropriately solemn, quotes and bible verses and a handful of pictures. The guy's name was Harold Sawyer. He was 66 years old when he died. I didn't know the man, but I suddenly felt very sorry for Harold.

The guy had obviously lived a long life, and this was the send-off he was getting from his family and loved ones. They couldn't even take the time to climb out of their cars for god's sake. I even saw one guy pull up who continued talking on his cell phone the whole time he sat there passing his condolences through the vacuum tube. It was times like that that I didn't recognize the world I lived in any longer.

As I turned to walk away, I was surprised to see a man standing right behind me. He smiled a smile that I would have associated with an insurance salesman – lots of teeth but no eyes – and he said to me; "Kinda disgusting, isn't it?"

A kindred spirit. "Yeah," I agreed, "I'd like to think that this isn't the wave of the future."

"Ain't that the truth," he agreed. For some reason, which became clearer to me later, the guy reminded me a little bit of my good friend Eddie.

We bantered for a while about the drive-thru and then he said to me; "Hey, you strike me as a guy who could use a little extra money, is that true?"

At first, I was offended by his remark, but then I did a quick self-scan – with my dirty clothes, greasy hair, stubbly face and tattered pack – and realized that I deserved it. Besides, he was right.

I shrugged indifferently.

"Yeah, I thought so." He flashed the salesman smile again. "I have a gig that'll pay you a few hundred dollars a night for just a couple hours work. You interested?"

I asked him what had become my standard questions – "Is it illegal and is it dangerous?" He said no to both questions, though I noticed a slight pause in his voice regarding the question of its legality. I asked him to tell me more. I saw very quickly why he hadn't listed this job in the local newspaper.

"There's a rather lucrative market for fresh tissue samples these days," he said in a conspiratorial whisper. "Underground researchers are looking for organs, stem cell samples and whatever else they can get their hands on that would help in their research." He placed his hand on his chest, almost proudly I thought to myself. "That's where I come in," he said.

It wasn't long before he stopped talking in riddles and gave me a full job description. I would be assisting him with a series of unapproved surgeries on dead bodies that would come through the funeral parlor in which he worked as an embalmer. He would remove organs and other tissue samples and my job would be to pack it all up in ice and prepare it for shipping. I shuddered at the thought. But I didn't turn and run. Big mistake.

As I weighed my need for money against the demands of the job, the man who would only identify himself as "Doc" told me a little bit about his background. Turned out that while he currently worked as an embalmer at the Shady Glen, he aspired to go to medical school at some point in the future. So, he performed these operations after hours in the basement of the funeral home to help fund his future education. He wasn't the least bit concerned about his lack of qualifications for such a surgical procedure. "Alive or dead, it's still the same thing – just cutting and sewing!" he told me.

Something about the guy made sense. Looking back, I think I was looking at him through jaded, cynical glasses as I was still reeling from Nancy's reaction to the locket and Harold Sawyer's fond drive-thru farewell. I accepted the job.

Our first "patients" arrived that night - two small boys who had died in a grisly car crash the day before - and I saw very quickly why Doc had a hard time finding reliable help. I wouldn't soon forget the smells, sounds and sensations associated with my first removal, preserving and, finally, packing of a human heart, liver and eyeballs. Suffice it to say that after two clients, and $200 cash, my career as an Organ Packer was over.

I took the cash from the Doc, who seemed proud of his not-everyone-can-stomach-this line of work, and headed out the door. As I walked out, I passed by the two small corpses that had been torn open; Doc was in the process of filling their now-empty chest cavities with some kind of foam and a saline solution. All I could think about was what if the parents of those two boys had walked in at that moment and saw their precious children lying gutted like that on the table. I felt a strong surge of shame ripple through my body.

I berated myself for many miles for giving in to the Gollum-like charms of the Doc and for playing a role in the mutilation of those two small boys. I had convinced myself at the time that the surgery would have taken place even if I hadn't been there, so why not cash in? But it took me just a few miles of walking to see the many errors in my line of reasoning.

"Just because people are being murdered each day, does that make it all right to shoot your neighbor?" I asked myself. It was one of those rhetorical questions that caused my mind to rewind to the days when my mother would ask me that classic motherly question about following a friend if he decided to jump from that hypothetical bridge. In its hyperbolic form, the question was always an easy one to answer; the tricky part came when that same hypothetical friend had less deadly adventures in mind. The gray line between "smart" and "stupid" had always been a confusing one for me.

CHAPTER 10

The $200 lasted me a long time, through Ohio and on into Indiana. It was during this part of my trip that I established my best walking rhythm. It was still summer but there wasn't any of the stifling heat and humidity that normally afflicts the Midwest that time of year. The skies seemed to be permanently blue and the air warm and fragrant. I didn't think it was possible to feel that good while walking through that part of the country. Even though I'd had limited personal experience with the Midwest, I'd always held a negative image in my head of the area from Ohio to Wyoming. I saw first-hand that my images were both inaccurate and unfair.

I also took better notice of what was around me during this stretch. The sights, the sounds, the smells - I couldn't get enough of any of it. Prior to that I had usually been too preoccupied with the search for money, food and shelter to even notice most of what was going on around me during the day. I would get lost in my own internal world of needs and fears until a pang of hunger or twinge of a muscle would pull me back to my immediate surroundings. The cash in my pocket and apparent promise of beautiful weather kept my fears to a minimum and allowed me the luxury of casting my eyes outward for a while.

I noticed, for instance, that I loved the time around sunrise each morning. I had slept through 99.9% of the sunrises in my lifetime, the few exceptions being an early morning flight to catch or some other such appointment that distracted me from truly *seeing* the sunrise. It was a quiet, magical time as the world stretched and awakened and I enjoyed being up and walking around in the pink and orange hues of dawn's early light.

I also found that I enjoyed observing people and forming little biographies around my admittedly limited snapshots of their lives. The man and the woman sitting on the bench are suddenly having a lunch hour affair. The sullen teen walking behind her mother feels misunderstood and frustrated with her parents' silly rules. The old man at the bus stop is contemplating a long-lost lover as he leans on his cane, waiting for the next bus. As silly as my little stories seemed, I also knew that these people's real stories would probably make my manufactured ones pale in comparison. I'd already gotten a glimpse at the true depth, and strange twists, of people's lives through the first part of my journey.

It also made me wonder what kinds of strange, untold stories existed behind the front doors of each house I walked by. I couldn't resist sneaking occasional peeks into some of the houses, especially after dark, to see if I could get some hints at the lives that were being lived within the walls. I would feel an occasional jab of guilt for being so nosy, but it was never hard enough to make me stop doing it. It was during one of my prolonged staring sessions through the windows of a house in eastern Indiana that I met Preference Quigley.

I was walking very slowly past an older home in what looked like a less desirable section of town, when a voice startled me from behind.

"What'cha doin' there mister!"

Caught by surprise, which had not been typical for me during my travels, I wheeled around to face the voice. I saw a woman standing there who seemed to be in her 50's but, judging from the way she held herself, she appeared to be sturdier than most 25-year-olds. Her voice and mannerisms said, "truck driver" but her blond hair and youthful figure said, "pure woman."

"If yer a Peepin' Tom, yer gonna be awful disappointed lookin' in those windows mister," she said as she nodded in the direction of the house. "That there is Gracie Miller's house 'n she's pushin' a hundred years old. Somethin' tells me ya might feel like pukin' in the bushes if ya ever saw *her* nekkid!" She laughed a big, hearty laugh as she stood in front of me.

"I'm not…" I tried to explain to the woman, but she wouldn't let me finish.

"Never mind, never mind," she said with a wave of her hand. "I don't really care if ya was or ya wasn't, to tell ya the truth." She eyed me up and down. "You look like a pretty interestin' character, what with yer backpack, greasy hair and all." She rubbed her chin. "I think I might want to buy you a drink."

I returned the favor and eyed her up and down, trying to size up her intentions. Even by the low light of the streetlights I could see that she was a pretty woman, in a rough-and-ready, pioneer woman sort of way. Her language was rough, but her eyes were soft and kind, so I nodded my consent to her offer of a drink.

"Great!" she bellowed as she extended her hand. "Preference Quigley's the name, but my friends call me Ren."

I shook her hand. Not knowing if I was a friend just yet, and not wanting to offend her, I replied, "Nice to meet you Ms. Quigley. My name's Dan Barnes."

"If ya call me Ms. Quigley again I'm afraid I'm gonna hafta slap ya. It's Ren to you!"

I smiled and nodded.

We walked together a short way and I told her an abbreviated version of my trip. This version included my story of Men's Pause and my Work Across America Plan, but little of the detail in between.

She guffawed. "Sounds like yer a bit of a lost soul Danny boy! To tell ya the truth, I'm a bit of a sucker fer lost souls, so how wouldja like to work fer me fer a spell as part of yer workin' 'cross America plan?"

Before I could get out my question regarding the type of work she was offering, we arrived at our destination.

She stopped and raised her arm as if she were Vanna White displaying that new car. "Well, here it is!"

I looked up and saw what looked like a bar with a big blue "Q" painted on the front window. The paint was a bright metallic blue and underneath it was written "The Blue Q" in script lettering.

"This is my place Danny boy. The Blue Q Pool Hall, get it?" She looked at me expecting something that I didn't give her initially because, truth be told, I *didn't* get it.

She looked disappointed and dropped her arm. "The Blue Q?!?" she said again with added emphasis. "Q?…Quigley?…pool cue?…get it?!?"

I finally got it. "Ahhh…I get it now." I tried to recover by giving her an extra big smile. It didn't work.

"Never mind. Let's go inside and get that drink." She was obviously hurt.

The Blue Q, if you had the opportunity to look up "pool hall" in the encyclopedia, would have been the color picture in the margin. It was dark, extremely smoky, reeked of stale beer and BO, and was packed to the gills. I liked it immediately. After being by myself on the road for so long I enjoyed being surrounded by people. The volume of the music and constant din of voices and laughter took some getting used to for my ears, but I adjusted quickly.

It wasn't a huge bar, probably a dozen or so tables scattered around, but it still took us a while to negotiate the small distance from the bar, where we'd picked up two bottles of beer, to a table in the corner. Negotiating all the bodies would have been a project by itself, but it was compounded by the fact that Ren knew everybody, and everybody knew Ren. We had to stop every couple of steps to talk about a new car, a new baby, the weather, and all sorts of other topics. People seemed to genuinely like Ren. I could see why. She was one of those people who made you feel better just standing next to her. She had a smile and a slap on the back for everyone she saw and there didn't seem to be an insincere bone in her body.

We finally made it to the table and, while Ren finished up one last conversation, I surveyed the room. I noticed right away that most of her patrons were men. By the looks of them, most were blue collar, pick-up truck driving types. Beer was the beverage of choice and pool and darts were the only games in town. This was not a pickup joint, like you'd find in Boston or New York. It was a meetcha-after-work-and-tip-a-few bar in which blowing off steam and having a few laughs were the priorities. Listening in on a few conversations, most of the talk centered around life in the local factories, fishing and hunting.

Ren sat down next to me. "So, what'cha think of my place?"

I nodded my approval. "Very nice. Nothing like the bars back home in Boston, but I like it." I smiled warmly, trying to make up for my earlier transgression.

"I'm glad t'hear that," she shouted over the din, "'cuz I want'cha t'come work fer me." She smiled as she raised her glass of beer in a toast.

I didn't hesitate. I smiled back at her and raised my glass to hers. Without even asking what the job might be, I said, "I accept."

CHAPTER 11

I spent the next couple of weeks sweeping floors, cleaning bathrooms, tending bar, stocking shelves, hauling garbage and basically doing whatever was necessary to keep the bar running smoothly. Turned out that one of Ren's regular bartenders had just gotten in a bad car accident and would be out of commission for a few weeks and I provided just the answer she had been looking for: short-term help with no strings attached.

I liked the work. It was a lot more social than any of the other jobs I'd taken, and I enjoyed it. Most of the places would tuck me behind the scenes, away from prying eyes, so nobody would ask any questions about who I was and how I was getting paid. Not Ren. She would do it whichever way she pleased and just dare anyone to say anything to her about it. Nobody ever did.

I also had a chance to get to know Ren a little better. We would talk whenever we had a chance, while cleaning up the place or over a drink after closing, and I came to like her even more as time went by. She was one of the most uncomplicated people I'd ever met. No hidden motives, no complaints about her childhood/parents/lousy luck/etc., no manipulations - just 100% pure Ren 100% of the time. It was refreshing to be around. And easy.

It was at the start of my third week, just about when I began thinking about grabbing my pack and starting to walk again, when I met another interesting stranger. I was wiping down the bar early one evening, before the arrival of the after-work crowd, when a man came up behind me and said: "So I hear ya been peekin' in on my Granny."

His voice startled me. I turned around and came face to face with a large, round man who was wearing a frown. "Ren tells me that yer the Peepin' Tom who's been stalkin' Granny Gracie. Is that true?"

I didn't know what to say. Thankfully, I saw his frown quickly turn to a smile as he said, "Ah, I'm just messin' with ya! Truth be known, I told Granny about it and she's tickled as can be that someone still wants to peek in her window at all!"

I laughed an uneasy laugh and didn't bother defending myself.

"Name's Zootie, Zootie Gibbons." He stuck his hand out and I shook it.

"My name's Dan Barnes."

"Yeah, I know. Ren told me all about you. She told me that you'd be a good person for me to talk to." He didn't say *why* Ren said that and that worried me a little bit.

We sat down and made small talk for a while. He had brought over a bottle of whiskey and a couple of glasses, which he soon filled. My instincts were on low alert, but I couldn't figure out why. There wasn't anything about him that seemed remotely dangerous to me. He was balding and grey with a well-trimmed salt-and-pepper beard and a huge belly that shook when he laughed. He had a jovial, talkative nature and I got the same easy-to-be-around feeling with him that I had gotten with Ren. When he spoke, he couldn't seem to make up his mind if he was Will Rogers or William Shakespeare as his pattern of speech alternated between backwoods hillbilly and Harvard professor. I guessed him to be in his late fifties, but the playful sparkle in his eyes took years off his age.

He told me that he lived in Seattle and that he was just back in Indiana for a short visit. He had grown up in Indiana, went away to law school many years ago and never came back, except for occasional visits. "Wouldn't come back here at all if it weren't for Granny and Ren," he said. Then he smiled at me. "Ren and I used to be married ya know."

It was easy to picture the two of them as a couple. "Oh really?" I replied.

"Yeah, but it just didn't work out. She wanted to stay here and run the bar for the rest of our days, and I wanted to go see the world. Familiar story, familiar sad ending." Zootie just shook his head.

"She's a great gal, though," he added, "and I'd hitch my wagon to hers again in a second if she'd make the move to Seattle with me." He chuckled. "But there's no way she'd do it. And there's no way the men in this town would let her do it even if she wanted to!"

We sat in silence for a moment.

"You married, Dan?"

"No, not anymore." My mind flashed on Mary and I felt old regrets that hadn't shown themselves for a long time. Zootie continued to ask me questions and my answers got increasingly honest. There was something about him that invited candor. I don't know if it was his easy manner, his pointed questions, the seemingly genuine interest he showed in my answers or the straight whiskey that he kept pouring into the glass in front of me. I suspect it was the whiskey.

I told him how Mary and I had been too young and much too idealistic about marriage. We kept on bumping up against each other's expectations, but we were too selfish and immature to talk about the hurts and frustrations, so the resentments just built up to the point that we had to push the escape button. "Same ol' story, same sad ending," I said with a forced smile.

Zootie nodded his agreement.

I went on to tell him about my trip, filling in all the small details that I had neglected to tell Ren. I even told him about the old woman and my cowardly response to her last dying moments.

"Don't go beatin' up on yourself for that one, Dan," he reassured me. "Nobody knows just how they're gonna respond to somethin' like that until they're nose-to-nose with it!" I noticed at the time, even through the whiskey haze, that he seemed particularly animated in his reassurances on this topic. I would soon learn why.

"So, what are your plans after you leave poor Ren in your rearview mirror?" he asked me.

"Oh, I don't know," I replied. "I thought I'd just hit the road again and point myself west."

Zootie shifted in his chair. "Well, actually, I might have somethin' for you to sink your teeth into, if you're interested."

I got an uneasy feeling in my belly.

"You see, Dan, I've got this project I'm workin' on, and it's provin' to be just a bit too big for one man to tackle." He leaned forward across the table and locked in on my eyes. "And I could use your help."

I didn't really want to ask the next question, but I did anyway. "What's the project?"

He reached around to his back pocket and pulled out a big wad of papers that were folded in half. He placed the papers on the table and, as he unfolded them, I could see that it was a list of some kind. He stacked the papers neatly in front of him and then placed his hand on top of them, sighing heavily. "This is a list, Dan, but not just any ol' list," he began. "It was handed to me just a couple of weeks ago by some agent of God or the devil, I still can't decide which just yet, and it's got the names of over a thousand unlucky souls on it." He passed one of the pages to me so I could examine it more closely. "I say unlucky because every name on this list has a date next to it and that date is the date that each of them will be breathin' their last breath on this earth." He paused to let his words sink in.

The words sank a little slowly due to the whiskey's effects, but they eventually hit their intended target. "It what?!?" I stammered as I scanned the page in front of me.

"I didn't believe it at first either. But sure enough, one by one, I saw each of those first names on the list show up in the Seattle Times obituaries and, by the third week, I was a believer!"

I looked at the list more closely. I noticed that the list was arranged in neat columns with the far-left column containing sequential dates, beginning with a date three weeks earlier. Next to each date was a name and an address, all of which I guessed to be in the Seattle area. Zootie had apparently jotted some notes next to some of the earlier names but I made no effort to decipher his illegible handwriting.

"Where did you get this list?" I muttered.

"The darned thing just showed up on my doorstep! Never saw hide nor hair of the author, just found a big envelope stuck inside my screen door when I came home one day. It took me a while to figure the whole thing out and, once I did, I wrestled with what to do with it.

"I thought about just givin' the whole mess to a TV station or newspaper and lettin' them figure it out." He heaved a deep sigh. "But then I got to thinkin' more about it and I realized a couple of things." He held up one finger. "One, I realized that if I was gonna find out the day I was gonna die, I wouldn't want to hear about it on the evening news or read it on the front page of the mornin' paper." He looked at me sideways with a "don't-you-agree?" look on his face and I nodded.

He held up a second finger. "Two, I realized that I'd been given somethin' pretty darned special and that this may be my one shot to do somethin' that might make a difference in the world. I had just been wonderin' to myself that week why the hell I was down here walkin' on this Earth anyway." His voice started rising. "Was it just to eat and shit my way through a lifetime and then feed the plants with my remains? Is that what this is all about?!?"

He pounded his hand on the table. "No, goddam it!!!" His eyes were ablaze. "Here I was finally gettin' a whiff of somethin' that was bigger than me and all I could think about was handin' the whole thing off! How pathetic am I?!?"

I flashed on the old woman and her locket. I felt pathetic.

Zootie's tone and eyes came down a few notches. "Do you know what I'm talkin' about Dan?" I nodded with more sincerity than he was able to see. "Do you understand that need to do something great so your life amounts to somethin' more than walkin' fertilizer?" I nodded again, more emphatically.

Zootie grinned. "Good. I knew you were the man I was looking for!"

My insides went crazy. *"Don't let him fool you - he's up to something!"* a voice whispered in my ear. Ignoring the voice, I asked; "Just what is it that you want me to do, Zootie?"

"I want'cha to come to Seattle with me and help contact these poor, unsuspecting folks to let them know what's in store for 'em! I want'cha to be another Paul Revere and sound the alarm!" He cupped his hands to his mouth and shouted the next words. "The Grim Reaper is comin'! The Grim Reaper is comin'!"

I looked around the bar to see if anyone else had walked in. We were still alone. I took a big gulp of whiskey. "I don't know Zootie…I'm going to have to think about this one."

Zootie shot down his last bit of whiskey and slammed his glass to the table. "I understand that Dan. I won't be leavin' 'till later this week so why don't'cha scratch your chin on it 'till then." He extended his hand across the table. "Fair enough?"

I shook his hand and nodded my agreement. "Fair enough."

CHAPTER 12

Zootie and I spent a lot of time together over the next several days. He hung out at the bar, helped out where he could, and we sat and talked for hours over beer, whiskey, and whatever else Ren decided to serve up to us. The words flowed as freely as the alcohol and we covered a lot of ground. Money. Sex. Politics. Nothing seemed to be off-limits.

"You a religious man, Dan?" he asked me one night, after several beers.

"No, not really," I confessed. "I find the whole religion thing to be a bit of a turn-off to tell you the truth." I then just pushed "play" on the religion tape that I'd played dozens of times, at countless parties and over countless drinks. I told him how religion seemed to be a crutch for some people and how I didn't buy the "God's will" excuse for everything good or bad that happened in life.

"Bible thumpers bug the crap out of me, I have to admit," I continued. "They're the worst! It takes a lot of arrogance for somebody to assume that they know the way to salvation for me!" I was putting my usual manufactured passion into my words, though any *real* passion for the words I was sharing had disappeared after the first few telling's many years earlier. "I believe that there is some Higher Being, but I don't believe that he wants credit for every little thing that goes on down here. Come on! If He's the all-knowing, all-wonderful, all-loving God that these people say he is, then why would he want to go stealing the credit for all this stuff that is the result of other people's hard work? It doesn't make any sense!"

Zootie just listened politely. After taking a couple gulps of beer I ranted onward.

"I've decided that I'm a practicing Chrizendian, Zootie." I paused for effect. He didn't furrow his brow or ask for an explanation, as most people had in the past, but I gave him one anyway. "I like the Christian concept of Love Thy Neighbor, I like the Zen concept of staying in the here and now, and I like the American Indian concept of honoring the Mother Earth. You add them all up and you have a spiritual quilt that I call Chrizendian, and that's what I believe." I took a big self-satisfied swig of beer and sat back in my chair, waiting for the inevitable questions and praise that typically followed my religious rants.

There was an awkward silence as he seemed to be digesting all that I had just said. I continued to wait for his admiration of my tremendous insights and obvious passion.

"So, what do you *really* believe?" he finally asked me.

I just about shot my gulp of beer through my nose. He saw the "What?!?" look on my face and explained further.

"I hear you saying the words, but I don't hear your heart behind the words," he explained calmly in his Harvard professor voice. "So, I'm just curious what you truly believe, behind all of your intellectual mumbo-jumbo."

I was speechless. In all my years of presenting my "Religious Views Tape," dating all the way back to my college years, nobody had ever asked me that question.

"What do you mean?" I sputtered. "That *is* what I believe!"

"Is it?"

"Yes!"

"Then you're tellin' me that you love your neighbor as yourself, warts and irritatin' habits 'n all, just as Christ directed us to?"

"Well, I try my best, but…"

"And that you don't allow past regrets or future fears to affect your present actions, as is practiced by Zen Buddhists?"

"Not *all* the time, but…"

"And, just like the Indians, you give thanks each and every day for the air that ya breath, the water ya drink and the food that ya eat?"

"Yeah, I'm a pretty thankful guy…"

Zootie smiled that mischievous smile of his. "I'm just messin' with ya again, Dan," he said. I felt the blood rushing to my face. "I'm just makin' the point that if you scratch a little deeper, lookin' past the answers that you always give to questions like that, you might be surprised at what you find." He smiled again. "Seems like sometimes there's a Grand Canyon between what we think and what we truly believe when the rubber hits the road." He threw me a playful wink.

While he talked, I managed to regain my composure. Part of me was embarrassed at having been challenged like that. Part of me was angry for having been embarrassed.

"So, what is it that *you* believe, oh Zootie-son?" I asked semi-sarcastically.

He was on to me but, to his credit, he didn't stoop to my level. "A year ago, Dan, I would have given you an answer much like yours: high on intellect, low on feelin'. But today," he looked at me solemnly, "and mind you, this is still bein' formed with each passing day." I nodded. "Today I believe in the inherent goodness in every human soul. And I believe that our one purpose here on Earth is to help each other out the best we can. The more we stray from that purpose, the more we suffer." He smiled warmly. "Simple as that."

He looked over at me and I felt a strange sensation run through me. It was almost as if his eyes were surveying my insides. It made me uncomfortable and I looked away.

"Wow," I finally said, trying to distract him, "sounds like you might have the beginnings of your very own church."

He let out a small laugh. "Anytime you try to take matters of the heart and turn them into a religion or a crusade, you lose the original message Dan. I think we both agree on that one. This is something that everyone has to stumble onto themselves - no churches, no revival meetings, no arm-twistin' - just a simple decision inside ourselves as to what's *really* important in life. After that, it's just a matter of havin' the courage to live it every day."

"Sounds easy," I lied.

"Yeah, ain't it though!" Zootie bellowed. "The knowin' and the doin' are kissin' cousins for sure, but sometimes they seem to live in different states."

We laughed and raised our beer bottles in a toast. I felt relieved to be off the hook from earlier. I had felt exposed and I was thankful that Zootie hadn't pressed me further. I noticed, too, that it was hard to get or stay mad at Zootie because everything he did seemed to be straight from his heart and it was hard to argue with a man's heart.

I didn't sleep well that night, or for the next couple of nights. I kept on rolling Zootie's comments, and his standing offer to join him in Seattle, over and over in my mind. The battle lines were quickly drawn. Courage versus comfort. Getting involved versus staying safely on the sidelines. The inner debate raged on and I couldn't get away from it. I would just lay in the bed that Ren had provided for me upstairs from the bar and agonize over each point that was made by my competing selves.

"You think you're ready to deal with a thousand people like that old woman?!? I asked myself.

"What else is it that you have planned for your life?!?" came the response.

"This isn't selling girl scout cookies!" I reminded myself. *"This is death, The Big D, lots of suffering and pain and other crap that's just gonna drag you down! Who the hell needs THAT?!?"*

"You do!" came the retort. *It's about time you invested yourself in something that mattered! Zootie was right about helping others!"*

"Who are you kidding? You couldn't even stick around long enough to help the Locket Lady! Just give the guy some money or something and wish him good luck. This ain't your thing, and it ain't your fight!"

I tried staying up extra late each night, so that I might fall asleep immediately and avoid the nightly dialogue in my head, but it didn't work. By the morning of Zootie's departure I was exhausted.

He came strolling into the bar that morning, whistling as if he hadn't a care in the world. I wondered to myself how he kept from becoming a sniveling wreck with that list in his possession. "So, how's it goin' Dan?" he asked cheerfully.

"Oh, not too bad I guess," I lied.

We made small talk for a while, but it didn't take Zootie long to cut to the chase. "So, do I have a partner?" He smiled a smile that seemed to assume he knew my answer.

"Well Zootie, it's like this…" I began hesitantly. His smile disappeared. "I'm thinking that I'm not really cut out for this Death Merchant thing and, well," Zootie was frowning now, "I think I'm going to have to turn down your offer."

Zootie didn't say a word. He just looked at me with those x-ray eyes of his, trying to discern my innermost thoughts, as if he didn't truly believe the words I was saying and he wanted to uncover the real truth that had been left unsaid. It made me a little uneasy and I began blabbering to break the uncomfortable silence.

"What I'd like to do though," I stammered, "is give you some of the money I've made here at Ren's to help you out." Still no response. I just kept talking, not quite knowing what would come out of my mouth next. "I also thought that I might look you up when I get out that way in a few months and see if maybe you might still need my help or something." I didn't mean it at the time, but it seemed like a good thing to say.

45

Zootie finally spoke. "You know Dan, I can't say that I'm surprised by any of this. Disappointed a little, but not surprised." He sighed and threw me a weak smile. "And you know what else? I'd already made up my mind that I wouldn't say a word to try to convince you otherwise if you turned me down. This list is gonna take too much outta you to be in it halfway and all my words would do is drag you over a line you didn't want to cross." He sighed again and placed his hands together, as if praying. "So," he stuck his hand out, "I guess this is goodbye."

I felt nauseous and empty.

"Zootie, I…" He wouldn't let me finish.

"Dan, don't say another word. Anything else you say will just be to make me feel better or to ease your guilt, and neither one is gonna help right now."

He was right. I just shook his hand and nodded grimly. As he turned and walked away, I managed to get out a weak, "Good luck!" to his back. I'm not sure he heard me. I stood there and felt like my aloneness spread far beyond the walls of the bar.

CHAPTER 13

I was miserable for days after Zootie left. Ren saw me moping around one day and came over to offer comfort. She patted me on the back and said, "Don't ya worry there, Danny boy. Ol' Zootie's got a heart as big as a mountain 'n he don't hold any of this against ya."

I looked at Ren with eyes that I'm certain were pathetic. "Ren, I just don't understand why the hell he chose *me* to help him with that list of his?!?"

Ren heaved a deep sigh, obviously trying to decide whether it was best to let me down gently or just give it to me straight. She gave it to me straight. "Well, Dan, it's because he saw in you a man who was searchin' for somethin' to give his life meaning and purpose. He thought that workin' on that list 'o his would give that to you." She paused. "To tell ya the truth, I see the same thing in ya, Danny."

Her words didn't give me the comfort that I think she had intended them to give. They just sent me into more of a tailspin. I let out an involuntary snort. "Yeah, well, you guys sure aren't doing me any favors, I'll tell you that! It's not bad enough that I let myself down all the time, now I gotta worry about letting you and Zootie down with my lack of character and chicken-shit, meaningless existence!" I all but screamed the last words at Ren and I felt sorry for it before the words had even left my lips.

"I'm sorry Ren, I..."

She held her hand up. "Stop right there, Dan! Don't you go apologizin' ta me for showin' some real emotion! Yer confused, yer frustrated and ya feel like yer whole life's been swung ass-side up! Ya got a right ta yell and scream and stomp yer feet a little!"

Her words completely deflated my anger. She reached over and pulled me into an embrace, and I didn't resist. She pulled me in tight and, as she squeezed me harder, I felt my body begin to tremble. I wanted to pull away but a voice inside me told me to stay where I was. Besides, she was stronger than I was. The involuntary shaking worsened as it felt like all my pent-up emotions were trying to exit my body through my pores. Looking back, it would have been easier if I had just cried it all out but, at the time, that wasn't an option - my cheeks hadn't tasted the salt of my tears for close to thirty years and I wasn't inclined to break that streak. I just trembled instead and, as hard as I shook, Ren wouldn't let go; she just kept squeezing me tighter and tighter and rubbing my back.

I don't know how long it was that we stood there, me trembling and her comforting me, but it was the sound of the front door opening that broke our embrace. A couple of the regulars walked in, saw us separate quickly, and headed for the pool tables. One of the men, who I knew was a little sweet on Ren, gave me a look that was filled with contempt. He thought I was moving in on his woman. I nodded and smiled weakly then turned to head for the bathroom.

Ren grabbed my arm and pulled me back. She pulled me in so that we were almost nose-to-nose. Her eyes were moist - it was obvious that she'd been crying even though I hadn't - and I could see the passion behind her tears. "Don't give up on yerself, Danny," she whispered to me in a soft voice that I'd never heard Ren use before. "You got a good heart in there," she reached up and placed her right hand on my chest, "and it's gonna tell ya everything ya need ta know." She smiled a soft, warm smile that filled her eyes. "You just gotta listen to it and not be afraid of what it tells ya." She patted my chest a couple of times and then turned to go deal with her two customers.

I stood there for a moment, feeling weak in the legs from all the trembling and a little taken aback by Ren's words. I finally noticed that Ren's suitor wanna-be was still staring at me and so, suddenly feeling like an idiot, I headed for the bathroom.

CHAPTER 14

I was packed and ready to leave the next morning. I felt like I needed to get out on the road and try to gain a perspective that only walking alone for a while could give to me. Ren got up early to see me off.

"You take good care 'o yerself, Danny boy," she said as she gave me a big hug.

"I will, Ren, don't you worry about that." I gave her a big squeeze. "And thanks Ren, thanks for everything."

She squeezed me back and I felt the same emotions from the night before charging up through my body. I pulled back, not wanting to make another scene.

She saw my struggle but didn't say anything, other than, "Good luck to you, Danny. I sure hope ya find what'cher lookin' for."

With that, and a wave, I was off.

The first few miles were just a blur as I struggled to get my internal bearings. After that, it became more of a physical struggle as I tried to find my old walking rhythm that had been put on the shelf for the previous few weeks. It had been my longest layoff from walking since my trip began and it took me a while to work out all the tightness and little kinks that had taken up residence in my legs and back.

By early afternoon I had re-discovered my rhythm.

My first day back on the road was pleasant enough, mid-seventies and clear skies, which allowed me to ruminate on some of the issues that had been raised back at The Blue Q. I didn't dwell on the issues too much, however, because, after recovering my gait and pace in the afternoon, I was too busy just enjoying being unencumbered on the open road again. I'd forgotten how much I enjoyed just putting one foot in front of the other, feeling my legs and lungs working together, and not having a worry in the world other than finding a suitable place to bed down for the night. It was a simple life and I was wallowing in its simplicity.

Day two was a different story.

I awoke the next morning to a whole different world. The weather had changed overnight from sunny, mild and clear to the dreaded three H's - hazy, hot and humid. It was mid-September and fall was supposed to be right around the corner, but summer had decided to assert itself one last time. The hot, sticky air descended like an invisible curtain by mid-morning and didn't let up for the next three days. This made ruminating quite difficult.

All I could think about for those three days was how to get comfortable, if even for just a few minutes. I took advantage of shade wherever I could find it. I slurped down whatever cold drinks I could get my hands on. I poured cups of water over my head and walked through sprinklers whenever I got the chance. I ducked into air-conditioned businesses as often as I could.

In the late afternoon of the third day of the heat wave, I desperately needed one of those air-conditioning breaks. I decided to buy my inside time with a cup of coffee and chose a small cafe in a small town in central Indiana. I walked in and felt instant relief as the cool air enveloped my hot, wilted body. I trudged over to the first available table and plopped myself into the chair. It was heaven.

There was no sign of a waitress for a while, so I picked up a newspaper that had been left on the table and began half-mindedly scanning the headlines. I was in mid-daydream when a waitress stepped up to my table.

"So, anything good in there today?" she asked.

She had caught me by surprise, which I noticed was happening to me more frequently lately. I set down the paper and said, "Excuse me?"

She nodded at the newspaper. "In the paper, anything worth reading?"

"Oh, uh, to tell you the truth, I wasn't really reading it all that closely."

She smiled. It was a smile that completely lit up the entire restaurant. "So, what can I get for you today?"

It took me a second to recover from her smile, as it had caught me by surprise. She had a round, almost ordinary face, but when she smiled it was if a switch had been flipped and her entire face radiated pure light. I was temporarily mesmerized. "Uh, how about a cup of coffee," I finally managed to say.

"You got it."

I looked down at her nameplate and saw that her name was Hannah. I smiled at her. "Thanks Hannah." She walked away and I watched her as she got my cup of coffee. She was probably in her mid-twenties and she had brown, curly, shoulder-length hair that was pulled from her face with a headband. She had full cheeks and radiant blue eyes that matched her smile. She had an average build, but it wasn't anything about her body or physical appearance that had me thinking what an attractive young lady she was. It was her energy. I swore that I could actually feel the energy around her. Or maybe I had just been in the hot sun too long.

"Here ya go," she said as she set my coffee on the table.

"Thanks."

"No problem." She smiled again and my heart smiled with her. She paused at the edge of the table for a moment. "You're not from around here, are you?"

I looked around the cafe and saw that it was nearly empty. I decided to give a bit longer answer than was typical for me.

"No, no I'm not," I began. "I'm actually from Massachusetts and am walking my way to the west coast."

"No kidding!" she gushed. "You know, I was standing over there thinking to myself that you were someone that I was supposed to talk to, I didn't know why, but now I do!" She looked at me kind of sideways. "Do you ever get those feelings, like you're supposed to meet some stranger because they have something important to say to you or some little piece of advice?"

I was hypnotized by her face. I couldn't stop looking into her eyes and smiling like an idiot. "No, I can't say that I do," I replied.

"I get those all the time. My mother says that I have a gift or something, where I can see inside of people and all that." She laughed. "If that were the case, I wouldn't have nearly the problems that I do with my love life!" We both laughed.

"So why are you walking across the country, if I may ask."

"You may," I said with a nod. "I guess you'd say that I'm looking for something, only I haven't found out what that is just yet."

"Sort of a mid-life crisis kinda thing, huh?"

Ouch. Here I had been thinking we were semi-flirting and then she basically calls me an old man. "Yeah, I guess it is a mid-life crisis kinda thing," I agreed reluctantly.

She saw my face drop. "Hey, it's okay! It's better to go out looking than to just be sitting at home being miserable!" She had misinterpreted my reaction, but her reassurances were still sweet.

"Thanks for the pep talk."

"I know *exactly* what I want to do with my life," she then said matter-of-factly.

"What's that?" I asked.

"After I save enough money, I'm going to enroll in the Journalism program at IU, get my degree, and then I'm going to travel the world and write for National Geographic."

Her enthusiasm was magnetic. At that moment I had no doubt that she would achieve every single one of her goals. "That's a great plan," I said with a smile. "Why don't you get started right now?"

The smile left her face. "I promised my mother that I wouldn't leave until my little brother graduates from high school and he's a senior this year. She can't make a go of it on her own since my father passed away and so I told her I'd help out until Jimmy's better able to." She sighed. "My mother always tells me, *Hope,*" Hannah looked down at me and rolled her eyes. "She always calls me Hope because those are the initials of my name - Hannah Olivia Penelope Edwards - and she tells me that that's what I gave her, hope, after Daddy died six years ago.

"Anyways, she says," Hannah crossed her arms and then raised her finger, imitating her mother I assumed. *"Hope, you're gonna have plenty of time to chase after those dreams of yours, don't you worry!"* She dropped her arms. "Sometimes I know that she's right, but sometimes I feel like I just won't have enough time, like every minute that goes by is so important and I'm missing out on such important things!"

I noticed that nothing about her tone was trying to solicit pity or sympathy from me. She was telling it in a matter-of-fact way that was free of self-pity. I was preparing to share a few words of wisdom with her when an older woman walked up to the table and cleared her throat.

"Hannah," the woman said when she had our attention, "you have some other customers over there who are waiting to give their orders." The woman, who I assumed to be the owner, looked at my pack and then looked at me with eyes that were familiar to me: the "I wish you'd leave my restaurant because you're not welcome here" eyes. I smiled at her with the biggest smile I could muster.

The woman walked away in a small huff and Hannah looked at me with a sorry-but-I-have-to-get-back-to-work face. I felt an impulse to reach over and grab her arm and wish her luck with her dreams, but I hesitated and, after exchanging quick smiles, she was off to the next table.

The cafe quickly got busier, as the seniors began coming in for an early dinner, so Hannah and I didn't get another opportunity to talk. She would come by to pour me more coffee occasionally but there was only time for a quick smile and then off she went to the next table. After a while, I decided it was time to start walking again as I had to find a place to bed down for the night. I got up, left the money for the coffee and a tip on the table, and headed out the door. Hannah saw me leaving from across the restaurant and gave me a small wave. I returned her wave and saw her radiant smile one last time.

Stepping outside, the heat was brutal. As I headed out of town, a quick dialogue took place in my head.

"Why couldn't you give that girl a little encouragement?" I asked. *"Nothing improper, just show her a little bit of human kindness. Is there anything wrong with that?"*

"Yeah, yeah, yeah, you make it sound so sweet and inno-cent," came the reply, *"but you know she would think that you were just some dirty old man trying to flirt with her."*

"What a shame," I thought, *"that I would have to hesitate about trying to be nice to someone."*

And on it went for several miles. I found a small field on the outskirts of town where I decided to make camp. I walked to the far edge of the field, out of sight of the road, and spread out my blanket under a large oak tree. I laid there for hours, eventually watching the day turn to dusk and the dusk turn to night.

I couldn't get Hannah's bright, smiling face out of my mind. I didn't feel any sexual feelings towards her, just an inexplicable attraction. It was like Hannah had said in the cafe -

I felt as if I was supposed to get something from her, only I didn't know what it was.

I also realized that I had repeated a past mistake. I had had the opportunity to do something kind and helpful and had, once again, slunk out the back door. I was hopeless. I fell asleep that night feeling like a complete failure as a human being. The unbearably thick, humid air served as an appropriate punishment for my failures.

CHAPTER 15

I hardly slept at all that night. When I did manage to fall asleep, I kept on going back to a recurring nightmare that I hadn't had since I was a kid.

In the nightmare, red-eyed rats kept coming at me. I tried running away from them, but my feet felt like they had been immobilized in concrete. I tried like hell to drag my feet across the floor, but it was no use, I was stuck. I would then fall to the ground, exhausted. After falling, I would roll over on my back and the rats would then start crawling up my legs. They tore at my pants until they found flesh. Dozens more crawled up to my mid-section and started gnawing on my shirt. I watched helplessly as they dug into the soft part of my belly with their big, yellow teeth. It wasn't long before they were feasting on my innards, blood and skin flying in all directions. I opened my mouth to scream but I couldn't muster even the smallest of sounds. I began to whimper in my nightmare as I lay there watching the carnage of my own body in front of me. Two of the larger rats would then pause and look up at me, their bright red eyes glowing with pure evil and their blood-soaked mouths grinning widely. Then the two large rats would start scurrying up my chest, towards my face, with dozens of other rats close behind them. They were going to start picking apart my face, I knew it, and that was when I would start screaming wildly and wake myself up. I must have gone through this cycle a handful of times over the course of the night.

Sunrise was a welcome sight the next morning. Exhausted and groggy, I got up and packed my bag. As I strode across the field, soaked with morning dew, I had an idea that I hoped would make things right for me.

I figured my sub-conscious was beating up on me because I had chickened out with wishing Hannah good luck with her dreams the previous day. So, I decided that I'd walk back into town, have breakfast at the same cafe, and try to un-do my mistake. It was a good plan. I had even overheard her mention to one of her co-workers that she had to work the morning shift this morning, so I knew she'd be working. Who said you don't get second chances in life?

The heat and humidity had seemed to back off a little bit which, combined with the excitement of my mission, made the walk into town quite pleasant. I even managed to come up with a small poem while walking, which I decided to jot down on a piece of paper and hand to her along with a twenty-dollar bill.

Though life can be tough
and unfair it seems,
I want to wish you luck
with all of your dreams!

It wasn't anything that Emily Dickinson would put her name to, but I liked it. I pulled out one of my journals and a pen from my pack when I got into town, wrote out the poem as neatly as I could, and then folded a twenty dollar bill up with it and put it into my pocket. I walked into the cafe feeling the kind of exhilaration that comes with preparing to give a gift that you know is absolutely perfect and will be appreciated by the recipient. It was my time to make things right with my conscience.

I walked into the cafe and set my pack by the door. I did a quick scan of the interior and saw no sign of Hannah. I walked to the center of the cafe and continued to look around. I spotted the older woman from the day before, she was standing by the kitchen door talking with someone, and I nodded and raised my eyebrows in an attempt at getting her to come over and help me. To my surprise, she did.

I noticed as she approached that her face had changed slightly from the day before. Gone was the pinched, never-pleased face and in its place was a sad, tired face. She looked like she'd been working way too hard.

"Can I help you?" she asked quietly.

"Yes, you can," I said with a smile. "I was in here yesterday, perhaps you remember me," she nodded slightly but didn't give me the same snobbish look that she had the day before. I pressed onward. "And, well, I was wondering if Hannah was working today, because there was something that I had forgotten to give to her."

The woman's face absolutely dropped to the floor. She then took in a small breath of air in a gasp and put her hand to her mouth as if horrified. "My goodness, you're not a relative of hers, are you?"

I couldn't figure out why such a thought would horrify her, but I answered with a polite, "No, I'm just an acquaintance of hers actually."

The woman looked slightly relieved, but I could tell that there was something else on her mind. "Then you haven't heard the news yet, have you?"

I felt a huge ache in the bottom of my stomach. "What news?" I asked, though I knew the answer before she got it out.

"There was a terrible accident last night, right at the end of Main Street," she pointed to some distant point, "and one of the cars went up on the sidewalk." The woman's eyes filled with tears. "That poor, dear girl was just walking home from work and didn't see the car coming and, well..." she paused, not sure what words to use next. The tears turned to sobs. "And, well...she was killed instantly."

The last few words thudded to the floor in front of me. *"Killed? How can that be?!? I just saw her yesterday and she was so full of life!"*

The woman must have seen my reaction and reached over and grabbed my arm. "She was such a sweet girl. I've known her mother most of my life and I just don't know how she's going to be able to live with another tragedy like this!"

"Dead?" I thought of the card in my pocket. *"But I have this gift that I have to give to her! How can that be?!?"*

The cafe suddenly started feeling very small and very warm. I began sweating profusely. The woman was still talking to me, but I wasn't listening. All I could think was, *"I have to get out of here!"*

I thanked the woman for her help and turned to head out the door. I couldn't get out fast enough. As I was picking up my pack by the door, I did hear her final words. "There will be a service for her tomorrow if you want to pay your respects," she shouted at my back. I didn't even acknowledge her words as I dashed out the door.

CHAPTER 16

I staggered out of town the same way I had come in earlier. At the edge of the downtown district I noticed something that I hadn't noticed when I came in: glass was strewn throughout the intersection. The thought hit me: *"This must have been where it happened last night!"* I felt chills despite the warm air. Unable to help myself, I started thinking about what her last moments must have been like.

Walking home from just another day at work, she was probably thinking about the day that had just ended and making plans for the day to come. Replaying small mistakes and maybe toying with a dream or two. Nothing to separate it from the thousands of other similar days that she had lived to that point. Then, out of nowhere, comes the end. No warning, no time to plan. Just the end. End of dreams. No more tomorrows. No more having to worry about stupid boyfriends, bad hair days or cranky customers. No more anything.

I flashed on her smiling face one more time and then, in my mind's eye, saw that smile turn to a look of fear and horror as she saw her fate in front of her. I swore that I heard a scream in my ears. I shook my head and started walking again, anxious to get out of that town as quickly as I could.

I trembled as I walked for the first few miles. I kept on trying to convince myself that I was being silly and sentimental, but it didn't work. Words such as, *"You didn't even know this woman for god's sake!"* did little to assuage my feelings of anxiety.

Another voice, much stronger than the one that had been trying to convince me how silly I was being, started to whisper in my ear. *"You're trembling for a reason,"* it said to me. *You're at a crossroads. You know it, and you're just putting off what you know you should be doing. Hannah's death was a sign."*

"A sign of what?" I wondered.

"Go to Seattle. Go help Zootie," came the reply.

Fear filled my belly. I thought about the old woman dying in front of me. I thought about the rats in my nightmare. I thought about my imaginary snapshot of Hannah's face, frozen with terror. I thought, too, about how I used to cry myself to sleep as a young boy.

When I was perhaps 8 or 9 years old, and had just learned about the finality of death, I obsessed on thoughts of my death every night before bed. I would lay there in the dark with my ear on the pillow and listen to my heartbeat reverberate through my ears. Thump, thump. Thump, thump. I would then think about how my heart would one day just stop beating. Forever. I then tried to get my young mental arms around the question of: "What then?" Not having been raised with any kind of religious escape hatch for that question, I had nowhere to run and hide. After my heart stopped, that would just be it. I saw nothing but blackness and the person that is me would just no longer be around. Then I would start to cry. Sob actually, as I became so afraid of the nothingness that lay off in my future. But it wouldn't end there. My heartbeat would then become the cadence for "The March of the Dead" in my head. Thump, thump. Thump, thump. Hundreds of gruesome skeletons and decomposing bodies would come marching by my mind's eye to the beat of my heart, giving me a horrific preview of my eventual fate. Thump, thump. Thump, thump. They kept on marching and I kept on crying until I would get so exhausted that I would finally, mercifully, fall asleep. That went on for several years.

I hadn't thought about that part of my childhood for a long time. As I thought about it, I realized that that was the last time I'd cried. Over a silly, recurring nightmare.

"Go to Seattle. Go help Zootie," came the echo in my head.

I thought about all the funerals that I had conveniently "missed" over the years. My neighbor Cal Perkins, who died of a heart attack when I was a teenager. My Uncle Bert, who died of lung cancer after a long, terrible battle that lasted for years. I never even went to see him in the hospital. Both sets of grandparents passed away without a goodbye from me.

The only funeral I'd ever gone to in my life was my father's and, truth be told, I had entertained selfish thoughts even then on possible ways to "miss" it. When I accepted the fact that I couldn't avoid it, I went through the motions with as much emotional separation as I could muster. I stayed away from the open casket and didn't so much as shed a tear the entire day, or for any days after that.

"Go to Seattle."

Why was all of this coming up now? Why did death seem to be taking over my life?

"Go help Zootie."

Why was I obsessing on the death of a girl who I had just met and who I had spoken with for less than ten minutes?

"Go to Seattle."

I stopped walking and looked up into the blue sky overhead. I stretched out my arms and yelled as loud as I could. "WHYYYYYY???????" It hurt my throat. No answer came raining down on my head.

"Go help Zootie."

I lowered my head, defeated. With a sigh I began walking toward the next town a few miles ahead. I had noticed at one of my earlier stops that it was a little bigger town and would probably have a train station.

I was going to Seattle.

PART II

Vidi

*"Our chief want in life is someone
who will make us do what we can."*
Ralph Waldo Emerson

CHAPTER 17

The train ride to Seattle was uneventful. I had enough money to get me as far as Bozeman, where I stopped and worked until I had enough to pay for the last leg to Seattle. The week in Bozeman was nice as it gave me time to think some more about what I was about to do. I went for several walks in the mountains during my stay in Bozeman and found that the cool, fresh mountain air agreed with my brain cells. It was also nice to get away from the oppressive heat of the Midwest and the time in the mountains seemed to solidify my decision. I was going to Seattle.

I called Ren from Bozeman and got Zootie's new address in Seattle. I wanted to surprise him, so I didn't bother calling ahead. I pulled into the Seattle Amtrak station, hopped a cab to Zootie's house in the Wallingford District north of Seattle, and was walking up his front walk 10 days after making my decision back in Indiana. I felt excited.

The house was located on a residential street and was quite large. I noticed as I walked up the sidewalk that the front yard was well-tended and there were birdhouses and flowers scattered throughout the yard. I strolled up the steps to the front door and pressed the doorbell.

Nobody answered, so I knocked.

Again, no answer, so I knocked louder. I was starting to feel my excitement turn to disappointment.

I stepped back a little and looked around for signs of life. Nothing. I did notice, however, that there seemed to be a worn path around one side of the house. I walked down the front steps and went over to investigate and saw that the path went through a series of arbors on the side of the house and seemed to end up in the back yard. There was no sign of a fence and no sign of any dogs, so I headed down the path.

The arbors were thick with what looked like grapevines. It blocked out all the sun and made the path shady and cool. When I stepped out from under the arbors and into the back yard I was hit with a wall of sound. It caught me by surprise, and I couldn't figure out where the sound was coming from at first. Then I saw movement, lots of it, and figured out the source of the noise.

It was birds - hundreds of them! They were flitting from perch to perch all around me and I felt slightly unnerved at first. Visions of some Hitchcockian nightmare danced across my brain. I'm not much of a bird expert but I noticed that there were birds of all sizes and colors in the trees and bushes. After my nerves settled down a little bit, I began to appreciate the uniqueness of my new surroundings.

Bushes, trees and flowers filled the yard, and everything seemed to be in full bloom. All the greenery prevented me from seeing the whole of the yard, but I did see a series of stone paths meandering throughout the yard, so I decided to start walking, hoping to run into someone.

As I walked, I took notice of a reality that took away a little of the luster from the magic of my surroundings. Bird crap was everywhere. I tried to step around it at first but soon saw that there was no way to avoid it. I had more than a few narrow escapes as I heard small splatting noises all around me as I walked.

Once in the back area of the yard, I noticed some movement - bigger than a bird - over in one corner. I headed over there yelling, "Hello! Hello!" as I walked. They couldn't hear me over the din of the birds. As I got closer, I saw that it was an older woman and she was filling bird feeders. The birds were singing and squawking all around her, but she just went on about her business. I could see the top of the dark, broad-brimmed hat she wore when she bent over, and it appeared that the birds had made her a target more than once.

I walked right up to her and yelled one last time. "Hello!" I startled her. She stumbled backward slightly and let out a squeaky, "Mercy sakes Marie!" I stepped forward to help her, but she regained her footing quickly.

As she gathered herself, I started talking, trying to introduce myself. "Hi there. I'm so sorry to startle you like this, but I knocked on the door and nobody answered so I thought I'd come back here and..."

"Don't you worry about me, m'boy," she said as she stood upright, brushed off her dress and stuck her hand out for me to shake. "Hyacynthia Ebbermeier's the name, but you can call me Hy."

Her lack of concern or questions after being startled by a stranger in her own backyard surprised me a little and caused me to pause before shaking her hand.

"What's the matter?" she asked me. "Are ya worried that I might have bird shit on my hands?" There was no mistaking the mischievous glint in her eye as she spoke.

I smiled and shook her hand. "Dan Barnes is my name. Nice to meet you, Hy."

"Dan Barnes!" she squealed as if she knew me. "Zootie said you might be showing up on my doorstep sometime soon!"

"Zootie? How did he..."

"Oh, sometimes that man seems to have a crystal ball stashed away somewhere, I'll tell ya that! He just seems to know things that other folks are left scratchin' their heads about."

"But I didn't tell anyone that..."

Hy waved her hand. "Never you mind about that! Fact is, you're standing here right now and that's all that's important right now, isn't it?"

I shut my mouth and just nodded. I wondered whether Hy was related to Ren or Zootie as she seemed to be cut from the same assertive, speak-your-mind cloth. She was probably in her 80's, judging from her size and wrinkles, but the way she moved and spoke took years off her age. She had a playful streak and I found myself smiling constantly while in her company.

"So, Dan Barnes, why'd you come out here to visit us?"

I didn't know how many people Zootie had told about his list, so I felt a little uncomfortable answering her question. "Well, I, um…"

"Was it the list that brought you out here?"

Saved. "Yes, as a matter of fact it was."

"Thought so," she nodded. She cocked her head and looked at me sideways. "You aren't on it, are you?"

"No, no," I said as I waved my hands. "I'm just here to help out however I can."

"I'm on it."

The three words carried a weight that hit me in the stomach like a wrecking ball, taking my breath away temporarily. I didn't know what to say. A voice from behind me took me off the hook.

"Danny! You made it!" I turned around and saw Zootie walking towards me. He walked up and gave me a big hug, which took me by surprise.

"Hey Zootie. How's it going?" I said as I hugged him back, even though it felt a little awkward.

"Life's grand, Danny, just grand!" He nodded toward Hy. "I see you've met my new landlady." They smiled warmly at each other.

"Yeah, Hy and I have met."

"I don't think he cares much for my little feathered friends, Zootie." I looked over and she winked at me.

I decided to play along. "Well, except for the wall-to-wall bird crap, I'd say they're the perfect backyard pets."

We all shared a laugh then Zootie motioned me towards the house. "Let's head inside Danny so I can show you around."

Hy followed us inside and on the way in I complimented her on her landscaping.

"Why thank you Danny! I like to keep a nice home for my little friends."

We walked in the back door and came into the house through the kitchen. The contrast couldn't have been more pronounced. I scanned the kitchen and saw dirty dishes stacked in the sink, old food laying on the counters and a distinct odor coming from somewhere. The story was the same when we walked through other rooms. I noticed that the dust was so thick on one windowsill that it appeared as if it had sprouted fur. Hy must have seen my jaw drop.

"A little different story *inside*, eh?" she said.

I didn't want to be rude, as I'd just met the woman, but an involuntary, "Yeah, that's for sure!" popped out of my mouth.

She wasn't insulted. "I made a decision many years ago Danny that I just couldn't do it all in my life. Something had to go, and I decided to spend my time with living, breathing things rather than keeping a never-ending river of dust at bay inside my house! Besides that, I hate housework! Did nothing *but* that for most of my 85 years and I just plain got better things to do these days!"

We finally walked into the front hallway and then into a den of sorts. "Like helping me with this list, for instance," Zootie said as we entered the room. I looked up where Zootie was pointing. One whole wall was covered with taped up sheets of paper. I walked closer and saw that it was a copy of the list

Zootie had shown me in Indiana. I scanned the list and was struck for the first time by the number of names that were on the list.

"How many names did you say were on this list?"

"We count one thousand four hundred and fourteen," Zootie replied. He paused for a moment. "And one mystery guest." I looked over at him and he nodded toward the sheets in the middle of the list. I walked over and looked at the names more closely.

The dates stretched from June that had just passed through to May of the following year. In the middle of the list, around the middle of December, there was a gap in the list. It was obvious that it was more than just an extra space between names as I could see little black ink remnants where someone had not quite whited out an entire name. I ran my finger along the space. It was smooth.

I turned around and looked at Zootie. "This list is a copy."

Zootie nodded. "And whoever copied it is probably the same person who made it, and whoever made it doesn't want us to see that particular name for some reason."

"Where'd you get this list again?" I asked.

"Just showed up in my door one day."

We were interrupted by a woman who came strolling into the room. "Hey Zootie! Hey Hy!" she said cheerily. She was a dark-haired woman with striking blue eyes that I noticed immediately. She was perhaps in her late thirties and had obviously taken good care of her body, which I also noticed immediately.

"Hey there, Trish!" Zootie replied as Hy gave her a hug. Zootie then hugged her and said, "Trish there's someone I'd like you to meet." She pulled out of the hug and stood right in front of me. Looking into her clear blue eyes I thought my knees were going to buckle. "Trish McConnell, meet Dan Barnes."

I shook her hand. "Trish McConnell, huh?" I said with mock contemplation. "So which part of Germany is your family from?"

She didn't miss a beat. "Southern part," she replied with a straight face. "And Barnes, what's that? Some Pennsylvania Dutch farmer name?" I love a woman who can play along.

Zootie broke up our conversation. "Well if you two are done flirting, I think I'll continue Dan's tour of the house."

We both blushed like a couple of school kids. It felt great.

"Well, it was nice to meet you Trish McConnell," I said as I walked out of the room behind Zootie.

"Likewise, Dan Barnes," she said as she smiled and nodded at me. "I'm sure I'll be seeing you around."

Zootie saw the smile on my face as we walked away. "Aren't you wondering why she's here, Dan?"

"Why she's here?" I thought for a second. Then, just as quickly, it hit me. *"Oh my gosh - the list!!!"*

"Don't worry though, she's not on the list," Zootie the mind-reader reassured me. "Her father was one of the early names on the list and she's been helping out with Project Hope ever since."

"Project Hope?" I mumbled.

"Yeah, that's the name we came up with for this whole crusade. What do you think?"

My mind flashed instantaneously to Hannah's face. *"Hannah Olivia Penelope Edwards is my name"* she had told me, *but my mother calls me Hope, because that's what I give her..."* Her words echoed in my ears so loudly she could have been standing next to me.

"It's a great name, Zootie," I muttered quietly.

"We all like it." He led me up the stairs and I noticed a large banner hanging from the ceiling. **"DO YOU HAVE ANY UNFINISHED BUSINESS?"** it asked in bold letters. Below it hung another sign. **"FINISH IT NOW!"** it read.

We walked down the upstairs hallway and stopped in front of a door at the end of the hall. "This will be your room while you stay here, Danny." He opened the door and we walked into a large, bright bedroom with two beds in it. I noticed that one of the beds had been slept in and there were clothes scattered throughout the room. "You'll be sharing the room with Brent." Zootie put his hand on my shoulder. "Don't worry, Brent's a good egg. You guys will get along splendidly.

"Now why don't you get settled in a little bit and rest up because I've got a little surprise for you tonight." He gave me one last pat on the back and then headed for the door. Before walking out of the room, he turned around and asked me, "You know how to play poker, don't you?"

"Sure," I replied. "And I've got a question for you."

"Fire away."

"How the heck did you know I was coming here?"

A big grin filled his face. "Ren called me and told me you'd called looking for my address and that you might be showing up here sometime soon."

"Ah, that explains it. So, you don't have a crystal ball after all," I said with a smile.

He turned again to go. "Don't be too sure of that, Danny boy. I may surprise you yet!" he said as he walked out the door.

CHAPTER 18

"You are bluffing, you filthy bandito!" Frank bellowed in his thick Spanish accent.

Zootie just smiled. "Time to put up or shut up, my good friend."

Frank squinted at Zootie and then slammed his cards to the table. Zootie took in his winnings and was obviously quite happy.

Hy was sitting next to me at the table and she leaned over to whisper in my ear. "So whaddaya think of our poker crew, Danny?"

I looked over at her and whispered, "Honestly? I feel like the mackerel at a shark convention!" We exchanged smiles and she patted my arm. I looked around the table. We'd been playing poker for several hours and I had already developed thumbnail sketches of each of my fellow poker players.

There was Francisco "Frank" Gutierrez, the Mexican, a former logger whose name was on the list. He struck me as an old lion who'd lost his teeth. He was close to Hy's age and, like Hy, he had strong opinions. He was coarse at the edges but seemed likable enough at his core. The man also loved to gamble.

Brent Haberman, my new roommate, was a bit harder to figure out. He was obviously an intellectual sort and he seemed to relish any opportunity to put his knowledge on display. He too was on the list, but he seemed a little more reluctant than the others to discuss that fact in this setting. He was close to

Zootie's age, somewhere in his fifties, but unlike Zootie he was fit and trim and obviously took great pride in his appearance. He liked to play the odds when it came to poker.

There was no doubt that Zootie was the man in charge. He presided over the table like a patriarchal pit boss, keeping everyone's attention focused on the game at hand. He raised with abandon and loved nothing more than to bluff his way to victory. Everything was done with a wink and a smile, however, as more than once I saw him slipping chips to different players who were running low.

Trish was a fish out of water. She obviously didn't understand the games very well but was still an eager participant. She could laugh and joke with the best of them, even Crusty Frank, and I felt my heart stop every time we made eye contact during the evening. I felt like I was in high school wanting to impress the new girl in my class.

Hy was seated next to me and she never stopped talking. She was constantly offering commentary or taking a good-natured jab at someone, never with ill intent. If Zootie was "the head" at the table then Hy was surely "the heart." She was part Granny from The Beverly Hillbillies and part Mother Teresa and it was a combination that made you glad she was sitting at your table. She made everything so much fun.

"So, are you ready to dive in tomorrow, Dan?" Zootie asked me between hands later in the evening.

"Uh, sure," I responded, having been taken by surprise by the more serious question amidst all the laughter and fun.

"Good, good. I thought I'd pair you up with Trish tomorrow and she can show you the ropes a little bit." Trish and I smiled at each other across the table. "That is all right with you, isn't it?" he asked. I looked over at Zootie and he gave me one of his trademark winks.

"Yeah, that'll be fine."

"Great! I think you two will make a dynamite team!"

I didn't feel like making the effort to try to find any hidden meaning within his words, so I just nodded. I glanced over at Trish as I fanned the cards that had just been dealt to me and noticed she was smiling. Good sign.

Later that night I was lying in my new bed when Brent walked into the room. We simply nodded and smiled at each other - a good smile, after a night well-spent - and then he grabbed his toiletries and went off to the bathroom down the hall.

When he returned, he let out a small laugh as he set down his toiletry bag. "I don't know why the hell I bother with flossing my teeth and eating chicken instead of beef; I'm certainly not going to die of heart disease or gum disease with the little time that *I* have left!"

I simply smiled an uncomfortable smile; this was all still too new to me to be able to joke about it.

Brent must have sensed my feelings of discomfort as he said; "You've got to loosen up Dan! All of us on the list have two choices - joke about it or take a flying leap into the canyon of despair, from which there is no return, and I for one am afraid of heights so I'm going to choose to joke about it." He flashed me a perfunctory smile.

"I guess I see that," I replied, "but this death thing is new for me and it's going to take me a while to adjust to having it in my face every day like this."

Brent walked over and sat on the edge of the bed next to mine. His face appeared sympathetic - almost fatherly - as he said, "Let me give you a quick primer on what to expect from life here at Hope House. A lot of what I'm going to say is borrowed from Elisabeth Kubler-Ross and others in her field, so please forgive me."" He looked at me like he would already know my answer to his next question. "You know who Elisabeth Kubler-Ross is, right?"

I gave him the answer he expected - even though it was a lie - as I nodded in affirmation.

He nodded his approval. "Good. Her book "On Death and Dying" is on the must-read list if you're going to be hanging around *this* place!"

I made a mental note to find her book.

"She talks a lot about the five stages of dying and you're going to see all of them on display around here."

"What are those again?" I asked as if they had once been known to me and were now simply forgotten.

Brent didn't seem to suspect my ignorance as he was more than happy to be in the role of the teacher. "First there is usually denial," he said as he raised one finger. "This is where they refuse to believe that they are going to die. They ignore symptoms, refute doctors' diagnoses and simply go on with life as if nothing is wrong." He raised a second finger. "Then comes the anger; they get mad at their disease or situation because of how it's disrupted their life and their plans." A third finger went up. "Next they begin the bargaining process; the old, if I go to church for the rest of my life will you please remove this cancer from my body type of thing." Finger number four. "Then comes the phase that a lot of people get stuck in - depression. It finally hits them that there's no way out and they're going to die. Most people are not equipped to deal with the realization of their own mortality, and they wind up feeling helpless and hopeless." Brent paused for a moment here, as if contemplating the meaning of his own words. "And finally," he continued, raising his thumb to join his four raised fingers," for the lucky ones, there is acceptance of their fate. This is the phase where all of the *I'm sorry's* and *I forgive you's* come into play as they prepare themselves for the end." He looked over at me and shrugged, as if to say, "there you have it!"

"So which phase are you in right now Brent?"

It took him a good minute to answer my question and I just stared at the ceiling in silence wondering if I'd offended him.

Finally, he said, "I guess, to be honest, I'm still a little bit pissed off at the whole thing." He looked at me with eyes that seemed to be asking for an affirmation of his feelings. "I'm still a young guy, and I had a good career, and I'm upset that all of that is going to be coming to such an abrupt end." Then his eyes took on more of a look of determination. "But I'll get a handle on this and - as Ms. Ross noted in her book - not everyone goes through all of these stages; once I get rid of this anger, I have no doubt that acceptance of my fate will be right around the corner."

"That's great that you feel that way Brent. I'm not so sure I'd feel that confident in the same situation."

He snorted involuntarily through his nose. "You'd be surprised what you learn to accept when you have no choice!"

"So what else should I know?" I asked, anxious to move on to a different subject.

He chuckled a wry, far-off chuckle. "Brace yourself for lots of hugs, buckets of tears and more gifts than you'll know what to do with." He looked over at me. "People who know they're dying are the most generous people in the world."

I just nodded, and I continued to nod as I laid in bed and listened to Brent's Death 101 lecture for the next couple of hours, until I couldn't keep my eyes open any longer and sleep overtook me.

CHAPTER 19

I met Trish in the front hallway the following morning after one of the best nights of sleep I'd had in a long time. We had a quick breakfast of toast and coffee, thanks to Frank, and then climbed in her car to head to our first "appointment" of the day.

"The way this is set up," she told me as she drove, "is that we all try to make an initial face-to-face contact with everyone on the list. We've started at the top, with the ones whose dates are coming up soon, and we're gradually working our way down the list." She looked over at me. "At first we thought there'd be no way we'd get in touch with all of them, but we're getting more and more people like you that want to help so now it seems more doable." She flashed me a small smile.

"So how is it that you ended up helping out?" I asked her.

"My father was one of the first names on the list."

"I'm sorry...I didn't know." I'd forgotten that Zootie had told me that just the day before. I felt like a jerk.

"No, it's okay," she reassured me. "If not for this list, I would have never had the goodbye that I did with him. I really owe Zootie for that gift."

"Wow, that's a great attitude to have about it."

She shrugged. "Yeah, well, it's an attitude that you're going to be seeing a lot if you keep hanging around Hope House." She pulled up to a curb. "Here we are."

She turned off the engine and shifted in her seat, so she was facing me. "So, here's the deal, Dan. We're going to be paying a visit to a woman by the name of Toby Liebman. I contacted her about her place on the list about a week ago and, like most people on the list, she didn't believe me at first. After sitting on it for a while though, and keeping an eye on the local obituaries for verification, she soon saw the light, so to speak. She's spent the past week going through all the stages of anger, denial, and the like and now she's at a point where she wants to talk some more. She called me last night and so here we are." Her blue eyes were fixed on mine. "Dan, all I want you to do is sit back and watch today. Toby's at a very delicate point right now and I don't want her to backslide, okay?"

I nodded.

We got out of the car, went up the walk and walked into the house without so much as a knock or a shout. We headed into the living room to the left and right away I noticed the smell. It was a vile combination of body odor, pee, poop and stale, heavy air. It took my breath away and it was all I could do to keep following Trish deeper into the smell.

Seated in a wheelchair on the far side of the living room was the largest woman I'd ever seen. The wheelchair was twice as wide as a standard one and it was still being stretched to its limits by her girth and weight. Her flesh spilled out everywhere. Her face was one big jowl and her eyes were all but invisible behind a pair of glasses that rested on her mountainous cheeks. Her large, blue legs stuck out from under her hospital gown and I could see right away why she was confined to the wheelchair. She must have weighed close to 400 pounds. The sight of this woman, combined with the strong smells, put all my senses on high alert. I felt my stomach start to do flip-flops.

"Hi Toby," Trish said sweetly. "How are you doing today?"

"Not so well, Trish." The woman took a deep, wheezing breath before each sentence and, when she exhaled, I could hear a loud rasping sound emanating from her throat. It was obvious that she was in a permanent state of discomfort and just the act of breathing was a chore for her. "I sent my nurse away on an errand so we could talk more freely." She looked over at me.

"Oh, don't worry about him, Toby," Trish reassured her. "He's a part of Hope House and is helping out with the list just like me."

This satisfied Toby and she turned her attention back to Trish. I sat down in a chair several feet behind Trish.

"So, what's up?" Trish asked nonchalantly.

"Like I told you on the phone Trish," deep, wheezy inhale...slow, raspy exhale, "I believe you about the list now, and," she paused to catch her breath..., "and now I'm having trouble getting to the point that I can just accept it." Wheeze in, raspy out. "You told me before that I'd go through all these feelings...and you were right...I've been doing nothing but crying these past few days...and I need your help."

Trish moved her chair closer to Toby so she could grab her hand and hold it. "What do you need from me, Toby?"

I saw tears begin to stream down Toby's cheeks. She made no effort to wipe them away. "I know that I'm going to die next week Trish...and I'm just so scared." The tears came faster.

Trish's back was to me, so I couldn't see her face, but I could hear a slight quiver in her voice as she spoke. "That's okay, Toby. What you're going through would scare anybody. It's okay to be afraid." She patted Toby's hand as she spoke.

"Yeah, but is everyone scared," wheeze in...raspy out, "of being carried out of their house with a forklift?" More tears dripped off her cheeks and onto her blue gown and her sniffling forced her to take recovery breaths more frequently. "And is everyone scared...of people laughing at them after they're dead...because of the size of their coffin?!?" Her voice was becoming more frantic. "I've seen those pictures Trish...of people my size being hauled out of their homes! People laugh and point and make fun of it!" She sobbed and sniffled for a while and Trish didn't say a word, she just let her cry it out. Before long, Toby regained control of herself and continued talking, though with a little more subdued tone.

"I wasn't always Tubby Toby, you know...I was actually quite thin and pretty up through high school...there's some pictures over there if you don't believe me." She took an extra big recovery breath as she pointed to another corner of the room.

Trish patted her hand. "I'm sure you were very beautiful, Toby, just as you are now."

Toby forced a smile at Trish's comment and then cast her eyes upward, as if watching an imaginary movie screen on the ceiling. "It was the summer after my junior year when it all changed...my boyfriend of two years, Bobby Mitchell, had just broken up with me...and I ran home prepared to cry into my mother's arms." She took a little longer pause to collect her breath and her emotions. "But when I got home, my Dad was there...and he told me that Mom had just died in a car accident." Toby stopped and stared blankly for a long while. "It was the end of my world."

She brought her gaze down from the ceiling and looked at Trish. "My Dad wasn't ready to be both my Mom and my Dad...so he started to withdraw from me and kept me away...by constantly criticizing me." Deep, wheezy breath. "He'd tell me that I was looking fat and that I should learn to take better care of myself...He stopped hugging me and would never acknowledge anything positive that I did." Another long pause. "That first summer felt like it went on for three years."

Toby tried to shift in her seat, but nothing really moved. The wheelchair let out a loud creaking sound. "I found comfort in cookies, candy, ice cream and chocolate...and by the time I went back to school in the fall, I had already gained 25 pounds...My classmates showed no mercy and it was in those hallways...that Tubby Toby was born."

"That must have really stung, Toby," Trish whispered.

She shrugged. "At first. But after a while I just stopped noticing...sort of a defense mechanism, I guess.

"Then came college, and fifty more pounds...and now here I am 25 years later at 390 pounds." She let out a deep sigh and tilted her head slightly. "The really pathetic thing is that I'd always believed that I would shed this weight someday." The tears returned and streamed down her cheeks. "And now I've run out of somedays." Her tears turned to sobs and it became harder to make out all her words.

"*Someday* is what's gotten me up every morning for my entire adult life!" Deep breath...raspy exhale. "*Someday* I would lose weight!...*Someday* I'd get to go to a movie like everyone else!" Her voice kept rising with each "someday" and the tears were streaming off her face. "*Someday* I would get out of this damn wheelchair and just go for a walk in the park!" She sniffled and wheezed and had a hard time catching her breath. "*Someday* I'd find a man that would hug me and hold me and make me feel beautiful and special!" As she struggled to catch her breath she was hit with an involuntary sniffle and a snot bubble shot out of her nose. She didn't notice. She was screaming now. "*Someday* I'd get to hold my baby in my arms and give it the love that the world never gave *me*!!!" This is where she completely lost it. She was sniffling and snorting as she muttered through the mucous around her mouth, "And now I don't have any more Somedays, Trish!!! *This is it for me!!!*" Her body was convulsing with the tears. "*Look at me, I'm pathetic!!!*" She started bawling uncontrollably and Trish just sat there rubbing her arm and hand.

Much as I hated to do it, I silently agreed with Toby. She *was* pathetic. Watching her sit there in her wheelchair, unable to move, her large face contorted with sadness and covered with snot, I felt physically ill. When combined with her profound sense of hopelessness, it was pathetic to the point of being grotesque. I had to avert my eyes or risk getting sick to my stomach. I looked down at the ground.

She wailed and mumbled indecipherably for a while and then let out a huge cry of pain. I looked up and saw Trish standing up and going to her side. She was hugging her from the side as Toby wailed. A new smell filled the air. It was the smell of a fresh bowel movement. Trish was looking over at me and signaling me to leave the room.

Toby had messed herself.

She couldn't even go the bathroom and clean herself up because of her size, and the nurse was gone, so Trish was apparently going to take on the project herself. I gladly left the room.

I walked out into the front hallway and then decided to just wait out on the front porch. The fresh air was like water to a man who had just trudged through the desert. I took in a few deep breaths on the front porch and then sat down on the steps, prepared to wait for Trish.

She surprised me and came out to see me just a few minutes later. "It looks like I'm going to be a while here, Dan," she said to me, "so why don't you just go ahead and head back to Hope House without me. I'll just call for a ride when I'm done."

A part of me felt relieved to get the green light to leave, but another part of me felt like I'd failed on my first mission. "It's okay Trish, I can just wait out here until you clean Toby up and then I can come back in and just keep watching and listening. You're doing a great job in there, by the way."

She smiled weakly. "Thanks Dan. But I'm thinking that I made a mistake in bringing you here today. I could tell by your body language that you're a little repulsed by Toby's appearance and I'm thinking that maybe I threw you into the deep end of the pool before I had you take your basic swim test."

I suddenly felt embarrassed. "No, I'm fine, really," I lied. "This is all just new to me and I'm trying to soak it all up as I go."

She put her hand on my arm. "It's okay, Dan. You don't have to lie to me. I know Toby's tough to listen to, with all of her layers of issues, and there's no shame in feeling a little put off by it all." She flashed a warm smile that made my heart stop beating for a moment. "Why don't you just head on home and I'll catch up with you later."

Her smile convinced me and the next thing I knew I was driving her car back the way we'd come earlier. I regretted the decision to leave almost as soon as I pulled away from the curb. I felt like a failure.

When I got back to the house I walked in and found Hy sitting alone in the living room. She was watching television with her feet propped up and the smell of freshly popped popcorn filled the air. She heard me come in and yelled to me from her chair.

"Hey there, Danny! Back so soon are we? Why don't you come on in here and watch Andy Griffith with me?" I shuffled over and sat down in a nearby chair. She must have read my body language as she asked me, "What's wrong with you? You're looking like a man who just got kicked in the shins!" She muted the television.

I took a deep breath and told her the whole story, about Toby and about my reactions and then Trish's comments. "I felt like a failure on my first day on the job with this whole list thing, Hy."

"Don't you go kicking yourself, Danny! This here list thing is a tricky business!"

"I know, I know. It's just that I guess I had hoped that things would be, I don't know, different somehow."

"Different how? Different, easier? Different, prettier? What kind of different were you looking for?"

I could sense that Hy was trying to comfort me but also trying to needle me a little bit too. "Different inside of me, I guess. I'm feeling like I'm letting myself down a lot lately, not to mention everyone else around me."

"Let me tell you a little story, Danny." She turned a little in her chair so she could face me. "I was married for many years to a man by the name of Jack. Jack was not much of a companion, truth be told, only I didn't know that until after he died fifteen years ago.

"When he died, I felt lost as can be for the next few months. All I'd known for over forty years was cooking, cleaning, taking care of him and the kids and all that other domestic crap. I didn't know what to do with myself!

"Then it hit me one day. I was sitting in my kitchen making a meatloaf when I realized: *I can do anything I want!* I kept on repeating it to myself over the next few weeks and you know what? I actually started to believe it! Here I was almost seventy years old and I was just waking up to all of the possibilities that life had waiting for me!" She leaned over and whispered to me, "I was a very pathetic old woman back then." We both smiled.

"Anywho, after convincing myself that I could do anything, I had to decide what that anything was! It didn't take me long to call up a dream I had as a little girl to create a secret place for myself, just like the one in The Secret Garden. Have you read that book?"

"No, I don't believe I have."

"Well you should! It's a magical book and one that I adored as a little girl. In it, this little girl Mary discovers a secret garden filled with beautiful plants and cute little animals and a mysterious boy named Dikon who played beautiful music on his flute." Hy paused, as if imagining the secret garden of her youth.

"So, anyway," she continued with a shake of her head, "I wanted to create a magical, secret garden just like the one in the book! Where the birds and animals could come and play and where I could go and just sit, away from all the hubbub and endless to-do lists. I got excited thinking about trying to create that right here in my backyard, but then you know what happened?"

She looked at me as if expecting an answer. I shook my head.

"When it came time to take my big plan off the drawing board and put it into action, I froze. It was like someone had just dipped my legs in concrete and attached me to the floor! I couldn't move! I was scared to death, Danny!"

"What were you afraid of, Hy?"

"You name it! Afraid that I would build stupid-looking birdhouses, and everyone would laugh at me. Afraid that I would dig up my backyard and nothing would grow back there. Afraid what my neighbors would think about me doing such a silly thing. Afraid what my daughter would think. Afraid that I would fall flat on my face and die a lonely old woman full of shame!"

"So, what'd you do?"

"I avoided the whole thing all together! I went back to my normal, old, boring, stable, predictable, life with no surprises and just danced around my dream for almost a year." She paused and shook her head. "Such a waste...such a waste..."

"Well, your backyard is beautiful now, so what got you to change your mind?"

"It was a TV show, Danny. I was watching a show that was talking about Gandhi's life. Do you know much about him, Danny?"

"No, just the basics, I guess."

"That's all I knew, too, but I saw so many other sides to him during this show. I won't bore you with the details," she smiled at me, "but there were two things that really struck me about that fella." She held up one finger. "One, is that he was just a regular person, like you and me, living a regular life for the most part when he got chosen by history to step forward." She raised a second finger. "And two, that he was just as afraid as any other person would be in his shoes." She cocked her head a little. "But ya know what?"

I shook my head.

"He stepped through that fear, Danny. And I saw that that was the only thing that separated that man - that great, courageous man - from you and me. He just closed his eyes and took that first step."

Hy clapped her hands together. "So ya know what I did? I shut off that TV and I went out into my shed and grabbed my shovel and started digging! Then the next day I went down to the hardware store and I bought everything I needed to start making my birdhouses. And you know what I found out?"

Once again, I just shook my head.

"I found out that all the fears I had were just little, pathetic paper tigers, Danny - all roar, no bite!" She slapped her leg. "Ya know what I think of when I think about my fears?" She didn't even look over for any kind of reply. She was on a roll and nothing was going to stop her. "I think about that "Back To The Future" movie where he goes into the future, you remember that one?"

"Yeah."

"You remember that part where he's walking by the movie theater and a giant monster comes jumping out at him from the theater?"

"Yeah, it was a big hologram."

"Yes, by jiminy, a hologram!" she yelled. "I can never remember that danged word!

"Anyway, that hologram had big, scary teeth and was tall as can be and the kid went skittering backward, didn't he?"

"Yep."

"But what was there to be afraid of really? Was it going to really bite him? No, of course not! Did it really have teeth or anything at all that might hurt him? No! So, what was there to be afraid of?"

"It surprised him."

"Exactly! But after the initial surprise, was there anything else to fear from that hologram?"

"Not really."

"I don't think so either. And that's exactly what I realized about my fears! They're big and they're hairy and they have these huge scary teeth that are dripping with blood, but when all is said and done, they can't hurt me!

"I finally saw that my fears are tall and wide but not deep at all! I had always tried to go over or around them, trying to avoid their claws and teeth, but there was no way because they were too big in those directions. One day I decided to do what Gandhi did and just take that step *through* my fears, and you know what?"

"What."

"I stepped right through! And on the other side I saw almost immediately how silly I'd been to be afraid of the hologram. After I'd done it a few times it got to be kind of fun and now I look *forward* to finding a new Fear Dragon in front of me so I can slay him with that one, magical first step into his two-dimensional, ugly face."

I thought about what she was telling me and how it might pertain to my own situation. It didn't take me long to see that she was right. I'd been running and hiding from my fears for as long as I could remember.

She continued. "Gosh darn it Danny, I got to do all kinds of wonderful things after that. I took cooking classes, I learned how to speak some French, I took a trip by myself to New England, I even changed my name to Hyacynthia!" She leaned forward and whispered to me, "it used to be Edna for goodness sakes." She leaned back in her chair. "Always hated that name, and always loved the small, sturdy hyacinth. You know that flower, Danny?"

"No, afraid I don't."

"I'll show you one out back some time. I think you'll agree with me that it's a fine, fine flower."

She reached over and placed her hand on mine. I squirmed a little but didn't move. Her blue-grey eyes looked into mine with unmistakable intensity. Her voice became gentler and more subdued. "That Fear Dragon chased me around for seventy years, Danny. He pushed me in all kinds of directions that I didn't really want to go. He's a heartless SOB, Danny, and I don't want to see you spend your life running from him like I did. My life didn't really begin until I stepped through him, Danny, and that was much, much too late in life. Don't make the same mistake I made. See him now for what he is: just a tall, scary looking hologram who has no bite." She gave me a warm smile and I could see tears forming in her eyes.

"You're a sweet boy, Danny. I can see that you have a good heart and you're just trying to find your way right now. Trust the compass in here," she tapped her chest, "and use the lantern that God gave you to light the way."

I was preparing to ask her about the lantern thing when we were interrupted. "Hey there Danny, I didn't expect to find you here!" It was Zootie.

I glanced quickly at Hy and then said, "Yeah, well, I didn't expect to find me here either."

Zootie must have seen that I didn't want to talk about it as he didn't ask any questions. "Okay, well, I'm heading out to grab Jennie at her parents' house. She's having a hard time with them right now and asked me if she could stay here at Hope House for a while." He turned and headed out of the room. "I'll see you guys later."

We waved to Zootie and then Hy turned her attention back to me. "That Zootie is good people, don't you think?"

"Yes, he is," I agreed.

"Seems like most folks these days are so quick to accept credit and stiff-arm blame, but he's different that way. He does exactly the opposite and it sure makes him a pleasure to be around!" I nodded my agreement. "The world could sure use more Zooties," she added with a sigh.

"I'm with you on that one."

Hy clapped her hands together. "Let's you and me engage in a little Mayberry Therapy together, whaddaya say?" Before I could answer, she added, "there's nothing like Andy and Barney and the gang to pick you up when you're feeling a little down! I tell ya that Barney just makes me hoot with laughter!"

I couldn't get the smile off my face. I'd learned in a short period of time that hanging around Hy was like having your own private circus. Her joy for life came pouring out of her and wrapped itself around any lucky people who happened to be in her company.

"So why don't you go grab yourself a cold Dr. Pepper out of the fridge, Danny." She put her hand on my arm. "I just love a cold Dr. Pepper out of the bottle, don't you?" I nodded. "And I've got plenty of popcorn here for the both of us," she said as she nodded at the big bowl sitting on the table next to her. "It could be like our own little pajama party without the pajamas!"

I laughed. "Hy, have you always had this much energy?"

"Oh no, Danny." Her brow furled. "I was an uptight old biddy who didn't have a clue about how to have fun. I'm just making up for lost time now!"

She shooed me with her hands. "Now go get your soda pop so we can watch Andy Griffith together."

I went and got my soda and came back to the room. When I returned, Hy had already turned the sound back on the TV and she was laughing uproariously at the exploits of Andy, Barney and the other residents of Mayberry. I sat down next to her and we laughed together, ate popcorn and sipped Dr. Peppers for the next half hour. All the dark clouds that had been hanging over my head got blown away by Hurricane Hy and I completely forgot about my problems for a short while.

CHAPTER 20

The following morning, I woke up and went downstairs to grab some coffee out of the kitchen. I was surprised to see an unfamiliar face sitting at the kitchen table.

"Hi there," the young woman said to me in a tone that suggested we were old friends.

"Good morning."

"You must be Dan. Zootie told me about you."

"Oh, he did, did he."

"Yep. Said you're helpin' out with the list. That true?" She talked quickly and in shorthand sentences.

I looked her up and down quickly. She was young, probably in her early twenties, and she had a kind of alternative look to her. Straight black hair, nose ring, grungy clothes. "Yeah, that's true," I replied as I made my way to the coffee pot.

"So, what's your DOD?"

"My dod?" I asked. I poured a cup of coffee and sat down at the table with her.

"Yeah, your DOD," she repeated for me. "Your Date of Death, D...O...D! You are on the list, aren't you?"

I finally understood. "No, actually I'm not."

"You're not? Then what the hell are you doing here? You got a relative on it or something?"

"No, no relative. Just helping Zootie out with the list, that's all."

She cocked her head, as if considering what I had just said. "I guess that's cool."

I decided to change the subject. "So, you know my name, but I don't know yours."

"My name's Jennie Morrissey." She paused. "And I'm on the list."

"Oh, are you," was all I could muster.

"Yep. And I got a DOD of November 14th to boot. Shitty luck, huh?"

Her words came quickly and without any emotion. I felt like I was talking to a female Joe Friday from Dragnet.

"That's terrible," I agreed.

"Yeah, but that's not the worst of it. The worst part is that my parents don't believe anything about this list. They think I'm getting sucked into this terrible cult that's gonna steal all my worldly possessions and then knock me off in some back alley."

Jennie had a nonchalance about her that I found common in people her age. She acted like nothing fazed her, but I couldn't help but believe there was more going on than what she was sharing with me. I decided to go against my nature and probe further. Hy's words from the day before were still fresh in my mind.

"So how does all of this make you feel, Jennie?" I asked as a first step.

"What are you, a shrink or something?"

Her comment knocked me off course. "No, I'm not a shrink. Just curious, I guess."

She cocked her head again. "You're not like the rest of them, are you?"

"Them, who?"

"Zootie, Hy and Trish and the rest of them that are helpin' out with this list."

"Why do you say that?" I asked a little defensively.

"I dunno. You just seem to be sittin' back from the whole thing a little bit, not really in the mix, if ya know what I mean."

I felt my face flushing, but I tried to hide it with a little bluster. "I don't know about that. I'm definitely new to this whole list thing, but I'm catching on more and more each day."

"Hey, don't go gettin' your boxers in a bunch! I was just makin' an observation, that's all."

I suddenly felt embarrassed at being thrown off course so easily. This girl half my age had gotten to me. My mind scrambled for a way to recover.

"I'm sorry," Jennie offered a few seconds later. "Here you are doing a good thing and I'm takin' jabs at'cha." She'd let me off the hook. "Forgive me?" She had a new look on her face, almost sweet, and I felt my body relax.

"Sure, no problem," I said casually.

"Great! So, let's start again, okay?"

I smiled.

She reached across the table with her hand extended. "Jennie Morrissey, nice to meet'cha."

I shook her hand. "Dan Barnes. Pleased to make your acquaintance."

"To answer your question Dan Barnes, about how it all makes me feel, I have to say I'm scared shitless." She forced a smile and I suddenly felt like I was sitting with a different person. Gone was the false bravado and sharp, staccato answers. In their place was confusion and fear. My heart instantly went out to her.

"Yeah, I can understand that," I said reassuringly. "I look on that list and ask myself how I would feel if I saw my name on it and I can honestly say that it wouldn't be pretty."

"I just don't have any experience with this death thing!" Jennie blurted out. "I'm twenty-one years old for crissakes! My biggest worries have been getting through college and figuring out ways to get my annoying parents off my back. Then Zootie comes calling and throws this whopper in my lap."

"I can't even imagine having to handle something like this at your age."

That did it. I looked over and saw her eyes watering up. It wasn't long before the tears began snaking their way down her face and I felt my body stiffen. I was heading into uncharted waters and I felt ill-equipped.

"I just don't know what to do!" she said through her sobs.

"Reach over and reassure her!" a voice inside of me yelled.

"You just met her, you idiot!" another voice countered. *"Just let her cry it out and she'll be fine!"*

I was frozen with indecision, so I just sat there, feeling helpless.

Jennie took a few deep breaths and composed herself after just a few minutes. "Whew! It doesn't take a whole lot to get me to do *that* these days!"

"Yeah, I can imagine," I offered weakly. I looked down in my coffee cup and silently berated myself for not being more of a help to her. I found myself wishing Trish or Hy were sitting next to me.

"Change of subject," she blurted out suddenly. I looked up and she was smiling. It was a nice, easy smile and, for the first time, I found myself thinking that she was kind of pretty, in a very alternative-girl-next-door sort of way. "Let's talk about *you* for a while, Dan Barnes!"

I returned her smile, happy to be off the topic of her impending death. "What is it that you want to know?"

"Are you married?"

"Nope."

"Got a special someone?"

"Nope."

"Any kids?"

"God, no!"

"Do you wanna have them someday?"

"Well, I'm certainly getting a little old to be starting a family, but I guess I wouldn't rule out the possibility."

"Hey, some of those guys in Hollywood are makin' babies when they're in their seventies and eighties!"

"True. But last time I looked I didn't have millions of dollars in my bank account and that always helps in attracting those pretty young things when you're an old fart with hair growing out of your ears."

"Good point. So, fact is, you'd better get going PDQ or you're gonna be SOL!"

"Do you always talk in acronyms like this?"

"Much as I can!" She got a playful glint in her eye. "So ya got any likely candidates in mind?"

"For?"

"Bearing your children!"

I laughed out loud. "Nope, no candidates. To tell you the truth, I haven't been in one place long enough to really meet anybody."

A contemplative look took over Jennie's face. "You know who I would want as the mother of my kids if I were a man?"

"No, who?"

"Trish." I felt my face flush. "She's the nicest person I've ever met and she's pretty too!" Jennie looked at me. "Don't you think she's pretty?"

"Uh, yeah, I guess so," I said, trying to appear disinterested.

"Do you think *I'm* pretty?"

"Well, yeah, sure you are." I was beginning to hate her line of questioning.

"My mother tells me I should wear makeup, that it would make me look more feminine. Do you know what I tell her?"

"What do you tell her?"

"That if I started wearing makeup it would mean that the ghoulish thief called vanity had won and that I would spend the rest of my life trying to extract myself from his sticky web as I stare for eternity down the bottomless well of self-absorption."

"Whew, that's a mouthful!"

"It's from an English essay I wrote in high school."

"You're quite a writer."

"Yeah, it's what I was going to try to do with my life." She paused. "Back when I thought I *had* a life." Her head dropped.

"A second chance!" a voice yelped from inside my head. *"Comfort her!"*

I started to reach across the table, but I was distracted by a noise behind me. "Mother of Mary, the plumbing in this house is so very bad!" It was Frank. He dropped a piece of piping that he was carrying into the sink and started washing it out. Frank served as the sort of ad hoc handyman around Hope House.

I pulled my hand back. "Good morning Frank," I said cheerfully.

He mumbled something at me in Spanish without looking up and continued to work on his pipe in the sink.

Jennie stood up. "Well, I guess it's time to get the day started," she said as she stretched.

"Yes, I guess it is," I concurred. I got up and put my coffee cup on the counter. When I turned around, Jennie was standing right behind me. *"Give her a hug!"* a voice instructed me. I felt the impulse but ignored it after another voice said, *"Frank's standing right there for crissakes! What's he gonna think if you're suddenly pullin' Miss Twentysomething into a clinch?"*

I looked at the ground and sort of shuffled my way past her.

Jennie took care of her coffee cup and then headed for the kitchen door. "It was nice to meet'cha Dan Barnes," she said with a wave. "And thanks for the ear!"

"No problem," I replied with a wave. She disappeared out the door.

CHAPTER 21

I spent the afternoon in downtown Seattle, by the waterfront, with Hy and her band of Grey Musketeers. She had recruited them from the local senior center and their mission on this day was to distribute donated blankets to the people living in the street.

We were focusing on an area around the Pike Place Market and there was no shortage of potential recipients. I had certainly become more aware of the homeless situation in this country during my travels, but Seattle seemed to have more than its fair share of street people. It seemed as if every doorway and alleyway was occupied with somebody curled up in newspapers or covered with cardboard. One of the women in Hy's troop told me that Seattle was an attractive place to be homeless because of its location next to the water and its temperate climate. It was usually possible to live in the streets year-round, a claim that many cities couldn't make.

The day itself was unusually gorgeous. It was a clear, sunny day with temperatures in the mid-seventies and a constant warm breeze coming in off the water. I wandered to the top of a grassy knoll in a nearby park and looked out over Puget Sound. The sunlight danced on the water below and the Cascade Mountains off in the distance cut a jagged swatch across the horizon. I was smitten with the view.

Hy came strolling up and stood next to me, looking out over the water. "Beautiful, isn't it?" she said wistfully.

"I'm not sure I've seen many things more beautiful than this."

"It's one of the things I love about living here," Hy said. "Seems like everywhere you look you see things so breathtaking that you can't help but believe there's something bigger than us at work in this here world."

"Amen," I murmured, still stunned by the vast magnificence in front of me.

"Well, Danny," Hy said with a sigh, "we've got some work to do!"

We walked back down the small hill and rejoined the group. We decided to work in pairs and then hook up at a nearby McDonald's restaurant in a couple of hours. Hy and I grabbed some blankets, put them into a small pushcart, and set off together.

Hy and I worked different sides of the street as we strolled up and down the many hills by the waterfront. After less than an hour my stamina started to subside. I'd handed out just a few blankets and I felt myself getting grumpy. I was tired of pushing the cart, I was hot, and I honestly didn't see the point to what we were doing. It seemed to me at the time that notifying the people on the list was a higher priority than handing out blankets. I looked across the street.

There was Hy talking with a woman pushing a shopping cart full of aluminum cans. She was gabbing away like she didn't have a care in the world and yet, truth was, she had a matter of weeks left to live. That realization was like a right cross to my chin. I suddenly felt ashamed for being such a whiner.

I decided to sit on the curb for a few minutes and attempt to adjust my attitude.

I sat there with the sun on my face and felt a puff of a breeze blow up from the water. It felt soothing on my face. I was just starting to feel my muscles relax a little when a scream pierced the air.

"YEEEEEEEEOOOOOOOOO…DAWGY!!!" came the yell from behind me. I jumped to my feet and went towards the scream, just a few doors up the hill from where I'd been sitting. I looked around as I walked up the hill to see if anyone else had heard the scream. Hy was still talking with the woman farther down the hill and nobody else was in sight.

I found the source of the yell without much problem. Tucked into a small alcove between buildings was a man in a wheelchair. As I walked up to him, he looked up at me with eyes that obviously didn't see anything. His right eye was completely sewn shut and his left one was a cloudy white color. The smile he wore revealed a deeply creased face and teeth that hadn't seen the bristles of a toothbrush in years. I also noticed that he didn't have any legs. He had a dark, dirty blanket across his lap and there were no bulges under the blanket where his legs were supposed to be.

"Hey there young fella, what's yer attitune today?" he said to me with what sounded like a lisp but was actually the result of talking through missing teeth.

"My what?" I asked, as I continued to look the old man up and down.

"Yer attitune m'boy! The tune ya play in yer head as ya stroll through yer day!" His voice was a little high-pitched, almost squeaky, but there was no mistaking his enthusiasm. "Are ya playin' a sad song that makes ya feel like yer draggin' a load o' bricks in yer britches? Or are ya choosin' ta play a tune that puts an extra li'l bounce in yer step that tells the world, I CAN'T BE STOPPED TODAY!!!!" He shouted the last part at the top of his lungs, and I looked around to see if anyone had heard him. An older couple had been walking by as he yelled and I just threw them a sheepish shrug with a "hey, what's a guy to do?" look on my face. They crossed the street immediately.

The old man began laughing which caused his rusty wheelchair to shake and creak. I was worried that he might fall out of it until I saw a makeshift seatbelt across his lap that had been hidden by the blanket.

I guessed the man to be somewhere in his sixties. He had a lot of grey in his thin, scraggly beard and in the greasy long hair that shot out the top and the sides of what used to be a purple visor affixed to his head. I would have guessed that the visor had last come off the last time he'd brushed his teeth.

"So, what's yer name, m'boy?" he shouted at me.

"Dan…Dan Barnes."

"Bowler Sims is m'name, Thomas Bowler Sims t'be precise. Nice ta meet'cha Danny." He stuck his hand out in my general direction.

I looked at it, thought about all the germs that must be living on it, and then shook it anyway. I made a mental note to wash my hands thoroughly when I got to McDonalds later.

"That's an interesting name," I said as I discreetly wiped my hand on my pants leg, "where did it come from?"

"I used to have a big ol' Bowler hat, Danny. Wore it fer years. But a few years back that dern thing got stolen and I had ta take t'wearin' this here visor in honor of my Minnesota Vikings."

"You from there?" I asked the question half-mindedly as I glanced over my shoulder to see if Hy was ready to move on. She was still talking.

"Yep, born 'n raised." The old man paused a moment and tilted his head. "Ya seem a little on edge there Danny boy, everythin' okay?"

His question took me aback. "Yeah, everything's just fine with me Bowler. Why do you ask?"

"I'm feelin' an edgy vibe m'boy, like ya got somethin' weighin' on ya right now." His insight, without having the benefit of even seeing my face, was uncanny. I looked at him, with his cloudy eye, greasy appearance and dilapidated wheelchair, and just shook my head.

"No, I'm fine, really," I assured him.

"Do ya feel sorry fer me, Danny?"

This one really threw me. Of course I felt sorry for him! How could I not? "No, I don't feel sorry for you Bowler," I lied.

"Yer lyin' t'me Danny!" He flashed his yellow smile. "But that's okay cuz yer intentions are good ones." He patted the blanket on his lap. "I gotta admit that I must be quite a pathetic sight settin' here in my busted-up wheelchair with m'greasy body, worthless eyes and not a leg t'speak of..." He trailed off for a moment and then rose up in his chair as far as his seatbelt would allow. "But don't you go wastin' a minute's worth o' pity on me Danny cuz, I gotta tell ya..." the last four words came out in a shout "...LIFE IS GODDAMNED GOOD!!!"

I glanced over my shoulder once again. Nobody around.

"Can you say that Danny?"

"Uh, well..." I stammered.

"If yer like most folks you'll probably choke on it halfway through. Or if ya do manage to squeak it out in a whisper you'll be lookin' over yer shoulder fer the upcomin' kick in the ass. It's like we think the Big Guy is up there with a wet towel in his hands ready to snap ya in the ass fer bein' so goddamned happy and, sin of all sins, so goddamned vocal 'bout it!"

He raised his arms to his side. "Go ahead Danny! Shout it out fer everyone t'hear!" He cupped his hands to his mouth. "LIFE IS GODDAMNED GOOD!!!!"

This time his shouts brought some attention. I glanced at the people walking up the street with the confused, and scared, looks on their faces, and knew I wasn't up to the challenge Bowler had put in front of me. I cared too much about what passers-by would think of me.

"I know it's a hard thing fer ya t'do, Danny, 'n I know I got a leg up on ya cuz I can't see the looks on folks' faces as they walk on by." He let out a small chuckle. "Leg up, that's a rich one, eh?" I laughed an uncomfortable laugh with him.

"Anyway, where was I?" he asked.

"You were lecturing me on how to enjoy life a little bit more," I said with a smirk.

"Rightyo!" he blurted out as he raised his hand in the air. "If yer gonna enjoy this ride, ya gotta tell yerself every dammed day that life is good 'n not feel guilty 'bout it! It ain't a crime ta enjoy life fer crissakes, but most folks live it like it is. Ya just gotta say fucket sometimes, Danny! Most folks just don't have enough fuckets in their lives!" He leaned forward in his chair and I would have sworn his cloudy eye was staring right through me. His voice lowered to a near whisper.

"'N don't ya go feelin' sorry fer me, Danny. If ya wanna throw yer pity somewhere, throw it in the direction of those poor slobs who trudge home from jobs they hate every day and then sit in front of the boob tube watchin' god awful shows just so's they kin fergit 'bout their misery fer awhile." He wagged a thin, greasy finger at me. "Now *that's* sad!"

He sat back in his chair and raised his voice to its usual bellow. "I'M ALIVE DANNY!!!!" Thankfully, he lowered his voice again as he continued. "Yeah, I got a few pebbles in my shoe..." he looked down at the ground, "well, if I *had* a shoe!" He chuckled. "But I'm still movin' Danny, 'n I ain't complainin' bout nuthin' jest so long as I'm breathin'!"

I glanced across the street and noticed that Hy was once again on the move. I prepared to leave, and Bowler must have heard my movements.

"'Fore ya go Danny," he flashed his yellow teeth and held out his hand, "ya got anythin' ya kin spare fer a homeless street philosopher?"

Ah, the pinch. It all made sense now. It was all an elaborate scheme to get some money from me. All my prior discomfort was swept away by my feelings of superiority.

"Well, Bowler, I do have a nice, new blanket for you if you're interested," I said in a suddenly confident tone.

Bowler cocked his head. "I'll take yer blanket, Danny, but I'm not sure I wanna take what yer thinkin' with it."

"What do you mean?" I asked, my discomfort quickly returning.

"Ya think ya got me figgered out now, don't'cha?" He took off his old blanket, revealing the stumps where legs once were, and handed it to me. "Ya think that everythin' I jest said was bullshit jest t'git a little money outta ya, eh?"

I took his old blanket and handed him the new one, unsure of what to say and unsure of what to do with the dirty, smelly blanket in my hands.

"Well, let me tell ya somethin' Danny boy" he said as he positioned the new blanket, "truth is truth no matter where ya find it 'n ol' Bowler always tries ta stick ta the truth. So, don't go thinkin' that ya kin jest wipe away everythin' a man sez cuz he makes his livin' on the streets! I'll have ya know that in some parts o' the world it's a very noble 'n proper thing fer a man my age t'be beggin' on the streets!"

I suddenly felt very embarrassed. I didn't say a word but reached into my pants pocket and pulled out a ten-dollar bill. I reached out and took Bowler's hand and placed the bill square in his palm. "You're right and I'm sorry."

Bowler took the bill and snapped it close to his ear. He smiled and his tone changed immediately. "A Hamilton, eh? Wellllll...fer that kinda money I'm gonna give ya Bowler's best!" He squared himself in his chair and sat upright. "Ya ready fer this one, Danny?"

I glanced again at Hy across the street. She had almost made it to the next street corner. I felt anxious to leave and catch up with her. "Yeah, I'm ready Bowler. Lay it on me."

"This here is Bowler's philosophy o' life 'n I don't jest tell this ta anyone, ya understand?" He had a mock serious look on his aged face.

"Yeah, I understand."

"Okay, here it is." He cleared his throat. "Remember that yer mind is nuthin' but the barkin' dog at the cave t'yer soul." He paused and had an unmistakable look of self-satisfaction on his face. "Made it up m'self, whaddaya think?"

"That's great, Bowler." I took a step to go. "Thanks for all of your advice, and I'm sure we'll be seeing each other again." I cringed at my stupid comment regarding seeing each other again. "I have to go now because I see the person who I was with starting to walk away." I took another step.

"Alright Danny boy, you go on yer way." He gave me a wave of his hand. "Thanks fer yer donation to the Bowler Fund and, remember, it's tax deductible on this year's return!" He smiled at his own joke. "'N remember ta keep that attitune in check!"

"I will, I will," I said as I took a few steps away. "So long Bowler!"

"So long Danny, and don't fergit t'get more o' those fuckets in yer life - you'll be a new man!" I heard him start to hum as I walked away.

I quickly caught up to Hy. I started to try to explain what I had been doing for the past half hour but realized, before I'd even uttered a word, that Bowler was inexplicable. You had to witness him first-hand to fully appreciate him. I just kept it all to myself and simply asked her, "How'd it go with the can lady?"

We walked, chatted, and handed out many more blankets over the next hour. I noticed that my attitude was much better than it had been earlier, thanks in large part to Bowler.

When all our blankets were gone, we headed to the designated rendezvous point, a McDonalds restaurant down by one of the piers. When we walked in, we saw most of our group gathered over in one corner, so we went over to join them. As we approached, I saw a woman named June Day, the self-appointed leader of the Grey Musketeers, standing up in front of the group. The rest were seated nearby, munching on their Big Macs and sipping on their Cokes. June appeared to be giving one of her Patton-esque speeches for which she'd become known.

"Now I know you're all tired," June was saying with her right index finger raised in the air, "but we've got a mission here today, and we've got to go out there and deliver the rest of those blankets!"

"Oh, give it a rest, June," a voice shouted from one of the far tables.

"Yeah, June," chimed in another, "who elected you Queen of the Nile?"

That brought a few snickers from the group. June appeared to have a small mutiny on her hands. Hy and I nodded at her and then sat down at a nearby table to watch the proceedings. There was probably a couple dozen women gathered in our little section. I stood out both as the lone male as well as the only person there under the age of sixty-five.

June Day was a feisty seventy-year-old who wasn't ready to give up the ship just yet. "Who else," she continued, "is going to stand in front of you whiners and try to get things done?"

Suddenly, out of nowhere, a french fry came flying through the air and bounced off June's forehead. It was so unexpected that June had to blink twice before she could process what had just happened. This brought uproarious laughter from the group. June scowled.

"All right," she screamed, "who threw that french fry?" Another fry came at her head, but she managed to dodge it. The laughter continued. June pounded on the table in an attempt at getting everyone's attention, but it was too late. Before you could say "quarter-pounder with cheese" there was an all-out senior citizen food fight in our little section of McDonalds. I hadn't seen the likes of it since Junior High.

Fries flew everywhere. Pretty soon, chunks of hamburgers and buns also became projectiles. June got the brunt of it at first but then it spread to all corners of our section. Nobody was immune from getting hit by flying food, including me and Hy. I looked over and saw a blob of ketchup on Hy's forehead and a smile on her face.

We dodged and ducked as best we could, but it was no use. After a while we just looked at each other, shrugged as if to say, "what the hell?" and then jumped into the fray. I glanced over in June's direction before hurling my first fry and saw a look of resignation come over her face just before a devilish grin replaced it. She reached over, grabbed a chocolate shake from the table in front of her, and dumped the whole thing over the head of the nearest woman. The woman was shocked at first as the cold, thick liquid oozed down her grey hair and onto her shoulders. But then she turned to face June and they both started laughing like little kids. She scooped up some of the liquid off her shoulder and flung it in June's face. More laughter.

As the battle raged, I noticed a McDonalds employee approach the group from one side. Judging from his shirt and tie, I guessed him to be the manager. He was probably in his mid-twenties and he was in way over his head. He raised his hand and let out a squeaky, "Excuse me ladies!" No response. He tried again, a little louder this time. "*Excuse me ladies!!!*" A french fry bounced off his head. He, like June before him, couldn't believe what had just hit him. "*I'm the manager for goodness sakes!*" was how I interpreted the open-mouthed look on his face. He seemed to think about attempting to restore order one more time but thought better of it. He simply shook his head at the group, as a disapproving parent would at their child, then turned and left. He was licked and he knew it.

I sat there with Hy, watched the food fly in all directions, listened to the giggles and screams, threw an occasional food grenade myself, and just laughed harder than I'd laughed in a long, long time.

CHAPTER 22

"You got a minute, Dan?" Trish had stopped me in the hallway one morning as I was heading out for a head-clearing walk. We hadn't really spoken at any length since the day I accompanied her to Toby's house and her voice caught me a little off guard. Truth be told, I had been avoiding her. The same eyes that had given me so much pleasure earlier now made me feel ashamed when I looked at her. Despite Hy's pep talk, I still felt like a failure that day at Toby's.

"Uh, yeah," I said as I glanced at the door.

"Hey, if you've got someplace to be, I understand," she offered with her hands up. "It can certainly wait until later."

"No, no," I assured her, "I'm all yours. What's up?"

"I just want to get your opinion on something." She looked over her shoulder and then lowered her voice. "But can we talk upstairs?"

I nodded and followed her up the stairs. We went into her room, at the opposite end of the hall from my room, and she closed the door behind me. I sat in a chair over by the window and she sat on her bed.

"First of all," she said with her head cocked to one side, "is everything okay between us?"

I could feel myself begin to blush. "Sure," I lied, "why do you ask that?"

"You just seem to be avoiding me lately and I want to make sure there's nothing wrong."

"Yeah, everything's fine."

A wry smile creased her face. "You're not still feeling bad about that day at Toby's, are you?"

My face got even hotter. "No, not at all. Hy gave me a little pep talk when I got back that day and everything's just ducky."

"*Ducky?!? What the hell is "ducky?"* AC wanted to know. *"You sound like a freakin' five-year-old!"*

Trish was a little more gracious, overlooking my choice of words. "That's good to hear. I would hate to think you were avoiding me."

"I could never do that." I tried to smile a warm smile, but I could feel that it came off as awkward. I needed to change the subject. "So, what is it that you wanted my opinion on?"

She slapped her thighs with her hands. "Ah, yes!" She reached over and grabbed a piece of paper from her night stand. "I've been trying to put together a special something for Hy and I didn't want her to overhear us talking about it." Trish looked up from the paper and I got to enjoy her blue eyes once again. I'd missed them. "Since she's only got a couple of weeks left, I thought we'd better do this soon."

I felt my heart plunge to my stomach. With all the commotion that filled Hope House I had forgotten that Hy's DOD, as Jennie called it, was rapidly approaching.

Trish continued. "So, I was thinking a picnic in the backyard, where she could be with her beloved birds as well as the people she cares about so much. What do you think?"

I was still reeling. "Boy Trish, that sounds like a great idea," was the best I could muster.

"I've made out a preliminary guest list and I've already got over two hundred names on it!" She shook her head in disbelief. "It's amazing just how many lives she's touched."

"Yeah, she's quite an amazing woman."

"Yes, she is." I wasn't certain, but it appeared as if Trish had started to cry. She was still looking down at her guest list so I couldn't see her eyes.

"I'm still so grateful for what she did for me and my father." She finally looked up and I saw the tell-tale tears filling her eyes. Her blue eyes had transformed into the most breathtaking color I'd ever seen. They glowed through the tears as she spoke, and I was mesmerized. "Did I ever tell you about my father?"

I simply shook my head.

She got down on her hands and knees and slid two banker's boxes out from under her bed. She took the lid off one of them and pulled out a handful of folders. I could see that the box had been packed to beyond full. She opened one of the folders and pulled out what looked like some old newspaper clippings and held them up for me to see.

"The Great Barrier Reef!" she said in a voice that hinted at frustration as she shook the clippings. She then put them back into their folder and pulled out another batch of papers, glanced at them, then held them up for me to see.

"Whistler Village, British Columbia!" Her voice was a little more frantic this time and I noticed the tears began to work their way out of her eyes and started streaming down her cheeks. I didn't know what I was supposed to say, if anything at all, so I just sat there and nodded at each fistful of clippings that she held up.

She held up several more, her voice raising higher with each one. "The French Riviera!" "The pyramids of Egypt!" "Bass fishing in Arkansas!" "Disneyland, for crissakes!" She had trouble getting the last one out as her tears turned quickly to sobs. She lowered the last packet to her lap and just stared at it as she sobbed.

I got up and went over to sit next to her on the bed. As I sat down, she was getting the tears under control and wiping her face. I suddenly felt very foolish for having moved.

"I'm sorry," she said as she used her shirt sleeve to dab her eyes. "I get on these crying jags sometimes and I just can't stop."

"No problem." I raised my right arm and patted her left arm a couple of times. I felt stiff as a board, but it still felt like I'd put my finger in a light socket when I touched her. I wanted to let my hand linger there a while, but I felt too self-conscious. I took it away and scooted a little farther away from her on the bed.

"It's just that I still hurt inside so much for my father's life of pathetic somedays." She turned and looked at me. "Do you know what all of these files are, Dan?"

"No, I don't."

"My father cut out every one of these articles himself because they were places and adventures that he wanted to experience someday. He created file after file over the years on thousands of places." She scrunched her face, obviously trying to force back more tears. "And do you know how many of these places he actually visited in his sixty-eight years of life?"

"How many?"

"*None!!!*" She spit the word out as one would a piece of spoiled food. "Not a single goddam one!!! How pathetic is *that?!?*"

This time I reached over and rubbed her arm before thinking. I didn't feel nearly as stiff.

"I pulled twenty-six boxes like these out of his house after he died, and I went through them and just cried and cried for days. Here was a man who wasn't poor, who had his health up until the end, and yet he never pursued a single one of his dreams! He just kept on collecting articles and information for an imaginary someday that just never came." She paused for a few seconds then turned her head towards me. "Why would he do that, Dan?"

I shrugged. "Fear, maybe?"

"I just find it all so sad." Her eyes went back to the boxes on the floor. "I remember when my mother was alive, they would always talk about going to the Caribbean someday. Mom loved the beach and she'd always wanted to see the blue waters of the Caribbean." Her head shook slowly from side to side. "Never happened. They never went anywhere. And now they're both gone. All that's left are twenty-six boxes filled with unfulfilled dreams."

We sat there in silence for what felt like several minutes. I continued to rub her arm and she continued to stare at the boxes.

Finally, she slapped her thighs firmly and said, "That's why I'm so determined to help people like Toby, Dan!" Her blue eyes fixed squarely on mine. They were filled with an intensity that was almost too much for me to look at. "I can't stand to see any more people die like my father, with all of their dreams and somedays boxed up in a closet. I want to help them to pull those boxes out, open them up and live whatever life they've got left to the fullest!"

Her shoulders suddenly slumped, and her voice became quiet. "Nobody else should have to bury a loved one like I buried my father. Hy, with this list of hers, allowed us a few last days to say our goodbyes and all, but there were far too many regrets left hanging in the air. And regrets are the worst, Dan, the *worst!*"

She stood up from the bed and kicked the boxes back under the bed. "So, no more looking back for ol' Trish! Eyes are forward and looking for ways to avoid the fate of my parents at all costs!"

"I'm sorry to hear that about your father, Trish."

"Yeah, it sure is a sad story, isn't it?" She heaved a deep sigh. "But sometimes the lessons we learn from our parents are through what *not* to do, aren't they?"

I nodded.

"Your parents still alive, Dan?"

"Just my mother. My father died ten years ago."

"Do you talk to her much?"

"Not as often as I should, but we stay in touch."

"Did you like your Dad?"

"Yeah, I liked him a lot." My Dad's face flashed in front of my mind's eye. I felt the salivary glands in my jaw begin to tingle, as if preparing me for upcoming tears, though none came. It was strange; I had never cried before over my father's death, so why now?

"You cry much?" Trish asked, as if she sensed my inner struggle.

I was glad for the distraction of her words. "No, not really."

"Why not?"

"Guess I just don't feel like it much."

She let out a small "hmph" sound, as if she were assessing what I had just told her. "I'd be surprised if you keep *that* trend alive much longer, Mr. Dan Barnes." Then she smiled.

CHAPTER 23

Hy's party was a huge success.

How Trish managed to keep the whole thing a secret from Hy I will never know. There were well over two hundred people packed into Hy's backyard and house that day and when Hy walked through the front door and heard the yell of "Surprise!" I thought she would fall down dead on the spot.

Trish's idea was to get everyone together to say their goodbyes to Hy while she was still alive, rather than wait until the funeral. It was a great idea and, quite honestly, I don't know why it hasn't caught on as more of a tradition. Hy loved every minute of it.

She flitted around from person to person like a princess at a ball. You would have thought she was fifty years younger. Stories were told, memories were shared, laughter filled the air and, whenever someone tried to get too morose or somber, Hy was quick to lighten the mood with a joke and a smile. I found it hard to believe that she had just a week to live.

The death sentence that hung over the day is what made it both wonderful and weird. Wonderful, because of the opportunities to share a final "thank you," "goodbye," or "I love you" with a very special woman. Weird, because Hy's casual, fun-loving manner gave the day the feel of a "Bon Voyage" party rather than a "Sorry-To-Hear-You're-Dying" gathering. If a stranger had walked into the party at its height, they would have thought Hy was going to Paris instead of the hereafter.

There was one moment, towards the end of the party, when I saw a side of Hy that better fit the occasion. The sun had set, many people had already left, and the ones that remained had moved inside. I noticed Hy slip out the back and I followed her out to the backyard. It was pitch black, there was no moon that night, so I used the little bit of light streaming from the house windows to find my way. I heard Hy before I saw her.

She was sitting back by the shed at the very back of the yard and she was crying. It was the first time I had seen or heard Hy cry and it caused me to stop in my tracks. I thought about turning around and leaving her alone, not sure if she wanted me to see her like that, but her voice told me otherwise.

"You gonna just stand there or are you gonna come over here and give me a shoulder for these tears of mine to fall on!"

I shuffled over to her and sat down next to her. I started to put my arm around her, but she held her hand up and said, "too late, the moment's passed." She wiped her face with her sleeve and let out a big sigh. I pulled my arm back.

"Just sittin' here thinking 'bout my daughter, Mandy." Another sigh. "Sure wish she coulda made it here."

"I didn't even know that you had a daughter!" I said, surprised by the revelation of this rather large secret.

"I don't talk about her much because it just makes my heart ache." She turned her face, so she was looking at me, and I saw the little bit of light from the house reflecting off the tears that remained in her eyes. "Ever since my husband, Jack, died she's all but disowned me as her mother. She thought I didn't take his death hard enough and that I'm not livin' the life that a grieving, old widow should live." She chuckled. "Guess as far as Mandy's concerned, I should just sit in a rocking chair with a black shawl over my head and wait for the Grim Reaper to come take me away!"

"Where is she now, Hy?"

"Oh, she lives down in Texas with her lazy husband and two bratty kids." I think Hy sensed my mild shock at her statement, so she added, "I know you don't hear me bad-mouthin' people very often, Danny, but if you met this family, you'd say the same thing. Mandy is an angry, bitter woman and it's spread like a cancer all around her. She was Daddy's little princess when Jack was alive and now that he's gone, she's findin' the world doesn't treat her quite the same way and it's made her an unpleasant human being. Her husband and kids have just followed her lead."

"So, does she know about all of…this?"

"If you mean about my death bein' around the corner and about this here gatherin', the answer is yes, she does know all about it."

"And what does she say about it all?"

"That I'm just a crazy, old woman who doesn't know my ass from a tea kettle."

"Wow, that's a shame Hy. It must hurt a lot to think about it."

"It's my only remaining regret, Danny, and I'm not sure I'll be able to get past it before next week." Hy's head sunk and she stared at the ground.

We sat quietly for a short time. Then I heard Hy begin to whimper and I slid over close to her, put my arm around her and held her tight. We sat that way, enveloped in Hy's quiet whimpers and the black of the night, for a long, long time.

CHAPTER 24

I was sitting in the kitchen the following morning, pushing around some eggs and thinking about Hy, when Zootie walked in. "Hey there Danny, we're heading off for a walk around Green Lake, wanna come?"

Behind Zootie stood Brent, my mystery roommate. "Sure," I said as I laid my fork on the plate in front of me, "I could use some fresh air."

Green Lake was a large lake in the middle of North Seattle and was a popular place for walking, biking, roller-blading or just hanging out and watching the people go by. I'd walked it several times since touching down in Seattle and I always enjoyed it as a place for a brief respite from the city.

As we walked toward the lake Zootie, as always, dominated the conversation. "So, how's it goin' Danny?"

"Okay, I guess." I was still preoccupied with my conversation with Hy the night before. "Zootie, did you know Hy had a daughter?"

"Yeah, I did. I saw a picture of her in Hy's living room and asked her about her. She told me the whole sad story. Really a shame given what a fine woman Hy is. That daughter, what's her name again?"

"Mandy."

"Yeah, Mandy, she doesn't know what she's missing! Having a woman such as Hy as your mother is a true gift and yet it sounds like Mandy is afraid to open the box."

"Hy said she's still too angry with her."

"Anger, fear, same thing."

This is where Brent chimed in. "Only forgiveness sets you free!"

"Who said that one, Brent?" Zootie asked.

"Mother Teresa."

Zootie laughed one of his hearty laughs. "I tell ya Brent, you got a quote for every occasion, don't'cha?"

Brent smiled. "All those years in academia put a lot of worthless information in my head."

Brent said the words as if he was humble, but it felt to me like he was anything but that. I hadn't had too many occasions to talk with him since that first night, as he rarely slept in our bedroom in Hope House, but I always got the vibe of "arrogant professor" with him.

I decided to try to get to know him better. "What was it that you did for a living, Brent?"

"I taught philosophy at the University of Washington."

"He wasn't just any old professor, Danny," Zootie interjected. "He was Professor Emeritus and gave lectures all over the world."

"Yes, it's true, I did enjoy some success within my field. That is, until this gentleman came calling." He pointed his right thumb in Zootie's direction.

"Sorry about that professor, just doin' my job." Zootie smiled a big smile.

"So, judging from the way you guys joke about it, it sounds like you're a little farther along in accepting your fate and your DOD," I said.

"My DOD?" Brent asked.

"Your DOD - Date of Death. It's an acronym that Jennie used, and she made it sound like everyone used it."

Zootie chuckled. "That Jennie is quite a gal, eh?"

I nodded. "Yes, she is."

"To answer your question," Brent jumped in, "I ascribe to the Frank Sinatra view on death and dying. He said, *"Dying is a pain in the ass"* and I couldn't agree with him more. But, like him, my fate has been sealed and now I must just accept its inevitability."

"That's admirable Brent," I said. "I just hope that I can have as calm of an approach to my death as you seem to have."

"I can howl at the darkness Dan or I can light a candle. I prefer to light a candle and go quietly into the gentle night."

Zootie slapped him on the back. "An inspiration to us all, Brent."

Brent gave him a slow nod of thanks.

Zootie then bent down and picked up a candy wrapper that was on the ground and stuffed it into a fanny pack that he had around his waist. He saw me looking at him and said simply, "Just doin' my part to save Mother Earth."

We continued our walk, talking the whole way and helping Zootie to fill his fanny pack with trash, which he would empty from time to time when we passed a trash can. After one lap around the lake Brent said that he had to go but Zootie and I decided to do one more lap together.

"So Zootie," I asked after bidding goodbye to Brent, "I've been wanting to ask you something."

"Fire away Danny."

"How is it that you can be so devil may care when you're surrounded by so much death and suffering?"

"Ignorance truly *is* bliss Danny boy!" We both laughed. "But I can tell that you're asking a serious question," he added, "so I'll honor it with a serious answer." He paused as we both stepped out of the way of an oblivious rollerblader who was barreling towards us on the path. Stepping back onto the path, he continued. "Many years ago, in what seems now like a previous lifetime, I was one of the best, and most obnoxious, lawyers in the Midwest. I was rich, successful, and rapidly climbing towards my own partnership. You just think about all the worst stereotypes of lawyers and that was me.

"So, one day this wealthy, ruthless lawyer decides to go for a joyride in his brand-new Porsche and guess what he does?"

"What does he do?"

"He rolls that sports car as he swerves to avoid a kid in the road, and he ends up in the hospital for a month." He smiled as he leaned over and whispered, "best thing that ever happened to ol' Zootie.

"I wasn't wearin' a seat belt when I rolled the car, so I got tossed outta the car and onto my head. I blacked out and my heart stopped beating. I was dead, Danny." He raised a finger and smiled. "And that's when it all started to get good! I had one of those near-death experiences Danny, the one where I go zooming through a tunnel towards the bright light. I won't bore ya with the details of all that cuz I'm sure you've heard it all before, but let me tell ya, it's all true!

"Once I reached the light, I was greeted by this old guy with the kindest air about him. I didn't recognize him and yet a part of me felt like I knew him somehow. He talked to me, but his lips didn't move. It was as if our brains were somehow linked together. And then he reminded me what I had to do next: it was time for my life review. Almost instantaneously my life played out in front of us, both of us watching without saying a word and yet both of us understanding the deeper meaning of what we were watching. It all just shot by like this," he snapped his fingers, "and yet we got to see everything."

Zootie stopped walking for a moment and looked over at me. "Basically, I got to see that I was blowing it in a big way, Danny. I saw how many of my thoughtless and selfish actions had hurt people over my lifetime and that I wasn't living the type of life that I was meant to live. What a gift that was!" He screamed his last words so loudly that several passersby gave him a strange look and a wide berth as they walked by. We started walking again.

"So, then I start asking this guy some questions. But the funny thing was that as soon as I asked the question, I already knew the answer." He shook his head. "Darnedest thing. It was like I was a big ol' encyclopedia and there wasn't a darn thing that I didn't know. It was during that time that the *BIG* answer hit me." He threw his arms out wide to emphasize how big it was.

"The *big* answer?" I asked. "That implies there's a big question."

"Of course there is, Danny! The big question that's on everyone's lips whether they know it or not. The big question that has inspired every religion known to mankind. The big question that sends most folks to their graves with a tinge of regret because they couldn't find the answer to it."

"Okay, okay, I get it! So, you going to tell me or not?"

Zootie stopped walking, smiled at me with his warm, almost fatherly eyes, and bent over to whisper in my ear. "What is the purpose of my life?" He then stepped back with his arms out to his sides as if to say "Voila!"

"Is there any question more basic than that, Danny? The ol' why am I here and what does it all mean question?"

"No, that's a big one all right. What was the answer you got?"

I could see small tears forming in Zootie's eyes. He crossed his arms over his chest, as if he was hugging himself, and said, simply, "Love." He said it with a reverence that one would use in church and he just stood there, allowing the word to hang in the air, for a couple of minutes. Then he let out a deep sigh and we continued walking.

"Such a simple answer, Danny, and yet I saw then just how powerful it was. I saw the entire history of mankind play out before me and I saw how many times we were given this simple message and yet we never managed to embrace it. We continue to choose the desires of our flesh over the desires of our soul and I saw what a huge price we've paid for that decision."

He let out a small chuckle. "Kinda funny that the Beatles had it right back in the sixties: love really *is* the answer! I've been on the other side, Danny, and, trust me, nothing else even comes close to mattering as much as the amount of love you can spread during your living and breathing years!"

"So what happened next?" I asked. "You obviously didn't die."

"No, I didn't. But, at the time, I sure wanted to. I didn't want to come back, It felt so good to be there in that place without any fear or pain or regret. Just simple *being* without all the baggage and I gotta tell ya, I'd never felt that way in my life.

"But then, out of nowhere, my *father* comes zooming into the picture! He'd been dead for over ten years and yet there he was in front of me telling me that I had to go back, that it wasn't my time to join him just yet. It wasn't like he was standing there wearing my Dad's clothes or anything, but I still *knew* it was him." Zootie stopped talking and glanced over at me sideways. "You thinkin' I'm crazy yet, Danny?"

"No, not at all Zootie. I'd read about stuff like this before, but I've never actually talked to anyone who's gone through it. It all sounds pretty amazing."

"Amazing it was for sure. And the most amazing part came when I woke up again and remembered all that I'd been through on the other side. Do you know what a tremendous gift it is to know exactly where I'm heading after I die? No doubts, no fears, nothing but a smile on my face because I know that the other side is filled with nothing but love and peace." Zootie had a smile filled with serenity on his face.

"I wish I could share in what you feel Zootie. Death is still a pretty scary topic for me."

"You aren't alone on that one Danny! Most folks avoid lookin' at ol' Mr. Death all together because they're just too darned scared to look in his eyes. That's why I'm doing all that I can with this list, Danny. I've been allowed to peek behind the curtain and cheat a little bit and I feel like it's my obligation to help as many folks as I can to see that what's behind the curtain isn't so scary after all. Matter of fact, it's pretty darned nice! We're just stuck here in this School For Lost Souls called Earth and all we see is fear and pain. Our job is to look past all of that and learn the one true lesson that lies at our cores before we get to graduate and move on."

"Boy, that all sounds appealing and all Zootie, but how do we get from here to there without having a near-death experience like you did?"

"Just *listen* Danny. I know you're gettin' the same message coming from inside of you, we all do, but you have to trust it enough to listen to what it's telling you. Everyone sees the Promised Land across the canyon of fear that's in front of them but you gotta be willing to take that first step onto the invisible bridge of faith that separates where you are from where you want to go."

I thought about my on-going internal dialogues and I chuckled. "How do you decide *which* voice to listen to?" I asked.

Zootie laughed out loud, one of his Santa Claus laughs that drew stares from all around us. "That's true, there can get to be quite a racket inside, can't there? But ya gotta learn to sort through the voices Danny and find the one voice that matters. He's the quiet one off in the corner Danny. The one who talks to you in whispers, not in shouts. If you're gettin' yelled at that's just one of your fears tryin' to be heard. Ignore him! He'll take ya nowhere but down Danny!"

I thought again about the various voices in my head and realized that my higher self did indeed tend to speak to me in a decidedly softer tone. "So, if all this is true Zootie," I asked, "and there's this wonderful after-life and all, why is it that more people don't remember it? Why is the knowledge of it reserved for just a select few like yourself?"

"I remember reading the Jewish myth that talked about how an angel of God used her forefinger to make the indentation on our upper lips at birth, as if making a "shhh" sound against our mouths. This was to seal the forgetting of our soul's origin so we wouldn't have the benefit of that memory during our lives on Earth. I certainly don't have all the answers Danny, but it seems like we have to come to this realization regarding the power of love on our own, without any outside help."

"A little test, huh?"

"Not so much a test, but a way to strengthen our soul. It's like if I were teaching my son how to do simple addition - if I did all of the problems for him and gave him all of the answers, he wouldn't learn a thing about addition, would he?"

I shook my head.

"Same with the lessons of the soul - we've got to learn the important lessons ourselves or we'll forever be relying on others to feed us the answers. That's why I've got such a problem with organized religions Danny: they make ya believe that they got the answer book right in their hands and if ya hang around 'em long enough, they might just feed ya a couple of those answers. Bullnuts! The only religion is the religion of love, Danny, I know that for a fact now. And the only church worth attending is the one ya got right in here." He tapped his chest. "No tithing necessary, no rituals to go through, no special books or prayers; all ya gotta do is take the time to sit down and listen!"

He gave me a playful elbow to the ribs as we continued walking. "'Course, no priest or minister is gonna tell ya that because there's no money in it. Nobody's gonna make a livin' off the religion of love because there's nothing to buy. You're self-contained Danny! Got everything you need tucked away inside and all ya gotta do is grab onto it."

As Zootie talked in his typical animated fashion, I couldn't help but think how dangerous he would be as one of those TV evangelists. The guy was so convincing and so magnetic that he would make millions. The old ladies watching at home wouldn't stand a chance; they'd be signing their life savings over to him before you could say "Amen!"

Zootie caught me smiling at the thought. "What'cha smiling at there, Danny?"

"Oh, nothing really. Just trying to imagine you as a pitch-man on TV. You'd be dangerous!"

He laughed. "Yeah, I guess I would!" he agreed as he stopped to dump another load of garbage into a trash can. "Good thing I no longer work for the dark side, eh?"

"That's for darned sure!"

The conversation shifted to lighter fare the rest of the way home. We bantered back and forth about baseball, failed relationships, and the aggravations that come with growing older as the sun sank below the western horizon. It had been one of the best walks of my life.

CHAPTER 25

"THOMP!"

It was a couple of days later that I was walking through the hallway, on the way out the door for a jog around Green Lake, when I heard a strange sound.

"THOMP!"

It sounded like it was coming from below me, down in the basement.

"THOMP! THOMP!"

I opened the basement door and stuck my head into the darkness to listen.

"THOMP!"

There was no mistaking it: it was coming from the basement. I went down the stairs to investigate. Once down the stairs I looked around and saw nothing at first, but then I heard a shout.

"Take that you mother fucker!!!" screamed the woman's voice. This was then followed by another "THOMP!"

I followed the sound to the back part of the basement. In the far corner I was surprised to see Jennie, standing with a young man I didn't recognize, and they were both standing in front of a suspended mattress with baseball bats in their hands.

"Come on David," Jennie screamed, "you can do it! Give that fucker a good ol' whack!"

"I don't know Jennie, I..." the young man started to say before he caught sight of me out of the corner of his eye. He put the bat behind his back as I walked up, as if afraid that he might be scolded.

Jennie looked over. "Hey there, Dan!" she said with a smile. She saw me looking at the bat in her hand and the suspended mattress behind her and explained, "We're just engagin' in a little therapy here, care to join us?"

"I've never seen this particularly therapy before, how does it work?" I asked with a small smile.

"It's really quite simple," Jennie began as she raised the bat to her shoulder. "You just think about how fucked up your life is, get good and angry and then..." she swung the bat at the mattress with seemingly every bit of strength she had. "THOMP!" Dust flew everywhere. She swung again, "Take that you mother fucker!" "THOMP!"

She rested the barrel of bat on the concrete floor. She was out of breath but still managed to smile. "See? Simple!" She motioned towards the bat. "Ya wanna give it a try, Dan?"

"No, that's all right. I'm not sure I've got enough anger in me to do the therapy justice."

Jennie looked at me sideways, obviously not believing what I'd just told her. "C'mon, everyone's got *something* to be pissed about!"

I shrugged. "Sorry."

"Fucked up parents? Lousy childhood? Broken heart? *Nothing?*"

"Nope, not a thing."

She shook her head in disbelief. "All right, I'll let ya off the hook this time. But *next* time I wanna see ya raisin' some dust with this thing." She lifted the bat and gave it a couple of shakes in front of me.

"Deal," I said.

The young man with her started to look even more nervous than he had earlier. I decided to introduce myself. "Dan Barnes," I said as I stuck my hand out.

He blushed as he shook my hand. "Dave Smith," he murmured.

"My bad!" Jennie blurted out. "I'm lousy at that kinda stuff, sorry about that."

"No problem," I assured her. Dave just looked at the ground.

"Dave here is on the list too," Jennie explained. "His DOD is a little before mine in November, isn't it Dave?" Dave nodded slightly. I looked at him a little more closely and saw that he was probably about the same age as Jennie, and yet he carried himself like a shy adolescent. He was tall and thin with sandy brown hair, cut conservatively, and was dressed in a t-shirt and jeans.

"He's a bit of a shy guy," Jennie continued, "but I'm tryin' my darnedest to cure him of that. I wanna get him to beat the shit out of this mattress cuz I know *he's* got a *boatload* of anger inside of him!" She gave him a playful nudge to the shoulder. "Don't'cha Dave?"

Dave didn't say a word, he just turned a deeper shade of red.

Jennie continued to serve as his mouthpiece. "Dave has AIDS" she said matter-of-factly, "not 'cuz he's gay but because he decided to try some drugs at a party and got stuck with an infected needle." She glanced over at Dave and saw that his expression hadn't changed, so she continued. "It was his first time doing it too - pretty rotten luck, huh?" She scrunched her nose and I nodded in agreement. "His DBD is to have his Dad tell him that he loves him, and his Dad isn't cooperating with that little dream, is he?"

This time Dave managed to shake his head.

"DBD?" I interjected. "Is that another one of your special little acronyms?"

"Dream before dying," she said with a shrug that seemed to say, *"isn't that obvious?"*

"So, if that's Dave's DBD, then what's yours Jennie?"

"I'm gonna keep that one a little secret for now, Dan." She smiled. "I can tell ya this, though: I've heard some pretty good DBD's from my fellow listmates! I'm keepin' 'em right here in this book," she patted a small notebook in her back pocket, "along with some other things that I'm learnin' along the way here at Hope House."

"Sounds like an interesting little book you've got there."

"Yessirree, it sure is."

I decided to change the subject. "So where did you come up with this therapy idea of yours?" I nodded towards the mattress.

"Read it somewhere. Good idea, huh?"

"Yeah, it is. I can see it helping to release a whole lot of anger in a healthy way that doesn't hurt anyone, except the mattress of course."

We exchanged smiles. "You'll love the next one I'm gonna use."

"What's that?"

"I'm gonna call 'em Mother Fucker Days. And on those days we don't have to be nice to anyone, we can just let our ugly, angry side come on out to romp around for a while and not feel guilty about it. Whaddaya think?"

"I think I'm going to make sure I don't cross paths with you on those days!"

"Smart man!" Jennie put the bat back on her shoulder and nodded in Dave's direction. "Now, if ya don't mind Dan, we gotta get back to our therapy here."

"Hey, no problem. I don't want to interfere with the work of Dr. Jennie!"

With that I turned to go. "I'll see you guys later," I said with a small wave.

"See ya," Jennie shouted. Dave just nodded.

As I walked away, I heard Jennie screaming again. "C'mon Dave, I know ya got it in ya! Just let it out!" I heard a muffled "Thomp" but it wasn't nearly as loud as the others had been. "What was that?" she screamed, "a freakin' love tap?!? Hit the mother fucker!"

I walked up the basement stairs to a series of much louder whacks. "THOMP! THOMP! THOMP!" After each whack Jennie was yelling, "That's it! That's it! Now you're gettin' the hang of it!" Dave appeared to have succumbed to the powers of Dr. Jennie's mattress therapy.

CHAPTER 26

"We are here today to honor the life of Toby Liebman…" the minister began. It was the start of two of the longest hours of my life. I fidgeted with my tie and shifted in my seat on the pew. I looked over at Trish seated next to me. She had already begun to cry. I felt like bolting for the door.

Trish had asked me to accompany her to Toby's funeral and, after having let her down the week before, I felt I had no choice but to agree. It would be only the second funeral I'd attended in my life, my father's having been the first, and I certainly wasn't looking forward to the experience.

The minister droned on with words that could have been said at any of a thousand other funerals across the country that day. I was ashamed of how I felt, but that didn't stop me from feeling it: I didn't want to be there. I felt like I was part of a huge lie, as first the minister and then members of her family got up and shared sentiments that couldn't possibly have applied to the woman I'd seen in the house that day. Words like "bubbly" and "vivacious" tumbled from people's lips and I wondered if we had come to the right funeral. Then Trish stood up and went to the front of the church.

I noticed people's reactions as she approached the podium; they would lean over and ask their neighbor, "Who's she?" The combined whispers created a slight buzz within the church and the sea of black in front of me, that had been stone still up until then, began to fidget slightly. Trish seemed oblivious to it all as she stepped up and shared what she had to say.

"My name is Trish McConnell and I realize that many of you don't know me. I've only known Toby for the last few weeks of her life, so I don't have the memories of her as a young woman that many of you have." She waved her hand in front of her, palm upward. "I regret that fact because it sounds as if she was quite a young lady." I could see that Trish was working to force back tears. I silently cheered her on. "The Toby I knew was a sad, regret-filled woman who longed for a better someday off in the future. Sadly, that someday would never come for her and I spent the last week of her life helping her to reconcile that fact within herself." Trish couldn't hold the tears any longer and she began to sob lightly. "I just wanted to tell all of you, her family and loved ones, that, in the end, Toby showed much courage and eventually found peace with her fate." She all but shoved the last few words out of her mouth in order to beat the wave of tears that was behind them. "I felt honored to have known her." She broke into heaving sobs as she left the podium and walked back to her seat next to me. I put my arm around her, and she cried into my shoulder. I felt like a jerk for my earlier thoughts. Leave it to Trish to find the half-full part of the glass.

After the service, on the way out of the church, we were stopped by several people as they wanted to thank Trish for her kind words. Her tears had subsided and she chatted with each of them at great length about Toby's last days. I just stood to one side and admired her kindness and graciousness. She was a truly exceptional woman and I had a ringside seat for watching her in action, doing what she seemed to do best: making people feel better about themselves. It was a gift that I found myself wishing I had as I could see what a difference she made in people's lives, even through a single interaction.

On the church steps we ran into Toby's father, who was shaking hands with everyone as they left. I thought about Toby's story regarding her father, and how it changed her life so dramatically, and I found myself having to get AC under control.

"Punch that mother fucker right in the face!" AC screamed at me. *"How can he even show his face here after what he did to that poor girl?!?"*

Fortunately, I let Trish do the talking.

"Mr. Liebman," she said as she grabbed his hand warmly, "I just want to tell you what a pleasure it was for me to get to know your lovely, courageous daughter, if even for a short while."

He was a little taken aback at first, but then he seemed to remember who Trish was from the service and a small smile curled on the corner of his mouth. "Thanks for your nice words in there about my Toby." His voice quavered slightly but there were no tears in his eyes. "It's true what you said, about her being a sad woman and all, but I was glad to hear that she felt some peace in the end." His eyes glassed over as he continued. "She wasn't always a sad girl," he said as his eyes focused on a point over Trish's shoulder, somewhere back in time. "She was the happiest girl you'd ever want to meet, full of life and dreams..." His voice trailed off and the tears began falling down his cheeks. "When her mother died, I know that I let her down, I wasn't there for her like her Mother had been." Now his head bowed, and he began sobbing. "I'd always meant to make it up to her someday, but now I can't..." He couldn't talk any more as he buried his head in his hands and sobbed like a child. Trish reached over and rubbed his back.

"For what it's worth, Mr. Liebman," she whispered to the back of his head, "Toby always spoke very highly of you and obviously loved you a lot." These words inspired even more tears from Mr. Liebman and a couple of people who had been standing with him led him off to a waiting car.

Trish and I made our way to our own car and headed back towards Hope House. "You're a pretty amazing woman, you know that?" I said to her as I was entering the freeway.

She looked over at me, smiled through her red, blotchy face, and said, "Thank you." She shifted in her seat, so she was facing me. "Why do you say that?"

"Because I watched you back there and you have this amazing gift for making people feel better. You did it with Toby, you did it with all of her friends and relatives, and you did it with her father, who I just wanted to punch by the way."

She let out a small laugh. "I see why you say that about her father, after hearing what Toby had to say about him, but he's just a struggling, hurting human being like the rest of us. You heard what he had to say about his regrets regarding Toby. That man must have some inner demons the size of watermelons!"

"Yeah, you're right. But that's what makes you even more amazing, you instinctively know all these things before you open your mouth. I would have gone in with my guns blazing and then felt like shit afterwards. But you, you always seem to default to thinking the best about people and they seem to prove you right most of the time."

"Yeah," she smiled, "I guess they do at that."

"Is there some book I can read or five-step seminar I can take to learn your secrets?"

She let out one of her laughs that made my knees buckle. It was a true, from the heart laugh that was absolute music to my ears. I found myself working hard to inspire those laughs as much as I could. "No big secrets to it, Dan. Just listen with your heart and you can't help but feel as I do. You see that people are all basically good and all they want out of life is to be able to push aside the curtains of hurt, pain and fear long enough to let that goodness out into the world." She shrugged, as if to say *"See? Simple!"*

"Sounds easy," I said deadpan. "So how much do I owe you for the seminar?" I gave her my best flirtatious look.

She seemed to return the look as she said, "how about a nice lunch somewhere?"

"Done! How about heading over to Edmonds and getting some seafood down by the water?" I was feeling as giddy as a teenager who had just scored his first date.

"Sounds great. I'm ready for a view of the water and a glass of wine."

"Your wish is my command." The rest of the drive to Edmonds was filled with laughter, obvious flirtations, and an unmistakable electric current that ran between the two of us. Our mutual attraction filled the car as memories of Toby's funeral quickly faded to the background.

CHAPTER 27

Trish had asked me to drop her at a friend's house on the way home from our lunch date, so I walked into the house alone a few hours later. I had a huge grin on my face as I thought back on a lunch that had been positively magical.

"Hey there, smiley. Where've you been?" It was Hy's voice and she was sitting in the living room.

"Hey there, Hy!" I walked towards her. "I was off having lunch with Trish." I sat down next to her.

"Trish, huh?" She had the same look that my mother used to have when I came home from a date in high school. "Did you two have a good time?"

"As a matter of fact, we did." I paused for effect. "Mom."

Hy laughed. "Just warms my heart to see two people I care about gettin' along so well, that's all."

"I appreciate your positive feelings." I noticed Hy rolling something around in her hands. "What's that you have there?" I pointed at her hands.

She lifted what looked like a glass bird. "Oh, this is something that Jennie had found in the basement yesterday." She looked at it as one would a prized photograph. "I forgot I had put 'em down there."

"What is it?"

Hy sighed and nodded towards a nearby bookcase. I looked over and saw many more of the birds, all different colors, placed on a shelf surrounding a picture of a young girl.

"My daughter, Mandy, and I used to paint these porcelain birds together as a sort of hobby." She nodded at the picture. "That's her there when she was about ten years old, back when she liked me." Another long sigh.

"They're beautiful Hy!"

"Yeah, we got pretty good at it." She held up the one in her hands again. "This here's always been our favorite. The bluebird." She handed it to me.

I looked at it more closely and saw the detail on it. It did indeed look just like a bluebird. "You've got some real talent, Hy."

She smiled. "More patience than anything else, Danny."

"Why were they tucked away in the basement?" I handed the bluebird back to her.

"'Cuz it was just too painful havin' 'em around all the time." I gulped, knowing my mistake as soon as I'd said the words. "They just reminded me of how much I miss havin' my daughter around, Danny."

"I'm sorry Hy."

"Don't be." She stared at the bird in her hand. "Jennie did me a favor bringin' these up here. It reminded me of what I had to do."

"What's that?"

"Give up on ever seein' her again and doin' any reconcilin' before I die. I just gotta focus my old eyes on the daughter I loved, and who loved me, and be content with that." Her face was very sad. "These here birds help with that."

"There's still a couple of days left Hy. Maybe we could hop a flight down to..."

Hy held her hand up. "No, Danny. It's no use." She reached over and patted my leg. "It's a sweet thought, but goin' down there would be akin to pokin' a stick into a hornet's nest and why would I want to do that in my last days?"

"Well, you certainly know best," I shrugged.

"Yes, yes I do indeed. And my place is here, with all of you." Her eyes went back down to the bird in her lap. "And my memories."

Hy just sat there, lost in her own world, for a while. I reached over and stroked her back in an attempt at silent support.

Soon, she lifted her head and looked over at me with one of the saddest faces I'd ever seen. "Danny, I wonder if you could do me a small favor."

"Anything, you just name it."

She reached her hand into a pocket on her dress and pulled out an envelope. She handed it to me. "I'm wondering if you could read this for me and tell me what you think."

I took the envelope. "Sure. What is it?"

"It's a letter I wrote to Mandy." I turned it over and saw Mandy's name on the front of the envelope. "For her to read after I'm gone."

I gulped. The envelope suddenly felt much heavier. I opened it up and took out the one-page letter inside. It was written in Hy's shaky long-hand but was entirely legible. I read it slowly, trying to fully absorb Hy's message.

> *My Dearest Mandy,*
>
> *When you read this, I will be gone. As I had told you several times, I knew my end was near and that's why I had wanted so badly for us to see each other again; to patch up old wounds, to express the love that I knew had always been there, and to hug once again as mother and daughter. Unfortunately, it was not meant to be, Mandy, and I'm sorry for that. It will be my biggest regret as I pass from this world to the next one that awaits me.*
>
> *I'm sorry that I wasn't the mother that you wanted after your father died, sweetie. I only did what I felt I had to*

do in order to be true to myself, I hope that you understand that. I never meant to hurt you and I absolutely never, ever meant to put any kind of wall between us. I wanted nothing more than for us to be as we were, "two peas in a pod" as your father used to say. I missed having you around Mandy. I missed painting with you. I missed watching you grow into a wife and a mother. I missed just sitting and sipping Dr. Peppers with you and chatting about nothing in particular. I missed my daughter, Mandycakes.

Along the lines of "being true to myself" I want to tell you something before my will is read. I have left the house to Zootie Gibbons and the other members of Hope House. I have left all my cash and the more personal possessions, such as our birds, to you my dear but the house will serve a much greater purpose in their hands right now. I hope you will understand this. Spend some time with them Mandy, you'll see what they're trying to do and how many lives they're impacting. I know you may feel a little hurt or angry at first, but don't blame anyone but me as it was my decision, influenced by nobody else. I hope you understand.

It's important that you know that as I sit here on the edge of death, I feel no blame or hard feelings in my heart for our years of separation. I feel nothing but love for you Mandy. I want you to know that, so you feel no guilt after I'm gone. As I write this letter, I'm looking over at our little flock of birds that we painted together. Remember those? I remember how we used to sit for hours painting them and how we'd try to make each other laugh so that we couldn't hold the brush still. Remember that? We loved each other so much then, as a mother and daughter, and I know in my heart that

that *love has never left. I feel it now, as I write this let-*
ter, and I will feel it in my heart for all eternity. I love
you my little Mandycakes.

Love Forever,

Mom

"That's a great letter, Hy," I said softly as I laid the letter in my lap. "I wouldn't change a thing."

CHAPTER 28

The two days leading up to Hy's DOD were pure chaos. Hope House became a kind of Mecca, with pilgrims coming from all over the place to pay their last respects to Hyacynthia Ebbermeier.

As was the case with her goodbye party, Hy was in her element. Even though her minutes of life remaining were now counting in the thousands, she was still generous with her time and attentive to all her visitors. It was still hard for me to believe that, in a few days, she would no longer be around.

I was paying a visit to the downstairs hall bathroom, the day before Hy's DOD, when I overheard two voices talking quietly outside the bathroom door. I instantly recognized the voices as Trish's and Hy's.

Hy spoke first. "You gotta get that boy's boat untied from the dock Trish and get him out into the river!"

"I know Hy, and I'm trying," Trish responded. "He's just so afraid of jumping in and I don't know what to do to get him off the sidelines." My face flushed and I caught my breath. "*My god, they're talking about me!*" I realized. I sat quietly and strained to listen, though a part of me wanted to just put my hands over my ears and shut out the whispers.

"He's such a dear boy and I hate to see him wasting this opportunity." There was a short pause. "You like him, don't you Trish?" I could practically *hear* Hy smiling through the door. I leaned forward involuntarily to hear the response, but it seemed an eternity before Trish spoke.

"Yeah, Hy, I guess I do." It was all I could do to not let out a yelp of excitement.

Another voice yelled to them from down the hall and I heard them walk off. I waited a minute longer before moving, then finished my business and left the bathroom, being careful to check in all directions before walking out. I headed straight to the backyard, feeling like I needed some time to digest what I'd just overheard. Once in the backyard I walked to a section in the far back corner that wasn't visible from the house. I needed to be alone.

I sat on an old stump and started to mull over Hy and Trish's comments. The excitement I felt at Trish's final comment regarding her feelings for me was quickly nudged aside by the embarrassment and shame I felt at their comments about my spot on the sidelines. Initially, I managed to mask my shame under a veil of defensiveness and anger. *Hadn't I been right there in the thick of things?* I wondered. *What do they want from me? It seems like they won't be happy until my name appears on the list!*

Then I thought about the source of the observations: Trish and Hy, two of the people I admired and respected above all others. The small escape hatch for my ego abruptly slammed closed.

"They're right, you know," a small voice whispered to me, adding further fuel to the "Dan-is-afraid-to-leave-the sidelines" theory.

I thought about how many people had come and gone on the list while I'd been in Hope House and how few I'd connected with in any real way. Hy, Jennie, Brent, and Toby to some degree; the list was indeed small. *"Why is that?"* I wondered. *"What am I afraid of?"* Besides the obvious reason of fear of death in general, which I already knew spooked the shit out of me, it seemed like I also had a deep-seated fear of commitment that was getting in the way.

It was such a cliché to say about men in general, "*you're afraid of commitment*", but Hy and Trish's comments made me want to scratch a little deeper. Where did it come from? I thought back to my childhood years to see if there were any long-standing trends in my life that would shed some light on it for me. I thought about my father, and how he tended to show his love for me through criticism, trying to make me a better person by pointing out my weaknesses. As I grew older, his voice in my head provided a constant reminder of where I came up short in life. It made me afraid to try new things for fear of "not doing it right" and looking like a fool. I didn't fault my Dad for this, as he was doing what he thought was best and he never did it out of spite or to try to intentionally hurt me. He was just loving me the only way he knew how.

I thought too about my string of unsuccessful relationships over the years. It would always follow the same pattern: date for a while, get closer, begin talking about "the future" and the "next level" and then it was "see ya later" time. I'd find one reason or another to sabotage the relationship and achieve my desired result: freedom. Not a healthy pattern according to all the self-help books but it worked for me.

But I saw now that it was just another branch on the same tree of fears that was now keeping from "going to the next level" at Hope House. To jump in, as Hy and Trish wanted me to do, would require looking closely at these fears and then be willing to lay them out on the table for all to see. Intimacy. Failure. Vulnerability. Those were the true enemies that I had to look in the eye and get under control before I could commit to anything worthwhile in my life.

A dark shadow rolled over my stomach as the reality of what I was proposing to myself stepped into the spotlight. *True intimacy?!? Making myself vulnerable?!?* I looked around, as if I'd been exposed and many eyes were now upon me. How would I begin? Then I thought about the conversation I'd had with Hy a week earlier.

"Step *through* your fears, Danny" she had said. I remembered the images she'd described of big holograms with no teeth, paper tigers she'd called them. I thought too of the Fear Dragons that she had slain in her later years, as an old woman, and I suddenly felt renewed shame for my hesitation at jumping into the fray regarding the list. It was time to take a stand. I stood up, took a deep breath, exhaled slowly, and walked back towards the house, ready to do battle with my own flock of Fear Dragons.

CHAPTER 29

Late that night Jennie summoned all the residents of Hope House into the living room. She'd told us that she had put together a ceremony to honor Hy, but she told us nothing more. As I walked in, I noticed a large paper dragon that had been taped up across the doorway leading into the hall. It had been painted on a large piece of paper and whoever had painted it had done a good job, I thought to myself. Its big teeth were bared in a snarl, fire was coming out of his nose, and its eyes glowed with pure evil. It caught the attention of everyone who walked into the room and caused much conjecturing as to its meaning.

Jennie stood in the middle of the room and didn't say a word as close to two dozen people filed into the room and found a seat, either in chairs or on the floor. After everyone had gotten settled, and the talking died down, Jennie began to speak.

"Thank you for coming everyone," she began. "Tonight, we will be attempting something that I hope will become a sort of tradition here at Hope House. The entire idea was inspired by our very own Hy," she pointed towards Hy and started clapping and everyone in the room clapped along with her.

"Nonsense dear," Hy said with a wave of her hand. "I just spewed out some silly thoughts! It was *you* that came up with this wonderful idea!"

Jennie's look turned sad for a moment. "That's why we're gonna miss you, Hy. Not only are you wise and wonderful in so many ways but you're so damned humble about it to boot!" That brought more applause from the group and Hy just looked at the ground shyly.

"Anyway," she continued, "for those of you who haven't heard of these before," she turned and pointed toward the dragon hanging in the doorway, "this is a Fear Dragon." She walked over towards it. "Notice the big, snarling teeth and the dangerous claws." She turned back to the group. "Pretty scary looking, huh?" Everyone nodded and smiled.

"Well, as Hy is fond of saying, scary as it seems, it's just made out of paper!" She snapped the piece of paper with her finger. "And it's kinda silly to be scared of paper, right?" Everyone nodded. "But that's what we're all afraid of - paper dragons!" My mind flashed to my session in the backyard earlier in the day. This was all way too coincidental for my tastes and I felt an involuntary shiver run through my body.

She nodded to Dave Smith and he stood up. Something about him looked a little different, but I couldn't put my finger on it right away. "Dave here is gonna show us all just how easy it is to step through this here scary dragon once and for all." She nodded again at Dave and, as if they'd rehearsed every step, he stepped forward to the center of the room, cleared his throat, and said in a loud voice that I didn't think he was capable of, "My biggest fear is that I'm unlovable." He started to choke up as he finished but he got it all out. I could see that he had begun to cry. I realized then what the difference was in Dave: confidence. Dr. Jennie had worked wonders with her therapy.

Jennie took out a big black marker and wrote in big letters, above the dragon's head; "I'M UNLOVABLE."

Everyone in the room then saw what was about to take place and they began to offer words of support to Dave. He didn't seem to hear anyone, however, as he maintained his focus on the dragon, and the words, in front of him. After a short time, he threw his shoulders back, took a deep breath and walked toward the dragon. He stopped right in front of it, mumbled what sounded like, "It's time to die, you bastard" and then walked right through it into the hallway on the other side. The room absolutely erupted into thunderous support.

Dave came back through the piece of torn paper and his face was positively glowing. He and Jennie embraced as the cheers continued. Jennie then broke the embrace, went over and tore the remnants of the dragon off the doorway, and replaced it with another big dragon that had been lying on the floor behind the couch. "I've got seven more of these that I made. Who wants to go next?"

It was only a moment before Hy's squeaky voice yelled out, "I'll go!"

Jennie grinned. "Come on up Hy!"

Hy got out of her chair and walked to the middle of the room. She waited until everyone quieted down and then said in a subdued voice; "I haven't told anyone this, but I'm afraid that my death will be painful." Hy began weeping softly and there wasn't a person in the room who wasn't weeping with her, except me. Hy, who had always been so strong for everyone else, suddenly looked very old and vulnerable standing there in the middle of the room.

Jennie wiped the tears from her face and wrote in big letters above the dragon, "PAINFUL DEATH." "Okay Hy, whenever you're ready," she said in a soft voice.

Tears continued to stream down the faces of everyone seated in the room as Hy stepped towards the dragon. She stopped in front of it, mumbled something that I couldn't hear, and then stepped on through it. Jennie had to help her just a little bit with the initial ripping of the paper, but she made it through to the hallway. Everyone cheered wildly as Hy came back into the room. She raised her arms like some champion boxer and then gave Jennie a big hug. She then walked back to her seat, acknowledging all the kind words and pats on the back along the way.

"Who's next?" Jennie shouted.

"C'mon, this is your chance!" a voice in my head suddenly pleaded. *"A chance to make a public statement about your new resolve."* I ignored it. It was all still too new for me to be standing up in front of a group and shouting it out for everyone to hear.

A middle-aged woman by the name of Shirley stood up. I hadn't really had the chance to get to know her, but Trish had told me that she was on the list with a DOD just two weeks away. She stepped to the middle of the room, still sobbing gently, and said for all to hear; "I'm afraid of being buried alive." Her voice cracked with emotion as she continued. "Ever since I was a little girl I've been afraid of this and now it's dominating my every waking moment."

Jennie wrote, "BURIED ALIVE" above the dragon's head and gave Shirley a small nod and encouraging smile. Shirley stood in the center of the room for several minutes before stepping towards the dragon. Everyone in the room could see that she was indeed looking inside of herself and trying to face down the fear that had been gripping her life since she was a child. She finally stepped forward, still sobbing, stopped in front of the dragon, and simply shook her fist at it defiantly before plunging through it. She too emerged to enthusiastic cheers.

The ritual repeated itself several more times. The next two I don't remember as my mind had been directed inward, doing battle with my own fears that were trying to keep me from going to the center of the room. My mind clicked back to the moment when I saw Jennie standing in the center of the room.

Her hands were shaking, and her face was streaked with tears, both old and new. Her voice was uncharacteristically quiet when she spoke. "All of you have been so brave, I figured it's my turn to step up here and share my BFD." She smiled through her tears. "That's Big Fear Dragon to all of you." Everyone chuckled. She looked at the ground and took a deep breath before continuing. "My BFD is that I'm going to be forgotten when I'm gone." She was trying to keep her emotions under control, but it was obvious that she was losing the battle. Her voice quavered as she spoke. "I'm afraid that, in the end, my life didn't matter to anyone and that any memory of me will just disappear right after I'm buried." The sobs soon won out and took over her body. She stepped in front of the dragon, wrote "FORGOTTEN!" across the top, tossed the pen aside, and then let out a yell that sounded like an Indian war cry: "AAAAAIIIIIIEEEEEEEE!!!!" She then turned her attention back to the dragon, raised both of her middle fingers in its face, and shouted; "Fuck you mother fucker!!! You aren't gonna lick *me*!!!!!" And then she disappeared through the paper into the hallway beyond. She walked back through the doorway afterwards, to the loudest cheer yet.

Wiping her face with her shirtsleeve, she went over and retrieved the pen that she'd thrown away earlier. She also grabbed the last paper dragon and taped it to the doorway. "All right," she yelled as she turned around, "who wants to take on the last BFD?!?"

Without conscious thought, I rose to my feet. Sweating profusely, I strode to the middle of the room and turned to face the group.

"All right Dan!" Jennie yelled from behind me.

I stood there, frozen, for what seemed like hours. All kinds of thoughts flashed through my mind, most of them voiced by AC, who had finally decided to show up to the party. *"Sit back down before you make an ass of yourself!"* he said to me. *"Nobody wants to hear you whine about your stupid little fears!"* he added. AC was being very encouraging.

I finally got my mouth to work and, with my voice trembling out of control, I said; "I wasn't going to come up here because even admitting this to myself is all so new." Hearing my voice work, and seeing that people were listening to me, emboldened me slightly. But my knees still knocked, and I could still feel the magma of suppressed emotions bubbling up dangerously close to the surface.

"But seeing all of you step up here," I nodded at Hy, Dave Smith, Jennie and the others, "inspired *me* to step up here." I paused. "Now I'm feeling a little sorry that I did." Laughter. That gave me a chance to collect myself for the final push. "I've discovered…" my salivary glands tingled but I held it together "…that I'm very much afraid…" my body trembled uncontrollably "…of commitment."

My mind went black and nothing around me existed for I don't know how long - I just stood there and shook. Finally, mercifully, the trembling abated, and I once again became aware of where I was. Looking around at the sympathetic faces, I decided then to finish what I'd started. Inhaling, in the staccato fashion of a boxer preparing to enter the ring, I felt the fresh breath of air clear my head slightly. I composed myself enough to walk over to the dragon.

Jennie had already written, "COMMITTMENT" across the top. I looked over at her standing next to the doorway and we exchanged warm smiles. I then focused my attention on the dragon. I looked closely at all the detail and color that Jennie had put into it. I smiled. *"Dr. Jennie has done it again,"* I thought to myself. Then, refocusing on why I was standing there, I felt a surge of anger boil through me. The anger caused my whole body to tremble once again. Then a voice, I still can't believe it was mine, yelled out; *"I'm onto you, you mother fucker!!!"* I punched the dragon in the face and then jumped through it like some high school football player at homecoming. I did it all so awkwardly that I tripped as I went through, stumbling face first into the hallway.

It didn't matter. I picked myself up, feeling exhilarated, and strode triumphantly back into the living room. I received slaps on the back, hugs and words of encouragement from everyone in the room. Finally, I came to Hy, who was beaming from ear to ear. She stood up and took me into a warm embrace, standing on her tiptoes so her mouth was next to my ear.

"Follow the tears, Danny," she whispered, "they're like liquid bread crumbs and they'll lead you right to the doorstep of truth deep inside of you." Her words surprised me a little bit, but I was feeling too emotional and euphoric to do anything other than squeeze her tightly. In the emotion of the moment I also whispered, "I love you, Hy" into her ear. She whispered, "I love you too, Danny" and then pulled back for a moment. She looked into my eyes and she had the warmest, most loving look I'd ever seen on a face. "And I'm damn proud of you m'boy!" she said emphatically.

As it turned out, those were the last words I'd ever hear from Hy's lips.

CHAPTER 30

On the morning of October 14th, Hyacynthia "Edna" Ebbermeier died quietly in her sleep.

Trish had found her in her bed, covers pulled up to her chin, with a small smile on her face. There was no sign that she had thrashed around when death had taken her, which was a relief to everyone in Hope House. Hy had apparently gotten the painless death that she had both wanted and deserved.

For myself, I felt a small twinge of regret that I hadn't had the chance to say one last goodbye to Hy. She had slipped off to bed amidst all the emotion and chaos the night before and I had fallen into bed exhausted many hours later. But that had been Hy's way in life - to try not to be a bother to anyone - so it was fitting that she had also been that way in death.

The doctor told us that it was Hy's heart that had eventually given out; "congestive heart failure" he called it. Many of us smiled at the irony that a woman with a heart as big as Hy's would ultimately be betrayed by that very same heart. The next several days were filled with planning for Hy's service. As per her request, her body was cremated, and we arranged to have a service in the backyard during which we would spread her ashes over her gardens.

Zootie had taken care of the cremation and Trish and I had made all the arrangements for the small service. The morning of the service was a gorgeous, warm fall day. The sun was blazing bright in a deep blue sky and it sounded as if every bird for miles around had come to roost in the trees around us to sing one last song of farewell for their beloved Hy. There were perhaps one hundred people crowded into the backyard and just about everyone had something to say about Hy.

I listened as person after person stood up and honored the life that Hy had lived. Every verbal stroke seemed to use the same brush and painted a picture of a woman who had lived a life filled with love, compassion and generosity of spirit. It was a wonderful service.

I had stood up towards the end and begun to share the words that I had written down the night before when a new face walked into the backyard. I recognized her immediately and it caused me to stop mid-sentence: it was Hy's daughter, Mandy. I gave her a slight nod of recognition, which she didn't return, and then tried to continue with my eulogy. But I was so disturbed by not only her *presence,* but also the obviously *un*mournful look she had pasted onto her face, that I just rushed through the rest of my words. Looking at her face, one would have thought she was standing and waiting for a bus, not mourning the death of her mother.

After the service was over people stayed and milled about both in the backyard and in the house. Mandy had quickly moved inside and was walking around the house like some inspector when Trish and I caught up to her in the living room. Trish stuck her hand out, "Hello there, my name is Trish McConnell." The woman didn't say a word. "You must be Hy's daughter Amanda," Trish continued valiantly, "I recognize you from the pictures. It's a pleasure to meet you finally and Hy would have been so happy to see you here."

Trish had kept her hand extended and Mandy looked at it like she had open sores that might ooze on her if she shook it. But she finally shook Trish's hand, reluctantly, and then turned her attention back to the porcelain birds she had been looking at on the shelves. I felt like I was invisible, but something inside of me said to remain that way, so I didn't bother to introduce myself to her. She obviously wanted nothing to do with any of us.

That didn't deter Trish from her appointed rounds. Hy had asked a favor of her before she died, and Trish was determined to follow through on her promise. She took an envelope out of her pocket and held it with both hands to her chest. "I just want to tell you that your mother died a very peaceful death, she didn't appear to experience any pain." Mandy turned and faced Trish, though the words she had just heard from Trish had not changed the indifferent look on her face. "I also want to tell you what an amazing woman your mother was and how many lives she changed with her big, generous heart and incredible wisdom."

These last words did have an impact on Mandy. Her face transformed from indifferent to bitter and she finally spoke. "You have no idea *who* my mother was," she all but hissed at Trish. I instinctively took a step backwards. "She may have fooled you and all of your fellow cult members, but I knew my mother for what she *really* was: a selfish fraud!" She screamed the last three words and little drops of spittle spewed from her mouth into Trish's face. Trish just stood her ground.

"I'm sorry that you feel that way," Trish responded quietly. "She had nothing but kind and loving words to say about you." She extended the envelope to Mandy. "She wrote this a few days before her death and she asked me to give it to you before the reading of the will."

Mandy snatched the envelope from Trish's hand and tore it open. As I watched her tear it open, I thought to myself just how *un*like her mother she was. *"How could she have come from Hy's womb?!?"* I thought. Looking at her smooth skin and tall, statuesque appearance, she could have been quite beautiful under different circumstances. But the bitterness in her soul had poisoned everything about her and all you could see now was the hate etched in her face and filling her eyes.

She stood in front of us as she read the letter from Hy and we could both see the anger building inside of her as she read. I don't even think she finished the letter before she crumpled it up in her hands and hurled it across the room. *"That selfish son of a bitch!"* she screamed. "I've been waiting patiently all these years for her to die so I could finally get what was rightfully mine and now she pulls this shit!" She went ballistic.

She looked around the room like a caged animal that wanted to sink its teeth into some flesh. Her eyes then came to rest on the porcelain birds, and she grabbed one. Without even pausing she hurled it across the room, smashing it against the far wall of the living room. *"Son of a bitch!"* she screamed. Then she grabbed another and tossed it even harder, yelling out, *"You selfish bastard!"* as it broke into small pieces against the wall. People scattered everywhere under the onslaught of the glass pieces.

We stood in stunned silence for a few moments as she smashed one after another of the porcelain birds that Hy had loved so much. Then a voice in my head said, *"Save the bluebird!"* It had been Hy's favorite and I looked down and saw it sitting just a few feet from me on the shelf. I stepped over slowly, not wanting to draw any attention to myself, reached down, and grabbed it in my hand. I tucked it behind my back and thought I was home free, until I heard a shriek from Mandy.

"What the hell do you think you're doing with that bird?!?" she yelled. I looked up and saw her stomping over towards me. She stopped when she was nose-to-nose with me. She was panting deeply, and I could smell the stale coffee on her breath. My heart climbed to my throat and sweat poured from my brow. I didn't realize how tall she was until she was standing there, eye to eye with me.

She put her hand out and said in a very threatening tone, through clenched teeth, "Give me that fucking bird!" Her eyes radiated pure hate.

I didn't move and I didn't say a word. All I saw was Hy's hurt face if her beloved bluebird ended up in pieces.

"I'm going to say it one more time," she said evenly as her eyes narrowed to slits, "give me the bird. It's mine, it said so in the fucking letter she wrote!"

I didn't know what to say or do. She was right, it was her property. Before I could consider that fact any further however, Zootie's voice broke in. He had probably heard the commotion from the smashing birds and had come inside to investigate.

"Actually, it all still belongs to your mother's estate until the will is read," he said calmly. I was never more thankful to hear the bugle call of the Zootie Cavalry coming over the ridge.

Mandy wheeled around to find the source of the voice. She zeroed in on Zootie and strode over to him, once again standing right in his face. "Who the fuck are you, fat man? The leader of this crooked cult?"

Zootie cocked his head back and let out a huge, deep laugh. "If that's true, I should be making a helluva lot more money! I understand that cult leaders actually do quite well as far as…" She didn't let him finish.

"Stow the bullshit, fat man!" she screamed. "I know exactly what all of you are up to here and you damn well aren't going to get away with it as long as I'm still alive!" She stomped out of the living room towards the front door. But once in the hallway she turned and, in the very same doorway where we had conquered Fear Dragons several nights earlier, she screamed for all to hear; "This house is *mine*." She pounded her fist in her hand for emphasis. "And I am going to haunt all of your lives until I get what is rightfully mine!" She wheeled and headed for the front door, but stopped short before opening it. She had one last verbal grenade to toss. "You have not seen the last of me! You can bet your sorry crooked asses on *that!*" Finally, mercifully, she opened the front door and walked out, slamming it hard behind her as she left. The entire room finally took a collective breath and let out a huge sigh of relief.

Zootie broke the stunned silence. He took in a couple of exaggerated sniffs and then said, "I swear I do smell a lawsuit in the air."

CHAPTER 31

Hy's death marked a turning point for me at Hope House. I felt like Dorothy in the Wizard of Oz after her house had touched down in the Land of Oz; suddenly everything was in technicolor. I *saw* more of what was going on around me, I *felt* more of the emotions that filled the air, and I *cared* more about what was happening. And, like Dorothy, I had my own Scarecrow, Tin Man and Lion to serve as friends and guides during the journey. Trish, with her huge heart was my Tin Man. Jennie, with her overactive brain, served as my Scarecrow. And Zootie, with his unlimited courage, acted as my Lion sidekick. Actually, Zootie even *looked* a lot like the Lion!

An early test for my new resolve came a couple of days after Hy's service. Trish was going to the hospital to visit a woman who was on the list. I asked her if I could go with her and she agreed gladly. During the entire trip to the hospital I noticed Trish looking at me sideways as I drove, probably wondering if this would be a repeat of what had happened at Toby's house. I was determined to not let that be the case. "Don't worry, I'll be okay," I finally said to her with a reassuring pat on the leg as we pulled into the hospital parking lot.

Once in the hospital we headed for the cancer ward. Trish had explained to me in the car that we were visiting a woman by the name of Ruth Cooper. She was on the list with a DOD a few weeks hence and Trish had already visited with her a couple times. She was losing a battle with breast cancer and was growing tired of her prolonged hospital stays.

"The odd thing with Ruth," Trish had said in the car, "is that both she and her husband Bill are on the list and they both have the same date next to their names."

As we walked down the hallway, I was struck by the sights and smells of the cancer ward. There was no mistaking the smell of death and the feeling of hopelessness that hung in the air. I saw room after room occupied by horizontal bodies that showed little sign of life. Loved ones were huddled everywhere and they all had the same looks of fear and sadness on their faces. My heart felt heavy.

"What the hell are we doing here*?!?"* AC wanted to know. I ignored him.

We finally arrived at Ruth Cooper's room and walked right in. She was sleeping. I looked down at her and felt pity; she looked half dead to me with her pasty skin, most of her hair gone, save for a few isolated patches, and her face and body withered down to just skin and bone. She looked like she'd just walked out of Auschwitz. My mind rewound instantly to the day by the warehouses, where I'd stumbled upon the dying woman on the ground. Liquid guilt surged through my veins, flooding every part of my body. I felt a quiet determination to not have history repeat itself.

I looked away from her pathetic body and scanned the room. There were flowers everywhere I looked and a few handmade cards, drawn with crayons, taped to the wall over her bed. There was a bed next to her, but it was empty, and the TV set was on, tuned into some soap opera. My eyes went back to Ruth. She had countless tubes attached to her body and I could see on her arms that she'd been stuck with many, many needles recently. Her lips were extremely dry and cracked and she let out small wheezing sounds as she slept. Though it was hard to tell, I thought she was probably in her early sixties.

Trish sat down in a chair situated next to the bed, up by her head. I grabbed another chair from across the room and brought it over to the same side of the bed, down by the foot. Once settled, Trish looked over at me, nodded, and then gently woke up Ruth. I felt a little uneasy about waking her up, given her condition, but I also figured that Trish knew what she was doing.

It took a few gentle shakes before Trish got Ruth to stir and then, once stirred, it took Ruth a few more minutes to gain any lucidity. She moaned softly as she scanned the room, her eyes still straddling the two worlds of dream and reality. Slowly, her eyes came into focus and it registered with her that she had visitors. A small crack of a smile formed on one side of her mouth. "Why, hello there Trish," she whispered. "So nice to see you again." Then she did an odd thing, as her eyes looked to the ceiling and she said quietly, "So long Mom and Dad. I'll see you again soon." She did it just as naturally as can be - as if they had been sitting right there with us and had to leave the room - and didn't offer any explanation to us. I cast my eyes to the ceiling, half-expecting to see two bodies floating above me, but saw nothing. I thought briefly about Zootie's words regarding an after-life and felt chills run through my body.

Her gray eyes then moved down to me. "Hello. Who might you be?"

Trish answered for me. "This is Dan, Ruth. He's a friend of mine."

Her eyes smiled mischievously. "What *kind* of friend?"

Trish returned the smile and patted Ruth's arm. "Just a friend, Ruth."

As Ruth raised her bed up in order to position herself more comfortably for entertaining visitors I marveled at her attempt at humor, however small, despite her situation. I quietly accepted the fact that I would probably be too immersed in self-pity to attempt humor - except perhaps occasional *dark* humor - if I were in a similar situation. I decided that I liked Ruth immediately.

Once in position, Trish helped her to adjust her pillows to which Ruth said a quiet thank you. "It's so nice to see you again, Trish," she said, her voice sounding more alive.

"I told you I'd be back to see you again soon."

"Yes, but there are a lot of people who have told me *that* lately and yet I see so few of them." She thought for a moment. "I guess it's just too hard for some people to see me like this."

"That's *their* problem Ruth, not yours."

"I suppose so, but I can't really blame them. I do look a fright," she looked over at me, "don't you think, Dan?"

She caught me by surprise. "No, not at all Ruth," was all I could muster.

She waved her hand at me in mock contempt. "Oh, pshaw! What else are you going to say to a dying old lady, eh?" Her smile told me that I needn't say anything more.

Trish, thankfully, changed the subject. "Look at all of these beautiful flowers and cards!"

Ruth scanned the room. "Yes, most of them are from my students," she said with a sigh. "Bless their little hearts, all they see is that someone they care about isn't doing very well."

"You're a teacher Ruth? I didn't know that!"

"I *was* a teacher," she said with unusually strong emphasis. "I had a classroom of second graders who can't wait to have Mrs. Cooper back because, as you'll read in some of the cards, the substitute isn't as nice as me." She chuckled.

"That's sweet."

"Yes, it is. I've always loved how simple their worlds are - everything is divided into things they love on one side and things they hate on the other." She sighed again, this time a more thoughtful sigh. "I'm finding that my world is becoming just as simple as theirs, divided into what I love and what I hate. The things that used to matter to me just don't seem to have the same appeal. Eating out in nice restaurants, buying new clothes, going on beautiful vacations..." Her voice trailed off. Then she cocked her head at Trish and said, "Do you know what matters to me now more than anything else in the whole world?"

"No, what?" Trish asked.

"A good poop!" Ruth said matter-of-factly. "Yes sir, you can take my car, have my entire wardrobe and feed me gruel for the next week just as long as you can guarantee me a good bowel movement! Those darn drugs that they're giving me have got me all backed up and it feels miserable!" She shook her head. "It's amazing what my life's come down to, isn't it?"

Trish stroked her arm. "I'm sorry Ruth."

She waved her hand. "Oh, don't waste any pity on me, Trish. I'm way past that. I'm looking at this whole thing a lot more matter-of-factly lately. For instance, just yesterday I decided to stop telling people that I'm a teacher." She paused for a moment. "I realized that I'll never teach again in this lifetime so why keep telling that lie? What I am is a cancer patient, plain and simple. That's my full-time job now and will be for the rest of my days."

There was an awkward silence as neither Trish nor I knew what to say. I thought about how Ruth sounded well-educated and was probably considered quite proper at one point in her life, but what shone through now was her practicality and subtle sense of humor that lay just below the surface. The silence that had filled the room was interrupted by another visitor.

"Hi honey, I see we've got visitors," the man's voice said. Trish and I turned to see an older man walking into the room. I noticed right away that he walked with a pronounced limp.

"Hi there dear," Ruth replied. "I want you to meet my friends Trish and Dan." She nodded at each of us. "This is my husband, Bill." We all shook hands. When he shook my hand, I felt his hand trembling in mine.

"Nice to meet both of you." This time when he spoke, I noticed that he tended to slur his words a little. What was wrong with him, I wondered? Did he have a stroke? Early stages of Parkinson's disease?

Bill sat down in a chair on the other side of Ruth's bed and right away he began stroking her head. He smiled at her with eyes that looked right past her bald head, gaunt face and all her other physical afflictions.

"I was wondering where you'd gotten off to," Ruth said.

"Just went out for a short walk, dear. You know I'll never be far from you," he said with a reassuring smile.

"Yes, I know," she replied with warm, soft eyes.

I suddenly felt awkward, like we shouldn't be intruding any further. I tried to catch Trish's eyes but then Ruth turned her attention back to us. "I was just telling my friends here how much our lives have changed lately."

Bill let out a snort. "That's for damned sure!" Bill was a man who seemed trim and fit for his age, save for the limp. He had a full head of hair that was graying only slightly around his temples and he had an air of intelligence and pride about him. He obviously cared about his appearance as he dressed very well, and both his hair and his mustache were neatly trimmed. Equally as obvious, he loved his wife very much.

"We've had quite a patch here lately," Ruth continued, "what with his Multiple Sclerosis getting worse and now my cancer coming back with a vengeance." She reached over and grabbed his hand and they interlocked their fingers. "Seems God has a plan for us, and he means business!"

Again, there was silence. I took Trish's lead and just sat there with my mouth closed. It wasn't long before Ruth picked up her thought again.

"Everything seemed to be going so well for us for a while there. We'd raised two beautiful kids, we had already welcomed our first grandchild into the world with another one on the way, we both had just a few years left to retirement...it was all going according to plan." She looked over at Bill, who had replaced his loving eyes with eyes that reflected a deep sorrow. "Then Bill started to have these problems with his hands and feet that just got worse. We went to a doctor and he gave him the diagnosis that he'd feared the most: Multiple Sclerosis." They held each other's gaze and I saw Bill's eyes misting over. "He'd watched his mother die of the same awful disease and it was his biggest fear that he would one day die the same way." With her other hand she reached over and stroked his face. Bill closed his eyes and leaned into her hand.

She pulled her hand away and turned back to us. "It got so bad that he had to quit his job as an engineer, he just couldn't handle the instruments any more, and he went on permanent disability. We were barely scraping by with my teacher's salary and his disability checks when we got hit with this whopper." She swept her free hand over the length of her body. "The doctor tells me that I can maybe live another year or two, with drugs, and there's even a possibility of a remission." She leaned over to Trish. "Of course," she whispered, "he *has* to say *that*, doesn't he?"

She leaned back and took her hand from Bill's, slapping the covers on her lap. "And, to tell you the truth, if my year or two of life is going to look like *this* then I want no part of it, I can tell you that!" Her eyes suddenly met mine and they were full of conviction. "Because this is no life at all!"

I felt the need to say something. "Aren't there other doctors you can see? Maybe a second opinion..."

Ruth laughed, not a mocking laugh but a laugh of resignation. "I've seen more doctors over the years than most folks see in *ten* lifetimes! This is my second go around with the chemo, the first time bought me another five years of remission, so I feel like I'm on borrowed time as it is. I knew that this was going to be it for me, and I wouldn't even have bothered with the chemo this time if it wasn't for my daughter's insisting so strongly." She nodded at Trish. "Then Trish came around one day and told me the story of your list, which just confirmed for me what I already knew: my time was near."

She took her husband's hand again. "The reason I'm telling you both all of this is that Bill and I have been talking a lot since your last visit Trish." They exchanged smiles and then Ruth turned her attention to Trish. Her jaw seemed to be set with determination and her eyes blazed with conviction. "And we have a favor to ask of you."

CHAPTER 32

"Hello! Hello!" Bill hollered out as he opened the front door of the house.

"Meme! Pappy!" The five-year-old squealed with delight as she ran to the door where her grandparents were standing.

"Hey there, muffin!" Bill said. "Come here and give your Pappy a big ol' squish!" The little girl ran into his waiting arms and he swept her up into a big hug. Ruth watched from her wheelchair and smiled at the scene in front of her.

It was several days later, and we were following through with part two of a promise we'd made to Ruth and Bill in the hospital room. Part one was getting Ruth out of the hospital without her daughter knowing about it, which we accomplished easily that morning. Part two required us to pay a visit to her daughter's house in Bellevue, across the lake east of Seattle, which was what we were doing now. I was feeling slightly tense as Trish and I were going to have to do a little role-playing at some point during the visit.

A woman, who was obviously quite pregnant, came around a corner and looked surprised to see her visitors. "Mom? Dad? What are you two doing here?"

"They gave me some time off for good behavior," Ruth said with a wry smile. "Now stop asking questions and come over here and give your poor old mother a hug." Her daughter obliged, then hugged her father and, finally, she cast a wary eye towards Trish and me standing off to one side.

"Hi there, I'm Ellen Harrison," she said as she offered her hand.

"Oh my," Ruth interjected, "put me in the hospital for a little while and I forget all of my manners!" She reached over and grabbed my arm. "This here is Dan Barnes and that's Trish McConnell standing next to him." Ruth winked at me as I shook her daughter's hand. "They're new friends of mine."

"Friends?" Ellen asked with a hint of suspicion in her voice.

"Yes, friends, dear!" She waved her hand in the air, as if to say it's time to move on to another topic. "I'll tell you all about them later, Ellen, don't you worry. For now, I'm wondering if maybe you can offer some weary travelers some cold refreshments."

"Of course," she replied as she continued to look me up and down, "let's head into the living room.

We all talked over iced tea and lemonade for more than an hour. Actually, Ruth and Ellen talked while Trish and I listened, and Bill played on the floor with his granddaughter, Merilee. The conversation eventually moved back to Trish and me.

"So, what is it that you do, Mr. Barnes?" Ellen asked casually, though her intermittent glances during the past hour told me she was very anxious to get some answers.

Once again, Ruth broke in and served as our spokesperson. "They both work at Hope House, over in Seattle, and that's part of the reason why I came to visit you today."

"Hope House? I've never heard of it."

"I'm not surprised because it's fairly new. But it's already got a reputation as one of the best assisted living homes in the Northwest."

"Assisted living? Mom, you know we've talked about this. You know I'd rather have you living with me here and, besides, there's no way any of us can afford anything like that." She cast a glance over at me and Trish. "Those kinds of places are priced way over our heads!"

"Now calm down dear, I know we've talked about it in the past, but some things have changed. First of all, there's no way that you would be able to take care of your father and me in your present condition - that baby is ready to pop out any day now! And besides, you already have your hands full with Merilee there." She nodded at the little girl giggling on the floor. "The last thing you need is more responsibility in your life."

"But Mom, the money..."

Ruth raised her finger in a shushing gesture. "Now don't you worry about that - we've worked something out with these kind folks and money will not be a problem."

Ellen looked over at us, her eyes and voice obviously full of suspicion. "What exactly have you worked out with my parents?"

Thankfully, Trish spoke right up because I'd never done well with play-acting. "Well, Mrs. Harrison," Trish began, "we see your parents as being very special cases. It's very rare that we see both adults in a relationship requiring the same level of care and, since we are still new to the area, we are looking to establish ourselves with a broad spectrum of people and circumstances." She nodded toward Ruth. "Having both your mother and father sharing a room at Hope House would give our facility more of the feel that we're looking to establish, with a sense of family and community." She paused for effect. God, she was good! "As such, we are prepared to offer them full care at a fraction of the usual cost. They could easily meet the monthly obligation using a reverse mortgage on their present home and still have plenty left over for down the road, should an unforeseen future emergency arise." Trish smiled sweetly.

Ellen let out a small "hmph" and shifted in her seat. "This all sounds just a little too good to be true. Is all of this going to be in writing?"

"Of course," Trish replied calmly.

She shifted her glance to me. My heart raced. "And just what is it that *you* do there, Mr. Barnes?"

Ruth, bless her heart, headed the question off at the pass. "He'll be Bill's personal care assistant and Trish there will be mine, Ellen dear."

Ellen was determined to hear me speak. "And where is it that you received your degree Mr. Barnes?"

This one I could answer, as it was the truth. "University of Connecticut, Mrs. Harrison," I croaked, as my voice had been dormant for too long. "Class of 1981."

She continued to eye me suspiciously.

"For goodness sakes, Ellen," Ruth broke in, "are you going to look this gift horse square in the mouth until it drops dead! Don't you think it's about time that your father and I got a little bit of a break from the world?"

Ellen's face softened and she turned her attention back to her mother. "I'm sorry, Mom - you're right. I guess I've become so accustomed to getting *bad* news that I don't even recognize the good news when it's right in front of me." She sighed a sigh that ran deep, obviously inspired by many layers of sadness. "I guess I feel a little guilty, too - like I should be doing more to help you guys."

Ruth wheeled over to her daughter and put her hand to her face, stroking her cheek tenderly. I could see that Ruth was beginning to cry. "Oh, Ellie, my dear, dear daughter. I knew that you would feel like you had to throw the whole weight of this square on your shoulders." Several tears ran down Ellen's cheek and Ruth wiped them away. "That's why I went and arranged all of this myself with Hope House, so you wouldn't have to be troubled with it."

"It's no trouble, Mom," Ellen replied through her tears, "you're my parents for goodness sakes!"

"I know, I know, but don't you see how this will work out best for *all* of us? You can continue to focus on your own family - your *growing* family I might add," Ruth nodded at Ellen's protruding belly, "and your Dad and I can be someplace where we don't feel like we're a burden or just getting in the way."

"But Mom, I told you..." Ellen began, but Ruth put her hand to Ellen's mouth.

"I don't want to hear another word about how we wouldn't be a burden to you, because the plain fact is that we *would* be a burden - there's no way to deny it! Two more mouths to feed, more laundry, more errands to run, more of everything!"

Bill finally spoke up, his slightly slurred speech adding more pathos to his words. "We love you deeply Ellen dear and we've thought about this a lot. It really will be best for everybody."

It all became too much for Ellen to handle. She burst into tears and replied, "I love you too, Daddy." Then she got out of her chair and went over to her father and wrapped a big hug around his neck. Bill wept softly onto his daughter's shoulder.

"Why is everybody so sad Mommy?" asked little Merilee as she watched her mother and grandfather hug.

"They're crying because they're happy, honey," Ruth explained. "Sometimes people do that."

Merilee walked over and looked at her grandmother's tear-streaked face. "Does that mean that you're happy too, Meme?"

Ruth pulled the girl up into her lap in the wheelchair and hugged her tightly. "Yes dear, Meme is very, very happy."

CHAPTER 33

"So, what do you think?" Jennie asked me.

I stood in the downstairs study looking closely at everything contained in the mini-shrine. A copy of "The Secret Garden." A bottle of Dr. Pepper. An old trading card from The Andy Griffith Show. Plastic flowers. Five cards arranged in a royal straight flush in hearts. A small dragon. A dried hyacinth. A photograph of Hy and Mandy. Birdseed sprinkled everywhere. And, of course, the porcelain bluebird. It was all contained in a small box that had been laid on its side and decorated with paper flowers and bright ribbon.

"Jennie, it's perfect!" I gushed. "Hy would have loved this!"

Jennie smiled. "Yeah, I think she woulda at that!" She turned to me, her look suddenly turning serious. "She was such a special woman that I didn't want to see her get forgotten."

I chuckled. "I don't think you have to worry about that with Hy."

"Yeah, well I just wanted to make sure." She looked around the room then whispered to me. "I also wanted to make sure that bitch of a daughter of hers didn't get her hands on any of this stuff if she came sniffin' around here again -that's why I put it in here instead of out there in the living room."

"Good move." Mandy's hateful eyes came flashing across my screen.

"Hey, by the way," Jennie said, "have we heard anything more from the princess?"

"No, not yet. Zootie figures that she's been meeting with lawyers and we should hear something soon."

"Great, can't wait!"

Suddenly we were interrupted by a muffled thumping sound and a slight vibration shook the floor. I recognized the noise immediately. "So, who do you have going through mattress therapy today, Dr. Jennie?" I asked with a smile.

"Oh, that's ol' Bill Cooper. He's really takin' a liking to beatin' the shit outta that thing! It seems he's got a real good supply of anger built up and he swings a mean bat!"

I smiled at the thought of Bill Cooper in the basement taking his swings at the mattress. He and Ruth had moved in to Hope House the week before and fit in right from the start. They moved into mine and Brent's room - Brent was rarely around anymore - and I moved in with Zootie. Both Ruth and Bill became fast friends with all the residents of Hope House and Jennie in particular seemed to spend a lot of time with them. Her own parents, Pat and Ronald, were still being difficult and Jennie appeared to enjoy Ruth and Bill's accessibility and their willingness to listen to her.

"You've really taken a liking to Ruth and Bill, haven't you?" I asked.

"Yeah, they're pretty neat folks." She let out a small sigh. "I wish Patton and Rommel would take a few lessons from them." I always smiled when she used her personal nicknames for her parents. She noticed my smile. "Hey, you wouldn't be smilin' if you had parental units like mine!"

"No, I probably wouldn't." I took the smile off my face and frowned slightly. "Have they budged at all with you Jennie, regarding the list and all?"

"Not a nit! As a matter of fact, they've gone so far as to threaten to call the police if I don't stop spending time with all of you cult members."

"The police?!?" I thought. *"Now that would introduce a whole new wrinkle to things!"*

"But I just told 'em that I'd already stopped comin' over here. I told 'em that I'm spending more time in the library 'cuz I wanna go back to school and get my journalism degree eventually." Her head bowed. "'Course, that is one of my BFW's, so it's not too much of a lie."

"Oh, oh - a new acronym…"

She looked up at me, her face regaining its brightness and enthusiasm. "BFW? Nah, I've been using that one fer over a week now! As a matter of fact," she reached into her back pocket and pulled out a small notebook, "I've got a couple dozen entries in my book already." She opened the notebook and found the page she was looking for. "Ah, here they are…Big Fucking Wishes." She glanced up at me and explained briefly, "these are wishes that probably won't come true for folks, especially if they're on that damn list, but they just can't deny that they're there."

She smiled, nodded, and then turned her attention back to the notebook. "Dave Smith's is to have sex just once before he dies. Zootie's is to remarry Ren. Mine is to get a degree in journalism and publish a book. Ruth's is to see her second grandchild be born. Bill's is that neither one of his kids gets MS." Jennie paused for a moment, her voice choking with emotion. She looked up, her eyes filled with tears. "Pretty amazing stuff, eh?"

"Yeah, I'll say! You seem to have quite a bit of information in that little book of yours."

"I've just been writin' down what people've been tellin' me, that's all. Their BFW's, BFD's, DBD's - you know, stuff like that."

We both smiled. It had become a little game between Jennie and me and she loved nothing more than to throw all those letters at me.

"By the way, Dan." She had a playful glint in her eye as she pulled a pen out of her pocket. "I still haven't gotten *your* BFW yet!"

"How about find a cure for cancer, will that do?"

"Nope, not good enough - I can tell you're not connected to that one at all. Try again."

I thought about her question for a moment. A month ago, I would have continued to parry with her until she gave up and left me alone, not wanting to reveal such personal things about myself. But now everything was different. I actually *wanted* to give her an honest answer. "Nobody has ever asked me this one before…" I said, trying to buy more time. Then it hit me. It was a wish that I hadn't talked about much before but had been coming more and more into focus for me lately. "I got it."

"Great, fire away." Her pen was poised.

"I want to father a child."

Jennie dropped her pen to her side. "Wow, my first repeat on the list!" She started scribbling it into her book, shaking her head the entire time. "Trish gave me the exact same wish just a few days ago." She chuckled and looked up from her notebook. "'Course she wanted to be a mother, not a father like you."

I felt slightly embarrassed and I didn't know why, perhaps feeling a little more exposed than I was accustomed to.

Jennie didn't help with my embarrassment when she said through a devilish grin, "maybe you two oughta work together on this one, eh?"

CHAPTER 34

"YEEEE-HAAAWWWW!!!!" Zootie screamed as he swung out over the pond on the rope and then fell to the water with a huge splash. It was late October, but the weather had been hovering near summer temperatures for the past week, so we decided to head out on a little mind-clearing field trip to Orcas Island in the San Juan Islands. The ferry ride over was gorgeous and I saw instantly why so many people fell in love with Puget Sound and the Pacific Northwest. The sun shone brightly, the ferry knifed through the clear blue water with birds flying everywhere, and the Olympic Mountains served as constant companions cutting their distinct and jagged swath across the western sky. I spent the entire ferry ride on the upper deck just taking it all in.

We'd decided to picnic next to a lake in Moran State Park on the eastern side of the island. Though the water was ice cold, a few brave souls, led by Zootie, had decided to go for a swim. The rest of us were content with hiking around the lake, paddling a canoe or just sitting and munching on potato salad and chips. I heard Zootie's scream of pain as he came back to the surface.

"WOOOO-WEEEEE!!! This water is liquid ice! I think my nuts have gone and left the building!" He swam to shore quickly and jumped out. "Good gawd! I am too damned old to be doin' this!" He grabbed a towel off the table and started drying off. He glanced back over to the rope swing and saw

Dave Smith having second thoughts about following him into the water. "Don't you worry 'bout a thing there Dave!" he shouted to him. "It only hurts for a minute!" He turned back to me and whispered, "Yeah, and then the *agony* takes over."

I sat and watched him towel off as I munched on some Fritos. Seeing Zootie standing shirtless in front of me, his huge hairy belly and sagging breasts jiggling with every movement, soon caused me to put the Fritos aside. "So, what do you hear from our friend, Mandy?" I asked as I wiped my hands on a napkin.

"Got some papers from her lawyers the other day." He finished toweling off and slipped his shirt over his head. "Looks like a pretty straight forward case - we took advantage of Hy and forced her, against her will, to leave the house to us. Mandy cries "No fair!" but then we show 'em what nice folks we are, not to mention the notarized signatures at the bottom of the document," he smiled and winked, "and, voila! - end of problem." He shrugged. "No big deal."

"Does she have any case at *all*?"

"Not unless she finds some mystery witnesses that can tell them what they want to hear - that we're no-good, scheming bastards who make a living preying on old ladies."

Zootie glanced over at the rope swing where Dave and Jennie were laughing and trying to push each other into the water. "Those two are gettin' kinda chummy, eh?"

"Yeah, they are," I agreed. "She's done an amazing job of bringing that guy out of his shell. The first time I met him I swear he'd rather chew light bulbs than even look me in the eye."

Zootie smiled. "Chew light bulbs, eh? I'll have to remember that one." He looked over at Jennie again. "That girl gets it, that's fer darn sure."

"Gets what?"

"Everything! What it's all about…what we talked about that day at Green Lake. Only she got it without havin' to cheat and go to the other side and back, like me." He shook his head. "I admire that."

"So, I hear that your BFW is to marry Ren again, is that true?"

He chuckled. "Jennie and her questions…" he pointed across the lake, "I tell ya, I love that girl!" He sat down across the table from me. "Hell yeah, it's true. I've never stopped loving that woman and I happen to believe that she hasn't stopped loving me either. I'd marry her again in a heartbeat if she'd just wander out this way for a while."

"Why don't you move back to Indiana and marry her?"

He got a far-off look. "No, I couldn't do that. Not now."

"Why not? We've got plenty of people helping with the list now."

"That's true." He smiled. "But then who the hell would hold *your* sorry hand if I left?"

As if on cue, Trish walked over to the table and sat down. "Hey boys! Hope I'm not interrupting anything, what with all this talk about hand-holding and such."

Zootie guffawed. "No Trish, go ahead and have a seat. I was just talking with Dan about who would take care of him if I left town and then, lo and behold, *you* walk over!" He got a look on his face that I didn't like. "Jennie tells me that you two have a lot in common, is that true?" He winked at me and smirked like a little boy who had just told a dirty joke.

I glanced over at Trish and then we both looked down at the table, too embarrassed to say anything.

Trish, bless her heart, changed the subject quickly. "Are you planning on leaving town, Zootie?"

"Hell no! That was just one of those hippo-thetical type questions, that's all."

I decided to turn the tables a little bit. "It seems that Zootie still has a thing for his first wife and is looking at the possibility of re-upping."

"Ohhh, is that so?" Trish chimed in. "And how does the former Mrs. Zootie feel about this?"

"He thinks she's on board with the concept, but location seems to be the sticking point this time around." I looked over at Zootie. He was sitting back with his arms crossed and a big grin on his face, enjoying mine and Trish's little exchange at his expense.

"Have terms been discussed? Is there a compromise possible?" Trish asked in her best lawyerly voice.

"Like maybe both of them meeting in the middle, say in Salt Lake City?"

"No!" Zootie thundered. "I will *not* agree to Salt Lake City!"

"I'm sorry Mr. Gibbons," Trish said with a straight face, "but this is out of your hands now; let the lawyers do their jobs."

"Lawyers!" he bellowed. "It's the damn lawyers that have ruined this great country of ours!" He leaned forward and whispered conspiratorially, "Why, did you know that they did a study in Sweden and found that exposure to lawyers can actually cause cancer!"

Trish put her hand over her mouth. "No!"

Zootie sat back and put his hands behind his head, nodding with his eyes. "Yep, it's a fact, look it up."

The three of us sat there talking and laughing for several hours. Not once did the topics of the list or Hope House or even death come up. It was a wonderful afternoon reprieve from what had been a very intense stretch of time for all of us.

CHAPTER 35

"Brent? Long time no see, how have you been?" I was helping Trish and Jennie put the finishing touches on another shrine in the study when Brent poked his head in.

"Fine, fine," he said absent-mindedly as he surveyed the dozens of mini-shrines throughout the room. He walked over to Hy's and smiled at the contents. "These are great. Whose brilliant idea was this?"

I put my hand on Jennie's shoulder. She was smiling shyly. "This young woman right here came up with the idea and it's taken over like wildfire over this past week."

"I just don't want people to be forgotten, that's all," Jennie said quietly.

Brent looked at several more of them. "Well, with these wonderful shrines in place they certainly won't be."

"So, what brings you our way, Brent?" I asked. "We haven't seen you around here since Hy's service."

He let out a heavy sigh and I smelled alcohol on his breath. "Yeah, I know. I've been busy with some things." I glanced down and saw that he was holding a book on cryogenics. He noticed my glance and casually put the book behind his back.

Trish reached over and put her hand on his arm. "Everything okay, Brent?"

"You mean besides the fact that I'm dying in a matter of days?" he said sharply, "yeah, everything's just fine!" There was a hint of desperation in his voice that wasn't hard to miss.

"Is there anything we can do to help?" I asked.

"Not unless you have some connections with the guy pulling the strings upstairs." He put his face in his hands and I thought he was going to start crying. "I'm sorry, I'm feeling a little out of sorts lately. Forgive me."

Trish rubbed his arm. "Absolutely nothing to apologize for Brent. We understand your situation and you're handling it beautifully."

Brent looked up, his eyes and face looking suddenly tired, but no tears were in his eyes. "The thing is, I'm *not* handling it beautifully - not by a long shot." He pulled the book out from behind his back and held it up. "*This* is the kind of thing I'm spending my time on! All I can think about is that there must be a way out - if I just apply myself, there *must* be a way to cheat death!" His shoulders dropped. "But all of my years of studying and training and teaching aren't worth a damn right now. I'm just another poor slob who's realizing too late in life that this whole death thing actually applies to *me!*" His words hung in the air for a moment and then a rueful, pathetic smile rippled across his face. "Ah, the arrogance of it all."

We all stood there in a silence that sat in my stomach like lead shot. Then Brent clapped his hands together and said, "Well, I'm sorry I dragged my dirty laundry in here and dumped it on your doorstep." He nodded to each of us and seemed to have his old air about him. "I will bid my goodbye and I thank you for your kind words." I shook his hand and off he went.

"Whew," I said after watching him walk out the front door. I turned and saw that Trish and Jennie had tears streaming down their cheeks.

"I worry about that man," Trish said quietly.

"Here I thought he was one of the Seekers," Jennie said sadly.

"The what?" I asked.

"Seekers. People who keep looking for truth and under-standing." She gave a small shake of her head. "I just had him pegged different, that's all. He might turn out to be a Runner, and that's the saddest one of all." She saw our confused looks and continued her explanation. "I see three groups of people forming off of this list thing - Seekers, which I told you about, Runners, who just want to keep running as far away from this whole thing as they possibly can, and Maintainers, who basically just keep up the ol' status quo as if nothing's changed." She shrugged, as if saying "*See? Simple!*"

"So, you think Brent may eventually run, huh?" Trish asked.

"I don't know..." her voice trailed off, "I sure hope not."

"Just where is it that you come up with these things, Jennie?" I asked.

She smiled and went back to work on the shrine she'd been working on. "I dunno, I guess I've always been like this. I like to watch people and kinda see what makes us all the same and what makes us all different."

"Well, you sure have a knack for it," I assured her.

She turned from her shrine and faced us both. "Hey, that reminds me!" She pulled her omni-present notebook and pen from her pocket. "I haven't asked you guys my question of the day yet!"

"Question of the day?" Trish looked at her sideways. "Is this something new?"

"Yeah, I just came up with it yesterday." She turned to the appropriate page and poised her pen. "Ready?"

Trish and I exchanged mock looks of disgust and, with a roll of her eyes, Trish turned to Jennie and nodded. "Fire away, Jennie."

"Okay Trish, you first," she said. She read the question from her notebook. "What is a habit that you have, that you do most every day, that you've never told another soul about?"

Trish laughed. "And what makes you think I'm going to tell *you* this information if I haven't told anyone else in all my," she paused and smiled, "in all my *years* on earth?"

"Hey, we already know how *old* you are Trish," Jennie laughed, "so don't think that *that* is some big ol' secret!"

"And how is it that you know *that*?" Trish asked with her hands on her hips.

"Hy told me." She winked at me. "And if you don't answer my question, I'm going to share that little piece of information with Dan here."

"Blackmail, huh?"

"Us journalists do what we have to do to extract the necessary facts."

Trish put her hand to her chin. "All right, all right, let me think."

Jennie turned to me. "You be thinking on this one too Dan 'cuz you're next."

I smiled and nodded.

"Okay, I got one for you," Trish said with an "aha!" tone. "I brush my hair exactly 24 strokes every morning."

"Why 24 times?" Jennie asked.

"I started doing it when I was a kid and now it's become sort of a superstitious thing that I always do."

"Fair enough. In the answer book it goes." Jennie jotted it down and then turned to me. "Dan?"

"Well, this is going to sound kind of weird, but I always put my socks and shoes on in the same order every time."

"What order is that?"

"Left sock first, then right sock, then left shoe, and right shoe last. Then I always tie my left shoe first."

"So, you're basically a left, right, left, right guy?" Jennie said matter-of-factly.

"Yeah, I guess I am. You make it sound like it's normal as can be, is that what you do too?"

"Hell, no! You're weird as shit Dan, but I just wanted to try to make you feel good." We all laughed.

"So how about you, Jennie," Trish asked. "What's *your* weird habit?"

"Sorry," she said as she snapped the notebook shut and shoved it back into her pocket, "I *ask* the questions around here, I don't *answer* them."

"Well that's a hell of an arrangement," I chided her.

We were interrupted by a knock at the front door. I walked over and answered it and came face to face with a young man dressed in a very nice suit standing on the front porch. "Hello, can I help you?" I asked.

"Yes." He pulled a card out of his suit jacket pocket and handed it to me. "James Barr, of Bergquist, Barr and Brand, here to see a Mr. Gibbons."

I glanced at the card. A lawyer. Probably here about the whole Mandy mess, I thought. "Come on in, I'll see if I can find him for you." I led him into the living room, throwing an "I-don't-know!" look to Trish and Jennie over my shoulder as I walked by the study.

I didn't have to look far for Zootie, as he came strolling down the stairs soon after Mr. Barr sat down. I nearly burst out laughing when I saw Zootie was wearing his bright red kimono that he favored when he was hanging around the house. I could see that he had nothing but his underwear on underneath it as his hairy belly and chest were protruding out the top of the gown above where he had tied the sash. He certainly didn't look very lawyerly.

He strode into the room and extended his hand to Mr. Barr. "Zootie Gibbons, and who might you be?"

Mr. Barr had been struck dumb for a moment but soon regained his lawyer's smirk and arrogance that he he'd had when he walked in. He stood up and shook Zootie's hand, looking him up and down with open disdain as he did. "James Barr, of Bergquist, Barr and Brand."

"Nice to meet'cha there, Jimmy," Zootie replied. "So, your Daddy owns a law firm, huh?"

This one threw Mr. Barr for a bit of a loop. "Uh, yes, he does, but..."

"Thought so," Zootie jumped in. "You're too much of a young pup to have your own name on the shingle so I figured it must be your Daddy or Grandpappy who put the Barr in Bergquist, Barr and Brand." Zootie sat down in a nearby chair and crossed his legs. "So how old are you, Jimmy, 27, maybe 28 years old?"

Mr. Barr sat back down on the couch. "I'm 27, but I don't see how that has any bearing..."

"So you must have just passed your boards, eh?"

"Last year, but..."

"Good for you, Jimmy!" Zootie leaned forward. "Those things are a bitch, aren't they?"

"I didn't think they..."

Zootie leaned back again. "So, what can I do for you, Jimmy?"

It took Mr. Barr a good solid minute to regain his composure. Then he seemed to click into the train of thought that he'd had on the front porch prior to entering Hope House. He reached into his briefcase and pulled out a sheaf of papers and, after ruffling through them, picked out the ones he'd been looking for. "My firm is representing Amanda Wiggins in the matter regarding this house and we have prepared what we believe to be a fair offer for you and the other residents." He handed the papers to Zootie with a small look of satisfaction on his face.

Zootie glanced at the papers and then tossed them on a nearby table. "Now I know that you probably went to a whole lot of trouble typing up this here term paper for your Daddy, but why don't you save us all a whole lotta reading of all that boring legal mumbo jumbo and just cut to the chase. What's the deal?"

Mr. Barr looked stung. He looked at the papers sitting askew on the table and then said reluctantly, "10% of the proceeds from the sale of the house, minus lawyer and realtor fees, would go to you, with the remaining 90% going to the next of kin."

"Specifically, Ms. Wiggins, eh?" Zootie asked with an arched eyebrow.

"That's correct."

Zootie erupted in laughter. He even scared *me,* and I'd gotten used to his loud, spontaneous eruptions. Mr. Barr looked at him with a combination of disbelief and a touch of fear. I think he thought Zootie was insane.

When he had gotten his belly laugh under control, he wiped his eyes and then rubbed his belly with both of his hands. "Oh my gosh Jimmy, that hurts the ol' belly when I laugh that hard! That was a good one, though - thanks for the joke, I really enjoyed it!"

"Mr. Gibbons, I can assure you that this is far from being a joke! This is a fair and decent offer and, I'm sorry to say that if you decide not to accept it then you will leave us no choice but to…" He never got to finish his sentence.

"No choice but to *what?*" Zootie fired back in a tone that was firmer than any I'd ever heard him use. He leaned forward and began bellowing at poor, overmatched Mr. Barr. "Do you think I'm stupid, Jimmy? Is that what it is? Do you think I don't know that the only reason you're even bringing this pissant offer to me in the first place is because you know you have no case? You know it, I know it and even your Daddy knows it - why the hell do you think he sent *you* down here?" He didn't wait for an answer. "Because he was too damned embarrassed to show his face here with that ridiculous offer in his hand!"

Zootie stood up and adjusted the knot on his sash. "So why don't you just get up, head downtown, and tell your

Daddy and his cronies to just leave the last wishes of poor ol' Hy alone." Mr. Barr stood up and Zootie placed his hand on his back as he led him out of the living room. "And while you're at it, tell Ms. Wiggins that it's time that she got on with her life and stopped wasting her mother's inheritance on silly lawyer fees."

Mr. Barr suddenly got his legs back underneath him. He turned and faced Zootie, his face red with anger. "Now wait just a minute Mr. Gibbons! I've sat here and taken everything that you had to dish out, including that ridiculous robe of yours, but you've gone far enough! I came here to talk to you, lawyer to lawyer, but you have obviously forgotten what that means." He looked Zootie up and down one more time with unchecked contempt.

"You don't like my robe?" Zootie asked innocently.

"No, Mr. Gibbons, I don't. And I have to say that I like *you* even less."

"Hey, now wait a minute there, Jimmy..." Zootie began, but Mr. Barr cut him off.

"And when I tell the partners what you had to say, I can assure you that your Hugh Hefner act will not be enough to save the day in round two."

"Threatening me again, eh?" Zootie stepped right into his face and put his finger up by his nose. "You should know your adversary a little better before you go throwing threats around, Jimmy boy." He stepped back and smiled a big, friendly grin. "That's your free lawyer tip for the day, no charge."

Mr. Barr stepped towards the door. "And here's my tip Mr. Gibbons: take the offer if you know what's good for you or you may find yourself with *nothing*." He wheeled and opened the door before Zootie could get off another word. "Good day," he said coolly as he walked out the door.

Zootie sighed and then turned to face me. "Well, that went well, don't you think?"

I had to laugh. "What happened to the spread the love thing that you told me about? I don't think Mr. Barr felt very loved when he left."

Zootie guffawed. "That only applies to interactions with fellow human beings Danny, and we all know that lawyers aren't human!"

CHAPTER 36

I was awakened a few days later by the sounds of construction. Saws were sawing and hammers were pounding and there was no way I was going to get anymore sleep. I got dressed and wandered downstairs, following the noise to its source. I opened the front door and was surprised to see a full-scale construction project underway in front of the house. I saw Zootie standing on the front lawn talking with a delivery person and walked over to him.

"What's going on here?" I asked Zootie after the delivery person had left.

"We're buildin' ourselves a front porch, Danny!"

"A front porch? Why?"

"Because I'd been thinkin' for a while now that the only thing this house is missin' is a front porch where you could sit in a rockin' chair and just watch the world go by." He turned to me. "Don't you agree?"

"Guess I'd never thought about it much to tell you the truth."

"Well, trust me - it will make a world of difference! Because there's a passel of things a man can learn through just settin' for a spell in a rockin' chair." He winked at me. "My Mama was from Georgia and those southerners are known for their rocker settin'."

"Where did you get the money for all these materials?"

"Didn't need any money; all of this was given to us by ol' Mr. Simmons. Turns out he was a bit of a lumber and hardware baron here in Seattle and he left us all of this in his will." He spread his arms wide. "I'd been talkin' to him about this dream of mine every time I went to see him in the hospital these last few weeks and I guess he decided that he wanted to help us out."

"Wow, that was generous of him!"

"Yep. Guess Christ was right on that whole thing about gettin' back tenfold of whatever you give, eh?"

I nodded as I scanned the front yard full of lumber and assorted building materials. "Looks like you got more than tenfold on this one," I mumbled.

"So, you ready to strap on an apron and get to work?" he asked me.

I felt my pulse quicken. "Uh, Zootie, I'm not of much use with this kind of thing. Truth is, I think I lost that whole fix-it gene somewhere along the way."

"Bullpuppies!" he thundered. "You're just afraid of it 'cuz you're not any good at it! Grab yourself a hammer and head over there and help Frank on the far end of the porch. He'll help you with the basics and, before you know it, you'll be swingin' that hammer like a pro!"

There would be no arguing with Zootie, I saw that, so I picked up a hammer and an apron of nails and headed over to Frank.

I was a bit sheepish approaching Frank as his head was down and he was hard at work. Frank had always struck me as the kind of guy who could fix *anything*; cars, plumbing, furniture, appliances, you name it. He was a person who you'd love to have as a friend or neighbor, as he was such a willing helper, and yet I had always found men like him extremely intimidating. Probably because men like him were so competent in areas in which I thought I *should* be competent as a man, and yet I was infinitely *incompetent* when it came time to do anything mechanical or construction-related. It was a part of me that I'd always tried to hide from the world and now here it was about to be put on full display.

"Hey there, Frank," I said apologetically, "Zootie sent me over here to help you out."

Frank stopped what he was doing and looked up. His face seemed happier than usual, the deep creases on his face forming a smile around his eyes. Though he was in his seventies, he moved around extremely well and had the work ethic of a mule. "Hola Dan! I'm glad to have the help." He nodded at the boards in front of him and went back to work.

The next words were hard ones for me to say. "Uh, Frank, what exactly do you want me to do? I'm kind of new to this whole carpentry thing."

Frank stopped pounding again and looked at me sideways for a moment until finally it seemed to sink in; *Dan is an idiot.* Then he set his hammer down and proceeded to give me a ten-minute tutorial on how to build a porch; taking measurements, squaring corners, how to properly nail a board - "the basics" as Zootie had said. It was helpful, but not nearly as helpful as just *watching* Frank after he resumed working following his brief explanation. I jumped in and worked elbow to elbow with him, keeping one eye on him and one eye on what I was doing.

After getting over my initial sheepishness, I enjoyed it. I soon saw that perfection wasn't necessary; if I didn't do it exactly right, nothing happened that couldn't be smoothed over, just as was the case with most things in life. My apprehension lessened and as the morning wore on, I took on more of a "teach-me" attitude which Frank responded to very well.

The morning went by quickly and around noon we took a lunch break under a tree in the front yard, munching on sandwiches that Trish and Ruth Cooper had prepared. Frank and I sat together, alone, for a while and I looked upon it as a good opportunity to get to know him a little bit better.

"So where is it that you grew up, Frank?"

He finished chewing on a bite of sandwich. "Small village of Patzcuaro in Mexico," he said, pronouncing the second syllable in Mexico with the characteristic "hee" sound of Spanish-speaking people.

"Patzcuaro? What's that near?"

"It is in state of Michoacán, in central Mexico."

"And when did you move up to the States?"

"After I was married. I went back and forth to Texas for many years to make money for my family. There was not enough work in Mexico." His face seemed to sadden noticeably. "Then my wife and daughter died, and I decided to stay." He took another bite of his sandwich.

"I'm sorry Frank," I offered quietly.

He shrugged. "It happens in Mexico. Doctors and medicine were not available in my village and I had no money to send them to a hospital."

"That's a shame. You must have been very angry about that."

He looked at me strangely. "Angry? No." He half-laughed. "That is where we are different, you and me. You gringos look at death and see just another problem to be solved. Mexicans look at death and see it as a part of life. There is no anger at death; it is just the way that it was meant to be. Who am I to be angry at?"

"The doctors, the lack of medicine; the fact that if you just had enough money you might have saved your wife and daughter."

"You see, that is what I am talking about; you see many problems that could have been solved. If only this and if only that. I don't see it that way. I see that my wife and daughter got sick and they died. Very sad for me, yes. But there was nothing more that could have been done."

"Wow, Frank, I'm not so sure I could feel the same way you do about that. I would just keep on thinking how *preventable* it could have been."

"That's because you and I were raised differently Dan. You were raised in this wealthy country where you think anything is possible and where you believe so many things are your *right* to have. I was raised in a country that had very little and we expected nothing other than what we worked hard to get. Most all gringos have car, house, TV, telephone, medicine," he listed these things on his fingers, "but in Mexico most of us didn't have these things. It was a different life."

"Does that make you bitter, that you didn't have those things when you see so many people in this country with all those luxuries?"

He laughed and his eyes twinkled. "No Dan, I'm not bitter. I wouldn't want the life of a gringo! Yes, you have all those beautiful things, but you use those things to protect you from the life around you." He shook his head. "No, I wouldn't want that."

"What do you mean by *protecting* us, Frank?"

"You norteamericanos are so afraid of everything!" Once again, he listed things on his fingers, this time smiling as he did so. "Afraid of getting old, afraid of getting fat, afraid of getting cancer, afraid of what people think, afraid of dying," he threw his arms up in the air, "where is the life in that?"

I chuckled. "Yeah, I guess you're right. You don't have those fears?"

"The fears of most Mexicans are simple fears; fears about getting enough food and making sure our families are safe. They are fears of living, but you gringos, your fears are all up here." He tapped the side of his head. "You have so much money that you can shield yourself from life, not feel it every day like Mexicans do. And that is why, when death comes to you, most of you are not ready for it; you don't see it and feel it every day as we do, and so you don't believe that one day it will come to you." He smiled broadly. "But it does."

"Yeah, you're right there, Frank. I know it's still a big hurdle for *me* to get over, and I see a lot of people here at Hope House struggling with it too."

"I see it too. I see death being such a mysterious stranger to many people and yet He is here among us all the time. It is sad."

At that point Zootie came walking over and sat down next to us. "How's the work goin' fellas?"

"Great Zootie," I said. "Frank here is teaching me all sorts of things about carpentry and throwing in some lessons on pampered Americans to boot."

Zootie laughed. "Well, he's right on that. I'll never forget a trip I took down to Mexico a few years ago." He smiled at me. "*After* my little accident, that is, so my eyes were wide open.

"Anyway, I went to the state of Oaxaca for a month and was struck by the simple, uncluttered lives the locals led down there. Yeah, they didn't have much in terms of material things but, boy, they sure were in touch with the world around them! I saw how uptight most of us Americans were and how most of us never even get to experience real joy because we're so determined to avoid the other side of the coin." He turned to me, his eyes ablaze. "I'm talkin' real, from the nuts, hold nothin' back, *joy!*" He motioned towards Frank. "Frank here has probably experienced more joy in his life than you and I put together." They exchanged smiles. "Kind of ironic, huh? We seemingly have everything in life and yet we're so damned afraid of losing it all that we never enjoy it! The Mexicans are one up on us there because they see that whatever they have, they're just borrowin' it and that the Grim Reaper always has the last say in everything." He let out a small chuckle. "If you want a real mind-blower, you should go down to Mexico for one of their Day of the Dead festivals; talk about looking death square in the eye!"

Zootie and Frank looked at each other and then shared a laugh. "Most gringos would not understand," Frank said flatly.

"That's for *damn* sure my Mexican amigo!" Zootie agreed. "I'd go so far as to say that most Americans would squirm like worms on a hook if they got plunked into one of those fiestas! They drag ol' Mr. Death out of the shadows and plunk him right in the middle of the damn spotlight; no sugar-coating, no holding back, he's right there for everyone to examine front and back, up and down." Zootie shook his head slowly at the memory. "Damnedest thing I've ever seen in my life."

Zootie clapped his hands together. "Well gents, it's time to get back to it; I want to get this porch done before the rain comes this weekend."

We went back to work, my mind swimming throughout the afternoon with random thoughts of our lunch-time conversation.

CHAPTER 37

Hope House, I noticed, had found its rhythm. I had wandered into the front study, where the shrines were located, one morning and saw the wheels of Hope House turning methodically.

Zootie had installed several more phone lines and there were now always a few volunteers sitting in the study contacting people on the list. Their job was to make the appointments for other volunteers - such as Zootie, Trish, Jennie and myself - to go out and have an initial meeting with the unsuspecting list members. Many of the volunteers were on the list themselves, but the vast majority were now like Trish; they'd lost a loved one who had been on the list, and now they wanted to help in some way. Rachel Mitchell, who was working the phones that morning, was a perfect example; she had been a good friend of Toby Liebman's and, through Trish, had signed on as a part-time volunteer.

The volunteers also helped in many other ways. Many of the family members and loved ones of the people on the list had a hard time adjusting to the news that their brother/mother/friend was going to die soon, so people on the list were forced to look elsewhere for help after they had come to accept their own fate. The volunteers thus became ad hoc trip planners, grief counselors, funeral planners and all sorts of other things. List members had many last requests that they wanted to fulfill - Dreams Before Dying, or DBD's, Jennie called them - so helping to find the cheapest airline tickets to Paris, or a good French tutor, or where to find the best deal on coffins were all challenges that filled the day of a typical Hope House volunteer.

What struck me that morning, and had struck me many times prior to that, was what an anomaly I was; I was neither on the list nor did I have a loved one on the list. There was, of course, Hy and others who'd *become* loved ones since my arrival, but, unlike the other volunteers, I had no *direct* connection to the list. No mother, no brother, no friend; just a conversation with Zootie back in Indiana tied me by the thinnest of threads to this list. *Why was I here?* I often wondered. *Why did Zootie think I belonged here, helping with this list of his?*

The other thing that struck me was the enormity of what was going on around me. I continued to see new faces entering, and hanging around, Hope House every day; to the point that I no longer even tried to learn all their names - there were just too many of them. I figured that I could be most useful by focusing my efforts on my own small sphere of people and not risk getting overwhelmed by the whole of the project.

Zootie, on the other hand, had an entirely different approach; he seemed to be involved in every detail surrounding the list and Hope House. He was tireless. He seemed to know everyone's name, no matter how new they were to the project, and he seemed to have his hand in every little side project around the house, from the construction of the front porch to the installation of new phone lines. After the front porch project was finished, he took the leftover building materials and, with Frank, began building a series of small rooms in the basement; the eventual idea being to have more rooms available for new residents. He'd also bought a cell phone and the thing never stopped ringing.

Seeing how completely immersed Zootie was in the project often made me feel guilty regarding my small role at Hope

House. I would tell myself that I was doing what I could to help and yet there was always this persistent voice in my head telling me to stop holding back and pushing me to do more.

As I stood in the study that morning, watching Rachel and the others working their way down the list, I was having a back and forth debate in my head. Then something Rachel said pulled me out of my trance. She was answering a question of another woman - I'd forgotten her name - who had come across a name on the list that she didn't know what to do with. Rachel's voice was deep and resonant and filled the room.

"What was the name? Sims? Thomas Sims?" she said to the other woman. "Yeah, his address is the mission downtown, by Pike Place Market, so there's no way to contact him. Just put the name on that list next to your phone and Zootie or someone will look into it."

"Thomas Sims?" I thought. "*I know that name, but from where...?"* It took me a minute, but it eventually came to me; *"Bowler!"* I walked over to Rachel. "Can I see the list for a second, Rachel?"

"Sure," she said as she handed it to me.

I scanned down to Thomas Sims and then looked at the date: just a week away. I handed the list back to Rachel and headed out of the room. I had to go find Bowler. I bolted down the basement stairs and found Frank and Zootie framing a room in the far corner of the basement, next to Jennie's mattress. I told them what I wanted to do, and Frank tossed me the keys to his pickup truck.

"Good luck," he said as I thanked him and headed back up the stairs.

I headed downtown, parked near Pike Place Market, and quickly made my way to the spot where I'd first met Bowler several weeks earlier. Thankfully, he was sitting in the exact same spot, as if he'd never left. I walked up quietly, trying to surprise him.

"Lordy!" he bellowed. "It sounds t'me like some injun is tryin' ta sneak up on me!" He turned his useless eyes in my direction.

I smiled. "How's the attitune today, Bowler?"

He returned the smile. "Why that sounds like my ol' friend Danny!"

"That it is." I put my hand on his shoulder. "How you doing, Bowler?"

"Life is goddamned good Danny!" He pointed to the top of his head. "Whaddaya think o' my new bowler?" he asked excitedly.

Sure enough, he had found a new bowler hat and it was a definite improvement over his old visor. "That's a beauty Bowler! Where'd you manage to find that?"

"Bought it used with that ten dollars you gave me! Ain't she a beauty?"

"Yeah, it really looks great on you!" My heart then sank as I remembered the purpose of my visit. I sat down on a nearby curb and looked around to see if anyone else was around. The street was clear. "Hey Bowler, I've got something I want to talk over with you," I began.

For the next half-hour I talked pretty much non-stop. I told Bowler the entire story, from my initial journey into Men's Pause to meeting Zootie to the struggles with the list. Bowler didn't interrupt me once and I wasn't positive he was listening to me until I had finished and I asked, "So what do you think?"

"I'm thinkin' I'm probably on this here list o' yers or you wouldn't be down here tellin' me all this," he replied evenly.

Once again, Bowler had me pegged. I lowered my head. "Yeah, you're right - you're on the list. I'm sorry."

"When?"

"A week from today," I said grimly.

Bowler turned his head away for a moment. "Well, then *fucket!*" he shouted. I looked up at him and he had the biggest, yellow-toothed smile I'd ever seen plastered on his face. "That gives me another week o' livin', 'n fer a man o' my age 'n my circumstances, that's pretty goddamned good, don't'cha think?"

I was stunned by his response but nodded anyway.

"I've had me a grand ride Danny boy 'n I got nuthin' ta complain about, that's fer damn sure!"

As he spoke, I was suddenly struck by an idea. I didn't pause long enough to think about it, I just blurted it out. "Why don't you come live with me for your last week Bowler?"

"Live with you? Now why would I wanna go 'n do a fool thing like that?"

I shrugged. "I don't know - maybe so you could eat a few hot meals, take a couple of warm baths, sleep in a nice bed, things like that."

Bowler rubbed his stringy, gray beard, as if in thought. "Ya say I could hop in a tub at yer place?" he asked suspiciously.

"Sure. You could take as many baths as you'd like."

"'N I could sleep in my own bed, with clean sheets 'n all?"

"You bet."

He stuck his hand out. "Well Danny boy, looks like ya got yerself a roommate fer the next week!"

I shook his hand. "Great!"

I stood up and grabbed the handles of his wheelchair. "Mind if I take you to my truck?"

"Hell no - you lead the way m'boy!" He adjusted himself in his seat and cinched his seatbelt a little tighter. "Just go easy on the bumps there Danny - this here chair's got a lotta miles on it 'n the warranty has done expired!"

I pushed Bowler - with great effort, as the chair creaked and whined its way down the street - to where I'd parked the truck by the market. During the short trip, we stopped a handful of times to talk to people who I hadn't even noticed were laying in other doorways along the way. They would yell to Bowler and he would instruct me to stop so he could say a hello or a goodbye. It was clear that, within the small community of the Seattle homeless, Bowler was both well-known and well-liked. Our last stop was just half a block from the truck; a small woman who had been picking through some discarded vegetables shouted a hello to Bowler.

"Winnie?" Bowler shouted back, "Is that you?"

She walked over to us, eyeing me with obvious suspicion, and then bent over and gave Bowler a hug. "How's the attitune my friend?" she asked with a warm smile.

"I'm feelin' Tommy Dorsey in my veins today, Winnie, 'n it feels pretty goddamned good!"

She glanced over at me and her smile faded, replaced by a concerned furl in her brow. "Everything okay with you, Bowler?" She was a younger woman, perhaps in her forties, and although her clothes were dirty and ragged, she had an air about her that was different than that of the other street people I'd met.

"Fine!" Bowler said with a wave of his hand. "I want'cha ta meet a friend o' mine Winnie." He reached out and grabbed my arm. "This here's Danny 'n I'm gonna be livin' with him fer a while."

Winnie's suspicious eyes seemed to soften a little and she nodded at me. I smiled at her and said, "Nice to meet you Winnie."

"Likewise," she said politely.

"Oh, Winnie, 'fore I fergit," Bowler blurted out as he reached into one of his pockets. He pulled out an old gold watch, complete with a long chain, and handed it to her. "I want'cha ta have this."

Winnie was obviously stunned. "Oh Bowler, I can't take that! That belonged to your Daddy and I know it means the world to you."

Bowler shrugged. "Ah, it used to, but I'm tryin' ta git rid o' some o' these things 'cuz it's makin' my chair too damned heavy." He extended the watch to her again. "Please Winnie, just take it. I mean it."

Winnie looked at him sideways. "There's something you're not telling me, Bowler Sims."

"What's ta tell? I'm an old man who knows that I ain't gonna live forever 'n I want ta make sure I give these things ta people who I know're gonna 'preciate 'em, that's all." I saw a look of sadness on Bowler's face for the first time. "I know you'd always admired this here watch Winnie, so I want'cha ta have it so ya kin take care of it fer me." He held it out in his palm and this time she took it.

Winnie was crying. "I don't know what to say, Bowler. Thank you. You know I'll take good care of it."

Bowler reached out and found Winnie's hand and grabbed it with both of his. "You've always been good ta me Winnie 'n I wanted to say thank you fer that. I know I'm a sight ta behold 'n I smell like yesterday's fish, but ya always were a help ta me 'n there aren't many folks who I kin say that 'bout."

Winnie tucked the watch into her pocket and then reached over with her free hand and stroked Bowler's face. "You're a sweet man Bowler and it was always my pleasure to help you out however I could. You know we have to stick together out here in the streets."

Bowler laughed. "True enough! But not everyone out here believes that m'dear 'n that's what makes ya so damned special!"

"Well, Bowler, take good care of yourself," she shot a look at me that told me to make sure I *also* took good care of Bowler, "and I'll see you around."

"I'll do just that Winnie, 'n you do the same, hear?" They exchanged hugs one more time, Winnie planted a small kiss on Bowler's cheek, and they yelled goodbyes as Winnie walked away.

"Quite a gal, that one is," Bowler said as I pushed him towards the truck.

"She seems different somehow from the other street people," I said.

"Aye, that she is!" Bowler agreed. "She had two small kids 'n lost 'em in a fire 'bout ten years ago. She blamed herself up 'n down fer their deaths 'n has never fergiven herself since." He shook his head sadly. "It's a shame, a woman as fine 'n educated as Winnie takin' ta the streets like that, but seems like everyone down here has a story just like that one." He turned and cast his cloudy eye at me over his shoulder. "Truth is, I don't even know her real name. She just told me one day that she's from Wenatchee 'n it's been Winnie ever since." He chuckled. "Ah, I'm gonna miss life here on the streets," he said wistfully.

CHAPTER 38

Jennie placed the framed picture on the table next to the coffin. She looked at it one more time - it was a picture of Sally Forget, a "list friend" of Jennie's, indulging in her DBD; bungee-jumping over a canyon up in British Columbia. Jennie had taken her up there a couple of weeks earlier and, according to Jennie, Sally had loved the experience. We walked past the table and stopped in front of the casket. It was a closed casket - Sally had been involved in a terrible car accident and the body was badly burned - so we paused for a moment and said our silent good-byes. I looked over and saw that Jennie was weeping quietly at the foot of the casket. I waited until she was done and then we walked together back to our seats.

"Did you notice the looks we've been gettin'?" she whispered to me when we sat down.

"No, what looks?" I whispered back.

"The *who-the-hell-are-you?* looks."

I scanned the church. I did notice that a few heads were inexplicably turned our way. All eyes snapped forward quickly, however, when the service began. Jennie told me that Sally Forget's family was very wealthy and they had obviously spared no expense on the funeral - the lavish bouquets, the ornate casket, the large candelabras everywhere you looked; it was like something out of lifestyles of the rich and famous. I also noticed something else unusual about the funeral: Sally was around Jennie's age - too young to be saying final good-byes -

and yet there was an unmistakable restraint that enveloped the church. I didn't hear any weeping throughout the entire service. It was strange.

Jennie and I left when the service was over and decided to walk home from the U-District, where the church was located. "Kind of a weird feel in there, huh?" Jennie asked.

"Yeah," I agreed, "I didn't feel a whole lot of grief in there, did you?"

"No, I didn't." Jennie looked at the ground as we walked. "I'm kinda worried that's how it's gonna be at *my* funeral," she blurted out.

I looked over at her. Fresh tears were winding down her cheeks. I put my arm around her and assured her, "Too many people care about you a whole lot to let that happen Jennie."

She wiped her cheeks. "You don't know my parents Dan. There were a whole lot of people who cared about Sally too, but they didn't get invited to *her* service."

"What are you talking about? *You* were invited."

She looked over at me and smiled weakly. "No, I wasn't."

"You weren't? But then how…"

"We crashed the service Dan." She shrugged coyly. "We had to! Sally told me that her parents would have a private service and she made me promise that I'd show up anyway, invitation or not."

I laughed out loud. "Wow! I've snuck into movies and concerts before, but never a funeral service!"

"Kinda sick that you even have to, don't'cha think?" She didn't wait for my answer. "I mean what kind of idiot even *thinks* about an invitation-only funeral service?!? What are they worried about - that maybe the wrong element might show up and give the funeral a bad name?" She scrunched her nose in disgust. "It's *just* the thing my parents would pull, I just *know* it!"

She pulled away, out from under my arm, and jumped in front of me on the sidewalk. Her face was dead serious. She wagged her finger in my face as she said, "You have to absolutely *promise* me that you'll show up at my funeral service with Trish and Zootie!"

I stopped in my tracks. I looked down my nose at her finger that was jammed in my face and smiled. "Jennie, I promise." I put my hands on her shoulders. "A thousand wild buffalo couldn't keep me away."

She dropped her finger and stepped back beside me. "Yeah, but two out of control parents might be able to," she mumbled.

We continued walking and talking through the U-District; the area immediately surrounding the University of Washington which was full of funky stores and tons of college students. We walked past one young woman who was walking alone, and Jennie suddenly stopped. She turned around and shouted to the woman, "Hey, wait a minute!"

The woman turned around and looked at Jennie, putting her finger on her chest as if asking; *are you talking to me?*

"Yeah, hold on minute," Jennie said as she walked up to the woman. They talked for a few minutes as I stood back and waited. I couldn't hear what Jennie was saying but I could tell from the woman's reaction that she didn't like everything that Jennie had to say to her. When they finally parted, Jennie patted the woman's arm and said, "Good luck!" The woman turned and walked away with a look that would best be described as bewildered.

"What did you say to that poor girl?" I asked when Jennie had caught up to me again.

"I just told her that she was wearing far too much make-up and that she didn't have to hide behind it because she was beautiful without it." Jennie flashed a devilish grin. "I'm getting a little outspoken in my old age, huh?"

"I should say so. That poor girl probably doesn't know *what* to think!"

"Hey, what can I say - I just can't stand to see that kind of thing with women my age and, with so little time left, I figure I gotta get my licks in while I can."

"*So little time left...*" As many times as I'd heard those words, they still caught me by surprise and served as a hard slap to my face. Did I have a curtain of denial up around me? I *knew* Jennie had less than a month left to live and yet the words still stung as if they were unfamiliar. Why?

"You okay?" she asked.

"Yeah, I'm fine - just thinking about what you said to that girl," I lied.

CHAPTER 39

"YEEEEE-HOOOOOO-DAAWWWWWGGGYYYY!!!!"
Bowler yelled at the top of his lungs. "Is there a finer thing in
life than this Danny?" He was up to his chin in bubble bath
and enjoying every minute of it.

I sat in the bathroom with him, watching him like a
lifeguard, as I didn't completely trust the harness system that
Frank had rigged up for Bowler. I had an unshakable image of
poor, legless Bowler slowly slipping out of sight under the
bubbles. I watched him frolic in the tub like a five-year-old and
I couldn't help but smile. The bubbles hung from his stringy
beard and sat atop his greasy head and slowly, layer by layer, the
thick dirt and grime fell from his body.

"When exactly was the last time you took a bath or shower
Bowler?"

Bowler stopped for a minute and looked off at the far wall
of the bathroom with his head tilted, as if deep in thought.
Then he burst out laughing, "Ya know what?" he hooted, "I
can't remember fer the life o' me when soap last hit this ol'
body o' mine!"

"I hope it doesn't cause any adverse reactions," I joked.

I watched him as he scrubbed his body while humming
some unknown tune; *he was one of the happiest, most positive
people I'd ever met,* I thought to myself. He had been a little
apprehensive earlier, as Frank and I were lifting him out of his
chair and into the tub, but the apprehension was soon washed

away by sheer joy. I thought back on the conversation I'd had with Frank and Zootie about joy while building the front porch; *"real, from-the-nuts, hold-nothin'-back, joy!"* Zootie had talked about. Bowler was experiencing that very kind of joy right in front of my eyes. He had been tasting life "on the other side of the coin," as Zootie called it, for so many years that he could access the joyful side of life in an instant. Bowler knew suffering - that much was obvious to me as I lifted his filthy, naked body, covered with sores, scars and signs of malnutrition into the tub - and yet it hadn't beaten him into submission. He seemed to have a spirit and a thirst for life that was inexhaustible. I envied those qualities in him, a thought that brought an ironic smile to my face.

"Hey Bowler, can I ask you a question?"

"Sure Danny - fire away!" he said as he scrubbed his back with a brush.

"Where the heck did you get your incredibly positive attitude?"

He continued scrubbing as he spoke. "Jest who I am Danny boy; can't help it any more'n a fish kin help swimmin'!"

"So, you've always been like this?"

He dropped the brush and turned to face me, the joyful look leaving his face. "Not always Danny. I had my dark years 'n it's those that eventually brought out this here side o' me." He threw his arms over the side of the tub so he could better face me. His one cloudy eye wandered everywhere but there was no doubt in my mind that he was looking at me as he spoke. "I had a wife and son Danny, back in Minnesota, and after fallin' off a roof I was workin' on, my legs didn't work worth a damn 'n I became a diff'rent man. I pushed 'em both away, drank my weight in whiskey every day, 'n eventually ended up out on the streets o' Minneapolis." He went back to the water in the tub, cupped his hands, and splashed a handful of water across his face. "You ever been in Minnesota in the winter Danny?"

"No, I haven't."

"Ain't a place t'be homeless, I kin tell ya that fer a fact! What little use I had o' my legs disappeared on those streets my first winter..." his voice trailed off. "Gangrene got the best o' them 'n I had t'have 'em cut off." He said the words without any detectable emotion.

"I'm sorry Bowler."

"Fer what? Fer somethin' that happened thirty somethin' years ago?" He laughed. "It all played out jest like it was s'posed to Danny. It took me a little while t'see that fer myself, 'cuz I was feelin' too damn sorry fer m'self, but then I saw it. After I lost m'legs I sat rottin' in a hospital for a long time until I met a nurse by the name o' Mercy Jenkins." He slapped the water as he guffawed. "Quite the name fer a nurse, eh?"

"Yeah it is," I agreed.

"Anyway, she took an interest in me 'n started talkin' me outta the dark hole I'd put m'self into. She was the one that got me m'nice wheelchair there." He smiled. "'Course, it was a mite nicer t'look at thirty years ago." I looked over at the wheelchair next to the tub and had a hard time imagining it ever looking nice. "She's also the one who got me out this way when she moved here herself some twenty-five or so years ago. Best thing that ever happened t'me 'cuz these here winters are a whole diff'rent animal 'n the ones in Minnesota! A man kin live on the streets here year-round without havin' ta worry 'bout losin' his parts ta frostbite."

"So you've been out on the streets ever since you arrived in Seattle twenty-five years ago?"

"Ol' Nurse Mercy took me in fer a short while but she passed on not a year after we got to Seattle - god bless that woman's soul - 'n I jest went back t'the streets 'cuz ain't nobody was hirin' men in my position back then." He flashed one of his big Bowler smiles. "Streets was all I knew Danny 'n the streets have been good t'me. I took my lumps in the beginnin' -

learnin' what's okay 'n what's gonna piss someone off - but it didn't take me long t'find my way." He raised one of his long, bony fingers. "But I tell ya what - I owe Mercy Jenkins my life 'n there ain't a day that I don't git up 'n greet the day that I don't say a big ol' thank you t'that woman."

"Yeah, you strike me as a thankful guy Bowler."

"Ain't no other way t'be Danny, 'cuz if ya ain't thankin' then yer complainin' 'n I ain't got any tolerance fer belly-achin'!" He pounded the side of the tub with his left hand. "'N kin ya tell me *why* we got nuthin' t'be complainin' about?"

I paused for a moment and then realized where he was headed with his question. I smiled as I answered, saying it with as much gusto as I could, "Because life is goddamned good!"

"That's right Danny boy - by god yer learnin'! Now come on 'n git me outta here 'fore the li'l bit o' stumps I got left shrivel on up to my nuts!"

CHAPTER 40

A couple of days later I had just gotten back from my daily walk around Green Lake when Trish spotted me in the front hallway and grabbed my hand. "You have *got* to come and see what Jennie's done down in the basement!" She pulled me toward the basement door and then down the steps. I was focused more on the feel of Trish's hand in mine than anything else as we descended the stairs.

Once in the basement I noticed that Zootie and Frank had finished the three extra rooms that they'd been working on. One was now actually occupied by Trish as she had volunteered to give up her room as part of a massive shuffling in order to get Bowler a room on the ground floor of the house. The other two rooms, as far as I knew, were still sitting empty. Trish stopped and knocked on one of the doors.

I heard a muffled "just a minute!" and then, a short while later, Jennie's face appeared in the doorway. "Hey guys!" she said. "Come on in, I'm just opening up another roll." We walked into the small, dark room and Jennie closed the door behind us.

The room was lit by a single red bulb that didn't throw off much light. The second thing I noticed was the smell - a strong chemical odor filled the room. "So whaddaya think?" Jennie asked excitedly. I continued to look around and saw pans filled with liquid sitting on waist-high shelves off to one side and what looked like photographs hanging from an overhead line.

"A dark room!" I blurted out.

"Yep," Jennie said proudly, "my very own dark room! Talk about a dream come true!"

"Look at some of these pictures she's taken," Trish said, motioning to the makeshift clothesline hanging across the room.

I went over and examined the pictures more closely. There were several of Dave Smith, a couple of Zootie and Frank working, a couple of Ruth and Bill Cooper and then an array of faces from around Hope House. One that struck me more than any of the others was one that she had taken of Bowler after he'd just finished taking his bath; he looked absolutely tickled to the bone as he sat in his wheelchair with his clean, wet hair slicked back and a fresh set of clothes on. I stared at that picture for a while.

"Great shot of Bowler, huh?" Trish said as she looked over my shoulder.

"Yeah it is. I still can't believe what a happy guy he is all the time."

"It's a gift he has, that's for sure."

"How sad is it that I actually feel *envious* in some ways of a guy with no legs, no eyes, no money, and who has less than a week to live?!?"

"Not sad at all Dan - he's a pretty special man."

Trish always knew the right thing to say and I loved that about her. "So how did all of this come together?" I asked, changing the subject.

"Well Zootie suggested it and helped find the money for the equipment and all," Jennie said, "and then that new guy, Red Williams, helped me to put it all together. I guess he's had his own darkroom before, so he showed me some of the tricks of the trade to get me started."

I had met Red Williams briefly the day before; he was a tall guy with thick red hair who had said he was an old friend of

Hy's. There was something about the guy that I didn't like or trust, but he seemed to know all about Hy, so I had just dismissed my feelings as being silly and paranoid.

"I swear I don't know where Zootie manages to find all of this stuff!" Trish said incredulously.

"He told me that people on the list keep donating things to the cause and he just tries to find a good home for them," Jennie explained. "The same guy that gave him all of this darkroom stuff gave him a real nice camcorder and so now he wants to start making videos of everyone on the list."

"That guy never stops!" I exclaimed.

"I don't think the man gets more than a few hours' sleep every night," Trish offered with a tinge of concern in her voice.

"He's goin' at it like he only had a little time left," Jennie said, "like *his* name was on the list or somethin'."

"Yeah, I worry about him too," I agreed, "but Zootie is *not* somebody who you can tell to slow down!"

Trish and Jennie both nodded and smiled knowingly. Then Jennie quickly asked, "Oh my gosh - do you guys know what time it is?"

I glanced down at my watch, tilting it towards the light so I could read it, "I've got 12:45."

"Damn! I was supposed to meet Dave for lunch at 12:00!" She quickly shoved some things in a drawer and then made her way to the door, Trish and I following close behind. She had just shut the door behind her when Dave Smith came bounding down the steps. He stopped right in front of us, not bothering to acknowledge Trish or me - he looked angry and all he seemed to see was Jennie.

"There you are!" he shouted in a strong, angry voice that I'd never heard from him. "Where the fuck have you been?!? I've been sitting at that fucking restaurant for the past hour waiting for you to fucking show up!"

"Now wait a minute Dave..." I made the mistake of saying.

He quickly turned his anger on me, and I saw that he was shaking. I also noticed that he now had several carcinomas on one side of his face - the first outward signs of the AIDS virus that was slowly taking over his body. "No, *you* wait a minute Dan! Because you see I don't have as many fucking minutes to spare as you do so don't go telling me what to do! You people who aren't even on the list make me *sick* with how you think you know what's best! Well, let me tell you - you don't know *shit!*"

I felt my heart racing faster as the spittle from his last word struck me in the face. Small fears of infection shot through my mind as I wiped my face. He was obviously angry, but it was to the point where I hardly even recognized him because his entire face was so twisted with rage. I was going to try to calm him down when I felt Jennie's hand on my arm. She patted my arm gently, as if to say, "Don't worry - I'll handle this," and then she stepped forward.

"I'm sorry Dave," she said quietly, "you're absolutely right to be angry and I have no excuse other than I just lost track of the time in the dark room." She tilted her head and smiled sweetly. "Can you forgive me?"

Dave kept shaking and I thought he was going to pop like an over-filled balloon when he abruptly turned around and ran back up the basement stairs without saying another word.

"My god, I've created a monster!" Jennie blurted out. She let out a sigh and turned to face Trish and me. "I got him to let out his anger but now I don't know how to stick a cork in the bottle."

"Whew!" I said. "That boy has enough anger to fill a *hundred* bottles!"

"Yeah, sorry about that," Jennie apologized. "It's not usually this bad, it's just that today is one of those Mother Fucker days that I was telling you about and he's really embraced the concept." She let out a small laugh.

"What are Mother Fucker Days?" Trish asked.

I put up my hand to let Jennie know that I would handle the explanation. "Those are days when they don't have to worry about being nice to everyone - they can just let all of their anger and bitterness hang out for all to see, without having to apologize for it."

"Very good Dan!" Jennie said with a nod. "The only thing I would add is that it just gets tiring having to be nice *back* to all the people who are being nice to *us* because we're on the list; sometimes I just don't *feel* nice and I want to be able to act that way, that's all."

"I can see that," Trish said with a nod.

"Yeah, me too," I agreed, "but a certain someone was going to *warn* me when these days came around." I gave Jennie a playful glare.

"Sorry about that, I forgot. Seems to be my day for forgetting." She looked at the stairs. "Now, if you'll excuse me, I have some bridges to rebuild." She clapped her hands together. "And I know *just* the building materials that I'm gonna use." She gave each of us a quick hug and then she was off up the stairs.

Trish and I looked at each other and shook our heads. "This place is certainly never *boring*," I said with a shrug.

"No, it's *never* that," she replied with a far-off tone. She waited a couple of moments and then asked, "Can I talk to you about something?"

"Sure."

"Can we do it down in my room," she nodded at the end room, "I don't want anyone to overhear what I have to say."

"Lead the way," I said with my palm extended down the narrow hallway.

She led me into her room, and I was taken aback by how much smaller it looked than the dark room; her bed took up more than half of the floor space. "You certainly traded *down*, didn't you?" I observed.

She looked around the room as if it had never even occurred to her prior to that moment that she now had a smaller, less desirable, room. "Yeah, I guess I did at that," she agreed with a small chuckle.

I sat down on the far end of the bed - there wasn't really any other place to sit down - and she sat on the near end. "So, what's on your mind?" I asked.

She stared forward as she spoke. "It's about Ruth and Bill Cooper." She heaved a deep, deep sigh. "They asked something of me the other day that I'm not sure I can do." She turned to me. "And I'm hoping that you can give me some advice."

This was a first from Trish - asking *me* for advice - and a part of me felt extremely flattered. "What did they want?" I asked as I leaned forward.

"You know their situation, with the MS and cancer and all, and how they don't want to be a burden to their daughter?"

"Yeah."

"Well, they came to me the other day and asked," her voice choked up and she couldn't finish her sentence. I saw that she had started to cry, and I moved closer to her on the bed so I could rub her back. She leaned forward with her head in her hands while I gently stroked her back. I could have sat that way for most of the day, but she got herself composed and sat up straight, took another deep breath, and continued. I took my hand off her back and folded them both in my lap. "They asked me if I would be willing to help them with something because they weren't sure that they could do it themselves."

Now I was extremely curious. "What is it Trish?" I asked calmly, when what I *really* wanted to say was: *enough of the preamble, what is it?!?*

She looked over at me with her moist blue eyes - the eyes that still never failed to make my knees wobble - and threw out a single, powerful word: "Suicide."

Not certain that I heard correctly, I asked "What?"

She nodded grimly. "You heard me right. They're both determined to end their lives before disease robs them of the option. Like I said, they're committed to not being two huge burdens on their daughter's life and they'll do *anything* to ensure that that doesn't happen."

I couldn't believe it. "Wow! What is it exactly that they want you to do Trish?"

"They want me to drive them up to a favorite lookout of theirs up in the Cascades, help them to the edge, and then just leave them there to do their thing." Her head dropped. "I just don't know if I can help them do that."

"What did you tell them?"

"I told them that I'd have to think about it and that they were asking an awful lot of me."

"Whew - that's an understatement!"

Trish looked at me, her eyes pleading for help. "What would *you* do Dan?"

The million-dollar question. I always hated that question because it was really asking, *"what do you think I should do?"* rather than, *"what would you do?"* I decided to buy more time to think. "Why are you asking *me* this question Trish? Why not Zootie or one of the others?"

The look she gave me then absolutely melted my heart - her eyes were soft, sad and vulnerable and it was all I could do not to grab her and hug her as hard as I could, trying to protect her from anything that might harm her in any way. "Because I trust you, Dan," she whispered softly.

I stared into her eyes for just a moment and then looked away - if I looked any longer, I would have kissed her for sure. "I don't know Trish - it seems like too much to lay on one person...." I started to say, but she wouldn't let me go any further.

She let out a small shriek of delight, jumped on top of me and gave me a huge hug and said, "I *knew* you'd help me out!"

CHAPTER 41

A couple of days later I found myself driving up Snoqualmie Pass in Ruth and Bill Cooper's 1974 Chevy Impala. They sat in the back seat - in silence for most of the trip - and Trish followed behind me in her car; that would be our ticket back to Seattle, as the plan was to leave the Cooper's car with them on the mountain so it wouldn't appear as if they'd had any help carrying out their plan. The sun was shining brightly and yet I felt an unshakable darkness filling the car. I was still having a hard time believing that Trish had talked me into being a part of this scheme.

"It's *their* choice Dan," she had told me, "and, besides, they're scheduled to die that day anyway, according to the list, so why not let them do it a way that they feel good about?" She had come a long way in her thinking since that first tear-filled session on her bed a couple of days earlier.

The silence that filled the car was the same type of silence that had filled many of the hospital rooms that Trish and I had sat in together over the last few days; it was heavy with thousands of unspoken words that wanted to be said. And yet, there was nothing really to say. It was times like that where words failed to measure up to the task in front of them - nothing seemed appropriate to say and so the empty space often got filled up with talk of the weather or some other mundane topic. I couldn't *begin* to think about discussing the weather as I was fulfilling my role as The Chauffeur of Death.

220

I looked in my rearview mirror to make sure Trish was still behind me - she was - and then glanced at Ruth and Bill in the back seat. They were sitting close to each other, hands locked together like two young lovers, and my eyes caught Bill's. He smiled at me. "I want to thank you again for your help with this Dan - we probably couldn't have done it without you."

"That's *exactly* what I'm worried about Bill." It felt good to finally be able to say it.

He let out a small chuckle. "So you're worried that you're the one pulling the trigger on our lives, is that it?"

"Well, in some respects, *yeah*! If not actually pulling the trigger, I'm certainly loading the gun and lifting it to your heads."

"Dan, let me tell you something that might help. Just yesterday Ruthie lost control of her bowels and it took me the better part of two hours to get her cleaned up afterwards. The cold, hard facts say that it's only going to get worse for us - her systems are shutting down one by one and my body's becoming more and more useless with each passing day. I ask you, man to man, if that would be any kind of life that *you* would be interested in living?"

"I don't know Bill. I guess a lot would depend on the people around me and whether or not I felt like I was making their lives better or worse with my being around."

"Exactly. And, to us, the answer is a resounding, *much worse!* Our son is in no position to help us out financially or logistically and our daughter, who has the heart of a saint, would run herself and her marriage into the ground before she'd give up on us. So, you see, we really have no choice but to take that choice out of her hands and make it ourselves - everyone will be much better off if we just end this ordeal before it gets much worse. Ruth and I do *not* want to get stuck in a hospital, barely alive, and watch our daughter get buried in debt just so we can breathe with a ventilator, eat through a tube and fill a bedpan twice a day. No thank you!"

"So, I'm doing you both a favor, am I?"

Ruth spoke for the first time, her voice quiet and weak but there was no mistaking what she said. "Absolutely." I looked in the rearview mirror and saw a small smile work its way across her pale, hollow face.

Bill patted her hands and, while gazing at her, said, "We've had a good life Dan. We've raised two children, traveled the world, known what love feels like, and now we get to pass to the next world from a spot that we've always loved." He looked back at me in the mirror. "Where you're taking us is where we said our wedding vows forty years ago."

"Are you sure it's still there?"

He laughed. "Oh, heavens yes - it's pretty hard to move an entire mountain! When we still had all our faculties, we used to go up to this spot every year on our anniversary to renew our vows as the sun was setting; this spot has beautiful sunsets."

"When's your anniversary?"

"Actually," he said with a smile, "it's *today* Dan. In about three hours we will have been married for forty years."

"You old dog!" I screamed. "So *that's* why you picked this day!"

He simply nodded and put his arm around Ruth, pulling her close to him.

We arrived at our destination a short while later and, after climbing a series of dirt roads, I parked the car in a small parking area that was empty except for us. I helped Ruth and Bill out of the car and Trish pulled up right behind us.

"You guys have certainly picked a great spot to be alone," Trish said as she got out of the car.

"We've always been alone up here when we came on our anniversary," Bill said. "Not too many people like to hike this time of year." He pointed to the far corner of the parking area where a small path wound its way into the woods. "That's the trail over there."

With me helping Ruth, and Trish lending a stabilizing shoulder to Bill, we made our way over to the trailhead. Once there, I looked at the old trail map that was posted and saw that the trail led to a lookout area called "Lover's Leap." I turned to Bill. "You can't be serious," I said to him.

He just grinned. "What can I say? I didn't make up the name, I just love the spot."

We stumbled our way over the well-worn trail for about a mile, stopping every 10-15 minutes for a short rest. Thankfully, we had left early and there would still be plenty of daylight left. After a mile the dirt trail ended, and we walked out onto a large rocky outcropping. We helped Ruth and Bill out towards the edge and then sat them down on a couple of makeshift seats made from large boulders. After getting them settled I looked up and out and felt myself gasp slightly - the view was breathtaking. I walked to the edge of the outcropping and felt like I was standing at the edge of the world. It was a bright, clear day and I could see the entirety of western Washington spread out before me; I could even see the hazy outline of the Olympics on the western horizon.

I turned to Bill and Ruth. "I can see why you two fell in love with this spot."

They were both still catching their breath, so they just smiled and nodded. I looked over at Trish and could see that she was as smitten with the view as I was. Then, as if choreographed, we both looked down at the same time; it was a straight drop of several hundred feet to the rocks below. We looked over at each other and didn't need to say a word - we were both thinking the same thing.

We turned and went back to Bill and Ruth. "No second thoughts creeping in?" I asked.

"If you're asking if we're afraid, the answer is yes," Bill said matter-of-factly. "If you're asking if we want to turn around and head back, the answer is no."

We sat down with them, mostly in silence, as they recovered from the short hike and then began to cast their eyes at the task in front of them. I looked in their faces for traces of the fear that Bill had spoken about, but I saw none. They seemed to be going through a checklist that they had established in their minds prior to the trip. "So, you're going to leave the keys in the car, right Dan?" Bill asked me.

"I sure will Bill."

He turned to Trish. "And you'll make sure that the videotape, that we made with Zootie, gets into Ellen's hands?"

"You can count on it," Trish responded with a warm smile.

"I'm warning you that Ellen's going to be madder than a hornet at you two for even allowing us to make this trip in our car," he winked at me, "but once she sees the videotape, she'll understand. Just realize that her anger comes from how much she loves us," he paused to wipe a tear from his eye, "and it's going to be hard for her to understand all of this at first."

Trish walked over and crouched next to Bill, putting one hand on his back and the other on his leg. "Don't you worry about a thing Bill - we'll help Ellen in any way we can to work through all of this."

Bill started to sob gently. "I can't tell you both how much we appreciate this. There aren't many folks that would be willing to do all that you've done for us." He reached over and patted Trish's hand and she pulled him into a sideways hug.

Then I heard a small squeak and I looked over and saw that Ruth was weeping into a small handkerchief that she had in her hand. Without giving it any thought, I went over and crouched next to her and put my arm around her. "Thank you," she whispered into my ear. Her words sent chills through my spine and I felt the familiar tingling sensation in my jaw.

"You two are very brave, loving people," Trish said through sobs, "and I feel honored to have known you and proud to help you in any way I can."

I looked into Ruth's face and saw the face of a woman with one foot in God's waiting room - there was no fear, only peaceful resignation with what needed to be done. Her eyes softened when she looked at me and she raised her hand with great effort to stroke my face. "Trust love," she whispered to me. I'm sure I gave her a strange look because I didn't think I'd heard her right. As if reading my mind, though, she smiled and nodded, as if to say, "*yes, you heard me right.*" I smiled awkwardly at her and nodded back.

"Now if you'll excuse us," Bill interjected with a determined voice, "we have a few words to say to each other before the sun sets." He wiped his face and eyes with his sleeve. Bill set his jaw and the entire mood changed instantly - it suddenly felt like we were simply dropping them off for a doctor's appointment rather than saying a final goodbye. We all exchanged hugs, I whispered a quiet "good luck" in each of their ears, and then Trish and I were waving goodbye as we headed off into the woods.

We both stopped part way down the trail and looked back at Ruth and Bill through a clearing in the trees. Bill was resting awkwardly on one knee in front of Ruth, as if proposing to her, and he was talking to her. "My god, they're renewing their vows one last time," I whispered.

"They're what?" Trish whispered back.

"Renewing their vows," I repeated. "Bill told me that they did this every year on their anniversary and today's their anniversary."

Trish began crying again while I just stared with my mouth hanging open in disbelief. "How incredibly sweet and romantic," she whispered through sobs.

We watched them for a little while longer and then, feeling like we were intruding, we decided to head back to the car. We didn't say a word the whole way down.

When we reached the car, the sun was beginning to set through the trees and a tremendous gloom climbed into the car with us; we knew exactly what was happening less than a mile away from us. I sat there for a moment, afraid to start the car for fear that I might pull away just as Bill and Ruth came stumbling out of the woods with news that they'd changed their minds. Trish's voice pulled me out of my trance.

"Let's not head back right away," she said without looking at me. "I need a break from all of this if just for one night." She then turned to me. "And I know just the place."

CHAPTER 42

Snoqualmie Falls Lodge sat atop a dramatic waterfall, all of which could be seen from inside an elegant restaurant. It was the most romantic setting I'd ever seen in my life. The entire restaurant was bathed in candlelight and Trish and I sat off in one corner emptying our second bottle of wine.

"You sure picked a winner here," I said to Trish as I looked out the window at the water cascading over the cliff into the blackness below. The sun had long since set and the night was clear and moonless. I looked up and saw hundreds of stars twinkling overhead.

"I love this place," Trish said as she followed my gaze out the window. "It never fails to make me feel better."

"You come here a lot?"

"I used to." She paused for just a moment, perhaps wondering just how much she wanted to share with me. I don't know if it was the wine or the setting or just the emotions of the day, but she decided to share it all. "Especially after Jerry and I started having problems."

"Jerry? Your husband?"

"Ex. We split up over five years ago."

A part of me did a backflip of joy. "What happened?" I asked casually, belying my inner excitement.

"I decided that I no longer deserved to be a human punching bag for him."

"Oh my god, he *hit* you?"

"Hit. Kicked. Slapped. However he felt like working out his anger that day." Her voice was emotionless.

"I'm so sorry Trish." I reached over and put my hand on hers.

"Yeah, me too. I'm sorry that it took me ten years to figure out that it was *his* problem and not *mine*."

"So, is he still around?"

"I left him down in LA five years ago and haven't seen him since." She flagged down our waiter and ordered a third bottle of wine.

"Do you think that's such a good idea?" I asked about the wine. "We still have to make that drive home."

She finished ordering the bottle of wine and then said to me; "No we don't."

CHAPTER 43

A couple of hours later I found myself lying in bed, quite drunk, next to an equally intoxicated Trish. She had insisted that we spend the night at the Lodge and, "not wanting to be alone," she had also insisted on getting just one room. As we laid in bed, looking up at the ceiling, the only thing that was spinning more than the room was my mind; I had a whirlwind of thoughts and AC was at the center of the vortex sounding the charge.

"This is your big chance lover boy! Make your move before she sobers up or falls asleep!" He was extremely convincing at that moment and it was all I could do not to roll over and press my body against hers. I turned my head and smelled her hair and her perfume, and they were both like magnets drawing me to her. I quickly hopped out of the bed.

"Where are you going?" Trish asked sleepily.

"I think I just need a little air," I lied, "this damned room seems to be on a merry-go-round."

She smiled at me - a sweet, flirtatious smile - and then rolled over to snuggle with her pillow. "Okay, but don't be long," she mumbled.

I took a deep breath and then headed out onto the balcony. It was a cool night, but the brisk air felt good on my face and in my nostrils. I heard the distant roar of the falls and the world stopped spinning for a while. It gave me a little time to think, though any thoughts I had were forced to first swim upstream against the strong current of alcohol that was flowing through my system. The two thoughts that had been strong enough to make the swim were: *"How long has it been since I've been with a woman?!?"* and *"Ruth and Bill are now at their final resting place at the bottom of some cliff!"* Completely discordant thoughts that struggled for my attention. I chose to focus on the first thought.

Since Mary and I had split up about ten years ago, there had been only two other women with whom I'd been physically intimate - Liz Walton soon after our divorce, and Becky Holmes a few years after Liz and I had broken up. Since Becky and I broke things off at the beginning of the previous year, and it was now almost November, that meant it had been close to two years since I'd even so much as *kissed* a woman. No wonder I was feeling so damned nervous! I was starting to feel sorry for myself when I felt two arms wrap themselves around me from behind.

"You took too long," I heard Trish coo from behind me.

I turned around and saw that she was naked except for her panties and she was wearing eyes that were screaming, *"kiss me!"* The only conscious thought I had at that moment was actually a quote from my good friend Bowler: *"Fucket!"* I pulled Trish into a full embrace and kissed her. Hard. All the small dams that had been put in place to keep my reservoir of emotions in check regarding Trish were immediately lifted out of the way by the alcohol and I felt a wonderfully overpowering torrent of emotion overwhelm my body. We slowly made our way to the bed, our lips in constant contact, and began exploring each other's body with hands that couldn't stay still. Every nerve-ending was on full alert as I stroked, rubbed, kissed and nuzzled every inch of Trish's body - the feel of her skin and the feel of her feeling *my* skin aroused me to levels I'd never experienced before in my life. I felt like a starving man who had just been placed in front of an endless beautiful buffet and I wanted to taste everything at once. We made love, off and on, several times until sleep finally overtook us just as the first slivers of dawn were starting to show themselves through our window.

CHAPTER 44

The drive back to Seattle the following afternoon was marked by an odd mix of extreme elation and profound sadness, all of which was shrouded in a thick, hangover-induced fog. As I drove, I tried to read Trish's feelings after our night of unbridled passion and personal revelations. We had talked little over our quick breakfast, both of us still feeling the effects of just a few hours of sleep, but now I felt ready to talk.

"So, how are you feeling?" I asked point blank.

"Besides my pounding head and strong feelings of lust for a pillow and bed, just fine." She flashed me a weak smile.

"Any regrets about last night?"

Her smile grew larger and she reached over and grabbed my free hand. "Not a one," she assured me. "You?"

I returned her smile. "None. I've been wanting to ravage your body like that for a *long* time. I'm just a little embarrassed that it took three bottles of wine to give me the guts to do it."

She laughed an easy laugh. "I feel the same way Dan - without the alcohol in me, I doubt very much that I would have walked out onto the balcony like that."

"I'm glad you did." I gave her hand a warm squeeze and looked at her with puffy, bloodshot, yet extremely loving eyes.

She acknowledged my look and then looked forward at the road ahead. "I still can't stop thinking about Ruth and Bill."

"Yeah, me too. I keep wondering how they felt during their final minutes together. They had to have been scared to death about jumping from that cliff."

"The only small consolation that my mind can grab at is that they were together in the end, just like they wanted to be."

"Yeah, small as it is, that's what I keep coming back to too."

The time passed quickly as we drove back. We pulled up to the curb at Hope House a little after 2:00 in the afternoon. Before I could even get the key out of the ignition, Jennie came bounding out of the house to greet us.

"Where have you two been?!?" she asked breathlessly. "All hell has broken loose here, and we didn't know where to find you guys!"

We walked up to the front porch and sat down so Jennie could fill us in on what had been going on during our absence. "First of all," she began, "Brent was found dead in a downtown hotel room last night." Trish and I exchanged looks of shock and sadness - in all the commotion, we had forgotten about Brent's upcoming DOD. "He had an empty bottle of bourbon in his hands," Jennie continued, "and two more empties laying nearby on the floor."

"How did he die?" I asked quietly.

"They think it was a massive stroke, but they're still not sure. His sister was the one who found him."

"Do you know when the service is going to be?" Trish asked.

"Tomorrow at noon, up in the Shoreline area."

"Man, poor Brent," I mumbled half to myself. I thought of how desperate and lonely he must have felt in that hotel room all by himself.

"Yeah," Jennie agreed, "by the looks of things, he was trying to run away from it all right up to the end."

Trish and I looked at each other and, without thought, reached over and grabbed each other's hand. I noticed right away that Jennie was staring at us and I quickly let go of Trish's hand. "What else happened?" I asked, trying to distract Jennie from what she had just seen.

I could tell from her small smile that my ploy hadn't worked, but she didn't say anything. "Ruth and Bill's daughter has been callin' non-stop for the past couple o' days. She said that they *always* talked to her on their anniversary, which was yesterday, and she was worried 'cuz she hasn't heard a word from them. Have you guys seen those two around at all?"

I didn't dare look over at Trish. I simply shook my head and said, "No, not recently."

"Well, that's real funny 'cuz they disappeared about the same time you guys did and their daughter says that their car is gone from their house too." She looked at both of us with eyes that were obviously trying to detect even the slightest clues, but we gave her none.

I just shrugged and said, "I don't know what to tell you on that one."

She just let out a small "hmph" sound. "And one last question," she added casually, "where the hell *were* you two last night?!?"

"What if we said it was none of your business?" Trish said sweetly.

"Well I'd say that I'll offer you a trade - you tell *me* where *you* were, and I'll tell *you* what happened with Dave and me last night." The big smile on Jennie's face told us that she was *very* anxious to tell us *something*.

"Okay, you've got yourself a deal," Trish said. "Dan and I decided to go off on a little retreat last night to Snoqualmie Falls Lodge to just clear our heads a little bit and get to know each other better." Trish looked over at me and we exchanged smiles and small nods.

"Well," Jennie said with a loud exhalation, "by the looks of your bloodshot eyes I would say that you didn't do a very good job on the whole head-clearin' thing." She looked at us both with impish eyes. "But judgin' from how cozy you two are lookin' right now, I'd say that you did a damn fine job on the whole gettin' to know each other better thing!"

Trish and I just shrugged at each other, as if to say, *"what the hell!"* and once again grabbed each other's hand. "Yeah," I agreed, "I guess we did at that."

"Thought so!" Jennie shouted. Then she leaned forward and motioned to us to do the same, to come closer, so she could whisper what she had to say. She glanced from side to side, to make sure there weren't any prying ears, and then whispered, "Dave and I did the nasty last night too." She pulled back and her eyes went wide in disbelief. "Do you believe it?!?" she shrieked.

"Wow, I don't know what to say," Trish mumbled in disbelief.

"Yeah, I know, it's kinda shocking and all," Jennie said with a shrug, "but I figured that this was the guy's BFW and there aren't too many BFW's in my little notebook that have much of a prayer of seein' the light o' day, so..." her voice trailed off and a smile overtook her face, *"...what the fuck?"* She laughed a high-pitched little girl laugh.

I flashed on Bowler, and my own thought from the previous night, and just smiled. "I say congratulations to you two Jennie - I think it's great."

"Thanks Dan." She shrugged a shoulder. "I mean, what the hell have *I* got to lose anyway; it's not like I'm gonna be dyin' of *AIDS*. And besides," a coy smile went up one side of her face, "I kinda enjoyed it." She looked over her shoulder again, to make sure she wouldn't be overheard, and then whispered, "I told him that it was my first time too - so he wouldn't feel so bad - but really it was my third time." She held up three fingers and scrunched her nose. She sat back in her chair and continued, "But I have to say that last night was the best time yet. He was so eager and appreciative and...considerate 'n all. The other two were about as considerate as dogs tearin' into a steak."

Trish and I snickered, and Jennie turned a devilish look on us. "All right you two, I've been sittin' here dishin' out all the dirty details and you guys haven't shared a word about *your* night!" She folded her arms and said emphatically, "It's time to dish!"

Trish and I looked at each other, smiled, and then turned back to Jennie. "We're too old to kiss and tell," Trish said simply.

CHAPTER 45

Brent's family had chosen to have a graveside service at a small cemetery in the north end of Seattle. Zootie, Trish, Jennie and I drove up together and, once there, Zootie and Trish walked up ahead while Jennie and I lingered behind. We were both looking at headstones as we walked toward Brent's gravesite. Jennie stopped at one that was for a young soldier who had died in World War II.

"Did you ever notice," she said to me without lifting her eyes from the headstone, "just how much these headstones look like hands rising up out of the ground? It's like they're saying, *"Hey, remember me? Don't forget that I lived here for a while!"* She heaved a deep sigh and looked around the graveyard. "Such a sad thing - all these forgotten people - with nothing left of them but a stone hand reaching up out of the ground."

I stepped over and put my arm around her. "Don't worry Jennie, I'll make *damn* sure that you aren't forgotten."

My words brought instant tears to her eyes - it was easy to see that this still hit a raw nerve with her - and she laid her head on my shoulder as she cried softly. I soon saw that Brent's service was starting across the way, so I nudged Jennie in that direction and we walked over arm-in-arm.

There were probably thirty or forty people gathered around the open grave and everyone's head was down as the minister who was presiding over the service said a prayer. I thought it odd that there was any type of religious invocation over Brent's grave, given that he was a very vocal agnostic, but I figured that it must have been a request of his family. I noticed that there was a handful of people - all dressed in black - huddled together at the edge of the grave and I figured that they were all members of his immediate family. None of them said a word throughout the short service, their only active involvement being to throw a handful of dirt on Brent's coffin after it had been lowered into the grave. As a matter of fact, the only voice that was heard during the entire service, except for the minister's, was Zootie's; he cleared his throat and squeezed in a few nice words about Brent towards the end of the service, after one of the minister's short pauses.

After the service was over, each of us stood over the grave and said our own private goodbye to Brent Haberman. My head was down when I heard a woman's voice off to my left. I looked over and saw one of the family members talking to Zootie.

"Are you Zootie Gibbons?" she asked with a slight quaver of emotion in her voice.

"Yes, I am," Zootie replied as he turned to face her with his hand extended, "and I just want to say that…" He was cut off abruptly by a hard slap across his face.

The woman looked up at him with extreme contempt. "That's for my brother Brent!" she screamed. "He was never the same after you told him about that damned list of yours, and he ended up just drinking himself to death!" Her eyes went to narrow slits and she spit the next words like venom. "You killed him just as surely as if you had put a gun to his head. Now you can *live* with that fact Mr. Gibbons!" She didn't wait for a reply - she just spun around and strode away with a man who shot his own looks of hatred at Zootie as he took the woman under his arm.

Zootie stood there stunned. There was a large red hand print on his left cheek that had to sting but he didn't even seem to notice that it was there. Trish, Jennie and I all went over to him to offer our own words of comfort, but he wouldn't have any of it. "Just let it be for a minute," he said. "I don't know as she's not right with what she just said." He walked back to the car and we drove home in complete silence.

CHAPTER 46

Zootie kept to himself for the next couple of days and it seemed to affect the overall mood of Hope House. If there had ever been any doubt about Zootie being the glue that held Project Hope together, there was none any longer - without Zootie's constant cheerleading, activity around the list slowed to a snail's pace.

It was during day two of "The Zootie Slump" that I was sitting on the front porch with Bowler. We had been talking about marriage when he got a strange look on his face.

"What's up, Bowler?" I asked.

"Oh, I was jest thinkin' 'bout a question that young gal Jennie asked me the other day."

"She does enjoy asking questions, that's for sure."

"That she does," Bowler agreed, "but one of 'em was 'bout my big fuckin' wish, or some such, 'n I told her then that I didn't have one." He reached his hand up to his newly trimmed beard and thought for a moment. While he thought, I sat there and marveled at the new and improved Bowler - trimmed beard and hair, clean body, clean clothes. His friends on the street probably wouldn't even recognize him. "Only now," he continued, "with all this talk 'bout marriage 'n such, I got ta thinkin' 'bout Jeanne 'n my son Tom Junior 'n wonderin' if they was still around 'n maybe..." he trailed off.

"Maybe what Bowler?"

He shrugged and I saw what I thought were tears forming in the corner of his cloudy eye. "I dunno, maybe it'd be nice to send them a letter or somethin' jest ta say I wuz thinkin' 'bout 'em, that's all." He looked away so I couldn't see his face.

"That's a great idea Bowler. You want me to help you out with it?"

He turned back to face me. "Truth is, even when I could see I wasn't much of a writer. 'N now, with both eyes gone, I couldn't write my way outta a bag o' wet worms if I had to!"

"I'll assume that means yes, you'd like me to help you."

He smiled. "If ya got the time, I'd be obliged."

I got up and patted him on the shoulder, then went inside to get a pad of paper and a pen. When I returned, paper and pen in hand, I scooted my chair closer to his wheelchair and said, "Okay Bowler, your personal secretary is ready and waiting."

"Tell me one thing first," he said.

"What's that?"

"Have ya got nice legs? I like my secretaries ta have nice legs." He let out a howling laugh that shook his wheelchair.

"They're okay," I replied straight-faced, "but if you lay a hand on me, you're going to hear from my lawyer!"

"Fair 'nuff!" he bellowed. "Now let's get down ta business."

For the next hour I sat there and just wrote down everything that Bowler told me. I changed some wording here and there - though not without asking him first - but in the end it was a letter that was unmistakably Bowler through and through. He told the story of how he had wound up on the streets, how he'd lost his legs, how he had been helped by Nurse Mercy Jenkins, and, through it all, how he'd come full circle to live a life that was goddamned good. The last couple of paragraphs were obviously the hardest for him as he talked about how he'd never stopped thinking about her and their son, and how he'd ended every day with a prayer for their happiness. It was a great letter and I felt proud to have helped him to compose it.

"Sign it *"Forever Yours, Tom"* if ya please, Danny."

"No problem Bowler."

"'N then we got one more small problem."

"What's that?" I asked, as I finished signing his name.

"Where the hell ta send the thing! I done lost track o' her over twenty years ago!"

"Hmm," I said, "that could indeed be a problem."

"Not to worry," came a voice from behind me. I turned and saw Trish walking over from a seat behind me on the porch. I had been so focused on Bowler's letter that I didn't even know she'd been sitting there.

"How long have you been there?" I asked her.

She wiped the tears from her splotchy face. "Long enough to get a good cry out of Bowler's words." She walked past me over to Bowler and bent down to give him a hug. "She's going to love that letter Bowler," she whispered into his ear.

"Mmmm..." Bowler said as Trish hugged him. "My secretary smells and feels better'n I thought she did!"

I laughed and said, "Just remember what I said about my lawyer!" Trish came over and sat next to me. "So, what's your brilliant idea?" I asked her.

"I can probably find her through one of those on-line directories," Trish said. "That is, assuming that she didn't re-marry or change her name."

"Ya can't be serious!" Bowler bellowed. "How could she take up with another man after havin' *this*?!?" He ran his hands up and down his body as if showing off a new silk suit.

Trish and I laughed. "You're right Bowler," I agreed, "chances are really good that she's still hanging on to that Sims name."

Trish went inside and returned a short time later with her findings. "Good news," she said with a big smile, "I found both a Jeanne Sims and a Tom Sims living in Mound, Minnesota."

"Mound?" Bowler yelled out. "Hell, that's where we got married!"

I read the letter one more time to Bowler, got his final approval, then went and found an envelope, addressed it, stamped it, then put it in the mailbox for pickup that afternoon. I sat back down on the porch. "So how does it feel to check off your BFW like that?" I asked.

He showed me his big yellow, gap-toothed smile. "Pretty damned good Danny boy. Pretty goddamned good."

CHAPTER 47

The next day - the day before Bowler's DOD - I was up in mine and Zootie's bedroom looking through some drawers to see if Zootie had any extra razor blades that I could borrow, when I came across something that caught my eye; buried at the bottom of one of the drawers was a stack of papers that looked strangely familiar. I pulled them out and looked at them more closely.

"My god," I murmured out loud, "it's another copy of the list." I wondered to myself why he had tucked a copy in the bottom of a drawer as I started flipping through it. Everything looked pretty much the same as the copy posted downstairs in the study except for two notable exceptions - it was printed on an entirely different type of paper and, as I flipped through, I saw that the whited-out name in the middle of the list had the original whiteout on it.

I sat down on the bed and looked at it more closely, wondering if it would provide more details as to the identity of the mystery list member. I held it up to the light and suddenly felt my pulse quicken and my skin go clammy. I looked closer, not believing what I thought I saw, but it didn't change. I dropped the list to my lap and mumbled an involuntary "Oh my god!" I looked down again, hoping that my eyes had just played a nasty trick on me, but they hadn't - there it was, clear as can be, a capital "D" and a small "a" at the start of the name and an unmistakable "s" at the end of the last name. I struggled to make out the rest of the name but that was all I could see, and it was all that I needed. I felt sick to my stomach.

Everything started to make sense to me - why Zootie wanted me to come out to Seattle with him, why he had brought me into Hope House with everyone else, why he had hidden this original copy of the list; it all flooded into my head at once. Another thought then crowded out everything else - I had to find Zootie and get some answers. I tore out the page of the list that had the whiteout on it and bolted from the room.

I ran down the stairs and went straight to the front porch where I knew Zootie had been spending most of his time the last few days, ever since Brent's funeral. I found him sitting in his favorite rocking chair. I thrust the page in his face, feeling as angry as I'd ever felt in my life.

"What the hell is *this*?" I shouted at him, unable to control my rage.

He looked at it with indifference - the same look he had given most everything the past couple of days - and said simply, "Looks like the original list."

"And when was it that you were going to tell me about *this?!?*" I jabbed my finger at the spot on the page with the whited-out name.

"Tell you about what exactly?" he asked too-calmly.

"*That it's my fucking name on the list!!!*" As I said the words, I felt a whoosh of blood rush to my head and the porch seemed like it was starting to spin.

Zootie stood up and stood nose to nose with me, his calm manner replaced with anger. "And what if it *is* your name? What then? It would be time to jump off the bench and get into the ol' ballgame then, eh Danny? No more whining, no more feeling sorry for yourself for no real reason - 'cuz now you'd have a *reason*, wouldn't you?" He had a look of contempt on his face that I'd never seen before.

I ignored his look - all I saw was my own anger - and managed to stop the spinning long enough to ask the question that I'd had on my lips ever since I saw the whited-out name upstairs; "So it *is* my name on there for December 14th, isn't it?" I asked desperately.

Zootie folded his arms defiantly. "I'm not saying it is, and I'm not saying it isn't right now."

I wanted to punch him right in the nose at that moment. But he'd given me the answer - in his own obnoxious way - that I'd come for: it *was* my name on the list, and I had a little over a month left to live. "You bastard!" was all I said, and I turned and ran from the porch. I jumped over all the stairs, ran down the front sidewalk and then down the street. I didn't know where I was going, but I just knew that I had to get as far away from Zootie and Hope House as I could.

After running hard for countless blocks, I felt my stomach churning and I stopped and puked into some bushes, gasping heavily between each heave in a desperate attempt at getting enough oxygen into my lungs. After retching and heaving myself into exhaustion, I slumped onto the sidewalk and dropped my head into my hands. The thought then hit me like an iron-fisted punch - *you're going to die.* I sat there on the sidewalk, feeling empty, for I don't know how long. The ice-cold hand of the Grim Reaper had a firm grip on my belly, and he wasn't letting go.

PART III

Vici

*"Don't wait for the last judgment,
it takes place every day."*
Albert Camus

CHAPTER 48

I awoke with a start from what had already been a fitful sleep. I was lying in bed in a downtown Seattle hotel; I had just seen Bowler in my dream, and he said goodbye to me. It wasn't an unreal, hazy, dream-like Bowler who had spoken to me, but rather it was a very vivid Bowler - minus the wheelchair - who had smiled at me and said, "See ya later Danny!" Then he said something else to me and the words were still echoing in my head; "Put the muzzle on the dog Danny and wander into the cave - you'll find yer answer there!" After saying those final words, he was gone and I bolted awake, half expecting to see Bowler standing at the edge of my bed.

I finally separated my mind from the dream world through which it had just been wandering and a thought fell onto my head like a piano of guilt: *"Oh my god - yesterday was Bowler's DOD!"* Amidst all the confusion and mind-numbing fear of recent events, I had forgotten about Bowler's pending death. Not only had I failed myself, but I had also failed a man who had trusted me with his life. I felt a cold emptiness fill my insides.

I sat up in my bed and shivered as a clammy river of sweat ran down my body. I looked around the room and saw nothing but blackness and the flash of a neon sign outside my window. I felt a strong urge to pick up the phone and call Trish or Jennie, both to check on Bowler's death as well as just to hear a reassuring voice. But I quickly decided that I wasn't yet ready to face the concerns and good intentions of others - there would be too many questions that I didn't yet feel ready to answer. I got up and went into the bathroom to splash some cold water on my face. Looking into the mirror, I felt ashamed at what I saw - a man who, two days earlier, had run like a frightened child from the news of his pending death and had been holed up in a cheap Seattle hotel ever since. The thought once again brought a lump to my throat and I had to fight back the tears of desperation that were waiting to burst forth. It was the true reason for my hesitation in calling Trish: I was ashamed. I splashed more cold water on my face and then did what I always did when faced with unpleasantness - I ran from it. I threw on my clothes and headed out the door, glancing at the clock on my way out: it was 1:15 in the morning.

The streets were still teeming with bar patrons, despite the late hour, and the distractions were welcome. The cold night air also served as a much-needed tonic to my dazed senses. I shoved my hands in my pockets and just started walking, much as I had many times before, away from the confusion and pain that haunted me. I hadn't gotten far before the darkness and my solitude were both broken by a woman's voice coming from the shadows of the buildings to my right.

"Hey you! Hey...*you!*" I turned to face the woman's voice and saw that it was the woman - I couldn't remember her name - to whom Bowler had given his watch the week before.

The woman walked over to me and asked without so much as a nod of acknowledgment, "So how's ol' Bowler doing these days?"

More guilt surged through my body as I struggled with what to tell her. "He's fine," I lied as I looked down at the ground. I didn't want to tell her anything more for fear that I would break down into a guilt-fueled hysteria.

She looked at me suspiciously. "Just where is it that you took my friend?"

"Up to a house in North Seattle," I replied.

"And you're sure he's okay?" she asked again, still looking at me sideways.

"I'm sure."

She let out a small sigh of relief. "Well that's the best news I've heard in a long time because I just had quite a start." She looked me up and down, as if assessing whether she should continue with what she had to say. She quickly decided to continue. "I was sleeping over there, peaceful as can be," she motioned towards a pile of boxes, "when I felt what I thought was Bowler hugging me and saying goodbye, only..." she paused again, for just a moment, "...he wasn't anywhere to be seen!" she finally blurted out.

I felt a chill course through my body. I wanted desperately to grab this woman by the shoulders and scream, *"I just had the same dream!"* but a bigger part of me felt like I'd just taken a big punch and I was staggering backwards trying to get my bearings before I blacked out.

She must have seen my reaction as she asked, "You okay mister?"

I didn't answer her. I just turned and ran as fast as I could, just as I had after Zootie had told me about my place on the list. I ran for a few blocks and then spotted a bar that was still open; I went in and threw myself into a booth. Still panting, while also trying to shake the guilt and strange occurrences from my brain, I put my head on the table in front of me and tried to keep from throwing up.

"Can I get you something mister?" I looked up and saw a waitress standing over me.

"Uh, just a beer," I mumbled.

She looked at me warily. "You sure you should have another one? You look like you've had enough to me," she said.

I sat up and took a deep breath. "Actually, I haven't had a single drink all night, so maybe you ought to bring me some scotch - make it a double - instead."

She gave me one last look and then, satisfied that it was all right, disappeared to get my drink. Soon after she set the drink on the table, I gulped it down and ordered another. I was in the middle of doing the same with the second drink when a man came over to my table and sat down. He was carrying what looked like a bible, which he set down on the table in front of him, and he was wearing a pious smile that I detested instantly.

"May I sit down," he asked as though he already knew the answer.

"What if I said no?" I asked without emotion.

He ignored me. "You look like you could use a friend," he said with a smile that seemed manufactured.

"No, actually I look like I could use a drink, and that's what I've got." I held up my drink for him to see.

"Alcohol is no way to solve your problems, my friend."

"Oh? And how do you presume to know what my problems are or how to solve them?" I was feeling irritated with his intrusion and with where I knew the conversation was headed.

"I can see that you're hurting, and I know from experience that any relief you get from the bottle is short-lived."

"What if short-term relief is that all I need right now?"

His eyes turned serious. "Nothing is ever short-term."

"So I suppose you're going to tell me that the real answer lies with Jesus and God, is that it?" I felt impatient and I just wanted to get rid of him so I could get back to my drink. "You know what?" I continued. "I get so tired of all of you born again Christians acting like you've got the inside track to salvation. What the hell makes you think that you've got it all figured out and that the rest of the world, that doesn't believe what you believe, is just clueless?" I took a self-satisfied swig from my drink and slammed it on the table. I expected to look across the table and see looks of confusion or anger on the man's face but instead I saw him smiling.

"So, is that why you think I'm sitting here - to bring another sheep into the flock?"

"Well, isn't it?" I asked, nodding towards his bible on the table.

He glanced down at the book on the table and laughed. "That's a copy of the Gnostic Gospels and some other ancient texts, some of which are about as *un*-Christian as you can get."

"So then why did you come over here and sit down?" I asked, feeling some of the steam leak out of my self-righteous rant.

"Because I saw a man who was hurting, simple as that."

"But what's in it for you?" I asked suspiciously.

He shrugged. "Nothing really. Unless you count the satisfaction that comes with helping another human being." He smiled again - more warmly this time - and I felt my defenses begin to drop. "So, is there anything that I can help you with?"

I looked at the man, more closely than before, and saw a man who was probably in his fifties, graying at the temples of his receding hairline, carrying a little too much weight on his short, stocky frame and who had sad, tired-looking eyes. "Thanks for the offer," I said as I drained my drink, "but my problems are ones that I have to work through myself."

He let out a loud "hmph" sound. "I've certainly heard that one before."

"Well, unfortunately, in my case it happens to be true."

"Try me," he insisted. "I can be an amazing listener."

The two drinks were quickly lowering any resistance I felt towards anything and everything, and I decided to just let him have it between the eyes. "What do you know about death?"

"Death?" he asked incredulously. "Shit, I know more about death than anything else." He leaned forward and his sad eyes suddenly burned with a fiery intensity. "It was death that brought me here mister, and it's the scent of death's stench that keeps me here."

"Amen to that," I muttered as I signaled to the waitress to bring me another drink.

The man's voice softened. "Hey, don't you think that you've had enough for one night?"

"Why is it that you're so damned concerned about my alcohol intake?"

"Because I used to be sitting where you are right now, trying to drink my problems away, and I had to learn the hard way that it just wasn't possible." He dropped his head and his voice lowered to barely a whisper. "I had just finished off my fourth drink after a hard day at the office about four years ago and went to pick up my eight-year-old daughter at a friend's house. On the way home I drove through a red light and got broad-sided by a truck." He lifted his head and I could see the deep sadness filling his face. "He plowed into my daughter's door and crushed her instantly. I woke up two days later and, after my wife told me what happened, I vowed to never touch alcohol again in my life. My wife left me soon after that - she told me that she could never look at my face again and not think about how I'd killed her baby - and, after over a year of grieving, I decided that I had to either find something to do that would honor my daughter's memory, or just say fuck it and join her on the other side. That's when I came up with this idea of working the downtown bars, just trying to help people to find answers that didn't involve alcohol."

"Hey, I'm sorry - that must have been a horrible thing to go through."

"Yeah, it wasn't a day at the beach, that's for sure." He turned his eyes to me. "But that's why I'm so damned concerned about the way you're drinking those scotches like water."

"Well let me tell you, you don't have to worry about me because this is the first drink I've had in months," I lied.

"Hey, we all started somewhere."

I was feeling frustrated with his seeming insistence that I was an alcoholic and asked him, "Do you really want to know why I'm sitting here drinking myself into a stupor?"

"Sure, if you want to tell me."

I took a big gulp from the fresh drink that the waitress had just set down. "All right, you asked for it. You'd better fasten your seatbelt because this one's a doozy." During the next half hour or so I ran through all the major events that made up my life over the past several months. I told him about my walk, about meeting Zootie, about the list, and about all the people who were on the list. And, finally, I told him about my place on the list and my projected date of death just a month away. I told it all with a detachment that masked the true emotions that were roiling under the surface. "So that's my story," I said as I finished off my third drink. "What would you do if you were in my shoes?"

He sat, seemingly stunned into silence, for several moments but then eventually found his voice. "Either you're one hell of a story-teller or you've got a pretty nasty bull by the horns mister."

"I've never been much of a story-teller."

"Then I would just say this to you: if your life has come down to a matter of days, then the *last* place I would be is here in this bar getting drunk with a bunch of strangers."

Even in my drunken state his words cut right to my core. I thought about poor Brent Haberman and how he had spent his final days - drunk and desperate - and I felt a cold fear fill my stomach. *I didn't want to end up like that!* I looked down at the drink in front of me and pushed it across the table. "Here, I'm leaving this drink in your able hands. You're absolutely right with what you just said, and I'm going to remedy that situation right now." I got up from the table and felt everything spinning around me, forcing me back into my seat. I took a deep breath to clear my head and tried again, this time managing to get to my feet.

"You're not going to be driving, are you?" the man asked me.

"Nope, just walking." I took a step and had to grab the back of a chair to catch my balance. "Or rather, staggering would be more like it."

"Do you need some help?"

"No thanks. Like I said before, my flight is going to be a solo flight."

"Good luck with all of it," he said. I turned and saw him smiling warmly and reached out and shook his hand.

"Thanks for your advice - you don't know how much that meant to me."

"No problem. I hope it all works out for you."

With that, I staggered out the door and that was the last I saw of the nameless man. I made my way back to my hotel room and threw myself on the bed. I closed my eyes and felt like I was on a ship at sea, in a very violent storm. As I adjusted to the motion, a moving collage of thoughts and feelings swirled through my head; I didn't linger on any of them for long, but rather just let them float on by like tiny thought bubbles.

A nudge of guilt for not having contacted Trish.

A small dart of anger at Zootie for not telling me about my place on the list.

A passing breeze of nostalgia for my old, boring life back in Boston.

A larger wind of regret for having let down Bowler.

Then came the main attraction, sweeping in like an emotional tornado, cutting a wide swath through my insides, picking up every other thought and emotion and tossing them aside as if they were weightless.

Death....*my death!*

Eternal blackness.

End of everything.

My stomach began to ache as it had never ached before. My heart pounded so hard that it echoed in my ears. I felt nauseous and yet I felt powerless to move. The cadence of my heart made me think back to my "March of the Dead" nightmare that had plagued me as a child. Thump, thump…thump, thump…I could see the faces of the dead marching in front of my mind's eye.

Bill and Ruth Cooper.

Toby Liebman.

Brent.

Hannah.

Bowler.

Hy.

They were all dead now. Buried, gone forever. A huge lump formed in my throat that threatened to choke off my air supply. I tried to shake my head and dislodge the images in my brain, but it was no use; they were like molasses, oozing through my mind and covering every part of my brain with thick, sticky blackness.

Then I thought about the little child - nine-year-old Danny Barnes - who had huddled himself under his covers, hoping to hide from the sinister darkness and the unrelenting march of the dead. So young, so helpless, and so very, very scared. It was then that the large, seemingly impenetrable dam that I'd had in place my entire adult life finally cracked; tears trickled down my face, slowly at first, as I started to cry for that poor boy. Once the tears started to flow, however, there was no stopping them. The dam began to crumble inside of me and, as it crumbled, the rush of emotions came faster and stronger. I cried long and hard for that frightened child, curled up and shaking under his blankets.

My cries soon became wails as I thought again about all the unfortunate souls who had been on the list. I cried for all of them; honest tears, from my soul, that fell like a hard rain on my insides, washing away all pretense and feelings of self-consciousness. My body convulsed with the tears, as if I couldn't get them out through my tear ducts fast enough. I felt the pressure building in my chest as I heaved and sobbed like a little child.

Then my mind suddenly shifted to thoughts of myself - a man who was being denied life just as he was starting to live it. It felt like more than I could bear and yet my mind locked in on the images and I cried for every one of them: my family, my friends, my memories, my dreams, my physical self, that gets to see, taste and feel. All of that would be dying with me in just a few weeks. The life that was Dan Barnes would cease to be. Forever. And it would all be traded in for...what?

I had always thought that I had a strong belief in an after-life and yet, at that moment, lying there with death lodged in my throat, I couldn't muster any comfort from those beliefs. They seemed like nothing more than cold, non-consoling ideas, made of paper rather than of the solid rock that I was seeking. I felt alone.

The feelings of aloneness - alone with the darkness and with the constant specter of death - began to deepen. Then an even deeper feeling, a feeling I'd never felt before, gripped my heart. It was as if all the tears that I'd just shed had simply washed a layer of dust off some larger, dormant feelings deep inside of me. These feelings had long tentacles that wrapped themselves around my soul and wouldn't let go. I felt an icy, all-consuming fear take over my body. I began shaking uncontrollably, just like that little boy did many years ago. Desperation filled my mind as I felt like I was free-falling into a bottomless pit of darkness and there was nothing I could grab onto to slow my descent. Fear and desperation were the shackles that bound my arms and legs as I fell faster and faster into the pit.

I pulled myself up out of the bed and bolted into the bathroom. I splashed handfuls of cold water in my face and down my neck, hoping to somehow break the hold that was on me. I looked into the mirror. "What the hell is happening to me?" I murmured to my image, half hoping for some sort of response. None came. Walking back into the room, I felt the deep tugging return to my insides. The octopus of fear had a hold of me and was pulling me down into his dark lair, causing me to feel frightened beyond words. The darkness that was enveloping me was more than just a simple lack of light; it was tangible - I felt it on my skin, I could feel it going into my lungs, and I tasted it on my tongue. I just stood in the middle of the room shivering uncontrollably, frozen in place by fear.

"What's happening to me?!?!" I finally shouted in desperation, the tears continuing their constant stream down my face.

CHAPTER 49

The next week or so was a blur of walking, crying, agonizing and soul-searching; I had no awareness of where one day ended and the other began. The anguish and distress became so overwhelming at times that I thought I'd never pull out of it. On more than one occasion I seriously considered renting a car and just driving; driving so far and so fast that the fear and the darkness would be left behind - finding some distant place where the list and Project HOPE and death would be a distant memory.

I also thought about things that had never so much as entered my brain before in my life. Things like suicide. I'd never tasted fear and desperation so strongly that the thought of taking my own life had some appeal, but I entertained that very thought several times over the next week. I saw very clearly why Ruth and Bill Cooper had decided to take matters into their own hands and approach death on their own terms. If I hadn't been so damned frightened of the very thing that I was looking to for relief I might have followed through on some of those thoughts. Instead, I continued to wallow in the fear and self-pity that enveloped me, and I struggled with overwhelming urges to either run as far and as fast as I could or sit on a bar stool and try to just dull the pain and sadness that I was feeling.

But then I would think of Brent. I would get an indelible image of poor, frightened, pathetic Brent, sitting on the floor of a hotel room, surrounded by whiskey bottles, whimpering his way into the next world. That was *not* how I wanted to spend my final moments - I knew that with all my heart - and that image provided me with strength when I felt myself faltering. *"I'm not a Runner...I'm not a Runner..."* became my mantra as I struggled on the wrestling mat with my multi-tentacled opponent named fear.

CHAPTER 50

As I was walking down by the waterfront one day at the
end of my Week of Blackness, I felt my first glimmer of hope.
It was a rare clear and sunny day in November in Seattle, and I
noticed that I truly *felt* the sun on my face that day. I had been
so numb and oblivious to anything besides the pain in my belly
for so long that the sensation came as a pleasant surprise. I
closed my eyes and turned my face towards the sun, wallowing
in its warmth and feeling its energy course through my body.
Then I heard a child crying and turned to look in the direction
of the sound. The child had fallen and skinned his legs and the
mother was down on one knee tending to his bloodied knees. I
felt my insides ache for both mother and child at that moment.

Continuing my walk, I took notice of many similar mini-
dramas being played out all around me. I seemed to absorb the
feelings from each situation - the pain, the pleasure, and all the
emotions. It was as if I had an invisible pipeline that allowed
me to tap into everything that was going on around me. I felt
so alive! I made my way to a bench that overlooked the sound
below, as well as the Olympics beyond, and sat down. I closed
my eyes and took in the ocean air; it filled my lungs with crisp,
delicious air and I felt like I wanted to lap it up like a thirsty
animal.

Bowler's face popped into my head and, instead of feeling
guilt, I felt love and compassion at his memory. I also felt an
invisible switch click on in my head, and I suddenly saw

Bowler's actions, and heard his words, with a new level of understanding. I saw his desire to keep life on his own terms and to live the life he thought he was meant to live right up to the end. I thought too about his advice that he had given to me - twice actually - to ignore the barking dog that is my mind and wander into the cave of my soul. He was right, I saw that now, as I had been staying away from the dark parts of my soul my entire life because I was afraid of the guard dog that is my mind. I saw now that my mind was indeed the enemy and that I needed to tame it in order to get to the "good stuff" down in the cave. I smiled and felt a wave of gratitude for Bowler and his words.

Then I flashed on Hy's face and I felt a deep appreciation for her kindness and all the sacrifices she made on behalf of me and the residents of HOPE House. Tears formed in my eyes as I thought about my dear, departed friend; they were not the tears of gut-wrenching anguish that had been my constant companion over the past many days, but rather they were the softer tears of love and joy and they fell gently to my shirt. Her final words came back to me in a rush and I smiled at how prophetic they had become: *"Follow the tears,"* she had told me that night, *"and they'll lead you like liquid breadcrumbs to the doorstep of truth deep inside of you."* I silently thanked her for her words of guidance.

I thought too about Brent and how he had, indirectly, taught me an invaluable lesson about how I wanted to die. I said a silent prayer for his soul and thanked him for the lesson he had given me. I also felt the pain and torment that had caused Ruth and Bill Cooper to take their own lives, and I said another silent prayer for them and for their daughter, Ellen.

I also saw how silly, naive and arrogant I had been all these months - thinking for even a moment that I could help these poor people find answers to their struggles regarding death. I saw that they were just being polite, allowing me to keep intact my self-serving, deluded notion that I was somehow being helpful. The truly funny part was that they were actually helping *me* all this time - helping me to prepare for this moment when I would be faced with the very same questions that had dogged *them*. I chuckled at my stupidity.

Thoughts of the living also crowded my mind. First there was Jennie, with her endless questions, quirky observations and original, yet effective, little therapeutic games. I smiled as I thought about her paper dragons and her mattress and baseball bat in the basement. I thought about Zootie and how his incredible courage and tireless support had changed so many lives. I then whispered a silent apology to him for my angry thoughts from earlier as I saw that he deserved nothing but my sincere thanks. And, finally, I thought about Trish. I saw what an amazingly kind and generous person she was and how lucky I'd been to have her in my life if even for a short while. I began to weep for the future that we would never have together.

After the tears had subsided, and I had wiped my face, I got up from the bench and continued my walk. A smile spread across my face as I noticed that the thick, dark fog had finally lifted from my heart and the sunshine of life was bathing me in its warmth. It felt like my soul had stepped out of the shadows for the first time in my life and it was now dancing in the sunshine. Incredible joy filled my heart and four words burst forth from my lips, almost involuntarily: *"Life is goddamned good!!!"* I screamed as loud as I could, not caring at all about the reactions from passersby.

CHAPTER 51

That night I fell into a deep sleep for the first time in days. In the early morning hours I had a visitor come into my room; I would say that I dreamt it but, like Bowler's earlier visit, it didn't feel like a dream.

"Hi Danny," Hy said to me. I saw her as clear as could be, and she was talking to me, but her lips never moved; it was as if we were reading each other's mind. I felt elated to see her again.

"Hy!" I said excitedly, "I'm so happy to see you!"

"We'll be seeing more of each other soon enough Danny," she said warmly, "but for now I just want to tell you a couple of things."

"What is it Hy?"

"First of all, don't worry so much about death Danny - when your time comes, you'll see that there's nothing to be afraid of." She smiled so warmly that I felt tears welling in my eyes as she spoke. "And the last thing I want to say to you Danny is to go home - they need you at Hope House right now."

"Okay Hy, I will," I promised. "But there are so many things I want to ask you; can't you stay a while longer?" I then noticed that she was joined by Bowler on one side of her and my father on the other side. They were both smiling warmly - almost benevolently - too.

"You'll get all of your questions answered soon enough Danny," she assured me. "For now, you must take care of the people you care about the most." Those were her final words as all three of them waved to me and then disappeared.

The next thing I remember is waking up and looking over at the clock: it was 5:00am. I jumped out of bed, threw on my clothes and bolted out the door. It was time to go home.

CHAPTER 52

I jumped on the first bus heading north to the Wallingford area and, while sitting in the bus, I realized that Jennie's DOD was the following day. I felt tremendous relief at that realization. After having let Bowler down, I silently vowed to not let anyone else down like that again during my last few weeks of life.

The bus dropped me in the center of Wallingford, and I ran the last several blocks to Hope House. I burst through the front door and was disappointed to see that I was greeted by an empty house - nobody was up and about yet. Before I could consider what to do next, Zootie came walking down the stairs.

"Dan!" he shouted. "Why if you aren't a sight for sore eyes!" I noticed immediately that his face had changed considerably from the last time I had seen him - gone were the tired, contempt-filled eyes and back were the lively, compassionate eyes that had always been Zootie's trademark. I dashed up the stairs and gave him a big hug.

"I'm sorry for running out on you like that," I murmured. "It won't happen again."

I pulled out of the embrace and saw that Zootie was crying. "Let's go sit down for a few minutes Danny, I've got a whopper of an apology to give to you." We walked down the stairs, went into the living room, and sat down next to each other in two of the chairs. My mind was swimming with things I wanted to say, and questions I wanted to ask, but I let him talk first. "I've been doing a lot of thinking since you ran out of here a little over a week ago Danny and I was hoping that I would get this opportunity to say some things to you before it was too late." He took a deep breath and, as he exhaled, a smile inched its way across his face. "First of all, Danny, I want to tell you that your name is not on that list." His words didn't register with me at first and so he repeated them: "Did you hear me? Your name isn't on that list!"

"How can that be?" I murmured. "I saw my name on there and…" He cut me off.

"What you saw on there was a name that began with "Da" and ended with an "s" and nothing more." He stuck his hand out for me to shake. "I'm not sure we've ever had the pleasure of being *formally* introduced: my name is David Gibbons, but my friends call me Zootie." He smiled at me as I struggled with all of the new information that he was throwing at me.

"I don't see what that has to do with…" I began. Then it hit me. Hard. *David Gibbons,* I thought - *it begins with "Da" and ends with an "s" just like…* "Are you trying tell me that it's *your* name on the list?" I blurted out.

The smile never left his face. "I am indeed."

"But why didn't you tell me that back when I confronted you with it?"

The smile left his face, replaced with a deep frown. "Because I was feeling sorry for myself Danny, simple as that. Brent's sister had thrown me for a bit of a loop at his funeral and it took me a few days to sort through everything. That slap on the face got me to wondering if I was doing the right thing with this list and, when you confronted me with the original list, I got a little defensive at your anger and thought I'd give you a little counter-punch by making you think that you were on it." He reached over and put his hand on my shoulder. "I didn't mean for you to *really* believe it for more than a minute or two, but you dashed off before I could set things straight. I'm truly sorry for that Danny."

Emotions that I couldn't even separate began competing for my attention simultaneously - confusion, relief, exhilaration - but the emotion that stood out in front, leading the charge, was compassion. I felt strong compassion for my friend Zootie and all that he had to shoulder regarding this list. I gave him a warm smile and patted his hand on my shoulder. "Don't even give it a second thought Zootie, because you know what?"

"What?" he asked as the playful glint returned to his eyes.

"Remember when you told me how that car accident you had many years ago was the best thing that ever happened to you?"

"Yes, I do."

"Well, this little car accident of mine was the best thing that ever happened to *me*. I feel like I've finally woken up after more than forty years of snoozing, and I finally get it!"

"What is it that you get?"

"Everything! Why I'm here at Hope House, why people on the list have done what they've done, why death isn't as big of a deal as I've always made it out to be...everything!"

Zootie flashed his paternal smile. "I'm happy for you Danny. And, for what it's worth, I can see the difference in you."

"Thanks."

"I had an epiphany of my own shortly after you bolted from the front porch."

"What was that?"

"That I'm nothing more than the messenger with this list. All I can do is give people the information and then it's up to them to decide what it is they want to do with that information. Poor Brent decided that he wanted to keep hiding behind a bottle of whiskey and, while that's very sad, it was his choice to make and there wasn't a damned thing I could do about it."

"I couldn't agree with you more Zootie. When I thought that I was on the list I did blame *you* for a short while." Zootie shrugged, as if to say *"of course!"* but I raised my finger for emphasis. "But! Then I saw that you had nothing to do with what I felt - it was all about *my* fear and my own unwillingness to really look at that fear." I smiled. "Finally realizing *that* was what started all of the *real* fun."

He nodded. "I'll bet."

I felt a thousand more questions bubbling up inside of me and I couldn't ignore them any longer. "So, are you ready now to give me some straight answers about this list?"

"Anything you want to know."

"Okay, question one - where the *hell* did this list *really* come from?"

He sat back in his chair and folded his hands behind his head, a broad grin dominating his face. "Good question. The short answer is that it came from *me*. The longer answer is that I don't have a clue where it came from." He saw my puzzled look and continued. "A little over a year ago I was messing around with hypnosis and past life regression with a woman I know and one day, as I was coming out of a trance, I started babbling these names, addresses and dates. She didn't know what to do at first but then she clicked on a tape recorder that she had and recorded everything I said." He nodded in the direction of the study. "When I was done, I had dictated that entire list that's hanging in the other room." He shook his head. "Only the funny thing is, I don't remember saying any of it or where those names came from." He shrugged. "So, in the end, it's as much of a mystery to me as it is to you."

"So you've known all along that you were on the list and that you were scheduled to die in December?"

"Yup." He leaned forward. "'Course, you have to understand that it took me a while to fully accept the truth behind this whole thing." He laughed a loud laugh. "Even for someone like me, who's had a chance to peek behind death's curtain, this was a bit of a mind-blower."

"That's for damned sure!" I quickly agreed.

"But, as I told you before, I eventually saw that this list was deadly accurate and, no matter *where* it came from, it couldn't be ignored. I knew that."

"So why did you keep your place on the list a secret?"

"Because I didn't want to have to deal with everyone's pity and such."

"Does Ren know that you're on the list?"

His eyes went to a corner of the room and I could see them misting over. "Nope."

"Why not?"

"Same reason as I said before."

"But don't you think that..." I was interrupted by a slam of the front door. I looked over my shoulder and saw Trish and Jennie walking into the front hallway. I stood up, so they could see me, and Jennie saw me first. Her eyes went wide with excitement and then, just as quickly, they narrowed to slits as a look of anger took over her face. She turned and headed for the basement stairs without saying a word. Trish hung her coat on a nearby hook and then turned when she heard the slam of the basement door. Our eyes met and I felt like a tractor beam locked onto me and pulled me in her direction.

"Dan..." she whispered and then we both lunged towards each other. I grabbed her and pulled her into a full embrace, our bodies fitting together like two broken pieces that were once again whole. We both started crying and I pulled her in even tighter.

"Trish, I'm so sorry that I ran off like that," I whispered into her ear. "I know that you were probably worried, but..." She pulled back and put her finger over my lips. I looked into her blue, water-filled eyes and I felt my heart dance with joy.

"Shhh...Dan," she said softly. "No apologies. Zootie told me everything and I understand completely." She smiled a smile so warm and loving that I began to sob like a baby. I felt so much love for her at that moment that I was sure my heart would just pop out of my chest. I kissed her tenderly several times and wallowed in the feel of her lips and the feel of her body pressed against mine.

I pulled back, put my hands on her shoulders, and looked deep into her eyes. "There is one more thing that I have to tell you, Trish."

"What's that Dan?"

My body began to shake and my voice quavered but I got it out. "I love you Trish."

Her face contorted, signaling the rush of more oncoming tears, as she said, "I love you too, Dan."

I thought my face would explode with the pressure of the tears I felt bubbling up, but I managed to finish what I had to say before the deluge hit. "I realized so many things this past week, but one of the most important things was just how lucky I was to have a person like you in my life." I reached over and wiped the tears from her face. "You're such a kind, thoughtful and beautiful person Trish and I can't believe my good fortune that you chose *me* to be with." The tears then won out and I wept uncontrollably as I pulled her into another embrace. We stood there like that - hugging and rocking gently to our own unspoken rhythm - for a while, until Zootie interrupted with a loud clearing of his throat.

"Ahem!" he said loudly. "Before you two forget where you are and start doing God-knows-what right here in the living room, I thought I might remind you about a certain person who has a certain big day tomorrow and who has a few certain feelings that she has to work through before that certain big day." He looked at us both and raised his eyebrows as if to say, *"do you know what I mean?"*

"Oh my gosh - Jennie!" Trish blurted out. She grabbed my hand and pulled me over to the couch where we sat down side-by-side. She held my hand in her lap and sat sideways so we could face one another as she spoke. "Jennie has had a bad week this past week Dan, and I want to bring you up-to-date on everything before you talk to her." Trish took a deep breath to compose her thoughts before continuing. "First of all, she's *extremely* upset with you. She felt very disappointed that you turned out to be a Runner, as she calls it, and feels like you've completely forgotten about some promise that you made to her. She didn't tell me what it was, but she said that you had given her your word and that it looked like you weren't going to *keep* your word."

I knew immediately what she was talking about - my promise to be at her funeral no matter what - and I knew that I would have much bridge-building to do with Jennie before tomorrow.

"The other thing that hit her hard," Trish continued, "was Dave Smith's death."

"But she knew that he was on the list," I pointed out.

"That's true, she did. But what she *wasn't* ready to deal with was Dave's decision to try to *test* the list a couple of days before his DOD by jumping off a building."

"What?"

She nodded. "He wanted to see if he could kill himself on a different day in order to prove the list wrong, but what he did was prove exactly the *opposite*. It turned out that the building he chose wasn't quite high enough to kill him, but it did a darned good job of breaking a bunch of bones and busting up his liver and other organs. He survived the jump - barely - and then spent the next couple of days in the hospital, never fully regaining consciousness, until they declared him brain dead two days later, right on his designated DOD."

"That poor guy," I mumbled.

"Yeah, it was pretty awful. Jennie took it really hard, because she felt like they were supposed to have a couple more days to be together and he just took those away without even talking to her about it. She was pretty devastated."

"Man, that girl is getting it from all sides, isn't she?"

"That's not all of it. Apparently, her parents have been putting a lot of pressure on her to move back home and get her life going in a direction that they deem suitable, so they're not even close to being where she wants them to be regarding her DOD tomorrow."

"That's too bad. I know how much she wants them to be on board with this whole thing."

"Yeah, she does, but it doesn't look like it's going to happen that way unfortunately."

"Anything else I should know about?"

Trish looked around before she spoke and then she lowered her voice to a whisper. "We've been getting some phone calls and visits from Bill and Ruth Cooper's daughter, Ellen, but I think she's still just trying to deal with their deaths." She nodded towards Zootie. "The video that they made with Zootie helped a lot, because she got to hear from their own mouths why they chose to take their own lives, but she still just plain misses them and is having a hard time reconciling the fact that they're gone now."

"Does she suspect that we had anything to do with it?"

"No, not at all."

Our attention was quickly diverted by a loud banging noise that came from the direction of the kitchen. All three of us got up to go investigate. We walked into the kitchen and found Red Wiggins in there standing at the stove. He was just turning it on and had an empty pan in his hand. "Just starting up some breakfast," he said quickly, almost nervously, "can I interest anyone in some eggs?"

We all just shook our heads - all three of us trying to make sense out of Red being in the kitchen that early - and then walked back out of the kitchen. "I just don't trust that guy," Zootie whispered to nobody in particular as we headed back down the hallway.

CHAPTER 53

After finishing my conversation with Trish and Zootie, I made my way downstairs to find Jennie. She was in the darkroom, the door was open, and she was pulling pictures off the drying line. "Hey there," I said as I walked up to her. No answer. I sat down in a small chair in the far corner of the room and planned to start babbling, hoping that I would stumble onto some words that might get her to start talking to me. As it turned out, it took far fewer words than I thought it would.

"Listen Jennie, I'm sorry that..." I began, but she cut me off sharply.

She wheeled around and put her finger right in my face as she spoke. "No, *you* listen Dan! I've only got a matter of hours left to live so I don't have time to be pretendin' that I'm mad at you and that's why I'm just gonna give it to you straight."

I nodded meekly.

"Truth is, I'm hurt more than mad." I saw the huge tears begin to form in the corners of her eyes. "Everybody that I care about seems to be leavin' me right now and I'm just not sure that I can handle all of this alone." I stood up and took a step towards her to hug her, but she stopped me with a stiff arm in my chest. "Don't you dare hug me yet! Not until you *swear* to me - on everything that's important to you - that you won't go MIA on me again!"

I stepped back and looked her square in the eye. "I swear to you Jennie that I'm back for good and that I won't leave your side. Not now, and not at your funeral." I made a crossing motion on my chest. "I swear it."

"Okay," she sobbed, "*now* you can hug me."

I stepped forward again and pulled her into a hug. I stood there, squeezing her tight and rubbing her back, until the tears eventually subsided. She pulled back after her final sobs and said, "Okay, that's enough of *that!*" She forced a small smile. "Who's got time for whimpering when I've got a death to plan?" She turned around and grabbed the pile of pictures stacked on a shelf. She straightened them all out and then handed me the pile. "I want you to have these," she said as she continued to wipe her face.

I took the stack of pictures from her. "Thank you."

"I also want you to have this." She reached around in her back pocket and pulled out her omnipresent journal and handed it to me. I could see the hurt and sadness in her eyes as she held the book out in front of her; she looked at it as a child would look at a favorite doll that they were being forced to give away.

"Jennie, I'm not sure that I'm the best person for you to give this to."

"Sure you are. Now that I know that you're not goin' anywhere you can keep adding to it for me." She nodded at the book that was still extended in front of her. "I even have a bunch of new questions already lined up in there for you. All you have to do is ask 'em, and then write down the answers. Simple."

I reluctantly reached out and took the book from her, feeling its weight in my hand much as I had felt the weight of the dying woman's locket many months earlier. "I'll do my best," was all I could think of to say.

"There's one more thing that I wanna give you - you'll find it tucked inside the front cover of the book."

I opened the book and pulled out a folded piece of paper. Opening it, I saw that it was some type of legal document. Reading further, I couldn't believe my eyes. "Jennie," I said, stunned, "this can't be what I think it is."

"Yep, it is. My grandpa left me a pretty substantial trust fund when he passed away a few years back and I want you guys to have it all."

I looked up from the paper, my mouth hanging open. "But Jennie, this is two and a half million dollars!"

"I know," she replied calmly. "Bop was pretty loaded."

I just shook my head, unable to comprehend what was in front of me. "Don't you have a cousin or somebody that this should go to?"

"Nope. I told you before, everybody I care about is right here in Hope House, so why not leave it with the people I care about the most?"

"What about your parents?"

She scoffed. "My parents?!? First off, they're already loaded - thanks to Bop - and secondly, they don't give a shit about me so why should I give a shit about them?" A sudden thought then seemed to enter her head. "But that reminds me. They're gonna be apeshit when they find out about all this, so I just wanna warn you so you can be ready for it."

"Apeshit? What exactly does that mean?" I asked suspiciously.

She waved her hand. "Oh, you know - lawyers and stuff, trying to prove that you had a gun to my head when I signed this." She pointed at the document. "That's why I got the whole thing notarized and had two witnesses sign it there at the bottom. I had a lawyer look at it and he said it was airtight."

"Who was your lawyer, if I may ask?"

She smiled. "Zootie."

I rolled my eyes. "Great!"

She turned very serious. "I want you guys to do something important with this money, Dan. I had all kinds of dreams for it before I knew about this list and all." Her head sank as she whispered, "Now all those dreams seem pretty shallow and unimportant."

I thought back to a conversation Jennie and I had a few weeks earlier. "Don't you worry Jennie - I'll make sure this money is spent in a way that assures you'll never be forgotten."

She looked up and her tear-streaked face brightened. "Thanks Dan. I knew I could count on you."

I laughed. "For a while there you probably weren't quite so sure about that."

"No, that's not true. Deep down I knew that you'd come back and do the right thing." She smiled. "You're one of those guys who's doomed to always do the right thing."

"I don't know about that, Jennie."

"It's true. Me, on the other hand, I'm destined to always be the fuck up who can't seem to get *anything* right."

I reached over and rubbed her upper arm. "Don't even *think* that Jennie, much less *say* it. You're one of the few people I've met in my life who I truly respect and admire. You have a heart as big as the whole outdoors and you know how to use it Jennie. That's a tremendous gift. Look at what you did for Dave Smith and so many others on the list." I caught myself short and swallowed hard when I realized what I'd said.

"Yeah," she said quietly, "look what I did. I pushed him off a damn building!"

I scrambled to find the right words. "You did not Jennie! You saved that boy, just as surely as," I took her chin gently in my hand and lifted her face so that I was looking in her eyes as I spoke, "you saved *me*."

"How the hell did I save *you*?"

I sat down in the chair and motioned for her to sit next to me. "I got to do a whole lot of thinking over this past week. As you already know, thinking about death as an impending reality is a whole lot different than thinking about it in the abstract, as a dinner conversation or a subject in a book."

Jennie nodded vigorously. "That's for *damn* sure!"

"Getting past all of my defenses, fears and other gatekeepers, what was it that I truly believed?" I stared off as I repeated the question, "What did I truly believe?" My eyes snapped back to Jennie's. "As I struggled with that question, I saw most of my previously held beliefs just whither away under the harsh spotlight of my pending death. They were like straw houses that got blown away in a storm of fear and doubt." I paused as I considered my next words. Tears formed in my eyes as the words of truth percolated to the surface. "What I ended up seeing was that the relationships in my life were the only thing that truly mattered, and I saw that I'd done a terrifically lousy job at them throughout the bulk of my life. All I could see were my own selfish, fear-based needs and that prevented me from doing the one thing that I was sent here to do." I smiled a contorted, emotion-filled smile. "Love."

I took a deep breath and continued. "But then, sitting alone in that hotel room, I realized that I'd been surrounded by the best teachers a guy could ask for and I didn't even know it. People like Zootie, Trish, Hy and *you*." I pointed at her for emphasis. "You know what it's all about and you show it every day with how you help people and give so generously to everyone around you." I scowled and wagged my finger at her. "So, don't you go saying that you're a fuck up because you are far, far from that Jennie. You're an amazing young woman who has helped to change my life and I can only hope that if I ever have a daughter that she would be just like you."

I looked over and saw that the tears were flowing unabated down Jennie's face. "I think those were about the nicest words anyone's ever said about me," she said softly.

"Well, every one of them is true."

She lunged forward and wrapped her arms around my head and neck and squeezed tight. "Thank you, Dan," she whispered in my ear. "That was the nicest going away present anyone could have given me."

CHAPTER 54

Later that afternoon Trish, Jennie and I were walking back to our car in the Ballard area after paying a last visit to Jennie's grandmother. "She seems like quite a woman," I said to Jennie as we walked.

"Yeah, she is," Jennie agreed. "Her and Bop have always been my only real allies in this fucked up family of mine."

"How old is she Jennie?" Trish asked.

"She'll be eighty-five next week. That's why I dropped off an early birthday gift for her."

"What's with this "Bop" thing?" I asked.

Jennie chuckled. "I had a hard time saying the word "grandpa" when I was a kid; it always seemed to come out sounding like "boppa." So I just shortened it to "Bop" later on and it just kinda stuck."

"Your grandmother seems to really love you a lot Jennie," Trish said.

"Yeah, I guess I should feel lucky about that." She stopped walking for a moment and looked at us both sideways. "I just can't figure out how a couple of great people like that could have had a kid like my mother."

"Strange how that happens sometimes," I said. "Look at Hy and the daughter *she* had for goodness sakes."

Jennie chuckled and started walking again. "Yeah boy, that Mandy bitch is definitely no chip off the old block." Jennie stopped again and froze, staring forward. "Hold on just a minute..." she mumbled and then dashed off. Trish and I watched her as she ran to a car a half a block away and put money into a parking meter. We then watched as a meter maid came out from behind the car with her ticket book in her hand. Trish and I walked up to them as Jennie was still pleading her case, which we both thought odd, because the car didn't belong to any of us.

"Come on, you gotta cut me some slack here," Jennie pleaded. "If my Dad sees another ticket, he'll take away my keys for sure!"

The meter maid looked Jennie up and down, the disapproving eyes never losing their glare. "All right," she said reluctantly, "I'll give you a warning this time, but pay more attention to your meter next time." The mini-lecture completed, she closed her ticket book and climbed back into her small cart.

"What was that all about?" I asked as the little cart pulled away from the curb.

Jennie smiled. "I just didn't think it appropriate that *anyone* get a ticket on my last day on Earth!" Her eyes continued to watch the meter maid's cart and then she murmured "oh,oh..." and was off like a shot. She had seen the meter maid pull over to ticket another car farther up the street, but Jennie managed to get to the meter and pump in some coins before the woman had time to climb out of her cart. This little cat and mouse game continued up the street for several blocks, and with each encounter we could see that the meter maid was getting more and more upset with Jennie. Trish and I hustled to keep up with her.

Finally, the meter maid pulled over to the curb, got out, and lit into Jennie. "Just what is it that you think you're doing young lady?" she asked with a definite edge to her voice.

Jennie smiled sweetly. "Just trying to help out my fellow human beings any way I can."

"If you don't stop this immediately, I'm afraid that I'm going to have to call a squad car."

"Why? Is there some law against putting money into other people's parking meters?"

The woman glared at Jennie without saying a word - though I could see that she had many words she would *like* to say to Jennie - and then with a small "hmph" sound she wheeled around and headed back to her cart. She started it up and bolted from the curb without another word and we watched as she went around the next corner on what looked like just two wheels.

"That was fun, huh?" Jennie said with a wide grin as she turned back to us.

"I'm not so sure that your friend the meter maid would use that particular word," Trish said.

"Are you done with your mission of mercy Jennie Hood," I kidded, "or do you want to head down to the waterfront now and start paying strangers' ferry tolls?"

"Hey! You know what," she said with a snap of her fingers, "that's not a bad idea - let's do it!"

Trish and I looked at each other, not knowing if she was serious or not. "Jennie, I'm not sure if..." I began.

She laughed out loud. "I'm just kiddin' with ya Dan. I'm done doin' my good deeds, we can head on back to Hope House now. I've got a few more letters I have to write." With that, we walked the last couple of blocks to the car, climbed in - with me at the wheel of Trish's car - and headed back to the Wallingford area and Hope House.

We hadn't gotten far before we hit a traffic jam caused by a car accident farther up the road. Being new to the area still, I didn't know many roads other than the main ones, so I resigned myself to just waiting it out as the tow trucks drove past us to prepare clearing the roadway. "Just take this left here," Jennie pointed from the backseat. "It's kind of a roundabout way, but by the looks of things it'll be quicker than just sitting here."

I took the left and followed her ensuing directions through a series of turns that eventually put us into an old warehouse section. I noticed too as we drove that the neighborhoods began looking more and more rundown. Finally, Jennie admitted what I'd already sensed: we were lost.

"Sorry about that guys," she apologized. "I've taken this route a couple of times in the past, but I guess I missed one of the turns."

"That's all right," Trish reassured her, "we'll find somebody and just ask for some directions."

I looked around. "I don't see any signs of life around here right now. This is like some scene in a movie following the apocalypse."

Trish looked out her window. "Yeah, this is definitely the low rent district."

A car then suddenly pulled out of an alleyway and came to an abrupt stop in front of me. I slammed on my brakes to avoid running into him. He then backed up until our bumpers touched and then, before I could even think of what to do next, another car pulled out of the same alleyway and pulled up right behind me. I was boxed in.

"Car jackers!" Jennie screamed as she looked out the back window and saw two large men getting out of the rear car with guns in their hands.

I wheeled around, my heart beating wildly, and saw the same two men. My mind raced, looking for a way out of our situation. Without thinking, I pressed my foot on the gas pedal and tried to push the car in front of us enough so that I could try to maneuver our car out of the box we were in. But Trish's small car was no match for the big car in front of us. The tires spun and I smelled the smoke coming from both the overworked engine and the squealing tires as I tried in vain to move the big car that blocked our path. Then a face appeared in my window - a smiling face waving a gun - and I took my foot off the gas pedal. He pointed the gun at my face and motioned for us to get out of the car. I saw no other alternative but to comply, so I put the car in park, turned off the car, and climbed out of the car with Trish and Jennie.

"Dat's better," he said calmly as we huddled together next to the car. "Ain't no use tryin' to git away mister - no use dyin' fer a piece o' metal, huh?" He smiled a confident, yet wicked, smile and motioned to one of the other men to get into Trish's car.

I heard Jennie mumble next to me; "Nobody's going to be stealing *my* friend's car today..." and before I could reach out to grab her, she ran forward and jumped on the back of the man trying to get into Trish's car. "That's not your car you asshole!" she screamed as the man fell forward with her added weight. He hit his head on the car door and then, dazed, began cursing wildly at Jennie.

"Get this bitch off my back!" he yelled to his friends as Jennie pounded on his head. I stepped forward one step, ready to jump into the fray to help Jennie, but the smiling man put his gun in my nose.

"Just stay right the hell where ya are mister," he hissed. I looked over at him and, at that moment, he reminded me a lot of my old friend Eddie from the deli back in Pennsylvania; same slicked hair, same arm full of tattoos, and same dark smile. I stepped backward and instinctively pulled Trish in behind me, to put myself between her and the man's gun. Then a gunshot rang out and everything stopped.

My head jerked to the right, in the direction of the gunshot, and I saw Jennie falling limply from the man's back. "What the hell did you do?" the smiling man shouted.

"I told ya to get her off my back," the other man said with a shrug, "but nobody seemed to wanna help me, so I helped myself." He held his still smoking gun up for the smiling man to see.

Everyone seemed to look down at Jennie at the same time and life suddenly went into slow motion. Blood oozed from a hole in her side and she lay on the road with a wide-eyed look of disbelief on her face. Trish screamed out and fell on her knees to Jennie's side. I looked over at the smiling man - his gun still pointing at my face - and he turned his head, so his eyes met mine. I could see it clear as could be in his eyes - he was thinking about shooting me right there in the street. A second passed - a second that took an hour to pass - and I didn't break eye contact with him, for fear that to do so would mean a death sentence. Then I saw his eyes suddenly change. The smile returned to his face and he said to me, "Today's yer lucky day mister. You get to live." With that he yelled to the other men to climb back into their cars and, in an instant, they sped off with all three cars. We were left there, alone, in the middle of the street.

After finally exhaling, my attention turned immediately to Jennie. I dropped down to my knees and assessed her situation: blood was filling the street all around her and she seemed to be in shock. "We have to get her to a hospital *quickly*," Trish cried out. She was trying in vain to stop the bleeding, but I could see that Jennie would bleed to death very quickly unless we got her some help.

Then I remembered something. "She's got a cell phone," I yelled out. I'd seen Jennie use it many times, so I knew she had one. The question was, did she bring it with her. I searched her pockets desperately and finally found the phone in her front pocket. I took it out and quickly dialed 911.

The ambulance arrived in a matter of minutes and everything became a blur as they loaded her up and sped off to the hospital. We told the paramedics about our plight and they allowed us to ride in the ambulance with Jennie. I was wiping Jennie's blood from my hands in the back of the ambulance when I heard her speak for the first time since the shooting. I went to her side and bent down so I could hear her.

"What the hell happened?" she whispered quietly.

"You were shot Jennie and now we're taking you to the hospital," I told her as calmly as I could.

"Shot?!? she exclaimed. "Didn't those mother fuckers know that my day to die is *tomorrow* not *today?!?*"

"Guess not," I replied with a forced smile.

She labored to reach her hand down to the spot where the bullet had entered her side and, when she pulled it back, it was covered with blood. "Damn. Is this all *my* blood?"

"I'm afraid so Jennie."

She wiped the blood on her shirt almost nonchalantly and then asked, "Did they get Trish's car?"

"Don't worry about my car, Jennie," Trish said from behind me. "It was time for me to get a new one anyway."

Jennie forced a small, weak smile. "Glad I could help you out." Then her face suddenly turned serious. "This sure puts a crimp in my plans for today."

"What can we do for you Jennie?" I asked.

She turned so her eyes met mine and her voice became suddenly strong. "Whatever you do, don't you dare call my parents!"

"I won't, I promise," I assured her. "What else?"

Tears formed in her eyes and began dripping down the side of her face onto the gurney and her voice softened to a whisper. "Please remember your promise about my funeral Dan, no matter what kind of hell my parents might put you through."

I reached over and grabbed her hand and gave it a hard squeeze. "Don't worry Jennie - I *will* be there, you can count on it."

She squeezed my hand weakly. "Thank you, Dan." They were the last words Jennie would ever say to me.

The ambulance then came to an abrupt stop and everyone began moving at once. Trish and I just stayed out of the way as they pulled the gurney out of the ambulance and rushed Jennie into the hospital. We climbed out after Jennie had been taken away and tried to follow their path into the hospital. By the time we got through the doors they had disappeared around a corner, so we asked for directions to the emergency room and made our way there as quickly as we could. Once there, I pulled out Jennie's cell phone and called Hope House to let them know what had happened. Zootie answered.

"She *what?*!?" he exclaimed after I told him the grim news. "I'll be there as quick as I can," he said hurriedly, and hung up.

"Zootie's coming," I told Trish as I put the phone into my pocket.

"Good," she said, her eyes forward, "we may need the reinforcements."

CHAPTER 55

Jennie was in surgery for over an hour. The doctor came out, looking fatigued, and walked over to Trish and me. Zootie had just walked away for a bathroom break. "Mr. and Mrs. Morrissey?" he asked.

Trish and I looked at each other. "Uh, no," I replied slowly, "we actually..." I was interrupted by a loud voice behind me.

"They're actually the reason our poor daughter is lying in there fighting for her life!" the woman's voice shouted angrily. "Don't you *dare* say another word to these awful people!" She shoved her way around us and stood between us and the doctor. "I'm her mother and anything you have to say shall be said to *me*." She took the confused doctor's elbow and turned him around so that they began walking back towards the emergency room. She turned sideways one last time, so we could hear what she was saying, as she said, "Thank goodness *someone* had the decency to call her parents to let us know what happened to our little girl!"

"Well, I saw the emergency number in her wallet," the doctor stammered as he looked over his shoulder at us, "and so I had the nurse call you immediately."

That was all we heard as they turned their heads and walked away. They were joined a few minutes later by a man who I assumed to be Jennie's father. We saw him talk with his wife briefly - as she nodded several times in our direction - and then they both shot us looks that should have been reserved for child rapists, murderers, and the like. Trish and I withered in their hateful stares.

"What's going on?" we heard Zootie ask from behind us as he returned from the bathroom.

"We're absorbing eye missiles from Patton and Rommel over there," I said as I nodded towards Jennie's parents.

He looked over and gave them a small wave which only seemed to anger them more. "So, we finally get to meet the parents, eh?"

"Yeah, and they seem to be every bit as pleasant as Jennie said they were."

"Well, I think you ought to go over there and introduce yourself Dan," Zootie said matter-of-factly.

"Are you crazy?" I blurted out. "They think I'm the reason that their daughter is laying in that hospital bed and you want me to go over there and introduce myself?"

"Yes," he responded simply.

Before I could form my next argument, Trish piped in. "Zootie's right, Dan. We have to start the thawing process with them *sometime*, so why not now?"

I looked at them incredulously, but saw that they were both serious. I swallowed all my arguments and resigned myself to the task. "All right," I muttered, "but if I motion for reinforcements, you guys come running!"

"We've got your back, Dan," Zootie assured me. "And while you're distracting them, I'm going to go over to that nurse's station and see what I can find out about our good friend Jennie."

I took a deep breath and let it out quickly. "Okay, here I go. Wish me luck."

Trish smiled sweetly. "Luck."

I turned and walked over to where Jennie's parents were standing. They seemed stunned that I was walking their way, but they also somehow managed to keep the hateful look in their eyes as I approached. I stuck my hand out, knowing that they wouldn't take it, as I introduced myself. "Hi, my name's Dan Barnes and I wanted to…"

"We know *exactly* who you are," Jennie's father said through clenched teeth. "And I must ask that you leave this hospital immediately."

He said it in a tone that suggested he was used to getting his way with people, and a part of me almost turned on my heels and walked out the door, just as he had requested. But then I thought of poor Jennie struggling for her life and it gave me the strength I needed to stand my ground and step through his bluster. "I'm sorry, but I can't do that. You see, I care about your daughter very deeply and I came over here to tell you that."

Jennie's mother shouted "Hah!" which caused all the heads waiting in the seating area to turn our way. "All that you care about is *money*, you shameless snake! You've been filling our little girl's head with all kinds of nonsense and now look where she's ended up!" She then became hysterical as she stepped forward and raised her hand, as if preparing to slap me. I quickly stepped back, out of her reach. "You ought to be ashamed of yourself!" she shouted. "Taking advantage of poor, young girls! You coward! You shameless, filthy coward!" Her husband put his arm around her waist to prevent her from coming after me and I took one more step backwards.

"I'm sorry that you feel that way," I said with my hands up in front of me. "But, trust me, you've got this all wrong." She didn't hear me. She continued to scream at me, and I could see that it was time to sound the retreat. I turned around and headed back to Trish and Zootie, ignoring the looks of the people seated around me.

"That went *extremely* well," Zootie said upon my return. I was still shaking from the encounter. "Doesn't feel so good to be accused like that when you feel like you're deserving of exactly the *opposite*, does it?"

I shook my head. "Now I know how you felt at Brent's funeral."

Zootie laughed. "Some days you're the pigeon m'boy and some days you're the statue." He put his hand on my shoulder. "And may I tell you what a fine-looking statue you make."

"Thanks a lot," I muttered.

Trish put her arm through mine and nuzzled close. "I'm proud of you for doing that," she said quietly, "I know it wasn't easy to do."

I patted her hand and said "thank you" then turned my attention to Zootie. "So, what did you find out about Jennie?" I asked him.

"Well, she came out of the surgery okay," he said before shaking his head, "but we all know how this is going to end up."

The three of us stood there, struck dumb by Zootie's words. Through the whole episode it had never occurred to me that all our efforts were to be in vain: Jennie would be dead in less than 24 hours. The list would have its way.

CHAPTER 56

Jennie's parents had her moved to a private room in the hospital and then notified the hospital staff that nobody was to visit her except her mother and father. We continued to maintain our vigil at the hospital, however, and, through a nurse whom Zootie had befriended, we received regular updates on Jennie's condition. She put up a valiant fight following her surgery, but the bullet had passed through several of her organs and the internal bleeding proved too difficult to stop. Jennie Morrissey died soon after midnight.

After receiving the news in the waiting room, we sat and cried in a small huddle for a long, long time. We cried not only for our good friend Jennie, but we also cried for a world that would no longer have Jennie in it - we knew it would be a world with fewer smiles, less kindness and it wouldn't be nearly as much fun. We each sat there and talked about the things that we would miss most about her and wept after each one. It was a cleansing time that was, unfortunately, cut short by the arrival of Jennie's parents. They strode up to us, looking tired and worn; the same hateful looks still plastered on their faces.

Jennie's father had his arm around his wife's shoulder - seemingly supporting her as she cried - and he stuck an accusing finger out as he said, "Don't think that this is over, because it's *far* from over as far as you three are concerned!" Then, without waiting for a reply, they turned and walked away.

"Seems like I've heard those words somewhere before," Zootie cracked as we watched them stride towards the hospital exit.

We spent the next couple of days trying in vain to find out when and where Jennie's funeral was going to be. The newspapers just said that it would be a private service - just as Jennie had predicted - and that people could donate in her name to the Catholic Church. My repeated phone calls to the Morrissey household were ignored as were our pleas to all the local Catholic churches asking for information on the service; the Morrissey's wealth had obviously bought them the silence they desired.

After two days of frustrating dead ends, Trish came up with a wonderful idea. "Let's call grandma!" she exclaimed. We quickly found her number, called her, told her who we were, and she told us all the details that we had been seeking. The service would be held the following day at the Catholic church over in Bellevue.

"Bingo," Trish said with a smile as she hung up.

"Good job!" I said to her as I gave her a big hug. I knew now that I would be able to keep my promise to Jennie. Then I flashed on the faces of her parents and I got a big knot in my stomach. "Something tells me that this was the *easy* part though," I said grimly.

The following day, Trish, Zootie and I piled into Zootie's car and we made the drive across Lake Washington to Bellevue. The church was in what was obviously an extremely wealthy neighborhood, and we looked in amazement at the large houses that sat back from the street as we made our way to the church.

"To think that I might be living in a place like this right now," Zootie mumbled to nobody in particular as we passed by mansion after mansion.

We arrived at the church a little bit early and sat in the parking lot, surveying the scene in front of the church. "Looks like they're checking invitations," I said dejectedly.

Zootie sighed. "Yeah, and I don't suppose that we'll be able to talk our way past those two big guys standing at the entrance." We all then watched as Jennie's parents stepped out of their black Mercedes and climbed the steps to the church. One of the men then took the keys from Jennie's father and, after exchanging a few words, he went down the steps and drove the Mercedes off to a parking spot, returning to his post at the entrance soon afterwards.

"Well, those guys definitely work for him," Zootie observed, "so bribery is not an option."

"How are we going to get in?" Trish asked.

"Let's drive around back and see what we can see," Zootie suggested as he started the car up again.

We pulled around the church and saw nothing but stone walls and locked doors, until Zootie exclaimed, "Aha - I just found our backstage pass!" He pointed off into a thicket of trees behind the church and, at first, Trish and I didn't have a clue as to what he was talking about. He pulled the car over, got out, and disappeared into the trees. Trish and I exchanged bewildered looks while we waited several minutes for him to re-emerge from the trees.

"Let's go," he said to us through the rolled down window after finally returning to the car, "we've got our way in."

"Did you find a tunnel into the church?" I asked jokingly.

"Better." He looked over his shoulder back towards the trees and then lowered his voice to a whisper. "I found an altar boy smoking some dope back in the trees there and we agreed to exchange favors."

"You blackmailed an altar boy?!?" Trish all but shouted.

"Shhhh," Zootie pleaded. "He's back there getting himself composed a little and no, I didn't blackmail him."

"Then what exactly do you call it?" Trish asked accusingly.

"I call it finding a way into a church so that we can keep a promise to our friend," he replied. "And besides," he added with a shrug and a smile, "I shared a few hits with the kid so he could see that I wasn't laying a guilt trip on him. I also told him not to get too hung up on all of the do's and don'ts of the church because God doesn't really give a shit if he smokes dope or not, He just cares what's going on inside his heart."

"A little Zootie sermon, huh?" I said with a smile.

"Sure, why not? I figure if I could save one altar boy from a lifetime of guilt, get a few hits on a doobie, *and* get us into the church at the same time," he shrugged, "that's a package deal too good to pass up!"

Trish shot him a playful smile as we climbed out of the car. Not two seconds later the boy emerged from the woods. Zootie walked over and put his arm around the boy's shoulder. "Jonathan, I want you to meet my good friends Dan and Trish." We all shook hands.

"Nice to meet you, Jonathan," I said. I guessed him to be in his early teens and could see that his eyes were still quite bloodshot from his sermon with Zootie.

"No problem," he said with a shrug as he glanced up at Zootie. "Not that I really had much of a choice."

Zootie laughed. "You always have choices m'boy - some are just better than others." With that, we all headed back towards the church.

Jonathan took us through a back door and then led us through a series of hallways until we came to the main part of the church. He nodded to us and we nodded back with whispers of "thank you." He smiled and then disappeared behind a curtain in the front of the church. We made our way, slowly and quietly, to the back corner of the seating area, away from the prying eyes of Jennie's parents. The service began soon after we sat down.

Relieved, I sat in my seat and said a few silent words to Jennie, forming them in my mind but keeping them from my lips. *"Well Jennie, I made it just like I promised."* I saw her face smiling at me. *"I hope you're making the transition okay, and you can trust me that I'll take care of things down here for you."* Small tears formed in my eyes. *"We're going to miss you down here, that's for sure."* I looked up at the high, domed ceiling and said the final words that I hadn't had the chance to say in the hospital. *"Goodbye Jennie - I'll never forget you."* I wept quietly for a while longer and then, after wiping my face, turned my attention to the service.

A priest was standing in front of the small group of mourners, and he was quoting verses from the bible in between spouting generic diatribe about death and God's will. I leaned towards Zootie and whispered, "Really makes you think about Jennie, doesn't it?"

Zootie looked at me, his face contorted with anger. "This is terrible! Jennie had shown me a copy of the letter she'd given to her parents regarding her funeral and it said *nothing* about a priest or any of this religious babble!"

Zootie was right. I had seen the same letter and the funeral Jennie described in it bore a striking resemblance to the one that Hy had requested - low on ceremony, and yet high on friends sharing stories and remembering the departed loved one. This service was probably the exact *opposite* of what she had wanted.

I sat there a while longer, listening to the empty words of the priest, and found myself getting angrier and angrier. *"How could her parents - who profess to love her so much - completely disregard her dying wishes?"* I asked myself. *"But what can I do about it?"* I wondered helplessly.

Then, as the priest asked everyone to lower their heads in prayer, a voice shouted in my head; *"Stand up!"* I looked around, half-expecting to see someone standing behind me. Nobody was there. *"Stand up!"* the voice shouted again.

Thinking about it, I quickly saw that I was guilty of the same thing as her parents - I was ignoring Jennie's dying wishes out of fear. It was hard to swallow, but it was true. Once again - more gently this time - the voice said to me, "*Stand up.*" Without thinking, I rose to my feet and started walking to the front of the church. I reached the front just as the priest said "amen" at the conclusion of his prayer. All heads then lifted, and I found myself staring into a sea of bewildered eyes. I glanced to my left and saw that the confused eyes of Jennie's parents quickly transformed to angry eyes when they saw who I was. I ignored them and cleared my throat.

"Most of you do not know me, and those of you who *do* think you know me," I said as I nodded at Jennie's parents, "think that you don't like me all that much." I set my jaw. "That's fine. I'm not up here to change your minds about that. I'm standing here to pay my respects to an amazing woman who changed my life in ways that I'm not sure I'm even aware of yet." I felt the heat of emotion welling in my chest. I swallowed hard, determined to keep the emotions at bay until I'd said everything I wanted to say.

"Jennie Morrissey swept into my life several months ago and my life has not been nearly the same ever since." My eyes gazed at the back wall of the church, although, in truth, they were surveying the inner landscape of my mind. I no longer saw the faces of the people in front of me - I saw only Jennie's face - and memory after memory drifted in front of my mind's eye. "She had a way of looking at the world," I continued, "that was irreverent, unique and highly entertaining." I smiled at the thought of all her acronyms and offbeat questions. "I could always count on Jennie to bring a smile to my face no matter how bad my day, or depressing my life, may have been."

Then I thought of Dave Smith and many others like him who were on the list. "She also had the biggest, kindest heart I've ever seen," I said somberly, "and she managed to change countless lives with that heart. I had the good fortune of watching her work her magic firsthand. Without asking for a single thing in return, she helped people tackle their fears, open their hearts, and live the lives they were meant to live." I couldn't hold back the emotions any longer and my voice quavered. "I was one of those lucky people," I said quietly. Composing myself, I continued. "I made a promise to her that I would be at this funeral and, despite many obstacles, I am here to fulfill that promise." I looked skyward as I said, "Goodbye Jennie Morrissey. The world is a sadder, less loving place today without you around and we're going to miss you down here." I smiled as I thought about my last words. "You may be gone from this world, but you will never be forgotten. I promise you that, Jennie." Then I lowered my head and walked back to my seat next to Zootie and Trish.

They were both wide-eyed when I sat down. "What the hell came over *you*?" Zootie asked in a loud whisper, as a huge grin spread across his face.

"I don't know," I replied with a smile, "a voice inside of me told me to stand up, so I did."

"That was beautiful Dan," Trish gushed. "Jennie would have loved those words."

"I hate to be a wet blanket," Zootie chimed in, "but I think we'd better beat a hasty retreat outta here before this service wraps up or we're gonna find ourselves facing down an angry mob."

I looked up and saw that one head after another was turning around and looking our way and not one of the faces appeared sympathetic. "I agree," I said, "let's head out the same way we came in." The three of us got up out of our seats and, as discreetly as we could, made our way towards the same back door through which we'd come in earlier. We got as far as the back hallway when we were headed off by Jennie's father and one of his henchmen.

"Just who the hell do you people think you are?" he spat out venomously as he stood between us and our exit. "You show up here uninvited to a private service and then have the nerve to stand up and pretend that you actually *cared* about my daughter." He spat out the word *cared* like he'd taken a bad bite of food. He stepped closer to me and I could smell the stale coffee on his breath as he spoke. "I received a copy of the letter regarding her trust," he hissed contemptuously in my face, "and I want you to know that you will never see a penny of that money. It doesn't take a detective to see what you did to my poor daughter; you forced her to sign over her trust to you and then you had her killed." He moved even closer to me, his nose nearly touching mine. "Or maybe you pulled the trigger yourself."

That did it. As intimidating as he was initially, his comments made me so angry that I couldn't contain it any longer. "You listen to me, Mr. Morrissey," I said forcefully as I stuck my finger in his chest. "I've had about all I'm going to take of your accusations and innuendo. If you want to sick a bunch of lawyers on me, be my guest and get in line. But know this," I hollered as I wagged my finger in his surprised face, "your daughter left this world feeling loved by very few people and the three of us standing in front of you," I waved my arm toward Zootie and Trish, "were among those few. I don't know where you get off thinking that you know more about your daughter than anyone else, but judging from this service you put together in there, you didn't know *shit* about your daughter!" I turned to Zootie and Trish and said, "Let's get out of here," and then brushed past Jennie's father and his hired hand as I led them out the door.

Once in the car, I felt myself calming down and I began to shake. Neither Zootie nor Trish said a word to me until I looked over at them. "Do you think he got my point?" I asked.

They both looked at each other and then started laughing. "Who the hell *are* you and *what* have you done with my good friend Dan Barnes?!?" Zootie screamed.

"Was I a little over the top?"

"Over the top?!?" Zootie exclaimed. "You were over the top, off the charts and out of this world m'boy, and I have to say that I loved every damned minute of it!"

I looked over at Trish. "What do you think?"

Her beautiful eyes sparkled with love. "I think you're my knight in shining armor," she said softly.

CHAPTER 57

I was numb for the next several days following Jennie's service. We managed to locate her grave site - again, contrary to her desire to be cremated - and the three of us paid a visit to her final resting place. It was depressing.

Her parents had placed a large, marble marker to mark her grave, complete with a large statue of the Virgin Mary looking down on her. It was large, I'm sure it was expensive, and it was very *un*-Jennie. I knew for a fact that Jennie would have laughed out loud at the sight of such a headstone hovering over her grave.

The three of us stood there, hand-in-hand, for over an hour, just talking, laughing and reminiscing about life with Jennie. It felt good, especially after the negativity of her emotionally-charged church service. There was nobody there to tell us what we could and couldn't do; it was just us, the birds, Jennie, and a cemetery full of silent observers.

When I got home that day, I felt the need to go to work on the promise I had made to Jennie. I went into her room, gathered up a bag full of mementos, photos, and other items, and brought it all downstairs to the front study. Once there, I spent the next couple of hours putting together the biggest and best shrine yet. I placed it next to Hy's - I thought that fitting - and found myself laughing and crying throughout the entire project, each item bringing back a flood of vivid memories. When done, I stepped back from it to see how the finished product looked.

While I was standing there, Trish walked into the room. I turned to her and asked, "What do you think?"

She looked me up and down and said playfully, "I think you look like hell!"

I wiped my face with my shirt sleeve. "Yeah, it was a bit emotional," I replied. Then I nodded at the shrine. "But, seriously, what do you think of it?"

She stepped closer to the shrine and examined its contents, lingering a little longer over some of the photos. Then she looked over her shoulder, her eyes misting over, and said, "You did good Mr. Barnes. Real good." I stepped over to her and put my arm around her.

"This was a great idea she had," I said as I scanned all the shrines.

"Yeah, that girl was a creative one."

I sighed deeply as I looked around the room. "I'm getting tired of all these goodbyes."

"Me too, Dan. Me too." We stood there for a while longer until we were interrupted by a knock at the front door. I went to answer it and, after opening the door, stood face-to-face with a man dressed in a suit. He looked like he was big enough to play linebacker for the local Seahawks football team.

"Can I help you?" I asked.

"Yes, you can," he said stiffly as he opened his wallet and flashed a detective's badge, "I'm Detective Steve Walker and I'm looking for a man by the name of Dan Barnes."

CHAPTER 58

Trish had run to get Zootie after hearing who the man was, and the four of us sat in the living room. Zootie and I sat next to each other on the couch while Trish and the detective sat in separate chairs across from us.

I looked over at Zootie, expecting him to initiate the discussion as he typically did, but he just sat there quietly. We all knew why the detective was there - Jennie's parents had obviously wasted no time in initiating an investigation into her death. But he didn't say anything at first, he just sat and scanned the living room. I finally decided to get things moving.

"So," I said as I cleared my throat, "what can we do for you Detective Walker?" I braced myself for the accusations - murder, extortion, who knows what else.

He brought his attention back to my face; his eyes were expressionless. He sat forward in his chair and rested his elbows on his knees - it was easy to see that our chairs had not been made for men his size. "It seems we've had some allegations made by a...," he took a small notebook out of his shirt pocket and opened it, "a Mr. Harold Baker" he read from the first page. He then shut the notebook, put it back into his pocket, and looked back at me. "Serious allegations."

"Harold Baker?" I thought to myself. *"Who the hell is Harold Baker?"* I glanced over at Trish and she just shrugged.

"It seems that he believes you had something to do with the deaths of William and Ruth Cooper some weeks ago and

I'm here to ask you a few questions about that." He smiled a manufactured smile.

I didn't even need to look at Trish - I could feel her eyes boring holes in the side of my skull. And I didn't *dare* look at Trish, for fear that any strange glance may give us away. *"Who the hell is Harold Baker and how did he know anything about the Coopers?"* I thought frantically.

"So, I understand that Mr. and Mrs. Cooper stayed here with you for a while prior to their deaths?" he asked calmly as he took out his notebook and pen.

"Yes, they did," I croaked as my mouth and throat had suddenly gone dry.

He wrote something in the notebook. "And what exactly was your relationship with them?"

"They were basically tenants here," I said, figuring that it was no use trying to maintain the charade of being a nursing home; he could have seen that for the lie it was by just asking to see our license.

"So, they paid you a rental fee?"

I paused. "Yes," I lied, "a small fee."

"And when was the last time that you saw the deceased?"

"That morning, at breakfast."

"And did they say anything to you that would indicate they were contemplating the taking of their own lives?"

I shook my head. "No"

"And where were you that evening between the hours of, say, five to eight?"

I nodded towards Trish. "I was with Trish all day."

"I see." He turned to Trish. "And your name again?"

"Patricia McConnell."

He wrote it down. "And you were with Mr. Barnes during those evening hours that I just mentioned?"

I could see that Trish was nervous, but she didn't even so much as glance my way. "Yes, I was."

"And where exactly were you two during those hours?"

"Oh, oh…" I thought. *"If she tells him we were at the Snoqualmie Falls Lodge, that would put us close to where the Coopers had died. If she lies, it would be an easy thing to trace our credit card records and see that we had been there. We were trapped."*

"Excuse me, Mr. Walker," Zootie interrupted. Good old Zootie - he knew we were trapped. "I happen to be Mr. Barnes' attorney, here on other business, and I'm sorry but I will have to ask that you discontinue this line of questioning until he and I have an opportunity to discuss these charges in full."

The detective eyed Zootie up and down, obviously finding it hard to believe that he could be my attorney. He snapped his notebook shut. "Fine," he replied evenly. "We can play it that way." He got up from his chair and extended his hand for Zootie to shake, which he did. "I'll be back here at the same time tomorrow." He started for the front door and then turned to face us. "Just so you folks know - this isn't Oregon, this is Washington. Assisting someone with a suicide *is* a crime here in this state." He nodded grimly and then continued for the door. Zootie showed him out, shook his hand one more time, and then closed the door behind him.

"Red!" he screamed after shutting the door. "Bet you every penny I've got that our man Red is actually none other than Harold Baker, husband of our favorite heiress, Mandy Baker. That little snitch!"

"Red?" I said out loud. Then I remembered: that day we'd found him in the kitchen, nervous as can be, after we'd heard a noise - he'd been eavesdropping and heard everything!

"Shit!" Zootie shouted as he pounded his fist. "I *knew* I didn't trust that guy, but I still let him hang around here!"

"Don't worry Zootie," I said as Trish and I exchanged warm, yet worried, smiles, "I'm ready to go to jail for what I did if I have to."

CHAPTER 59

We spent the next twenty-four hours trying to figure out a way out of the corner we were in. We discussed countless alibis, created elaborate lies, and even went over potential defenses, in case it eventually came to that. Nothing we came up with held up under scrutiny, however, and we arrived at the same dead end every time. We were stuck.

I went for a long walk the following morning, to clear my head prior to Detective Walker's arrival, and it was during that walk that I finally found my answer. And it came from a most unlikely source. I had walked down to Green Lake and then sat on one of the benches to just think for a while. I sat down on a large bulge in my back pocket and reached around to pull out the offending bulge; it was Jennie's journal. I had put it in my back pocket the previous day while I was assembling her shrine. I opened it up and began leafing through it. Embarrassingly, it was the first time I'd opened it since the day she'd handed it to me.

In it I found all kinds of buried treasure. There were all the answers to Jennie's many questions. There were quirky observations about people and the world around her. There were assorted pictures and doodlings. There were many personal journal-type entries. I sat there on that bench and leafed through it for an hour, unable to restrain my out-loud laughs or my gentle sobs. Some of her words all but leapt off the page and pulled me into an embrace, they were so heartfelt and real. I found myself both missing and loving my departed friend Jennie.

I paused for a long time at the section where she had written down people's BFW's - Big Fucking Wishes. I saw Bowler's, Dave Smith's and several others that had little check marks next to them, which I assumed meant that their BFW's had been fulfilled. Curiously, Zootie's BFW - to re-marry Ren - also had a check mark next it, though I knew for a fact that that had never happened. I also felt another wave of embarrassment at mine and Trish's matching BFW's. The embarrassment turned to a smile, however, as I recalled the day that Jennie had pointed that out to us. I saw that there were many other BFW's like ours that still didn't have a check mark next to them. Jennie's was on that list. I choked back the sadness as I read her BFW; "I want to write a book that gets published someday" was what she had written in response to that question. I felt a pain in my heart for her wish that would now remain unfulfilled for all of eternity.

Finally, I turned to the back of the book, where she had assembled a variety of her favorite quotes. There was one about courage, and one about love and, finally, there was the one that jumped from the page and shook me to my core: "The truth will set you free." A well-known quote that I'd heard many times before and yet - in that place, at that time - it seemed as if it had been written just for me. *"The truth will set you free."* I thought about it for a while and realized that it was the answer that I'd been looking for. Of course! I slammed the book shut, put it back into my pocket, and all but ran home to Hope House. On the way, I took a moment to say a silent "thank you" to Jennie. *"Thank you, Jennie!"* I said to her in my head. *"You're never going to stop helping me, are you?"*

When I got back to Hope House, Detective Walker was already there and sitting in the living room. Trish and Zootie flashed me a *"where the hell have you been?"* look as I walked into the living room.

Zootie was sitting across from the detective and turned his attention back to him. "As I was saying Detective Walker, we need just a little more time to discuss these accusations, so if you could…"

I stepped forward. "Don't worry Zootie, I'm ready to talk to the detective now."

Zootie looked up at me, his eyes - which only I could see - were obviously asking me; *"Are you crazy?!?"*

I ignored him and sat down on the couch. I took a deep breath and let it out slowly. "Detective Walker," I began, "make yourself comfortable, because I have one hell of a story to tell you."

"But Dan, don't you think that…" Zootie interjected, attempting one more time to bring me to my senses.

I simply raised my hand and said, "Zootie, it's okay." He nodded and just sat back, though I thought I might have detected a small smile on his face as he repositioned himself in his chair.

I turned my attention back to the detective. "As I was saying, I have a long, amazing story to tell you Mr. Walker." With that, I jumped into the story of Hope House, Hy, Zootie, Jennie, and, of course, the list. I told him how I'd come to be involved, how I was reluctant to get too involved at first, and how - with the help of some small nudges from deceased friends in my dreams - I managed to work through my fear and get to the point where I could actually embrace the mission that had been placed in front of me. I used few details at first, as I saw in his eyes that he wasn't believing any of what I was telling him. But then, about halfway through my monologue, I detected a small but noticeable change in his eyes - they switched from being detached and dispassionate to being interested and almost sympathetic. This encouraged me to add more detail about my dreams, Jennie's funeral and other events, including Bill and Ruth Cooper's suicide.

When I was done, I took another deep breath and said, "Well, there you have it Detective Walker. The 100% unfiltered truth."

He didn't say a word for a long, long time - he just lowered his head and wrung his hands. Zootie, Trish and I sat there, exchanged confused looks and mouthed some words back and forth, anxiously waiting for his reaction. Finally, mercifully, he looked up.

"If you had laid this story on me a couple of years ago, you'd be in cuffs right now and we'd be on our way down to the station," he said slowly, still not looking me in the eye. He paused and looked down at his hands. "But about a year ago I lost a partner of mine." Another pause. "He got shot in the gut and he died in my arms, before the ambulance could get there." I could see that he was wrestling with some strong emotions as he spoke, but his voice stayed even. He looked up at me and I saw the intensity in his eyes. "After he died, he came and talked to me in my sleep every night for a week. At first, I thought it was just because I felt guilty or something, but by the third night there was no doubt in my mind - it was Jimbo." He shook his head and I thought I detected a slight quaver in his voice as he continued. "He told me that he was lost, didn't know what happened, and he needed my help. Finally, during that last night, I just told him that he'd been shot and that he was dead. I told him that he had to find his way to heaven because he wasn't supposed to be hanging around here anymore." His head bowed once again. "That was the last I saw of him."

Trish got up from her chair and went over to sit next to him, where she comforted him by rubbing his back. The room was silent as he hung his head for a while longer.

"You did the right thing," Zootie said softly, "it's easy for a soul to get lost and confused when death comes so sudden like that. You helped him to find his way."

The detective inhaled slowly and exhaled quickly, making a loud noise as he blew the air out. He raised his head and said with an ironic smile, "This didn't turn out quite like I thought it would."

"Most things don't," Zootie said gently.

"If any of the other detectives saw me now, they'd pull my badge for sure."

"Nobody but us will ever know about what you just shared," Trish reassured him as she continued to rub his back.

Detective Walker shifted his large frame in his chair, cleared his throat a few times and seemed to get back into character. Trish sensed this and stopped rubbing his back. "So as far as I'm concerned," he said with an authoritative voice, "this case is closed, and I see no need to press any charges."

Trish, Zootie and I smiled as one. "That's great news," I said calmly, masking my true excitement, "thank you for your understanding, Detective Walker."

"Hey," he replied with a wink, "us loonies have to stick together, right?" He stood up and we all shook hands, except Trish who gave Detective Walker a big hug. He seemed to be genuinely surprised by the display of affection and stammered, "I don't know all of what you guys are doing here, but you seem to have your hands full with it and I wish you the best of luck with it."

"Thank you, Detective Walker," I said, "that means a lot to us."

"And by the way," he added as he strode to the door, "the name is Steve, and if you guys need any more help in the future, here's my card." He handed me one of his business cards from his shirt pocket. "Call me anytime."

We all thanked him as he left, and waved goodbye as he headed down the front sidewalk. After he'd driven off, we looked at each other and burst out laughing. "Aren't you just the man full of surprises!" Zootie kidded.

"That was brilliant Dan," Trish gushed. "Where did you come up with *that* idea?"

"Our good friend Jennie gave it to me," I replied as my eyes went skyward, "and something tells me she's not quite done helping me out yet."

CHAPTER 60

The following morning, I read through Jennie's journal in greater detail over my breakfast. I was still feeling the glow from the day before and wondered if there were more hidden messages for me contained within her journal's pages.

I smiled as I read through more of the responses to her questions of the day. I laughed out loud at Zootie's response to the question of, *"If you could change one thing about your body what would it be and why?"* His very Zootie answer was; *"I'd move my ass to the front of my body to make it more accessible and shift my big belly to the back because I'm tired of looking at that thing and not being able to see my toes!"* I made a silent promise to keep the tradition alive for her by asking the questions that she had written down for me prior to her death.

I flipped to the Big Fucking Wish section and my eyes went to a name that I didn't recognize: Elena Camandona. Her BFW was to return to Italy - her home country apparently - one more time before she died. The entry had three exclamation points next to it but no check mark. I set the book down and wondered to myself if Elena Camandona had managed to make that trip prior to her DOD.

I turned to her personal journal section and scanned the entries. I was once again struck by how sensitive and perceptive Jennie had been for someone so young. One entry bemoaned the fact that we were all doomed to forever be surrounded by strangers despite our strong desires to the contrary. While still considering the implications of this entry I read another that started me chuckling: she wrote about her desire to get some tears out that she knew she needed to cry and yet they felt stuck, so she wrote how she was going to go rent a sad movie which would hopefully act as "emotional bran" and allow her to have a "bawl movement." I laughed until tears streamed down my face.

Trish heard me laughing from the other room and came into the kitchen. "What the heck is so funny in here?"

I pointed to the journal and read the entry to her; she laughed right along with me. Then I remembered my silent promise and flipped back to the Question of the Day section. "Hey, while you're here," I said to Trish as I scanned down to the questions that had yet to be asked, "I've got a question to ask you."

She smiled. "Decided to keep it going for her, huh?"

"Yeah. She worked too hard on this book to just have it sit in some desk drawer somewhere."

"So, what's today's question?" she asked as she settled into the seat next to me at the kitchen table.

I ran my finger down and stopped at the next question. "What three things would you like to hear said about you at your funeral?" I looked up and smiled. "Good one, huh?":

Trish looked down and stared at the journal. "Yeah it is," she said absently, obviously thinking about the question. It took her a few minutes, but she finally said, "Okay, I've got it." Everyone in Hope House had grown accustomed to the unspoken rule of Jennie's questions - be honest. We had all taken the time necessary to consider the question she'd asked and then give a thoughtful response. Jennie could smell a throwaway response from a mile away. I took the pen that was tucked inside the journal and poised myself to record her response.

"Fire away," I said.

"Number one is that I'd like to hear people say that I tried at my life. I don't want to be seen as someone who was always standing at the water cooler talking *about* life."

"Good one," I said as I wrote.

"Number two would be that I knew all about love and matters of the heart - that I wasn't afraid to love, be loved or to extend my heart to the people around me."

"I'd say that one's already a safe bet to be heard at your funeral Trish," I said with a warm smile before starting to write. After I finished writing it down, I looked up and saw that she was staring at the far wall and crying.

"Number three," she said softly, "is that I was a good mother to my children."

Love filled my heart and tears quickly filled my eyes. Slight embarrassment also tugged at the edges of my emotions, but I ignored it as I reached across the table and grabbed her hand. "You're going to be the best mother the world's ever seen," I assured her.

She wiped her eyes. "I don't know Dan. The more I think about it the more I think that I'd better brace myself for the possibility of a life without children."

"Nonsense!" I said firmly as I slapped the table, which had the desired effect of startling her. "You're younger than I am, so if you're giving up the dream then that means it's time for me to be giving up mine, and I'm not ready to do that just yet."

She smiled tenderly and squeezed my hand. "You're sweet."

"Now let me write that one down so it becomes a matter of public record."

As I wrote, she said, "I hate to cut this short, but I have to get going to the hospital."

"Who are you going to go see today?" I asked with my head still down.

"A woman who Jennie used to visit. I want to make sure she doesn't just slip through the cracks and get forgotten."

"What's her name?" I asked, still writing.

"Elena Camandona."

I stopped writing and looked up, my mouth hanging open. "I'm going with you."

CHAPTER 61

Elena Camandona, we soon found out, had checked herself out of the hospital several days earlier. After a few white lies regarding our intentions, one of the nurses was kind enough to give us her present address. We headed straight to her house in the Northgate area.

It was a small, one-story house - much smaller than the three-story behemoths that surrounded it, which made me think that her house had been built earlier than the rest - and it was framed by nicely kept gardens. We knocked on the door and waited for an answer.

The answer came in the form of a brusque, middle-aged man who opened the door with a very unwelcoming, "Yeah?"

"Uh, we're here to see Elena Camandona," Trish offered politely.

He opened the door wider so we could enter. "She's in the bedroom," he said impatiently as he pointed his thumb over his shoulder. After we had entered the house, he walked out the front door and closed it behind him without another word to us. Trish and I looked at each other and shrugged.

"Hello?" Trish said loudly, hoping to get more direction as to what to do next.

"Hello!" came a weak, squeaky reply from just down the hall. We followed the voice and walked into Elena's bedroom. She was lying in her bed, propped up by several pillows. She was a woman who had obviously seen at least eighty years, possibly more, and who, equally as obviously, had one foot firmly planted in God's waiting room. Her small, emaciated body all but disappeared under the covers that she had piled on top of her.

We quickly introduced ourselves and explained that we were there to visit her in Jennie's stead, due to her recent passing. "She was a dear, sweet girl and I'm looking forward to telling her thank you when I see her again," Elena replied matter-of-factly.

"Uh, maybe you didn't hear me Elena," I said somberly, "but Jennie passed away last week."

She chuckled. "I heard you dear boy." She adjusted her covers a bit and then asked, "Did you meet the gardener?"

My mind flashed on the brusque doorman. "Yes, I guess we did," I replied.

"Isn't he a grump?" Elena asked with a small scowl.

"Warmth didn't seem to be his strong suit," Trish replied with a smile. She sat down in a small chair by the bed and I did the same over on the other side of Elena's bed.

"My neighbors hired him to tend my yard," she squeaked as she fussed with her blankets. She stopped fussing for a moment and looked at Trish. "They told me that they just wanted to help me out, but I know they were just worried about the old lady's yard becoming an eyesore and spoiling their view." She winked. "I swear, young people seem to think that being old means being stupid too!"

Trish and I exchanged glances and smiled. We both liked Elena immediately.

"So why did you come home?" Trish asked.

"Oh, I guess I just didn't want to die with a tube up my nose," Elena replied; again, with the same matter-of-fact voice, as if she were explaining why she preferred butter over margarine.

"I guess I can understand that," Trish agreed with a nod.

Elena reached over and put her hand on Trish's forearm and leaned forward conspiratorially as she whispered, "They'll tell you what a big mistake it is, those doctors. As if going home to die were akin to putting a revolver in my mouth." She winked again as she leaned back. "I'm telling you, I don't know what it is that they teach these young doctors in medical schools, but they sure don't know diddly poop about dying."

Trish smiled a gentle smile. "I think that they get so focused on saving peoples' lives that they forget sometimes about the possibility of death. I think they see that as a failure on their part."

Elena let out a shrill cackle, reminding me a little bit of the witch in Wizard of Oz. "Anyone with one good eye can see that death is a very *real* possibility for *me*."

"What is it that's wrong with you, Elena?" I asked.

She turned and looked at me. "Cancer m'boy. Started in my left breast and spread every which way from there."

"You must be in terrible pain," Trish said softly.

"Nope. I've got so many pain pills in me now that you could probably kick me in the shin and I wouldn't even bat an eye."

"Is there anything we can do for you to make you more comfortable?" Trish asked.

"Not right now, dear girl. I've just got a week left, from what Jennie told me, and I don't plan on doing much more than saying a few goodbyes and looking through my photo albums over there." She reached up a bony finger and pointed toward a dresser behind Trish that had a tall stack of albums on it. She sighed. "At my age about all I have left are memories."

"No family members who we can contact for you?" I asked.

Another deep sigh. "No…" her voice trailed off. "My husband, Bud, passed away four years ago, and I've been a lonely, old woman ever since that day." Her eyes met mine and a slight frown etched its way across the thin skin on her forehead. "I think that's why I got this cancer. God knows that I'm done down here and it's time to head home so I can be with Bud again."

"Sounds like you two really loved each other," I said.

Her grey eyes lit up. "Oh yes! We met in the seventh grade, back in Ely, Minnesota, and we were together most every day after that. Except for the war - he had to go overseas for a few years then. But when he got back, it was if he'd never left and we never slept a day apart after he got off that ship. More than fifty years we were together, and I can tell you as God is my witness that I loved that man just as much the day he died as I did back then in the seventh grade." Her eyes got a far-off glaze and Trish and I took the opportunity to exchange loving glances.

Elena's eyes re-focused on the present and she turned her attention to me. "I still sleep with him, you know."

Inexplicably, a small chill crawled up my back. "You do?" I asked, trying not to give away my surprise.

"Oh yes," she replied in her butter vs. margarine tone, as if *everyone* sleeps with their dead husbands. "He's still with me all the time. As a matter of fact, he told me you two were coming today and that I shouldn't be frightened because you're both such nice people."

I smiled. "It's good to hear that we got such a nice endorsement."

"Hmm, hmm," she said as she went back to fussing with her blankets. Without even looking up, she said, "He's standing right behind you right now if you'd like to say a thank you."

The small chill became a full-fledged shudder. "He is?" I replied with a crack in my voice. I had the same feeling coursing through my body as when I saw "The Exorcist" for the first time.

She looked up from her blanket-fussing and, with reassuring eyes, said, "Bud says to tell you not to be frightened. He's standing there with a friend of yours and she says that you've done a good job of following the bread crumbs."

CHAPTER 62

It was several hours later, and I was still shaking. After leaving Elena's place, Trish and I headed to a nearby coffee shop to debrief. I needed help making sense of what had just happened.

"I mean, I definitely believe in the whole life after death thing now," I sputtered as I took a small sip from my vanilla latte, "but I've never been around anyone who could actually *talk* with somebody from the other side!"

Trish grabbed my hand from across the table and gave it a gentle squeeze. "Didn't you say that you saw Hy and Bowler in some dreams not too long ago?"

"Well, yeah, but that was different - I was asleep! The whole thing still had a "*were-they-or-weren't-they-there*"? kinda feel to it. This thing with Elena didn't have any fuzz around the edges - she was *talking* to them Trish!"

She smiled at me as if I were a small child who had just realized that there was no Santa Claus. "Pretty amazing, huh?"

"You say that as if it's something that *you* can do too."

"No, not yet - though I sure wish I could. But I've been around a lot of dying people who can do the same thing." She took a large sip of her kiwi Italian soda. "The first time I was around somebody who did that, I thought for sure they were hallucinating or something; I mean, come on! Talking to the dead - that's something you read about in Stephen King novels!"

"Exactly!"

"But the more times I saw it the more I realized that these people *weren't* hallucinating - they were seeing something that was as real as this glass in my hand."

"But why is it that only *they* can see them? Why didn't we see Elena's husband or Hy today if they were standing right there in the room?"

Trish shrugged. "I certainly don't have all the answers on this topic, but I imagine it's sort of like those hidden pictures - you know, the ones where you have to stare at them a while before you can pick out the 3-d picture buried inside? I think it's as simple as some people can do it and some people can't. Like those hidden pictures, it's probably a matter of just relaxing your eyes a little bit, not fighting it so much, but I know *I* haven't mastered the technique yet."

"So, do you think that Hy and Bowler and Jennie are here with us right now?" I looked around the room, half expecting one of them to come strolling up to our table.

Trish had a large grin on her face as she replied, "I *know* they are."

CHAPTER 63

Several days later I received a phone call from a man named Jack Beck. Jack was a man whom I had contacted six or seven weeks earlier - prior to my "awakening" at the hands of Zootie's little lie - regarding his place on the list. He had given me a big stiff arm back then and I had given up on him; he was a middle-aged, hard driving type who let me know, quite bluntly in fact, that I was full of shit and he had no time for whatever it was I was trying to sell him. After returning from my pilgrimage, however, I had decided to give him another try.

I had called him several times recently - each time getting his secretary or his answering machine - and this was the first time that he had decided to return one of my calls. "Hello Jack," I responded after he identified himself, "how are things going?"

"Uh, not so well actually," he replied, with a quiet, sub-dued voice that I hardly recognized as belonging to Jack Beck.

"What's the matter?"

There was a long pause. "I'm...I'm in the hospital." Another pause. "I had a heart attack two days ago."

"I'm sorry to hear that Jack." I sat down in a nearby chair. "What are the doctors telling you?" It was a stupid question and I knew it as soon as I asked it.

"What does it matter?" he replied quietly. "You already told me everything I need to know. I was just too stupid to listen to you." I heard his labored breathing on the other end of the line, but I couldn't tell if he was crying or just struggling for oxygen.

"That's not true at all Jack. It's a lot for anyone to take in - trust me, I know what I'm talking about on this."

"Yeah, well, I believe you now," I could hear unmistakable sobs this time, "and now I just got two days to set things straight."

My heart broke for him as I thought about how far the Jack Beck I had met before had fallen to get to this point in his life - calling a relative stranger and breaking down into tears over the phone. "Where are you right now Jack? I want to come see you."

"The UW Medical Center," he said between sobs, "room 104."

"I'll be right there." I hung up, hopped in Trish's car and was walking the halls of the UW Medical Center in less than twenty minutes. I found his room quickly and knocked softly on the half-opened door.

"Come in," came the weak reply.

I walked in and sat down next to his bed. "Hey Jack," I said with a smile, "good to see you again."

His eyes were at half-mast - probably some drugs that were beginning to take effect - but he managed a weak smile and a "thanks for coming."

"No problem." I looked him up and down and was struck by how frail he looked lying there in the hospital bed. Here was a man who had just climbed Mount Rainier the year before and wasn't much older than me and yet he looked twenty years older.

He must have noticed me checking him out as he whispered, "Pretty pathetic looking, huh?"

"Hey, you just had a heart attack - you're allowed to look a little pathetic." My words hung in the air for several minutes as we did the unspoken guy-dance; wondering how much to reveal and what to say next. I decided to just cut to the chase and save him from having to make the effort. "So, what can I do to help you Jack?"

He turned his head to look at me. He had a tube hanging from his nose and a bandage on his forehead, probably from falling down after having his heart attack. His eyes still seemed unsure as to how much to say to me. Then he let out a big *"what the fuck?"* sigh and said, "I don't know how to die."

I didn't know what he was trying to say, so I asked, "What do you mean?"

"I mean, I don't know how to die," he repeated. I sat there in silence - the value of which I'd learned again and again at Hope House - and he finally elaborated. "All I've known for the past thirty years is work and getting ahead. I've got my next five years all planned out in my Day-Timer at home - right down to the vacations I'm going to take and where I'm going to build my retirement home." A single tear rolled down his cheek. "That's why I told you to take a hike when you first came around about that list of yours; it just didn't fit into the plan." He turned his head and looked at the far wall, seemingly too embarrassed to have me see him cry. "Pretty arrogant, huh?"

"I wouldn't call it arrogant," I reassured him. "Most people think that death applies to everyone else but them." I paused for a beat and then added, "I know that was what I thought prior to this list coming into my life."

He rolled his head back to look at me. "Really?"

"Sure. Who has time to think about something like death? All it does is make you feel like shit, so why bother?"

I could see his eyes trusting me more - he saw that I was a kindred spirit of sorts - and he said, "Yeah, that's what I thought too. And I also thought that if I kept running fast enough, and stayed busy, that death wouldn't be able to catch up to me. He'd have to take a number like everyone else and just get scheduled in."

I laughed at that thought. "Wouldn't that be nice? Schedule death in like a dentist appointment." I held an invisible phone up to my ear. "Oh yes, hello Dr. Death. What's that?

Thursday? No, no I'm sorry but Thursday just won't work for me - I have a tennis game that morning and a very important meeting that afternoon. Why don't I look over my schedule and just give you a call back with some possible dates? Okay, talk to you later. Bye." I hung up my invisible phone and saw that Jack was smiling.

"Yeah, that would be *much* better," he said. Then his face went somber. "Only it *doesn't* work like that, and I'm feeling lost about what to do."

"What is it that you *want* to do?" I asked him.

He let out a wry chuckle. "Wave a magic wand and make all of this go away." I opened my mouth to speak but thought better of it and just waited. "Other than that," he soon continued, "all I can think about are appointments that I won't be able to keep, people I need to call, and other business stuff." He began fiddling with one of the tubes running across his lap. "Only, none of that matters anymore. I just can't seem to get my mind around the idea that my future doesn't extend past two days from now." His voice got quieter and more tears formed in his eyes. "I've been so geared to my future plans my whole life that I don't know how to think any other way." He turned and looked at me with sad, pathetic eyes. "That's where I need your help."

CHAPTER 64

Zootie and I were sitting on the front porch - rocking our way through an unseasonably warm November day, when the topic of Mandy Baker came up. We had just been talking about Jack Beck, as I was looking for some advice from Zootie on how I could best help the poor guy, but I could tell that Zootie was distracted, so I asked him what was on his mind.

"Oh, I was just thinking," he said as he watched a bird eating at one of the nearby bird feeders, "that maybe we can find a way to make Mandy happy without giving up the house."

"What were you thinking?"

"Well, you know how much I want her gone from our lives before I leave Hope House for good in a few weeks?"

I absorbed the body blow regarding his imminent departure and responded calmly, "Yeah."

"Well as stubborn as she is, and as bent on revenge as she is, I don't see her calling off her lawyers until she gets either this house or a serious pile of cash in her hands."

"So, what are you proposing?"

He swiveled his head and winced at me as he said, "Cash her out."

"Cash her out?" I asked. "How?"

"Use some of that money that Jennie left us and make her an offer. Not full market value of the house, but enough to make her feel like she made us bleed a little bit."

I was taken aback by his suggestion. "I don't know Zootie," I said as I shook my head. "Jennie left us that money to do some good with the list and have her memory live on to some extent. I'm not sure that tossing some money at Mandy Baker to keep her off our backs qualifies on either one of those counts."

His eyes went back to the bird feeder and he rested his chin in his hands. "Yeah, I suppose you're right. I have another meeting with her lawyers the day after tomorrow and I guess I'm just grasping at straws trying to find a quick way to end this whole mess. That woman is such a..." His voice trailed off and his eyes went wide; I thought, from his reaction, that maybe Mandy Baker was walking up our front walk. I turned my head, to follow his eyes, and saw right away why he'd reacted the way he did.

"Omigosh!" I shouted as I leapt to my feet. "Is that really *you*?" I ran down the porch steps and pulled the surprise visitor into a big hug. "What the heck are you doing out *here*?!?" I asked incredulously.

"Got a call from Jennie to come a runnin' as quick as I could," she responded as we embraced. "Took me a while, but here I am." We broke our embrace and she looked up at Zootie, her face beaming. Zootie just continued to sit in his rocking chair, mouth open, unable to believe that Ren Quigley was standing on our front sidewalk.

CHAPTER 65

The next several weeks seemed to go by in a flash. After Ren arrived it was if someone had hit the cosmic fast forward button and life's events blurred together as if viewed from a speeding car.

There were dozens more deaths and, along with them, dozens of futures that came to an abrupt end, dozens more dreams that died on the vine of possibility, and dozens upon dozens of other lives that were forever changed by the death of a loved one. I will forever remember each one of them, for their own unique pieces of humanity, but there were two deaths that stood apart from the rest during that period of time.

Jack Beck died from a blood clot that had traveled from his heart to his brain two days after I had initially visited him in the hospital. What I learned during those two days was that he was completely alone in the world - not a single relative or true friend to speak of - and all he was looking for was someone to sit by his bedside and listen to him; listen to his regrets, listen to his fears, and listen to his pain. So, listen to him I did, for 48 hours. During those 48 hours I heard the profound hurt of a man who had bet all his Life Dollars on the wrong horse.

Jack had been a living cliché of a man who seemingly had it all and yet had nothing. His work had been his life and he had achieved much - both in dollars and prestige - within his work world. But it had come at a price. Good business sense dictated a life played out close to one's chest and that approach, while effective in the boardroom, tended to keep people at arm's length.

"I had always thought that I'd have time to make friends and all that after I retired at age fifty," he had whispered to me at one point during our 48-hour confessional session. Tears filled his eyes as he told me, "I didn't realize how important friends were until I was lying here, helpless. I just never thought I'd ever *be* helpless." He looked up at me with eyes that were begging for answers. "Did you know that I could bench press 250 pounds and run a 10k in under 45 minutes?"

I just shook my head. He wore a wry smile framed with sadness. "Now, all I can think about is how I'm going to have the first funeral ever where nobody shows up." He cried - hard - for several minutes after expressing that fear. I cried right along with him, realizing that he had just expressed a fear that resonated with many people, including me.

The amazing part of those two days with Jack was being able to watch a man completely transform right before my eyes. I watched a man who I would have described as arrogant, driven, selfish and obnoxious prior to his heart attack, slowly morph into a humble, gentle, kind soul who cared about nothing more than "getting it right" in his last hours. And get it right he did as I took dictation on countless letters of apology that he insisted on sending out to a variety of former friends, business associates and even neighbors. He also called many people, insisting that they come to see him, and he presented them with all types of gifts and endowments that I had helped him to assemble. The reactions were priceless.

After his 48-hour sprint toward redemption was complete, he died peacefully, his final words being a quiet, "Thank you, Dan." And then I watched as the light slowly faded from his eyes. It was beautiful. What was equally as beautiful was seeing the number of people who had decided to show up at his service. It wasn't exactly a crowd, but I knew that it was more people than would have shown up had he not had his 48 hours of getting-it-right time. Peoples' capacity for forgiveness and seeing the best in others moved me on several occasions during his service.

At the other end of the spectrum was Elena Camandona. She was a woman who had lived a life filled with love, generosity and kindness and was thus spared a heart heavy with regrets or fears. There was no last-minute scrambling for redemption by Elena - quite on the contrary, during her final days she behaved more like a person who couldn't wait to leave on an exciting trip that she'd been planning for years. She had no unfinished business to take care of prior to her departure so Trish and I just basked in her glow, sitting at her bedside listening to her stories and insights, as much as we could. She continued to chat with her dead husband, Bud, and it was his name that she had on her lips when she eventually succumbed to death. There was no struggling for last gasps of air, no fighting for another minute of life; her breathing just got shallower and shallower until it stopped all together and she died with a small sigh and a serene smile on her face. Elena finally got to take the trip of her dreams, to be reunited with the man she loved above all others.

A more tangible love story was also simultaneously being played out within the walls of Hope House during those few weeks. Ren and Zootie became instantly inseparable and the love they shared was on constant display for all to see. They were like teenagers discovering love for the first time and it brought smiles to the faces of anyone lucky enough to witness it firsthand. Watching them together, I thought how perfectly matched they were, and I couldn't help feeling sadness at the thought of this romance ending so abruptly.

"Yeah, it's sad," Zootie agreed one day, after I'd shared my observation with him. "We blew it this time around, but I'm determined to get it right the next go-round."

"But even if you believe in reincarnation and all that, how do you know that you're going to find each other again?" I asked.

He gave me a big Zootie grin and said, "Oh, we'll find each other, I'm almost certain of that. One of the many things I learned during my peek behind the curtain is that our little spirit families stay close together from one life to the next - that's how we keep building on the lessons we learn."

"So, what's the big lesson you're going to be bringing from *this* lifetime?" I asked, though I thought I knew what his answer was going to be.

He thought for just a moment and then said, straight-faced, "Move my ass around more." Zootie surprised me once again. "It looks like I'm going to die a pretty early death," he continued, "and that's probably because of this." He grabbed a couple fistfuls of fat from his mid-section and jiggled it up and down. "Next time around I'm gonna go easy on the beer, cheeseburgers and chocolate."

It was that same day that we received our first correspondence from Jennie's parents. It came in the form of a letter from their lawyers notifying us of their pursuit of wrongful death charges against us. The letter had been expected at some point, but it was still deflating to all of us. Zootie had taken it particularly hard as it became one more thing that he felt the need to get settled prior to his death. We all knew that there was little hope of that happening, barring a small miracle.

The letter prompted me to get to work on something more *positive* regarding Jennie's death. The "what to do?" was answered by Ren as she had taken one look at Jennie's journal and said: "This should be published!" It was a brilliant idea and a great way to fan the flame of Jennie's legacy to the world. I put together a packet of her entries, along with a cover letter, and mailed it off to a dozen publishers. Zootie also had a friend, Amber Reed, who worked as a literary agent, so we put a packet in her hands and asked her to see what she could do to get it published.

It was a very full three weeks at Hope House, but nothing compared to the week before Christmas - Zootie's final week of life.

CHAPTER 66

"We're going to get married," Zootie announced with a huge smile. He and Ren had asked Trish and me to sit down and that was the bomb that they dropped on us.

"That's wonderful!" Trish shrieked.

The two of them - Ren and Zootie - sat across from us and glowed. I was stunned. "Married?" I said, trying to mask my surprise. "Why would you get married this...uh...late in the game?"

They looked at each other, as if sharing the unspoken intimacy of an inside joke, and then Zootie looked over at me and said, "Because we're *supposed* to be together, simple as that. We don't care if it's for seven days or seventy years, we know now that we're *supposed* to be together and the sooner we rectify that, the better."

Ren's look then turned serious. "'N we want you two t'be our best man 'n woman at the ceremony, if yer willin'."

Trish didn't even look over at me. "Of course we will!" she responded. "We'd be honored, wouldn't we Dan?"

I smiled. "Of course we would. Watching you two together these past few weeks has been downright inspiring and I can't think of two people in this world who belong together more than you two."

They both smiled warmly and Zootie said, "Thanks Dan, that means a lot."

It turned out that they had planned the ceremony for the following day so there wasn't much time to prepare. We had helped to plan many, many funerals at Hope House, but this was going to be our very first wedding, so we were all a little clumsy with the details at first. But we pulled it all together and it turned out to be a beautiful, touching ceremony. They said their vows in the living room, in front of a minister friend of Zootie's and a few dozen people, most of whom were involved with Project Hope. Afterwards - due to the steady flow of Seattle liquid sunshine outside - everyone just milled around the house, content to munch on hors d'oeuvres and dispense well-wishes to Zootie and Ren. The most surprising dispenser of well-wishes showed up at our doorstep later in the day, as the festivities were winding down.

When the knock on the door came, I was standing at the edge of the living room and so, being the closest to the door, I answered it. I was taken aback at first by who was standing on the porch, dripping wet, but I managed to get out a "Hey Red" to our visitor.

"Hey Dan," he replied sheepishly. "Do you mind if I come in for a minute?"

I looked over my shoulder, wanting to make sure Zootie wasn't nearby, as the sight of Red would only remind him of a festering boil on his now-short life, and I didn't want to ruin his wedding day. I turned back to Red. "I don't know if you should come in, Red. This is Zootie's wedding day and I don't think..."

"Please?" he begged. "This is kinda important and I'm leaving tomorrow morning to head back to Texas."

I looked him up and down, weighing what to do next. He looked different to me now - perhaps because of our suspicions regarding who he was and what he'd done - and my first impulse was to tell him to take a hike. Instead, I said, "I'll let you in if you first answer a couple of questions for me."

"I have a feeling that I know what they are, and that's the reason I'm here, but go ahead and ask away."

"First question - are you Mandy Baker's husband?"

"Yes, I am," he replied with a sigh, "for better or worse."

"Second question - did you sick the police on us regarding the Coopers' death?"

He looked at the ground and shifted uncomfortably. "Yes, I did."

I felt my face flush with anger. "Then why the hell should I even be talking to you?" I asked, barely able to contain my anger.

He looked back up at me, his eyes filled with remorse. "Because I fucked up, and now I want to make things right."

Before I could get out another word, Zootie came walking up behind me - he'd probably heard me shouting - and asked, "What's all the ruckus about here Danny?" He stepped past me and saw Red standing on the porch. Zootie's mood changed instantly from jovial to enraged as his fists clenched and his body stiffened. "What the hell are *you* doing here?" he bellowed at Red.

Red instinctively took a step backwards, perhaps fearing that Zootie's clenched fists were intended for his face. He probably wasn't too far from the truth. I stepped in front of Zootie and said, "He was just getting to that Zootie. Maybe the three of us should step out onto the porch and get to the bottom of this."

Zootie's scowl went down a notch to just a frown and he nodded his assent. I motioned to Red to sit in one of the rocking chairs then led Zootie out and closed the door behind us. I made sure that I sat down between Red and Zootie. "So why don't you finish what you were saying Red," I said after everyone was settled.

Red didn't look at us when he spoke - his eyes seemed fixed on the steady rain falling beyond the porch. "I came up here from Texas not too long ago with one goal in mind - get this house back and then sell it so Mandy and I could have some cash for once and pay off a few of our debts." He heaved a deep and prolonged sigh. "But after spending some time here..."

"As a spy!" Zootie interrupted.

Red nodded. "Yeah, as a spy. I was supposed to gather as much rope as I could to hang you guys with," he said as looked up at me with sad, contrite eyes. "And that's why I was eavesdropping on your conversation about the Coopers."

I could hear Zootie shifting in his chair, probably preparing for another verbal strike, but I tried to head him off. "So, what made you have a change of heart, Red?" I asked.

"That hasn't been determined yet," Zootie muttered.

"I don't blame you for not trusting me Zootie, but like Dan said, I have had a change of heart," Red said earnestly. Once again, his eyes turned outward, towards the rain. "I felt like shit after telling the police about the Coopers..."

"I'll bet," Zootie interjected.

Red ignored him and continued. "I looked inside myself and saw I actually agreed with everything you guys were doing here. Seeing firsthand how you guys are using Hy's house and her money to help so many people made me feel awfully shallow for wanting it to just pay off my credit cards." He bowed his head. "So, I decided that the best way for me to help you guys would be to just disappear and let you keep doing what you're doing."

"What are you saying Red?" I asked.

He looked over at me with a determined resolve on his face. "As of this morning I've called off the lawyers and at this time tomorrow Mandy and I will be back in Texas."

I was stunned. I flashed on Mandy's face that day in the living room - the anger and hate spewing out every pore of her body - and I asked, "How the hell did you convince Mandy to agree to this?"

He chuckled a wry chuckle that was obviously filled with many unspoken thoughts. "Let's just say that she was reluctant at first, but I eventually convinced her to see it my way."

I looked at him sideways, all kinds of follow-up questions filling my head, but I could see that he didn't want to betray his wife any further, so I just said, "I don't know what to say, Red. So, I'll just say a huge thank you on behalf of everyone here at Hope House." I extended my hand and he shook it. I glanced over at Zootie, who had been strangely silent, and saw that his face had transformed from anger to shock. "What do you think of all this, Zootie?" I asked.

He closed his mouth that had been hanging open and replied, "I guess it's safe to say that I'm pleasantly shocked." He then smiled and extended his hand to Red. Red returned the smile and shook Zootie's hand vigorously.

"I'm sorry for everything that I put you guys through and I'm sorry that it took me so long to see the light," Red said.

"Hey," I said to him, "we're just happy that we're going to have a few less lawyers in our lives."

"Amen to that," Zootie concurred.

With that, Red rose to his feet, shook our hands one more time and said, "Well, I don't want to keep you guys from your party, so I'll just say so long and good luck."

"Thanks Red, we appreciate that," I said. "And good luck to you with everything."

He knew exactly what I'd meant by "*everything*" and he smiled. "Thanks. I just may need a little luck for the next few months." Then he turned and headed out into the rain. And, just like that, Mandy and Red Baker, and all their accompanying lawyer-filled baggage, were out of our lives forever.

I had all kinds of thoughts and emotions coursing through me as I watched him walk away, but Zootie summed it all up best when he said, "Well, that certainly rates a huge checkmark on the ol' to-do list."

CHAPTER 67

It was several days later that I had "The Conversation" with Zootie - an exchange that was short on words but long on meaning. It had begun innocently enough, with a simple question: "So how's married life treating you?" I asked him as we were walking around Green Lake that day. Trish and Ren had been walking with us and had gone off in search of a bathroom.

"I feel complete Dan," he responded. We sat down on a nearby bench to wait for Ren and Trish to return. "The right person has a way of making sense out of a senseless world and that's what Ren does for me."

"Any regrets about not getting married sooner?"

He sat silent for a moment, carefully considering my question. "You know what? A part of me sure wishes that we had more memories of being together tucked away - exotic vacations, raising children and such - but another part of me, the bigger part I think, wouldn't trade away any of the lessons that I got to learn on my own while we were apart." He looked over at me. "Sometimes one person can travel a lot quicker than two, if you know what I mean."

"Yeah I do know what you mean," I said as I reflected on my own life of predominantly solo flight. "But how do you know when it's time to take on a co-pilot?" I asked.

"When you start asking questions like that," he replied quickly. Then he flashed his paternal smile and said, "Marry her Dan."

"What?" I asked, more to borrow time than anything else.

"I've got just a couple days left so I'm not gonna wax philosophical or try to talk around it in hopes that you'll see it for yourself, I'm just gonna say it." He reached over, put his hand on my shoulder, and then looked me square in the eye. "Don't wait any longer Dan - marry Trish."

I exhaled loudly. "Whoa! Where is *that* coming from?"

"It's coming from a friend who's seeing things pretty damned clearly right now and I see that you two belong together and the only thing holding you back is some old fear you have about commitment."

I had to admit that I'd been toying with the idea of pro-posing to Trish ever since Zootie's wedding. But in my mind, the decision was still sitting off in the future at a safe distance. "But there's still so much going on at Hope House," I sputtered.

"That's just an excuse," Zootie replied quickly with a shake of his head.

"And I don't have any real income right now," I added.

"Excuse!"

"And I…" I began.

"Excuse, excuse, excuse!" he bellowed. "You can trot out all of the feeble excuses you want Dan, but the truth is that you're scared shitless to even *say* the word, never mind actually *doing* it."

He was right and we both knew it. "Okay, I admit it," I said with a sigh. "But that's another good reason *not* to do it right now."

"Bullshit!" he thundered. "If you've learned one thing since coming to Hope House, I would hope that it would be to *not* give in to fear simply because it's there in front of you. Like Jennie showed us all so well that night in the living room, the best shit is sitting just one step *past* our fears!"

I didn't have a chance to respond as Ren and Trish came strolling up to our bench. "What are you two talking about?" Trish asked as she sat down next to me. "You looked like you were into a pretty intense discussion."

"I was just sharing with Dan why I thought *buying* a car was better than *leasing* one over the long run," Zootie replied with a small wink.

"Are you going to be buying a car?" Ren asked me.

"No...well, maybe..." I stammered. "Actually, I've been thinking about it for a while now and Zootie helped me to clarify my thinking." I glanced over at him sitting on my right and returned his wink. "He's just got a lot more experience with this kind of thing than I do."

We continued our walk, content to talk about things other than marriage, much to my relief. That night, however, as Trish and I sat having dinner at a local restaurant, I wandered back into the hornets' nest. "Have you given much thought to us ever, you know, making our arrangement more...permanent?" I asked her.

"Just every day," she replied without hesitating, which kind of surprised me. "Why do you ask?"

I poked at the salad sitting in front of me. "I don't know. I guess seeing Zootie and Ren together just got me to thinking about us and the future, that's all."

She stopped eating and reached across the table to grab my hand; she was also wearing a highly flirtatious grin. "Is this what's known in the trade as a backdoor proposal?"

I didn't answer right away, as dozens of possible answers competed for my attention. All of them got muscled aside however as one answer came marching up from the back of the line and headed right for my lips; I said it even before I thought it. "Yeah, I guess it is." My voice quavered and I felt an immediate impulse to suck it back in after I said it, but it was too late - I said it, and she definitely heard it.

Her expression changed to doubt. "Do you mean that?"

I didn't hesitate this time. I nodded and said, "Yeah, I guess I do."

She still wasn't entirely convinced. "You guess you do *what?*"

I didn't understand what she was asking. "You know," I said with a shrug.

She wasn't buying it. "No Dan, I don't know and, to tell you the truth, I need to hear you say the words."

I knew the words she wanted to hear, and it was no use trying to dodge it any longer. I took in a deep breath and said the words quickly as I exhaled, "Will you marry me?"

The doubt instantly left her face and there, in its place, was unmistakable love and joy; it was the face of hers that I loved the most. My heart melted and I knew right away that I'd made the best decision of my life. "Oh Dan, you don't know how much this means to me," she whispered. Tears filled her eyes and, as they raced down her cheeks, she said, "Yes. Yes I will marry you Dan Barnes." I began to cry too and we both jumped out of our chairs simultaneously, rushing into an embrace next to our table. We stood there and held each other for a long time - crying and whispering soft *"I love you's"* in each other's ear - unaware of the dozen or so sets of eyes that were watching us from the other tables in the restaurant.

After finally breaking the embrace, we sat back down at the table, wiping our faces with our napkins. We talked about the question of when to have the ceremony, and even toyed with the idea of doing it the following night so that Zootie could be a part of it. But we eventually decided that we'd rather wait until sometime in the new year, so that we could do a little more planning. *"Zootie will be tickled that I even asked the question,"* I thought to myself.

Trish then suddenly went silent. She had a look on her face that I'd never seen before - sort of a guilty, yet reticent, cocktail of an expression; as if she'd just tossed a baseball through my kitchen window and she was afraid to tell me about it. "What's wrong?" I asked.

She wouldn't look at me. "There's something that I'd been wanting to tell you, but I wanted to wait until the time was right to do it." She looked up and her eyes were soft but determined. "And I think now is the right time."

I suddenly felt very nervous, but I didn't know why. "What is it, Trish?"

She grabbed both of my hands in hers and pulled them across the table so that they were resting in front of her. She clutched my hands hard and, once again, began to cry. "You're going to be a daddy," she then blurted out.

The words hung in the air, as if suspended by helium, and reverberated around us: *"You're going to be a daddy."* They didn't penetrate all the way to my brain at first, but they kept on trying, desperate to make contact: *"You're going to be a daddy!"* Time seemed to slow down - perhaps some Greater Being saw that I needed the extra processing time - as what was probably mere seconds stretched like taffy to feel like minutes. *"I'M GOING TO BE A DADDY!!!"* The words finally hit their mark. "Oh my gosh, how?...when?..." I sputtered helplessly.

Trish smiled warmly. "I think it was during our first drunken tryst up at Snoqualmie Lodge. I've known for a while, but I didn't want to say anything to you until I knew that you wanted to be with me for me, not out of a sense of responsibility to an unborn baby." Her smile got bigger as she added, "And now I know."

Looking across the table at her at that moment - the candlelight dancing on her tear-streaked face and her blue eyes looking at me with a love that was so intense I almost had to look away - I knew right then that everything was going to be okay. I smiled back at her, squeezed her hands in mine, and said, "You've made me a very happy man." And I meant every word of it. We sat in that restaurant - crying, talking and hugging - well into the night.

CHAPTER 68

"I'm going to be an uncle!" Zootie shouted after hearing the news. "This calls for a celebration!" Classic Zootie. He's the one who's going to die the following day and he decides to throw a party for somebody else. That's why he was one of a kind.

"But Zootie, tomorrow is your day to..." I began in protest.

"Nonsense!" he interrupted. "I don't give a flyin' fuck about tomorrow - *today* is what matters, and today we're gonna celebrate!"

I knew there was no arguing with him, so I just nodded my consent. That evening we went into downtown Seattle and had a wonderful dinner at a fancy restaurant on Lake Union and then went to a dance club that played big band music. "I love dancing to swing music!" Zootie had announced over dinner. It was his way of mentioning a sort of "last request" so we were all more than happy to accompany him to the dance club.

It was a lot of fun. The four of us danced for an hour or so, switching partners frequently - there were even a couple of songs during which Zootie and I paired up - and none of us could stop smiling and laughing. It was a great time.

Until a little after midnight.

We had just finished a particularly lively version of "Chattanooga Choo-Choo" and had made our way back to our seats for some refreshments when I heard a dull thud from behind me. I looked down on the floor and there was Zootie lying on his back clutching his chest. Slow motion took over for the second time in less than twenty-four hours as I went to my knees and lifted my friend's head into my lap. He was struggling for air, and I could see that he was in a lot of pain, but then I saw his eyes suddenly grow calm. "Guess this is it…" he whispered between chest pains. Ren was on her knees at his side and she was sobbing into his right hand, which she was clutching to her cheek.

"I love you, sweetie," she whispered through her tears. She then reached down and began stroking his forehead, which was beaded with sweat.

"Love…you…too," he managed to force out before his body was overcome with a huge wave of pain. His breathing then became sporadic, but he managed to force out two more words, which I'll never forget; "Damn…cheeseburgers…" was all he said.

Then everything seemed to shut down at once as his face turned blue and then grey and his breathing stopped all together after a few last pitiful attempts at pulling in oxygen. I thought about trying CPR but a voice inside of me told me that it was no use; it was simply his time to die. Zootie took in his last breath right there in my lap.

After he stopped breathing, I lifted him up, pulled him into an embrace and whispered, "I love you Zootie." Somebody in the dance club had apparently called 911 because it wasn't long before a couple of paramedics were peeling my arms from around his body and lifting me up and out of the way so they could begin their life-saving efforts.

They tore open his shirt and tried everything from paddles to needles but nothing brought Zootie back. He was gone. I stood there looking down at his lifeless body - with Ren crying into one of my shoulders and Trish the other - and it struck me once again, for the hundreth time, how strange death was.

Despite the huge advantage of forewarning we had with the list, Zootie's death played out as it did for most people - one minute we were laughing, sharing stories of yesterdays and dreams of tomorrows, and then he was gone. No long goodbyes, no final words of wisdom left behind for the living to consider - just gone. In its wake was a huge hole - the hole that Zootie used to occupy in the world - and we, the living, were now left to figure out how to fill that hole.

I thought too how Zootie had been the first person to actually die in my arms. Strange as it sounds, it was - as it had been with Jack Beck the week before - a beautiful thing to be a part of. Watching the transition from life to death, while it is undeniably sad and tragic at times, is also an extremely powerful and one-of-a-kind, indescribable experience that stirs parts of ourselves that we didn't know we had, or that we tend to ignore in our day-to-day lives.

The part of us that feels tied to all living things.

The part of us that knows we are mortal beings and that every day of life is an incredible gift for which we should always feel thankful.

The part of us that feels compassion for even the smallest of hurts or briefest moments of suffering in the world around us.

The part of us that feels unbridled love for all who touch our lives.

And, finally, the part of us that wants to cry and cry and cry, not stopping until all of the pain that we feel inside is sitting in a puddle of tears in front of us.

I felt all these things as I watched Zootie's lifeless body being taken away. As they carried him past me on a stretcher I reached down and grabbed his hand - it was already feeling colder - and said a final goodbye to my friend Zootie Gibbons.

EPILOGUE

Zootie had requested that his body be cremated and then he wanted the ashes stirred into a can of varnish which would then be applied to his favorite rocking chair on the front porch of Hope House. Leave it to Zootie to put a smile on our faces even after he was gone. We did as he had requested, and it is in that chair that I am sitting as I write this final chapter, almost a month to the day after Zootie's death and nearly a month into the new year. The weather is gray, and the air is cool, but I felt it fitting that I have a piece of Zootie next to me as I write down my final thoughts on this incredible year.

Zootie's service, held at Hope House the last week of the year, had attracted a standing room only crowd numbering in the hundreds. The number of lives he had touched was staggering. There was much crying but, to be honest, the laughs outnumbered the sobs by at least two to one. Zootie had always inspired more laughter than tears during his lifetime and it was fitting that the same be true after his death.

It was at Zootie's service that I ran into Amber Reed - his literary agent friend - and she had informed me that she'd found a publisher who was interested in Jennie's Journals. It was a great piece of news. Trish convinced me that I should call Jennie's grandmother to share the good news, since she had always been Jennie's biggest fan, and I did just that the following day. She was of course overjoyed to hear that her favorite granddaughter was going to be published - knowing full well that it had been a lifetime dream of Jennie's - and then she asked me a question that, ultimately, served to remove a large black cloud from the skies over Hope House.

"Did you tell her parents yet?" she asked me.

"Uh, well, you see…" I stammered, realizing that she was in the dark regarding the pending lawsuit against us, "we're not exactly on good terms with them right now," I eventually said.

"Oh? Why is that?" she asked.

I made the decision to tell her the entire story, which I did, including everything from the hospital scene to the letters from their lawyers.

"I see…" she said simply when I had finished. "Can I call you right back Dan?"

I thought that maybe she had a cake in the oven, or perhaps I had offended her in some way, but I said, "Sure," and hung up. It wasn't twenty minutes later that she called me back.

"Good news," she said cheerily. "My daughter has decided to drop all charges against you, and you can expect to see a formal letter of apology in the mail within the week."

"How…?" I began.

"I never told you this Dan," she said as she cut me off, "but the words you shared at Jennie's service were the only words I heard that entire day that had anything to do with my granddaughter. That was a brave thing you did that day and I admired the hell out of you for doing that for her. I'm just sorry I didn't get a chance to pull you aside that day and tell you that."

"Thank you for saying that," I responded. "It was part of a promise that I'd made to Jennie quite a while ago."

"She had told me prior to her death what she had planned to do with her trust money and I told her I thought it was a grand idea; better to go towards changing lives than buying a new boat or a vacation home in the Caribbean, which is what my daughter would have done with the money if she'd gotten her hands on it." I could hear her let out a long sigh. "I love my daughter Dan, but I have to say that I sometimes cringe at the priorities she has in place for her life."

"I'm sorry to hear that," I said.

"Yeah, well, I'm sure a big part of it is my own damn fault - too easy on her when she was a child and all that - but I saw an opportunity to redeem myself as a mother a little bit during our earlier conversation."

"How was that?"

"Knowing that what she was doing to you was wrong, and also knowing that she couldn't wait to get her hands on my money after I'm gone..." she paused for a moment to consider her words, "...well, let's just say that I helped her to see the error of her ways."

I let out an involuntary laugh. "You blackmailed your daughter?" I asked.

She chuckled. "Yes, well I guess I did at that!"

And so, just like that, the final item on Zootie's checklist had been checked off. I knew that, wherever he was, he too was smiling at the news.

So now here I sit, at the start of a new year. The black clouds are gone - at least the figurative ones - and the skies ahead are looking brighter. The year that just passed was, by any standard, *THE* year of my life, and the year to come has the potential to surpass it. There are still four more months of names on the list, names that contain, I'm sure, stories every bit as compelling and life-changing as Zootie's, Hy's, and Jennie's. I'm excited to continue down the path that they had started on with me, and eager to build on the many lessons that I've learned from each of them.

I'm also excited about being a father. Trish has a small basketball protruding from her belly now and pregnancy seems to be making her more beautiful with each passing day, though

I wouldn't have thought that possible. Being a part of so much death has caused me to be more in tune with the cycles of life and I'm looking forward to being a part of a joyful beginning after experiencing so many sad endings. I should also mention that our wedding date has been set for the middle of June - a few weeks after the final date on the list, and a couple of weeks before she is due to deliver our first child.

More than anything else, as I sit and watch the rain on this cold January day, I feel thankful. I feel thankful for all the blessings of life, the many lessons of death, and the magic of love. I find love to be the engine that drives my life right now and I think back to just a year ago and how far I'd been from that truth. But, thankfully, the journey that I began back in May of last year - to find a soul that had been quieted to a whisper in my chest - has been successful; I found my lost soul, and the love that fills it, and I can now say with all my heart, *Life is goddamned good!*

www.ingramcontent.com/pod-product-compliance
Lightning Source LLC
Chambersburg PA
CBHW070734180626
46818CB00007B/2835